TRIAD

By

Lyndi Alexander

Science Fiction Novel from
Dragonfly Publishing, Inc.

TRIAD
Science Fiction Novel

Paperback Edition
EAN 978-1-936381-32-6
ISBN 1-936381-32-X

Published in the United States of America by
Dragonfly Publishing, Inc.
Website: http://www.dragonflypubs.com

To the brave men and women of Maquis Universal, who taught me everything I know about flying a spaceship, what it takes to survive on the raggedy edge, and how to remain cool and (mostly) collected when someone's trying to kill you and yours.

Acknowledgements

Thank you to MU and DF and UEP castmates, who shared many happy and creative times with me during the genesis of this story: Kellie, Sue, Jeff, Susie, Chad, Charles, Youlanda, Tim, Gus, Tasper, Eric, John, Luc, Dawn, Stacy, Sebastien, Jen, Katrina, Jordan, Josh, Robin, Dacie, Brian, Roberta, Matt and so many others who passed through. Some of the names in the story have been changed to protect some of the innocent. The rest of you are guilty. You know who you are.

Thanks also to Cierra and the art crew, my editor Glenda and my publisher Terri for their belief in me and the work they've contributed to this novel.

And a huge thank you! as always to my critique partner and dedicated red-pen-wielder Jean, who helped kick the manuscript into shape, despite her general disinterest in science fiction. Huzzah, madam! Huzzah!

Major Characters:

SOLARII:
Trezanna Len (Solarii Commander)
Rumadan (Solarii Officer)
Chase Austin (Solarii Security Chief)
Matthew Juri (Solarii Security)
Julian McKinley (Solarii Engineer)
Monty Winston (Solarii Pilot)
Shelby Hussard (Solarii Pilot)
Eugene Boring (Solarii Doctor)
Shahla Talib (Solarii Doctor)

DRAGONFLEET:
Estrella Drake (Dragonfleet Leader)
Hawk Kenton (Dragonfleet Officer)
Gustave Henry (Dragonfleet Engineer)
Krainel (Deposed Dragonfleet Leader)

KHIMEYR:
Catava Rolon (Khimeyr Leader)
Darien Pomeroy (Khimeyr Officer)
Xiu Qiaolin (Khimeyr Officer)
Lily Renard (Khimeyr Pilot)

ARKOSIAN PIRATES:
Yves Marcand (Arkosian Pirate)
Andaeus Meda (Arkosian Pirate)

MERCHANTS AND MERCENARIES:
Marus (Waypass Station Computer)
Piper Donovan (Mercenary Pilot)
Stefan Ciro (Waypass Merchant)
Yanoro Ciro (Waypass Merchant)
Vanyakin of Myana (Mercenary)

CHAPTER 1

NEW blood. If we don't get it soon, we're finished.

Trezanna Len watched the large monitors of the Solarii command center, her breath coming in tight gasps as she willed her remaining fighters to stay in the sky.

She had assigned fifteen ships to battle the Arkosian space pirates. Seven were still holding on. To their credit, they had knocked out a dozen smaller pirate craft. Two pirate ships continued to drop hydro-bombs, the impact of the deadly missiles registering in cold numbers on the radar.

The thought of the destruction of her colony made her stomach turn. For so long hundreds of people depended on her to keep them safe. Now she may have run out of luck.

"Incoming!"

The alert caught her off guard.

"What? Where?" Trezanna jumped out of her chair, running across to the command center's main viewer. She didn't wait for bad news. "Get out! Everyone out!"

The half-dozen people who manned the center scattered out the doors. With headset in hand, Trezanna made sure she was the last to leave. As her hand left the doorframe, the command center exploded into shards of plasteel and krete. She stumbled into the corridor, the shock driving her into the wall opposite. Her nose and eyes filled with a sharp, choking smoke.

Almost immediately, the hallway went dark.

Think, damn it, think!

No power. That meant no radar, no communication, no ability to monitor. She had to find out what was transpiring overhead.

Head spinning and her shoulder aching, she shoved off the wall in the direction of the nearest set of computers she knew of, the rec-room. People screamed in the distance, the sound echoing along the halls and rattling her spine. Despair stalked her like the trails of smoke and dust in the passageway. She did her best to ignore it as she felt her way through the dark until she reached a junction with power.

Eyes burning, she tried to focus on her goal. Left, then another left, halfway down that hall and a sharp right. *Now.* More people of the Induna colony could die with every second that passed. She couldn't let that happen. She forced herself to keep moving.

If she had been on the small command deck of her fighter, she would have blasted the pirates for all they were worth. She had chosen to stay on the ground this time, since the number of command officers not confined to the infirmary was growing short. If she could keep the generator from crashing and the shields fully operational, there was a chance to keep the base viable. How much damage did the bomb do to the command center? Did the Arkosians now have entry?

Trezanna hurried across the debris-cluttered floor to the games console and pushed aside the remnants of a child's birthday celebration. Her priority now was to make sure that young Jahn survived to see his next one.

She tapped in her command password and the screen blanked. The lights overhead flickered. "No, damn it! No! You hold on, you sorry piece of crap gennie!"

She held her breath a moment, glaring upward as if she could force the current to remain by sheer will power. A few seconds later, the lights stopped their intermittent blinking and the screen flashed, first with her command link, and then current status. She surveyed the base's remaining power supplies. Nearly gone.

Her arm ached from where her shoulder had hit the wall and her fingers shook, making her typing erratic. Almost twelve hours since the attack began in the dark of the early morning. The Arkosians were old enemies. They vacated this sector years ago. Now they were back and without even a greeting or a demand. Just the blast from their weapons.

Her fingers couldn't seem to hit the right keys, so she gave up on the keyboard. "Marus, voice mode," she snapped, waiting for the computer to process her orders. When its red light flashed, she stood back, able to give vocal commands.

"Marus, cut lights to fifty percent base-wide. Transfer power to shields. Display current tactical data."

Trezanna focused closely on the screen as the overhead lights dimmed. Other than the command post, the attack had not damaged anything crucial. Seven ships now occupied the air space directly over the base, four pirate ships and three of Trezanna's. The Solarii ships, the *Whirlwind,* the *Tiboron,* and the *Blaze,* smaller and more maneuverable, circled the larger attackers like wild dogs, taking bites out of their hulls with each pass.

Running a hand through her hair and shoving it out of her face, she loosed a shower of krete debris. Trezanna tuned the controls, trying to catch the frequency her fighters used. Barely able to hear at first, she leaned in close, the blue light from the screen dimly illuminating her face and body. Static phased in, and then sharpened to a war whoop.

"Beat it, Winston, she's gonna blow!" came the triumphant voice of Shelby Hussard, the spitfire teacher-turned-pilot of the *Tiboron.*

"Cheeky bit." Monty Winston swerved the *Whirlwind* from its path, swinging wide to avoid the coming explosion. His voice was warm and amused, despite the stress-inducing situation he was in. Trezanna noted with approval that he avoided Hussard's trajectory, preventing pirate gunners from acquiring an easy shot at them both.

Hussard counted down. "Three. Two. One. Now!"

The on-screen trace of the larger of the pirate cruisers wavered and vanished.

"Yes!" Trezanna waved a fist of satisfaction as she imagined a silent shower of fire and sparks bursting into the vacuum of space only to be swallowed by the black. "Well done!"

She leaned against the edge of the console, her body aching. The smell of burnt plastic and wiring filled the room.

"Give it up, you bastards," she whispered. "Call it a day. Go home."

Winston reported one pirate lightship decimated by a large piece of torn metal. Apparent chaos reigned overhead as the debris from the cruiser scattered. Then he and Hussard turned their ships to dog the rest until they turned and fled.

The *Blaze* hung in space, power readings flickering. Dr. Shahla Talib was in the cockpit, reluctantly pressed into service after two pilots had been killed the week before. Talib had been through Space Force training before joining the Solarii and assured them that she could handle the controls of a small ship.

Trezanna frowned and thumbed the com-unit. "Talib? Solarii base to *Blaze*, come in. *Blaze?*"

No answer. Had Talib been sent up there to die?

The Solarii personnel roster had counted about seven hundred at the beginning of today's attack, approximately two hundred on the compound itself, another several hundred in support personnel, farmers, artisans, metalworkers, living outside the compound on Solarii-claimed territory. Trezanna was responsible for all of them. She couldn't afford to lose anyone else, especially someone on the medical staff.

Perhaps the flickering power interfered with communication. Ship-to-ship might be more effective. "*Tiboron,* what's Talib's status?"

"Reading one life sign through explosion residue, but it's faint, ma'am." The *Tiboron* swooped closer to the wounded ship. "I can send someone to tow her home."

"Do that. We can't afford to lose the doctor, or the ship. Rendezvous in thirty minutes in the conference room. Len out."

"Understood."

Trezanna waited for Winston to acknowledge the order, and then cut the frequency. Time to regroup and see what the pirates had left them. Why had the Arkosians come back after being defeated so soundly years before? Why now?

"Marus, show the command display stats."

Trezanna studied the information coming in from the ships and the local outposts. Only when she had made sure all her chicks were safely headed home did she notice the blood soaking her right sleeve and the piece of metal poking through her upper arm. Buzzing filled her head until everything went black.

* * *

TREZANNA Len awoke, lying on her back, unsure of her whereabouts.

From nearby she could hear someone crying out. She was in the infirmary. The room was lit only by blazing emergency lights that dazzled some sections of the room, but left the rest in darkness. She tried to push herself upright, but found herself restrained on a medical table. Her navy blue jumpsuit had been cut away in the upper right quadrant, and she was freezing.

"Boring!"

Her chief medical officer appeared from behind a blood-flecked curtain under the lights at the far end of the room. Eugene Boring was humanoid-bipedal, nearly human but his Eponan physiology dictated he was short, squat, and hairless with skin that gave him a slightly jaundiced appearance. His eyes, a deep piercing violet, sparkled with good humor as he scanned her. "Ah, Len, you're among the living. Nice for you."

"What's wrong with me?" Trezanna growled. "I'm scheduled for a debrief." She struggled with the restraining field, while the doctor blithely continued his scan. Irritated, she tried to identify the wounded on the beds around her. "How many did we lose?"

"Hmmm," Boring said, focusing on his handheld monitor. A dark-suited ensign came up, whispered in his ear, and then walked away at a quick pace. The doctor finally turned to her and smiled, releasing the field. She hated that smile. She really did.

"Hmmm what?" Trezanna pushed herself upright, brushing bits of plascrete from her shoulders. "How did I get here?"

"Beck went looking for you when you didn't show up at your meeting. Thought it was rather rude of you to throw a party and not appear." Boring smirked. "Nearly bled out, yes you did, and what would have been the state of affairs then, hmmm?"

Trezanna muttered something uncomplimentary.

"I have excellent hearing, Dearie. Don't you worry about that." His eyes twinkled.

"What time is it?" she managed, looking around the infirmary.

Nearly every bed was full. Half her ships had left the fight due to damage and injuries. Others must surely have been injured on the surface. The tech staff would have to get the shields bolstered right away. If any remained upright.

So much to do. And how much time had they lost?

"Just before dawn. You've had quite a nap. It's a shame. The rest of us are working so hard."

Trezanna glared at him. "You knocked me out."

"Needed your sleep. Nothing others couldn't handle for you."

"But it's my job." She tried to pull together the stringy remnants of her jumpsuit. "How many did we lose?"

"Nine only from the ships, and a family living out near the generator. Most were repairable injuries." Boring sketched a wave toward the other beds. "Be good as new, these, before you know it." He positively beamed, making her wonder if he had slipped a gear or two.

Trezanna slid off the table, wincing at the sharp pull in her back as she twisted her bandaged shoulder. Her injury must have cut deep. "Why are you so blasted happy? We could have been wiped out today. Damned pirates."

"Reinforcements." Boring rocked on his heels. "Waiting to meet with you."

Trezanna's eyes opened wide. "From where?"

"You won't believe it." He just smiled. *That* smile. Then he walked away to answer a nurse's summons.

There was no time to return to her quarters. Trezanna peeled off the bloody remains of her uniform and grabbed a surgi-suit from the medical supply closet. Not fancy, but it would do.

Reinforcements. Unbelievable. Space Force must have answered her request for help, despite what she had done to them.

Better not keep them waiting.

Seeing Boring once again lost to his work, Trezanna rolled up the loose sleeves of the surgi-suit, and then lifted a spare com device from the doctor's desk before heading to her office. In the base's main building, the halls were mostly empty, their muted gray surfaces absorbing the sparse overhead light. No doubt the rest of the survivors were occupied in recovery efforts. There was a lot to do. Too much.

The Solarii base covered about ten square kilometers, including all the outbuildings and farm areas, where the descendants of the Terran Diaspora planted corn, soybeans, and rice. The group's claim was staked in ink and blood, their home for more than seven years a small section of the easternmost continent on the planet Induna. The climate was temperate, their needs minimal. All they wanted was a chance to enjoy life free of interference from the sector overlords, too much bureaucracy, and the damned pirates.

Random thoughts passed through Trezanna's mind as she walked. Dr. Talib must have been rescued, or else someone in medical would have told her differently. She had an idea of the extent of damage to the main base, but reports on the two larger complexes, status of the shields and other repair work would be waiting for her review. The command center would have to be reconstructed first. If they were lucky, maybe the bomb didn't take out any important couplings, and they could make it work on a shoestring. On a more personal note of irritation, Boring's incessant good humor had to go.

She rounded the corner to her office and stopped short as she found the passage crowded with perhaps two dozen people. The air was close with the odors of those under stress for too long, without facilities to care for themselves. The babble of voices stopped as they saw her.

One of her security officers stood with the group. He nodded as she approached and then moved off down the hall.

Whoever these people were, they had apparently been cleared. Trezanna eyed the crowd for any sign of the dark green uniforms of Space Force but saw none. Had Gene been jollying her along about the reinforcements?

This raggedy group looked as useful as a bunch of unwanted kittens. If they were refugees, they had come to the wrong place. Trezanna needed warriors, more ships, and more supplies, not more mouths to feed and people to protect.

A woman emerged from the center of the group, clad in a stark gray jumpsuit streaked with dust and oil. Ash blonde hair and pale aquamarine eyes left no doubt who she was.

Trezanna had only ever met one woman with eyes like that. "Catava Rolon," she whispered.

The former pampered beauty had changed in the last five years, now thin to the point of hollow cheeks, her clothes hanging like draperies on her bones. A wry sparkle appeared in Catava's stunning eyes as she met Trezanna's gaze. "Never thought you'd see me again, did you?"

CHAPTER 2

"CAN'T say that I expected to," Trezanna said.

She watched Catava Rolon for a moment, wondering if a handshake would be acceptable. Catava's stiff stance suggested the answer was no.

Looking at the rest of the group Trezanna found no warmth in their expressions. Perhaps they were as worn out as they appeared, or perhaps they still carried old resentments from having once been part of Dragonfleet, the Solarii's sector rival. Either way, finding Catava, the once unapproachable daughter of a high-ranking Dragonfleet officer, on the doorstep of her office was a shock.

"I didn't expect to be back," Catava said. "When we left Dragonfleet for the Zeta system five years ago, we believed our Khimeyr would be able to establish a colony and begin again. But things didn't work out like we hoped." She paused, her eyes filling with pain. "We've suffered unspeakable losses."

"Why are you here?" Trezanna asked.

"We saw you'd been attacked."

"This? No, this is new. Estrella hasn't been brave enough to strike on our soil yet. Mostly skirmishes in space, territorial bickering. This is something else altogether." Trezanna eyed her. "So why are you here?"

"We want to come home. Estrella ran the Khimeyr out of Dragonfleet space, and we shouldn't have let her. We're ready to put her in her place. We can help you do it."

"Incredible." Trezanna struggled to keep her face composed. As much as she needed help, could she trust someone so close to her enemy? Surely Catava's ties to Dragonfleet ran deep, even if she now belonged to the splinter faction Khimeyr.

Debating the best course of action, Trezanna reached for Catava's arm. Perhaps they should speak in private. It tended to promote plain speaking.

"Come in my office," Trezanna said, opening the door.

The crowd fell back. Their eyes were haunted and their faces gaunt, like people who had lived among the dead.

As Catava walked toward the office, she touched several of those she passed with a reassuring hand.

The office was sparsely furnished with gypsy bits and pieces of equipment. At least there was a fresh coat of pale blue paint. Trezanna felt self-conscious about the room's haphazard appearance. What did that say about her leadership ability? Wasn't she supposed to be competent, in charge? A small voice in her head mocked her for being ridiculous. Who expected a command to be picture perfect during a pirate raid?

Least of all this broken woman before her.

Catava stood awkwardly in front of the desk, looking closer to Trezanna's forty-five years than her own age, somewhere near thirty. She cleared her throat and glanced at Trezanna. "Not your usual uniform, I take it."

Trezanna closed the door and looked down at the scrubs ruefully. "No. I'm afraid mine was damaged by the pirates today. The Arkosians are back."

"Ah. That explains what we've seen, then. When we arrived last night, everything was still smoking. Between that and Estrella's temper, how many personnel do you have left?" The woman lowered herself into a chair with arthritic slowness, crossing her legs, leaning forward to listen.

The question pinged Trezanna's radar. The situation was much too irregular to be handing out information like holiday gifts. Last they had heard, someone else led the Khimeyr. Could Catava, the Khimeyr second-in-command, be trusted?

"Where's Luca?" Trezanna countered.

Catava looked away, out the window. "Dead."

"I'm sorry. Luca was a good man."

When Trezanna joined the Solarii, Luca Strada was Dragonfleet liaison to the group, back when both fought the oppression of the pirates that terrorized this sector for thirty years.

The Solarii banded together on the small planet of Induna, brave individual souls who challenged the despots, gathering members as word of their alliance spread. Dragonfleet held a small outpost on the planet's largest moon, which was large enough to hold an atmosphere, often geosynchronous over the Induna colony. They were a vicious bunch, but grew even more so under the petulant, tumultuous leadership of Estrella Drake. Dissatisfied with the bounds of Dragonfleet territory, Estrella would use any excuse to carve a larger section of the sector for herself.

As allies with a single cause, the two groups fought and won, ousting the pirates in a bloody victory. But the celebration and peace had been short-lived. Without the constant gnawing of pirate fangs in her side,

Estrella instigated bickering within Dragonfleet which ultimately spawned the rebel faction Khimeyr. Strada took nearly two hundred of those unwilling to live under Estrella's *prima donna* rule and moved them to the next planetary system, Zeta, promising them a new colony, a place to enjoy the free life they had earned.

But apparently that peace, too, had been denied.

"Something got Strada on a scouting mission seventeen months ago, an animal or—" Catava shrugged. Her voice was devoid of emotion, but the sorrow in her eyes was unmistakable. "He wasn't the only one. Zeta Colony was never the paradise we hoped it would be. Many dreams died there."

Were the rumors true? Trezanna had heard that Catava turned down countless offers of marriage, hoping Strada would woo her, even finally abandoning home and family to follow him to Zeta's shattered utopia. No wonder Catava seemed sad at Strada's loss.

"Let me get your people settled." Trezanna slipped the borrowed com from her pocket and called her security office.

The accent in the voice that answered told her it was Winston. His Terran heritage came from an area called Down Under, and his speech was quirky.

"I need some room for new recruits," Trezanna told Winston through the com. Then she turned to Catava. "How many?"

"Ninety-two." Catava dropped her eyes, as though ashamed to come begging.

Trezanna passed that number to Winston. "C-Wing is still standing, right?"

"Last I saw the place, ma'am," Winston's voice echoed. "But ain't checked yon since yesterday mornin'. Stand by." After a murmured conversation in the background, an affirmative response came through. "Rightio. Send 'em on along."

"Will do."

"Glad yer back amongst the livin', ma'am." Winston's voice held genuine warmth.

"Thank you." Touched by his concern, Trezanna thumbed the receiver to neutral and set the device on her cluttered desk. Taking a paper and pen, she scribbled directions to C-Wing and slid the paper across the desk to Catava. "That should get you started. Anything else I can do for you?"

"You still don't trust me, do you?" Catava stood, the lines on her face telling the hard tale of those five years more clearly than words.

"Trezanna, there are ninety-two of us left. We have a couple dozen ships and a history with Estrella. You can take us or leave us. But you should take us."

Trezanna knew Catava was probably right. Reluctant to make a commitment, she chose to deal with immediate needs. She was good at that. The rest could wait.

"Let your people get settled in and relax as long as the pirates let us. Estrella has kept her sniping to harassment of our ships away from the safety of the planet, but I wouldn't put it past her to come at us, knowing we've been hit by the pirates. Never a dull moment, right?" Her smile felt stretched and tired. "Extra clothing stores are in Cargo Bay four. Galley ports operate fairly standard, and the food supplies aren't too low. Power is iffy."

"I've got people who became expert in saving failing systems. I'll make sure they pitch in."

"Appreciated. We'll talk once I get a chance to take stock of our situation, all right?" Trezanna stood up in dismissal.

Catava took a deep breath, let it out. "Thank you," she said quietly. "If you hadn't welcomed us…." Her voice trailed off, flooded with deep relief, and Trezanna sensed how close to the breaking point she must be, responsible for so many and nowhere safe to turn.

"If the pirates kill us all, I'm not sure you'll be so grateful to be here," Trezanna replied in a sharper voice than she had intended. Damned pirates. Damned Estrella. Damned life. Sure seemed like it.

The Khimeyr woman left the room. Amidst murmured rumblings and questions Trezanna couldn't quite make out, the group dispersed slowly in the direction of the empty wing.

Trezanna slid into her chair, closing her eyes, her injury draining her energy. Despite her reservations, the new recruits would seriously bolster Solarii forces and equipment. She had no choice. She had to accept them.

She and Catava would have to watch each others' backs, while at the same time each protected her own.

CHAPTER 3

TREZANNA ran hard, boots pounding the cold ground as she traveled the forest path.

On this, the second morning following the attack, she had come outside to make inspection of the damage in full light. The sight of the outlying buildings was almost more than she could take. The huge metal shop adjacent to the main hangar that contained all their spare ship parts, equipment and tools, was spared, but the textiles unit had taken a hit. Reports indicated the machinery that sewed their clothing and built their small furniture was intact, but some of the stores were wiped out.

Trezanna continued running, feeling the pull of her healing injury. In some way, she was hoping the physical activity would dull her vision to the sight before her, the burial grounds on the outskirts of the base. Seven new graves were obvious with their upturned soil. She could recall the faces and the names of those that died. She had let them down, all of them.

And for what? The pirates claimed rights to a huge portion of the space that surrounded Dragonfleet and Solarii territory, an area including several asteroids rich in mineral deposits, part of the original grant given to the Solarii by Space Force. If it were only space, the Solarii ruling Council would have let it go. But they needed the ores and metals for their own survival, and for trade. No possibility of capitulation.

So they refused to adjust the border.

Six years before the pirates had fought them for it. Fought them and lost. Since then, the Solarii maintained a tight vigil. The pirates had been seen only seldom in the intervening years. Much more likely their attacker would be Estrella in her sleek *Talon,* using Trezanna's ships for target practice, mocking the Solarii and directing her subordinates with her sharp tongue.

Though the old Terran roots of her name might have suggested the soft glow of a star in a night sky, those who personally dealt with Estrella knew the slight brunette to be fiery, crafty and slick as an avaricious opportunist could be. The occasional defector spoke of a huge physical plant under her main base that produced all the supplies they needed and built their ships, but it was staffed by people who were hardly treated better than slaves. Her years in power had created a political structure which reinforced her strengths and covered her weaknesses. So far, she had gotten her own spoiled way.

The Solarii were not likely to get help from outside, either. Most had families reckoning back to the Diaspora, a time years before when Terra ejected millions of its overcrowded residents into space to find their own way. Those old Earth residents clumped into groups, determined to keep their heritage alive. In the vastness of space, most of them concentrated on maintaining themselves and their families in whatever small corner of the universe they could conquer.

Space Force had ostensibly been set up to monitor and assist the Terran colonists, smoothing contacts with other races, and providing support under threats of attack. Trezanna had done her share when she worked for the Force. But she really couldn't think that they would come to help her after she had been summarily cashiered.

Stumbling over a root, Trezanna finally slowed to a walk, breathing hard. The arrival of the Khimeyr was perfectly timed, providing a small window of hope. Together, they might form a plan to best fight off the pirates, before they turned their attention to the containment of Estrella. She would call a meeting of the Ruling Council that afternoon, she decided, and then invite Catava Rolon and her advisors to join them.

Taking a deep breath of the crisp air, she felt better. Rebuilding was already underway and soon everything might be back to what they considered normal.

"Perhaps the pirates were just testing us," Trezanna murmured, looking out over the crop fields to the west. "We showed them we weren't slacking. They can just move on to someone less prepared."

On the way back to the main facility, Trezanna reflected on the changes in Catava. Personal ties had a way of complicating life. Various liaisons over the years had taught her that. She was no celibate.

She even had a child.

McGregor Donovan, leader of a small outpost in the Grand Duchess sector and her lover of two years, had charmed her into letting their baby daughter Keridwen stay with him for several months while Trezanna handled a crucial mission for Space Force. When she had finally finished her assignment and flown home to make sure the visit was going well, she found his house abandoned. No one at the outpost was willing to give her any information on their whereabouts. Heartbroken, she searched for her daughter for years, using the resources of Space Force as long as her superiors would tolerate it. After months of distraction and sorrow, her career vanished as surely as McGregor had.

My little girl would be twenty-one now.

Trezanna frowned and slammed the mental door on that memory. She couldn't allow her personal pain to interfere with her job. Better to shut distressing feelings away. Keep everything painful hidden, which was easier to do some days than others.

Entering the administration building, she found people busy cleaning up debris. The Solarii, all of them, were full of heart. Trezanna spoke words of encouragement to each person she passed. Her destination was the main lounge, a room best described as a family room, where crew and staff spent their off-hours. It was a place to relax and talk about the day's activities and release steam. Some twelve meters square, the room had a thick brown carpet, its white walls decorated with artwork created by the base residents. Tables of all sizes were scattered across the room, along with worn couches and chairs in whatever haphazard configuration the room's occupants found useful at the time.

The usual gathering spot was the three-meter brown plasteel bar Winston and his buddies had installed soon after their arrival. The Bar was stocked with intoxicating beverages, as well as other less dangerous liquids. It was also the home of several hotpots, where inhabitants made their derivatives of Terran coffee, tea and other brews to warm and stimulate themselves.

When she volunteered to become administrator of the Solarii, Trezanna mainly kept to her private office, preferring to work in order and solitude. But she soon realized that everything important was discussed in the lounge. That was when she decided to have her tech people wire an auxiliary console into the corner behind the bar. Now she could monitor morale, while picking up information that might not make it up the usual chain of command.

This day, the only occupant of the room was Bethany Garcia, one of Boring's nurses, who nodded a blonde head wearily at the administrator, and then returned to her cup of tea and the stack of charts balanced on her round belly.

"Things calming down?" Trezanna asked, as she slid onto her firm-backed broad stool.

"Some." Bethany pointed to the top chart. "Dr. Talib isn't doing so well. But Dr. B says she'll pull through fine." She turned her round face to Trezanna and shifted uncomfortably on the hard chair. "You're looking better than yesterday, ma'am."

Trezanna smiled. "Let's hope so. You're still feeling all right?"

Bethany nodded. "Dr. Boring says work is good for pregnant women. I'm not due for weeks yet." She ran a hand over her bulging abdomen. "But this little one doesn't know he's supposed to rest sometimes."

"It'll all happen soon enough," Trezanna said. She smiled as she booted up her console to read the daily reports. She struggled with a burst of envy for the young mother-to-be. But all was not rosy in Bethany's future. Her husband Raimundo had been killed several months before in a surprise Dragonfleet attack near one of the asteroids, so Bethany would be raising her child alone.

Security reported some trouble between the Solarii and Khimeyr officers during the moving-in process. Despite her welcome of Catava's people, it would take time to establish a good working relationship and trust. Solarii personnel had good reason to dislike those of Dragonfleet. Whether the Khimeyr were different remained to be seen. She sent a memo she hoped had been upbeat to all personnel, inviting them to take advantage of the opportunity to work with the newcomers.

The counter was still covered in dust from the attack the day before. Absently, Trezanna brushed it away. Just within reach was the galley window. She reached over and nabbed a piece of havafruit and some water. Then she turned her attention to the survey of Solarii resources. Food was at an acceptable amount. They had fifty ships of assorted sizes. Twelve were under repair. All together, they were seven hundred and forty one adult crew and staff. Nearly a hundred more if they counted Catava's people. All the same, their stores would become strained with the advent of the Khimeyr and the extra supplies needed for repairs.

Trezanna studied the staff list. The five members of the Ruling Council had thankfully survived, including herself and Dr. Boring.

Chase Austin, a young woman, tall and willowy with green eyes, with no family or ties other than the Solarii, led the Solarii security force, including traditional purser duties of billeting of troops. Keeping track of where people belonged tended to give the strawberry blonde a valuable edge in heading off squabbles.

Technical Director Julian McKinley maintained the internal systems of Marus, the Solarii computer system, and communications, as well as overseeing the shipyard and fleet. He was young, just a year into adulthood, but he was so apt that he managed to snatch the position from others that were older and more experienced. With thick black hair and an Asian tilt to his dark eyes, from his mother's heritage, belied the

Scots name his father had left him.

Operations and Intelligence was staffed by Rumadan, an antennaed Viorn, a lavender-skinned humanoid with feline characteristics and markings, her eyes solid black with no iris. That ebony stare had put Trezanna off at first, as it did most humans.

The rest of Trezanna's people were divided among the departments. She was fortunate that so many who believed in individual freedoms also believed in feeding intelligence and education. Many skilled people had found their way to the Solarii over the years.

Three doctors and four nurse-techs worked under Dr. Boring's direct supervision. The extensive medical department seemed like a luxury during the peaceful times. She often toyed with the idea of scaling back expenditures, but now she was glad that idea never took form. If the infirmary had not been fully stocked, the loss of life during the pirate attacks would have been much greater.

Several Solarii engineers were killed in various attacks as they worked on site trying to save shielding or weapons. Tech was down to three. Hastily, they added some general workers to the security force, while some were pressed into combat duty, as was the case with Dr. Talib.

Now another group of space survivors would help swell the ranks, though it was hard to guess from the ragtag Khimeyr mob Trezanna had seen outside her office the day before what skills might emerge. She sent a second memo to convene a meeting of her staff, and was in process of sending one to Catava Rolon when the door opened abruptly and the Khimeyr spokeswoman walked in.

Overnight a transformation had occurred. It would seem that a full night's sleep, along with some fresh wash facilities and a clean navy blue uniform, did much to restore the Khimeyran's dignity. Blonde hair was piled neatly on her head in a loose knot, and her nails were tinted a soft pink. Dark circles remained under her eyes. Whatever damage the failure of Zeta Colony caused would take more than one day to heal.

"Good morning," Catava said, walking briskly across the room. She nodded to Garcia and took a seat at the counter.

Trezanna raised an eyebrow and gave a slight smile. "Kafee?"

Catava looked wistful. "Real kafee? It's been so long. All we had at Zeta was a kind of bitter herb that we brewed into tea."

"Don't give it a second thought," Trezanna said, making her way over to the kafee maker. She poured a steaming mug full and then brought it back to Catava. "I'm sure it was difficult surviving day to day, even without thinking of luxuries. Right next to you, in the galley window, is a tray with milk and sugar."

Catava clutched the cup in her hand, just inhaling its fragrance for a few moments. When she looked up, her eyes were wet. She wiped them roughly in frustration. "I shouldn't. I'm sorry."

"No, no. Don't apologize."

With the arrival of the Khimeyr, Trezanna thought she would have to deal with the spoiled woman-child she had once known, but time had changed Catava. What could have happened to bring about such an alteration? It could have been the loss of so many comrades. And she couldn't help speculating on what happened between Catava Rolon and Luca Strada. That would be a story worth hearing. But now was not the time for storytelling.

Trezanna looked away, finding a scratch on the counter to scrub at as Catava sipped the kafee with a grateful sigh. "I've been reviewing troop strength and supplies so we can discuss them when we meet."

"Of course. When were you expecting to compare notes?"

"Early this afternoon some time." Trezanna pursed her lips thoughtfully. What better way to establish the Khimeyrans' commitment than to move them to the front line? "Would your people be willing to mount the afternoon patrol? The pirates haven't attacked again today."

Catava gave a soft laugh. "They probably won't." Her eyes took on the hard consistency of gems. "I'd be more prepared for Estrella to come poking around. She has to know we're back. Believe me, she's not expecting us, and she won't know how to react."

Trezanna shrugged. Catava's statement didn't ring of arrogance, but of familiarity with the enemy. She could be right. Estrella was nothing if not predictable. "The morning sweep didn't show either of the fleets. Maybe it's just going to be a quiet day."

"Well, that's up to you. My pilots will fly, if you need them to." Catava took another sip of the hot kafee. It seemed to melt the chill from her eyes. "With us working together we'll have to come to some kind of arrangement. A mutual respect, if you know what I mean."

Trezanna felt her lips curl into a strained smile. "I know. It will take time." It was already in her plans to ease the tension between them. With a few delicate touches to her console, she printed off a copy of the staff list and handed it to the Khimeyr leader. "This is our roster."

Catava glanced at it. "All adults?"

"I didn't list the children. We've got sixty-two at last count."

"We've brought three," Catava said, looking away for a moment.

"We'll add them to the care facility list." Trezanna tried to guess the mystery behind Catava's look. A colony would not have survived without a healthy number of children to populate the next generation. Perhaps that was why they returned.

"All right." Catava finished her kafee and set the cup on the dusty counter. "What time?"

"Thirteen-hundred."

"I'll let my people know." Catava, ever the Khimeyr officer, nodded and left the room.

Trezanna sat back on her stool and considered the exchange. *Unexpected.* She shook her head and moved on to her agenda for her staff meeting.

CHAPTER 4

CATAVA Rolon walked back to her assigned quarters.

The gray walls of the hallway reflected little personality or warmth. Functional, just like the Solarii. Trezanna Len seemed no less efficient or driven, as the Solarii and Dragonfleet fought side-by-side. Perhaps the woman had never enjoyed a day of passion in her life.

Catava remembered having heard that Trezanna thrived on work and remained distant from those around her, never becoming too involved. Luca Strada had always respected those ethics. Despite the haphazard appearance of the base, Trezanna looked fit. Not even a streak of gray showed in that auburn hair.

Maybe this could work.

C Wing was abuzz with the voices of her people, most looking more rested and like themselves. Catava even found an occasional smile. *Much better.* Inside her suite, the largest of the wing, she peeked into the bedroom, finding the bed still occupied.

"Come on, little rascals. Time to find something to eat!" Catava pulled the covers back to find two small bodies in tucked positions. "Rise and shine, now."

The boy, Chad, just short of four years old, rolled over and groaned. "Momma Cat, not hungry."

Catava laughed and sat on the bed to tickle him. "You will be soon." She turned her attention to the toddler girl next to Chad and smoothed rumpled dark curls back from her face. "Come on, Suzi. We've got things to do today." The girl whimpered and reached for Catava, who scooped her up into her arms. "It's all right, Suzi girl."

The boy struggled the rest of the way awake and crawled into her lap, too. She held them both close, gaining as much comfort from their tiny warm bodies as she gave.

They should have been mine. It wasn't the first time that thought plagued her.

When they began squirming in her arms, she knew they were fully awake. The previous day, she had managed to pick up some bright new clothing from the store before stopping by the galley port for some breakfast grain and a fruit juice she didn't recognize.

With nimble fingers Catava helped them dress before setting the table. "Here you go. Yummy!"

Chad took the long way around the room, finding a multitude of other things to pick and poke at. Finally, he climbed up to the small table to stare at the bowl suspiciously, and then drank some juice. "Good," he announced.

"Told you." Catava set Suzi in a chair. The girl selected a handful of grain from her bowl and lined them up in a design on the table. The activity seemed to please her. "Suzi," Catava scolded, but her frown only brought a radiant smile to the face of the child, her eyes like chocolate drops lit from within. When was the last time the child had smiled? She couldn't remember.

Catava grabbed more kafee from the galley port, and then joined them with a pad of paper to plan what information she would reveal to Trezanna.

They had arrived with twenty-five ships, just as she told Trezanna. But the words she had used purposely glorified the machinery they brought with them. Most of their ships were held together with the equivalent of spit, heavy tape, and adhesive wire. Only prayer kept them working until their arrival at the Solarii base.

In the tropical forest where the Zeta Colony was built, they never expected to find thieving native tribes, animals, and humanoids. In the last two years their parts for repairs were either stolen or simply worn beyond usefulness. Of course, the Solarii would have the means to repair them, which meant within days her offer to help would be legitimate. Her people were capable of flying the ships. There were no niceties about the last year at Zeta. Everyone did what they were assigned, regardless of any prior specialty.

The Khimeyr had become experts in making do, searching out possibilities, scouting territory, and surviving. The people? Ninety adults plus these two children and a new baby born on the Crossing back. After Luca's death, she had taken over as leader, but her true government was shared with two others of the Khimeyr.

First was Darien Pomeroy, a lean sober Space Force renegade who saw ghosts and devils behind every tree. His instinct for danger had saved lives on countless occasions.

The other was Xiu Qiaolin, a woman Catava considered as a sister. Both were raised within the privileged class of Dragonfleet, both willing to plunge into the unknown Zeta to escape Estrella's obsession for power. Trained by Dragonfleet as a combat pilot, Qiaolin had been a lieutenant and a frequent mission companion of Estrella.

The Khimeyr medical staff was decimated, and many non-assigned crew spent the last year as hunter-gatherers to assure the survival of the others. It remained to be seen how the two groups could fit their personnel puzzle pieces together.

Chad's clear voice interrupted her reverie. "Are Papa and Mamma going to find us here?"

Catava looked at him, struck to the heart. Despite her father's angry words of discouragement, she had longed for a love between herself and Luca. She had left her rank, her privilege, her family at Dragonfleet to follow Luca to Zeta, hoping that when they arrived there he would see her, really see her, and realize how she felt.

Instead, on the crossing to Zeta, Luca fell in love with a doctor named Theria, leaving Catava no chance, not even a hope. By then, of course, her pride would not let her turn back. Instead she buried her pain, working as hard as the rest to make the Zeta Colony succeed and never wanting him to know how much she hurt.

But somehow Luca knew.

Some months after his death, Theria came to Catava, her serene manner making it impossible to resent her intrusion into such personal pain. She explained in her soft, warm voice that Luca knew of Catava's feelings. In light of Zeta's troubled circumstances, the two of them decided to ask Catava if she would care for Chad and Suzi, if anything should happen to them.

"Please say you will," Theria asked, touching her with a smooth, pale hand. "I've had a dream. My time is near."

Theria's people placed great faith in dreams. If the doctor felt her death was near, in all likelihood it was. Catava's mind spun at such an arrangement. It wasn't like she had children of her own. She never felt an attraction toward another man, not with Luca so nearby and yet untouchable. But could she do it? Luca was gone and now she would never have him. The least she could do was raise his children. She accepted the offer.

Theria died two weeks later in a ground-quake as she searched for a new settlement. No one raised an eyebrow when Catava gathered the children's things and moved them into her quarters.

Catava studied the brown-haired boy who had shared her last six months. "No, sweet. They've gone on to a better place."

The boy's hazel eyes, Luca's eyes, seemed to pierce her. "But you said *this* a better place. You said it safe and warm. You *said*."

She fumbled with the literal-mindedness of small children. "It's true, I did."

Chat waited, watching her. Catava glanced at Suzi, and found her also watching, wide-eyed.

"They're gone." Catava spoke firmly, watching the flicker in Chad's eyes. "They passed on. They won't come back, sweet. There is nowhere you can find them, not in this life."

A tear ran down Suzi's cheek and her little spoon shook in her hand. Catava reached out to pat her arm softly. "But I'm here. Momma Cat will care for you always, I promise."

Chad appeared unmoved. "When I'm dead, too, then I see them?"

Now how should she answer that? Unfamiliar with children's ways, she certainly didn't want to encourage him to harm himself. Maybe he wasn't thinking that. Maybe he was just asking a simple question.

"That could be, sweet. None of us know what happens after we die. But that won't be for a long time. I certainly hope not, anyway, because then you'll be gone. And those of us left behind will be sad, like you're sad about Papa and Momma."

A serious look on his face, Chad straightened his red over-shirt. With a nod he went back to his bowl and finished his breakfast without further comment.

Suzi slid down from her chair and came over to climb in Catava's lap, giving her a milky kiss. She hugged the baby, rocking her gently until she felt better.

The door com beeped. The children had been timid since their departure from Zeta. At the sound of the beep they quickly hid behind the table. Catava cleared their bowls away, and then answered the door. Darien Pomeroy lounged against the doorframe, unsmiling, eagle-like eyes burning.

"Dare?" Catava eyed him, not seeing anything obvious wrong.

With his black hair trimmed close and no facial growth cluttering craggy looks, Darien Pomeroy was still handsome at age forty-seven. He stubbornly wore the remains of his Dragonfleet leather pilot's jacket, the collar and elbows worn and ragged. He had obtained new pants from the Solarii stores, but it was clear from his taut muscles and clenched jaw that every fiber rebelled against even wearing anything Solarii.

"This was a bad idea," Pomeroy grumbled, pushing past her to enter.

The children scurried to the other room. Their high-pitched squeals and screeching springs clued her they were jumping on the bed, but

Catava didn't think they would hurt anything. She was learning to balance her leadership responsibilities with her care-giving ones and at this moment her leadership role was called for.

"What makes you say so?" Catava retreated to the table with her kafee and offered him a cup, black, which he took with grim thanks.

"Things locked up tight. No computer access. Rationed supplies. There are seven new graves. Mayhap we came to die with them, eh?"

"No." Her tone was firm. "No more dying. We've got to turn this around."

Pomeroy snorted. "And their better-than-you attitudes? Worse than old Space Force days. Like as not they're asking for an ass-kickin'."

Catava frowned and straightened her collar. "I know it's not easy. Dare, I'm counting on you to set a good example for the rest. We've got a bigger battle ahead of us, dealing with Estrella." She stared at him, eyes hard. "Isn't she the target? Isn't Dragonfleet our enemy?"

"Don't mean I have to like it," Pomeroy growled. His hands fidgeted, straightening his collar and picking at his shirt.

She allowed herself a smile. "No, it doesn't. As long as you do it."

Pomeroy stalked around the room, full of nervous energy. "So when we going after her? We gonna attack? Take Miramar back for our own?"

Catava slipped into one of the cushioned chairs at the table, hoping her own visible attempt at relaxation would encourage his. "I'm meeting today with Len to discuss our plans."

That stopped him. "And who'll make the decision? Miramar is *our* home. No hoity-toity Solarii woman'll tell me when I can take it back."

"I'm not saying she will. I said we'll discuss it."

Pomeroy's quick retort was cut off by the door com. Her gut twisting, anticipating it would only be more of the same, Catava went to answer it. As she had suspected, she was met by a parade of people, each with some complaint about the facilities or questions on how to operate the galley ports, or whether they were allowed to access their ships. She dealt with each in an efficient way that would have made Trezanna proud. One by one the room cleared, except for Darien. She went to him and took his arm, feeling his tense resistance through her fingertips.

"We've brought them here. We are their mother, father, brothers, and sisters. I need you to help me lead them, keep them strong, keep them proud. We will handle Estrella in time, and win our place back on Miramar. But now we are weak, and the Solarii are weak. Together we must build each other's strength for the coming battle." She squeezed his arm and looked into his eyes. "We need each other, for now."

"Mayhap," Pomeroy snapped, yanking his arm away from her. He made a gesture, pulling his finger across his throat. "Once that's done, we're done with the Solarii."

She studied him, not wanting to encourage mutiny. "If that is what the future brings."

He nodded once and stalked out.

Catava wondered what that future might be and returned to her list. She had three hours until her meeting with Trezanna Len. She expected it would be a rocky one. If her own people were of an insubordinate mind when it came to a joint effort, she could only guess Trezanna's would be as well.

Somehow the Solarii had to be convinced this venture was the only way they would all survive. Somehow.

CHAPTER 5

SO they had come crawling back.

Estrella Drake tapped the tip of her carved black dagger on the wooden table, trying to comprehend the implications of the Khimeyr return. Luca Strada and his people, incapable of living under *her* rule, now enjoyed Solarii hospitality?

It made no sense.

The tapping grew more agitated until the dagger actually stuck into the tabletop. The petite brunette growled and leaped to her feet, hurling her cup behind the bar, where it broke with a satisfying crash.

Her early morning patrol of the borders of Solarii space had revealed the presence of the Khimeyr ships. The blaze of her anger had burned so hot that none of her people dared to venture uninvited into her private chambers.

A black leather jumpsuit held her slim body close, the familiar feel comforting her. The broad mirror on the far wall reflected the flash of anger in her dark eyes. Unlike the other female social butterflies of the Dragonfleet, Estrella wore her hair in a pixie cut, which required little physical maintenance. She looked like she meant business, all the way to the tips of her polished black boots.

Her rooms, on the other hand, dripped with decadence. Power colors of red, black and deep violet covered velvet cushions, brocade coverlets and plush pillows, along with a fully stocked bar. The furniture gleamed with a shine of perfection, polished by whoever was on her black list that week. She wanted her followers to know whom they served.

Her first response after returning from her morning flight had been to shred a feather pillow, tearing it to bits with her fingers. Its remains lay on her bedchamber floor, gray fluffy bits covering the area like debris from a ship's explosion.

Frustrated by the lack of answers, Estrella channeled her anger into the question of two ships she had lost to the Arkosian pirates the week before. One a cruiser. How had that happened? Supposedly, the shields failed.

"Shields?" Estrella screeched in frustration. "What has *failed* is my engineering crew!" She slammed a fist on the intercom button and summoned Gustave Henry to her chambers.

Pacing, constant movement, seemed to calm her frantic mind.

"I'm in control," Estrella muttered, her hands clenching into fists. "I'm in control."

Whispers seemed to come from the shadows around her, attempting to shake her confidence, but she resolutely shut them out.

Estrella had been taken in a pirate's raid when she was just ten years old. For fifteen years she had been thief and trader. Back then, all that saved her during a cold, hard initiation into a pirate camp were her wits and the possession of a quick knife stolen from an unwary captor. After that, she attached herself to a succession of mentors, learning what she could from each and then discarding them for more useful ones.

She escaped in her late teens. For several lean months, she lived off what could be stolen or bartered for. Then she came across the group now called Dragonfleet. There, among the politics and intrigues, she found a home with the Dragonfleet combat unit.

Used to manipulating others, she moved up through the ranks by guile, or sometimes assassination, if that was more efficient. She had fought in the battle against the Arkosian pirates. While the Solarii made feeble attempts at assistance, Estrella was convinced that it had been the power of Dragonfleet that vanquished the foe.

Estrella had led the final assault which cremated the Arkosians' headquarters and ended their occupation of the sector. And she made sure everyone knew it.

Back then her goal had been simple. Unite the group and then rule them all. Only one blot marred her ambition, the defection of the Khimeyr led by Luca Strada. He had managed to leave with the most talented techs and a selection of equipment that devastated Dragonfleet stores. She had nearly murdered him on the spot and would have if his armed followers had not been there to back him up.

"Then you get out!" she had told him. "Get out and take your traitorous believers to hell with you!"

"Hell would only be ours if we remained, Estrella," was his reply. Though he wore his usual disarming smile, the condemnation glared from his eyes. Then he and his followers were gone.

Now they were back.

Estrella continued to pace, scheming, wondering how to discover Strada's plan, curious what incentive the Solarii might have offered him. Stepping around the detritus of the pillow, her boot heels echoed off the polished floors. Ten steps left, ten steps right. Ten steps left, ten steps right. After enough repetition, she finally achieved a modicum of calm.

The entrance of the roly-poly engineer provoked her angry glare. He bowed deeply when she noticed him, with a sharp "Ma'am!" Then he waited, uncertainty reddening his chubby face.

Estrella approached him, every muscle taut. She pinned the man with her stare, like a dead insect. A dark smile came to her face when she paused behind and noticed as he twitched. She knew he was wondering whether her legendary dagger would be plunged into his back.

It should be. The man was sloppy. But he was a wonder with a dead engine. Damn him.

Coming around to face him, she examined his visage closely, still silent and disapproving.

"Ma'am, I—"

With a single wave of her hand the man's jaw snapped shut. Gus had joined the Dragonfleet as a young man. He had been with them way before she had arrived. But he knew her ways. She even heard he chose to work the hangars to avoid coming under her eye. In all honesty, other than the maintenance of her precious *Talon*, she paid very little attention to the mechanics, preferring to leave that duty to a subordinate. Unfortunately, that long-suffering fellow was on the cruiser that had been destroyed by the Arkosian pirates.

So she needed this little worm.

She studied his eyes, ready to catch a lie if it slipped between his lips.

"The shields failed?" Estrella asked, an edge in her low voice.

"That was the report I got, ma'am." His gaze remained steady into hers. She respected that. Estrella only respected backbone or muscle. Anyone who had neither was useless to her.

"And?" She poked him in the chest.

"And what? I maintain our ships to the highest standards!" Gus snapped. "Our materials have become substandard and supplies and parts scarce. We can't do much if your suppliers sell you garbage, and you don't demand better."

Estrella's dark eyes blazed. She slapped him so hard he staggered back. "How dare you speak to me in this way?"

Gus straightened, wiping a trickle of blood from his lip. "I tell you the truth. Or does the great and powerful Estrella of Dragonfleet hide from reality?"

She growled. "I hide from nothing."

"I didn't think so. Apparently you haven't been told that what you've taken in trade is of inferior quality."

She tried to remember where they had purchased the parts. Normally, they would have ordered them manufactured by her people. But she recalled the last supplier made her an excellent deal. Possibly too good. "I shall deal with them. They will not have the opportunity to cheat anyone again."

"Ma'am." Gustave 'Gus' Henry stood respectfully but not cowed, waiting to be dismissed.

"Do not fail me again," Estrella warned.

"No, ma'am."

"You may go."

After he left, Estrella made her way to the bar and poured a fluted glass of a strong green liqueur rumored to be addictive. Its flavor burned sweetness and lit a fire of confidence in her heart. She savored it, pleased with the encounter, and wondered whether Gustave Henry would prove as satisfying an ally as her last engineer. She could smell his fear. He was probably envisioning his death, she thought. Yet, he found the courage to stand up to her. He was no coward.

The most important thing was how she maintained her authority during their conversation.

Ultimately, that was how Estrella gained her leadership of Dragonfleet. Krainel, the one called the Braveheart, led the group when Estrella wormed her way into the organization. She observed his style, finding a pattern of soft treatment of certain members. Over a matter of time, quietly calling attention to his favoritism and patronage in the right quarters, undercut his authority. Soon the warriors changed their allegiance, openly challenging Krainel's orders in council. Once she acquired enough support, Estrella proclaimed herself leader of Dragonfleet. She challenged him to a fight for the honor. And fight he did. But he was older, slower and drained by the constant conflict. It took hardly an effort to finish him.

Then she was Empress. Queen. Lady of all the Heavens.

Estrella laughed at her own characterization. The commander's seat at Dragonfleet was hardly royal. But there were comforts, including her choice of the eager young men vying for her attention. She tried to keep several on the hook at any given time. It made for interesting competition, but also opened the possibility for some young thing coming up through the ranks with his or her eye on Estrella's ruling seat. Of all people, she should know those dangers.

Her mind turned back to the problem of Strada's people. Had he taken back all two hundred which had left with him? Qiao? Jack? She remembered Darien Pomeroy's beady eyes, ever vigilant, greedy, and nosy. Men like that could survive anything. For certain, he was among their number. She knew it.

Now that the green and her conversation with Henry had released some of her tension, she sat at the table and retrieved the dagger, idly flipping it in her right hand as she scribbled out notes with her left.

This new information necessitated changes in her plan of attack. The addition of the Khimeyr ships to the Solarii forces would change the balance of power. She would have to wait and see how aggressive the refugees would be before she could decide how to proceed.

And I nearly had them, too.

Estrella growled and tossed the dagger across the room where it pierced the wall with a satisfying thud. She might even have to resort to diplomacy. She could try talking. Anything to buy time before she blew them all to hell. A sly smile crossed her face, as she headed out to announce the Khimeyr return.

CHAPTER 6

TREZANNA could tell by Rumadan's plum skin-tone that the council talks were not going well.

They had been at it for a while at the large round table in the stark conference room, long enough that the first pitcher of citrus drink was gone and the second invaded.

Trezanna stood and stretched her aching legs hoping to ease the tension within. Instead of her stiff uniform, she wore a soft green jumpsuit that was at least comfortable. Reading the others' postures revealed a lot about how the Solarii would deal with the return of the Khimeyr.

Julian McKinley sat straight as a board, the uniform he insisted on wearing pressed but grease-stained, railing at length about the Khimeyr ships cluttering up his hangar bay. "I can't do anything with these crates of bolts!" he protested as his stylus playing a nervous staccato rhythm on the datapad in front of him. "Do you have any idea what poor condition they're in? I might be able to build two good ships out of the lot of them!"

"It can't be that bad, Jules." Chase lounged slightly in her padded chair, having already voiced her opinion of the potential security problems, projected from the several violent encounters she had handled between the Solarii and the newcomers. She, like Trezanna, wore a more relaxed jumpsuit, hers a pale yellow, specially made for her with concealed pockets for weapons. "They've been flying them for the last six months. Do what you can to keep them in the sky a little longer. We need all the birds we can get."

Trezanna agreed, sipping a lightly sweetened green herb tea that Dr. Boring prescribed to promote calm. It wasn't working. She idly stared out the window across from her chair, the midday sun providing brilliant light. She imagined the feel of that sun on her skin, knowing it would be warm and comforting. Their base, located in the southern hemisphere of Induna, experienced longer days and warmer nights as their planet rotated its axis away from their star. It would be some time before the coming of the frozen season.

Where will we all be by then? Will we survive that long?

She caught Boring's amused eye. The Eponan found it hard to contain himself at the prospect of having enough bodies, ships and equipment to end the war, and stated he found the rest of the details insignificant.

"We must work together," Boring announced cheerfully. "The good of the many is the ultimate goal."

"They ar-r-re an unknown quantity," Rumadan shot back, ears flared and bent slightly backward. Her accented speech rolled the R's like a cat's purr. "They are Dr-r-ragonfleet."

"They are Khimeyr," Trezanna prodded softly.

"Unknown." Rumadan's black eyes glittered with insistent suspicion.

Trezanna held enough suspicion for all of them. She understood the feelings of each of her council members. But the doctor was right. If they lost the war, the rest was irrelevant. She turned back to McKinley. "Your cooperative attitude will do much to convince the Khimeyr that we are to be trusted as well. I'm sure with some patience and parts...."

McKinley was not persuaded. "And where am I to get these parts? I've been scrounging for enough just to keep our own ships flying. You wouldn't want to see some of the crap I've been...." His voice trailed off, as if he just realized to whom he was speaking.

"A marvelous job you do, yes young Julian!" Dr. Boring bubbled with encouragement as he smiled at the engineer's agitation. "When you make something from nothing, you are a magician, or a miracle worker at the least."

Rumadan scowled at the doctor, and then turned to Trezanna. "What access do you intend to give them to our computer? Shall they be able to steal our deepest secrets?"

"That's something I want the Council to decide. I'm sure Catava Rolon will ask when we meet." Marus held strict safeguards. Many Solarii didn't have clearance for information about troop strength, enemies and other important data. But the Khimeyr? Another story as far as Trezanna was concerned, at least until they proved themselves.

Chase's green eyes studied them. "I was someone unpredictable, an orphan. An unknown." She looked pointedly at Rumadan. "Yet I was welcomed here as a new link in a bigger chain. I earned responsibility, but it didn't take long. And it was because the Solarii were open to immigrants. They had a cause at heart, the cause of fighting against oppressors, whoever they might be. Since I have become one of you, we have aided many in their battles. Can you say that's not what the

Khimeyr need?"

"They don't have to seek it at our cost," McKinley grumbled.

"Exactly. Likely steal it and take it back to the Dragon Queen." Rumadan, practically twitching in her seat, finally rose abruptly and started to pace.

"Possible," Trezanna said. "But I suggest we give them a chance. Limit their access at first, control the amount of damage that can be done, without insulting them. Unfortunate as it may be, Catava is correct. We need the Khimeyr right now. If the pirates decide to engage us, Marus' projection shows we could be *finished* in less than six months."

A long silence was broken at last by the doctor's buoyant voice. "If we're decided, I have patients waiting for my healing touch."

"We haven't decided anything." McKinley ran a hand through his shaggy hair, the corners of his eyes crinkled with frustration.

"Then let's decide," Trezanna said. "Do we accept the Khimeyr offer of help?"

The final answer was three in favor, two against. Trezanna nodded in dismissal, and her Ops and Tech directors virtually bolted for the door. The doctor smiled as he came around the table to pat Trezanna on the shoulder. "Mount Hunter wasn't formed in a day."

"What?" Trezanna frowned.

"The Doc's right." Chase got to her feet and laughed. "These things take time. Let's see what Catava says. If she turns you down, she may make your decision a lot easier."

Chase walked out with Dr. Boring, who started a joke about two Rigellian salesmen. As the door closed, their laughter echoed.

Trezanna drank the rest of her tea, desperately seeking calm. A knock at the door let her know the Khimeyr leader was ready. *Round two.*

"Come in."

* * *

TREZANNA watched Catava slip inside the conference room.

After looking over her shoulder at those who had just left, Catava turned back to Trezanna. "From the looks of things, your people aren't any more enthusiastic about working together than mine."

Trezanna studied the woman who managed to make a standard dark blue jumpsuit look tailored and sexy. How did she do it? Perfect proportions, like a child's doll. Suppressing a flash of envy, Trezanna shrugged and gestured for Catava to help herself to refreshment.

"I don't blame them," Trezanna said. "No one's had time to adjust to your arrival." She cocked a brow at Catava, wondering how much of her officers' thought process to share. She shifted in her chair, trying to look relaxed. If she could project a superior attitude, perhaps she would shake the feeling of being needy. "If we'd known your plans, we could have prepared. Why didn't you warn us you were coming?"

The Khimeyr leader smiled. "We didn't want to get blown up before we had a chance to talk." Catava took a glass of tea from the tray and then sat directly across from Trezanna. "So is it worth talking? Or have you already made up your minds to toss us out?"

Trezanna pursed her lips, and then nodded. "I can't say it will be smooth, but reality is what it is." She replayed the council discussion quickly in her mind. "Tell me if I'm wrong. Your ships are in horrendous condition, our supplies are short, and we're both down a lot of personnel. All of this in the face of dealing with a mad woman and some space-grabbing pirates."

Catava pulled a small datapad from her jumpsuit pocket and handed it to Trezanna with a tight smile. "No, that about sums it up."

"Good. Just as long as we both know how screwed we are." Trezanna returned the smile in kind and turned her attention to the information on the unfamiliar datapad. Hard to believe a group existed that was worse off than hers was at the moment.

The other woman added wildflower honey to her tea. "From the list you gave me this morning, I think our crew will complement yours."

"I see that." Trezanna tapped a finger on the small screen, tipping it to catch the dimmed overhead lights. Even though the command center was quickly being repaired, the base was only operating at seventy percent overall power. They would have to exercise special caution.

"What does Estrella have in the way of staff? Do you have any idea?"

Catava shook her head, fingers tugging idly at the zipper on her jumpsuit. "When the Khimeyr left, we took the majority of the tech types. We never received much news from her base." A hard light entered her eyes. "She received some from ours. For a while."

At Trezanna's curious look, she reached for her cup, her fingers white where they held it. "Estrella managed to smuggle someone aboard the Zeta transport. Nearly six months he lived side by side with us, sending her reports about everything. We found copies of his com-spools." She let her cup brush against her lips, something in her eyes lost in memory. "Luca killed him on the spot."

"I'm not surprised. Estrella's a devious bitch." Trezanna set the pad down. "Can we really do this? At least long enough to assure all of us will survive?"

"It is the only logical option. But I'd be foolish to promise it will happen smoothly."

Trezanna reviewed the staff list, seeing a couple of familiar names, but none that leaped out as known troublemakers. "Anyone in particular we need to handle with a gentle touch?"

"Darien Pomeroy is a good man, but not a trusting one. Others resent being here as well." Catava slumped back into her chair. "I think we'd be better served to concentrate on those who will work together. Pair them up, yours and mine, let the others see by example that we can succeed."

Trezanna considered the suggestion in light of her council's split vote. What choice did she have? "Sounds reasonable. We could use people in medical and security? If trouble breaks out, having someone from each camp involved in quelling the outbreak might prevent claims of favoritism."

"Exactly."

"I've got a couple of pilot-mechanics I could send to work on your ships. My chief engineer is swamped at the moment." Trezanna already had people in mind. Winston was a friendly sort. He and Shelby Hussard would be good ambassadors.

"I'll choose some likely candidates." Catava sat back in her chair, a look of cool assessment in her eyes.

How much of Catava's cooperation was born of desperation? Once the Khimeyr had the chance to defeat Estrella, would they turn on the Solarii? Trezanna didn't want to think about that.

"What are we up against?" she asked. "Tell me how to gain an edge over Dragonfleet."

Catava hesitated. "Five years since we've been there. I'm not sure what to say. Estrella's ruthless, aggressive, and every step she's taken as Dragonfleet's leader has built her image bigger and stronger. I'd say she genuinely considers herself invincible."

That, Trezanna believed. She still felt Catava held back, but her memories of this woman were of a much different person. She was unsure how far she could push. "And what benefit do the Khimeyr get from this? You said you wanted to go home. Surely you don't believe she will just vacate the premises and hand you the security codes?"

"Hardly." Catava's voice was dry as a winter wind.

"It's not that I'm not grateful you and your people are here to help. I'd been praying for some relief, though the Holy knows I would never have expected this." Trezanna paused, sharing a hint of a smile. "I suppose what I'm asking is what you've considered doing after we battle Estrella. If we send her packing, you could take Miramar. If we don't, there are other places."

"We don't intend to give up the fight for our home until none of us remain." The Khimeyr woman's voice was dark with grim conviction. "I owe my people more than the promise of death. We must defeat her. We have no choice."

Depressed to hear their bleak outlook put so bluntly, Trezanna nodded. "Neither do we. All right. Our mutual need and mutual goals will have to sustain us for now."

Trezanna let herself leave the table to busy her hands with a fresh cup of tea. The herbs totally failed to provide any calming influence, so she switched to a black tea with a smoky undertone, taking it with no sweetener.

"Did your people get settled in? I heard about a couple of scuffles, but nothing major. Enough food and supplies?"

"Sufficient for now." Catava watched her thoughtfully. "But they're restless. That's the reason I want to get them blended with your people as soon as possible. We've been in a fight for our very existence every day for the last two years. They need occupation, before their nervous energy boils over into...." She trailed off with a shrug.

"No end of work that needs done here. Those who aren't flying can join repair crews. Once all your ships are restored to good working order, we can assign your pilots into regular patrol rotation. Pomeroy and others wound a little tighter can take reconnaissance missions into Dragonfleet space, since they'll know some ins and outs over there."

"If Estrella has left everything as it was. You shouldn't expect too much at first." Inquisitive eyes turned to Trezanna. "And me? What do you think you'll find for me to do?"

Now that was the real question, wasn't it? If either group leader took a subordinate position, their people would be up in arms. Induna was Trezanna's to command, but if she truly intended to be fair, she had to acknowledge Catava's right to lead. Shared leadership at this level of trust, however, would be touchy.

"What do you want to do?" Trezanna asked.

"Not as easy as it sounds, is it?" Catava gave a laugh that hinted of some private joke. Her long fingers captured a shred of plastic on the table, worrying it between them. "I'm catching flak already because I haven't just taken over." Her eyes flicked to Trezanna, her foot tapping in disjointed rhythm. "You lead the Solarii. We're here at your sufferance."

"But they don't want to follow my orders, do they?"

Catava smiled, shrugged. No answer was needed.

Trezanna would have been sure at this time yesterday that they shared nothing in common. The Catava Rolon she remembered from the previous alliance between Dragonfleet and the Solarii was a daughter of privilege, spoiled and poisonous.

Trezanna had also changed. The first time they had fought the space pirates, she could have been considered idealistic and naïve. But day-to-day details of ensuring the safety and existence of a transplanted culture wore that optimism thin, as a rock could be worn away by repetitive falling of single water drops over time. Now she and Catava seemed more alike than different, at least on the surface. It was plain there were unknown depths to Catava. Trezanna held her own secrets, as well.

Taking a deep breath, she cleared her mind. A solution must be found. One came to her and she plunged ahead.

"What if I named you temporary commander of the offensive forces?" Trezanna paused, trying to judge the reaction on Catava's face. "You'd report directly to me and be responsible for both Khimeyr and Solarii personnel involved in the Dragonfleet conflict. I'd continue as administrator and make all other decisions for the whole group. But I want to have the final word on major initiatives."

Catava gave a smile that looked forced. "Don't trust my judgment?"

"I don't know your judgment," Trezanna countered.

In the brief silence that followed, the women eyed each other, taking full measurement. Trezanna didn't allow herself to relax until she saw Catava's frozen smile melt into something more genuine.

"I'll inform my people," the Catava said.

"Fine. I'll let the council know ASAP. We should start making joint assignments as soon as possible. Estrella may be cautious, now that circumstances have changed, but she won't be shy for long."

"Exactly." Catava reached out her hand. "Thank you."

Trezanna, surprised, shook her hand. "For what?"

"Taking the Khimeyr, or their remains at least, seriously."

Trezanna could have sworn Catava's lip trembled on that last part. Who would have believed that loss of arrogance? Some day she would have to find out what happened at Zeta, what burning fire had seared away the selfishness and reduced Catava Rolon to her core.

"Your group may be all that stand between the Solarii and

extinction." Trezanna straightened her jacket, feeling a chill crawl up her spine at the thought of her base being wiped out. "We need you. I, for one, am glad you're here."

"Frankly, I hadn't known what might happen when we arrived. This is a far cry from the response Estrella might have given to a request for alliance from one in need."

On that, they agreed as well.

Trezanna nodded. "I'll have Winston stop by this afternoon."

"Darien can watch for him. Make sure he doesn't have trouble." Catava smiled faintly and set her cup back on the tray before leaving the room.

United we stand, divided we fall. Just because the maxim predated them by centuries didn't make it any less true.

Trezanna tapped a finger on her lips. Deep in thought, she offered a small prayer to the Holy that together they would stand against Estrella.

Certainly she had more confidence than from two days before. Maybe now it could happen. She allowed herself the satisfaction of believing it as she headed out to find Winston.

CHAPTER 7

MONTY Winston grumbled all the way into C-Wing.

"Bloody hell. Make nice with the Khimeyr? What she thinks I am, blasted Welcome Buggy?"

Winston's black leather coat, knee-length, whooshed as his strong legs carried him down the hall. The place was already cluttered with old sacks, hunks of metal and other Khimeyr trash. He even imagined the wing smelled bad. He didn't like it.

"Hush, Monty," Shelby Hussard chided.

"Don't you hush me!" Winston snarled.

Taking pity on his young companion, he slowed his stride to match her shorter legs.

Winston had to admit that Shelby cleaned up pretty, dressed in plain clothes for the occasion with her dark blonde hair loose about her shoulders. She looked like a Welcome Wendy, all right. But nothing she wore would stop a bloody Khimeyr bullet, if they felt unfriendly. And he had never known anyone who came from Miramar to be anything but unfriendly.

"Consider it an honor we were sent," Shelby persisted. "Trezanna must think we're going to succeed. Julian was really too hostile."

"Killed his sister, didn't they?" Winston said with a shrug. "Bloody Dragonfleet."

"These are not Dragonfleet, they are Khimeyr," Shelby murmured. "Remember, they *left* Dragonfleet. They're here to *fight* Dragonfleet."

Winston just growled and kept walking. It made no difference to him. The Khimeyr complicated things. He didn't like complications. He also didn't like the looks he and Shelby received from Khimeyr members alerted to their arrival. They didn't look very friendly at all.

"What is it? Just men? I had the same damned conversation with Julian an hour ago. Not like I don't have things I should be doing. I could be out giving Max a good run. But we've got our orders, Monty."

"If Trezanna wants to make nice with them," he said, "she should be here."

Dressed in a gray flight suit, a short, trim woman, black hair cropped straight and boyish, stepped into the doorway before them. Her almond-shaped eyes were a peculiar shade of chestnut, and the fire in them blazed so warm it was hard to ascertain if she was friend or foe. Winston noticed that the others stepped aside to give her room, so he assumed she was some sort of authority figure.

"Looking for someone?" the woman asked.

"Ma'am," he said with a sharp nod of his head, a ribbon of dismay passing through his midsection as he acknowledged silently that he found the Khimeyr woman attractive. Now that was a twist he had not expected. "I'm Monty Winston, Solarii engineering. This be Shelby Hussard, one of our pilots. Admin sent us to check out your ships, see what's to be done to get you flyin' again."

The woman smiled, the warmth extending to her whole body. "Xiu Qiaolin." She took each of their hands briefly.

Remembering those of Chinese descent shared their surname first, he greeted her with what he hoped was appropriate dignity, considering her warmth had awakened something in his own body. "Qiao, a pleasure, ma'am."

Winston noticed rough calluses on her hand as they touched. So Qiaolin was a true working woman. He liked that, too.

"I'm glad you're here," Qiaolin replied. "Catava said to expect you. Darien should be here momentarily."

"Here." The gruff bark echoed, as Darien Pomeroy came out of the same room where Qiaolin had been. His bright eyes were unforgiving as he studied the Solarii pair.

The challenge in Pomeroy's stance raised the hackles on Winston's neck. He found it hard to offer a welcome, even though those were his orders. This was his base. *Let Pomeroy make the first move.*

Shelby elbowed Winston. "I'm Shelby Hussard. You must be Mr. Pomeroy." She looked up at the man, fixing him with a stare until sheer politeness forced him to acknowledge her.

"Must be," Pomeroy grunted, staring back.

Winston bristled as the grudging look on the man's face. How did Trezanna think these two groups would work peacefully together? Here this bloke was dependent on the Solarii dime and he spent it on a chip for his shoulder big as a wild pig.

Qiaolin put a hand on Pomeroy's arm. "This is Monty Winston," she said gently. "Why don't you show them to our hangar area, Dare?"

A door opened behind the Khimeyrans, spilling the giggle of small children. Looking past Pomeroy, Winston noticed two little heads peeking out, blinking at the commotion. Pomeroy growled at them, and they peeped and vanished.

"They're cute," Shelby said to Xiu. "Are they yours?"

Qiaolin shook her head. "Darien?" she asked again.

He waited until the door closed behind the children. "C'mon then," he growled, half-turning to lead the way, but obviously not intending to leave his back exposed.

That's what we needed, a bloody prima donna. Winston didn't have to take this crap. "If you don't need our help—" Another pointed elbow jabbed his ribs. He turned his glare on Shelby. "Hey!"

"Sorry, Monty. I tripped over a tear in the carpet there. Base is in terrible shape after that last attack." Shelby's expression was apologetic as she stepped out of range of retaliation.

Knowing exactly what she had done, Winston gritted his teeth and followed Pomeroy.

"Don't worry," Qiaolin said. "They'll either hit it off like old pals, or tear each other to bits."

Their shared giggle burned Winston, and he stomped up the hallway, knowing which of the two choices he expected. He tried to condense his assessment of Pomeroy into concrete terms. Something nagged at him about what the man wore. He walked faster and maneuvered himself into a position where he could see the man's left shoulder. There. That was it. A piece of worn insignia on the lean man's decrepit jacket.

"That a Space Force Special Ops badge?" he finally asked.

Pomeroy's shoulders twitched. "Mayhap it is. Ancient history, that. What's it to you?"

"Naught, really. Just thinkin' I knew some people worked Ops with us in the Western Alliance."

"New Terra?" Pomeroy jammed his chapped hands in his pockets. Winston heard the note of interest in his voice, no matter how he tried to look like he didn't care.

"Aye." Winston walked half a step faster, catching up with Pomeroy. "Ten year ago, thereabouts. Scrapping an Eastern Bloc takeover under Melat leadership."

"Had some comrades there. Rough crossing, what I understand." Pomeroy held the heavy door to the hangar bay open for them to pass through, and then let it shut with a metallic clang behind them. The hangar's outer doors were open to the field. A fresh cool breeze blew in from outside.

Winston nodded, his mind filling with memories of the conflict, his role as a ground fighter that time, not in the air. The smells of exploding gunpowder, burnt flesh, screams of the wounded, all of the horror rose before him again, fresh as if it were the day before. He shoved it back inside the box in his mind, where he would be safe from it. "Lost most of me mates. Spec Four blokes, though, worth their weight in bloody gold."

The lips of the Khimeyr security man twisted with the effort to fight a smile. "Not Space Force, then?"

"Me? No way." Winston shook his head with a snort. "Too many rules."

"Too right, too right." Pomeroy waved an agitated fist in the air. "Couldn't stand it myself, had to blow. Man can't do his job less'n some officer jump on him for hair too long or boots what been in the field unpolished."

"Bloody bureaucracy!"

"Exactly."

Shelby left them and moved on to meet and greet. Not Winston's cup of tea. One of the Khimeyr pulled Pomeroy aside to ask something, so Winston took advantage to assess the people and equipment in the wing. Everything and everyone looked worn almost beyond value, especially the rank and file. But even that didn't prepare him for the condition of the ships.

Winston's opinion of Khimeyr bravery, or perhaps foolhardiness, increased as he studied each one. Julian McKinley didn't exaggerate his complaints about the ragtag fleet. Likely held together with stretchy bands and baling wire, if he had to guess. He needed a closer look.

"May I?" Winston asked.

Pomeroy waved him on.

Choosing one of the better candidates, the name *Odyssey* painted on its side, Winston started up the shadowed ramp. He avoided the piles of debris outside the hatch and continued into the cockpit, which he found dimly-lit and empty. And a disaster.

He spoke to the computer without response. Manual access yielded a couple of blinks from the control panel lights. Under the panel, multi-colored wires connected to access ports on both sides, for no reason Winston could think of. He leaned over the pilot's seat to key in a test launch pattern, frowning as the sequence didn't work.

"What a rotting piece of crap."

"Don't move." Cold metal touched the back of his neck. The voice was female, its edge as sharp as her blade. "What do you think you're doing in my ship?"

Winston froze, his hands still on the panel. "No harm done, love. Just checkin' things out."

The woman snorted. "I'll be the judge of that."

As she came around the far side of the nav chair just out of reach, Winston caught a glimpse of blue eyes under a frizz of thick brown hair and shaggy bangs. She wore a nondescript flight suit that might have been gold once, but was now mostly shades of faded brown. A curved bladed knife was in her hand. A wicked weapon, indeed. He didn't dare flinch. No sudden moves, he thought.

The woman turned up the lights. She examined the panel for sabotage, tested several buttons, and then turned a simmering glare on him. "What you *doing* here?"

Winston gestured toward the ramp. "Sorry. Didn't know anyone was inside. Pomeroy told me I could check it out."

"Dare?" The woman twitched, lowering the knife a few millimeters.

Winston nodded, hoping he wouldn't have to deck the girl to avoid being stabbed. Now that he could see the slim figure clearly, he estimated her age as just out of her teen years. All the hair and the old clothing disguised her pretty well. He didn't hurt kids.

"He's out there. I'm Monty Winston. I'm one of the Solarii pilots, here to help." He eyed the panel ruefully. "If that's possible. Are they all like this?"

"For the most part. Been a long time since we had new parts." She put the weapon down on the panel. "They call me Lily Renard."

Winston reached for her hand and shook it, feeling the dry cracked skin of her palm. Another working woman. "Nice to meet you, Lily. I'm Monty Winston."

Lily reached behind the seat and grabbed a bundle, unrolling a thick olive green jacket which she wrapped about her shoulders, looking as though she hoped it would camouflage her. "Good enough for me."

"This is your ship?"

"My husband's. But I been flying it when it runs. Brought it from Zeta in one piece."

"Then you're one hell of a pilot." Winston straightened and finally smiled. Lily responded, confirming his guess. Definitely younger than his original thought. "We need good pilots up against the pirates."

"And Dragonfleet? It's why we're here. It might take all we have, but we will go home," Lily said, her jaw set with determination.

"You'll go back to Miramar?"

"We have nothing else." Lily's tone hinted of desperation, the pleading of those cast in the role of wanderers and nomads, wanting nothing more than a place to call their own.

And the Queen of Hell standing between here and there, Winston thought. Not that Lily didn't already know it. "Is your husband onboard too?"

"No." Lily whipped around and grabbed the weapon again. Winston stepped back out of reach, but Lily intended only to put the blade back in its sheath under her jacket. "He got other things on his mind."

Lily turned and stalked out, heading below.

"Well now, what's that about?" Winston wondered aloud, hearing her puttering. None of his business, that was for sure.

He shifted his focus back to the mechanical aspects of the ship. He followed Lily to the lower deck and found the business sections of the *Odyssey* pretty much as expected. He stayed out of Lily's way and out of any compartments that looked personal, letting her know when he left the ship. At least the husband hadn't showed up with a knife of his own.

Winton squared his shoulders as he stepped onto the ramp, his attention drawn by a commotion in the middle of the hangar. A crowd of about twenty had gathered around a scuffle. Spectators, both men and women, encouraged the combatants. One of them was Shelby Hussard, the other a Khimeyr woman Winston didn't know. He yanked his com from his jacket pocket and entered the emergency code, then headed into the crowd at a run.

"Break it up!" Winston roared. He spotted Pomeroy standing across the makeshift circle, arms folded. "What are you doing? Get your skirt there under control, mate."

Pomeroy shrugged. "They're grown. Leave 'em be."

Winston felt annoyance growl up through his throat. "Bloody hell."

He reached for Shelby, intending to drag her out of the brawl, taking his eye off the other woman for a split second. A mistake, as it turned out. She hit him square in the chin with a fist of bloody knuckles. Pain shot through his head. As the onlookers cheered, his knees buckled and blackness enveloped him.

Some time later, Winton's eyes opened to find Shelby bending over him, her shirt bloody. His jaw ached. Pomeroy waited there too. The others were gone.

"What happened?" he mumbled.

Shelby winced. "I'm sorry, Monty. I didn't mean to start it. I just said something about the ships to one of the women there." She shrugged. "All hell broke loose. Are you okay?"

Winston grunted. Lying on his back in enemy territory wasn't the wisest idea. He shoved himself upright, surprised when Pomeroy stuck out a hand to help him up. After a moment's hesitation, he took the hand. His legs were still a bit wobbly. The woman Shelby fought was nowhere in sight.

Pomeroy reached out and helped Winston to his feet.

"So you broke it up?" Winston asked.

Pomeroy shoved his hands in his pockets. "Not so much. Everyone kinda lost interest after *that* got here."

"That?" Winston eyed Pomeroy a moment, and then turned to see what he meant. His stomach knotted up as he saw Rumadan. He would have thought Austin would show up to his coded call, not the Ops Director. Either the situation had truly gotten out of hand, or Trezanna decided to send the big guns because this was the Khimeyr.

Rumadan noticed Winston looking at her and the strip of violet darkened along the short fur of her exposed face, arms and legs. The rest of her body was covered by a long jacket with Solarii markings, which he knew protected her soft belly. She walked upright, although many of her characteristics were feline and her accent was as distinct as his own.

"Ma'am," Winston said, trying to look as if he were in control of the situation. The twinkle in her eyes let him know he had failed.

"Humans are such a difficult race." Rumadan studied the three of them. "Even when they choose to bond for the greater good, they cannot resist the battle."

"Hey, I didn't choose anything!" Pomeroy said, crossing his arms.

Rumadan studied the man for several long seconds, her eyes, all black with no irises, unblinking. Finally he looked away and Rumadan turned to Winston, ignoring Shelby Hussard for the moment. "Report."

Winston straightened, fighting off dizziness. "The ships are in poor condition. McKinley's right to be concerned. But they don't seem too worried. Guess they can fly their birds held together with a prayer and twine."

"Perhaps they have heart. It may be enough." Rumadan eyed Pomeroy a moment, then turned away to walk through the hangar.

Winston hurried to catch up, knowing that reasonable tone, the one that meant the Viorn perched on the verge of an angry outburst. Pomeroy might think he had gotten off easy, but repercussions would show up, somewhere. They always did.

"Tell me about the ships," Rumadan said.

Winston filled her in on the state of Lily's ship, as a prime example.

Rumadan walked slowly with him, pointing out old damage and other notes of interest on the six ships housed there. Winston noted as well the distrustful eyes of the Khimeyr working on them. "I shall expect a full report."

"Yes, ma'am."

"Including why Hussard felt it necessary to get into a fist fight on the first day." Her tone shared her irritation.

"I'll try to find out, ma'am." Winston glanced over to see Shelby was gone. He would have to track her down.

Rumadan's fur flushed a lighter shade of lavender, showing she was amused. "If it wasn't the two of you, it would have been someone else. With you, at least, the damage has been contained." She let a soft hand pet his arm, then she left the hangar.

"What the—" Frustrated, Winston walked back over to the scene of the crime, where Pomeroy waited, his dark eyes dancing with glee.

"Hope she didn't ream you too bad, pal."

Winston shrugged, the movement wrenching his neck and jaw. Swallowing a curse, he eyed the other man. "Weren't ordered to come here and fight. Orders were to make friends."

Pomeroy grinned suddenly. "Bureaucracy, again, right? All about orders, not so much about reality."

"Too right." Winston rubbed his chin. "Your woman's got one heck of a left cross."

"Lucy? That she does. No one talks bad about her ship. Ever."

"We'll make a note." Winston eyed the other man, feeling that wall between them had thinned somewhat. "So. Let's get to work on your birds, hmm?"

"Ready when you are, *mate*."

Darien's emphasis on Winston's own slang brought a smile to his lips. Maybe the meet wasn't what they planned, but then they came expecting an enemy and instead found some of like mind. No one would declare an end to arms anytime soon. But it was a beginning.

Winston pulled a datapad from his pocket to take the estimated list of parts they would need. "Ready for the rundown."

CHAPTER 8

THE attack came without warning, without even a hint of impending danger. Estrella's Dragonfleet warriors appeared fully veiled already over the base, strafing the compound with brutal rounds of laser fire.

"Battle stations!" Julian McKinley called. Caught in his seat in the makeshift command center, a former conference room outside the hangar area, he was the first stunned officer to react. "In case anyone hadn't noticed," he muttered to himself.

He sent the call base-wide, and then his feet hit the floor for the hangar bay. Rumadan would hold the center until Trezanna could get there. Scrambling to ships, to consoles, was second nature to the Solarii at this point.

* * *

CATAVA had been up early and dressed, taking only a moment to wrap her hair tight before she ran toward the main base.

At the entry to C Wing, she met Trezanna Len, who was yanking a leather flight jacket over her soft blue blouse as she left the commons. A piece of latticed ceiling caved in almost over their heads. Catava ducked and cursed as debris fell around them.

Trezanna grabbed her arm and pulled her in the other direction. "We'll have to cut through the hangars to the new command post!"

"Is it Estrella?" Catava asked, as the two of them ran the long way around. She would have put down money that it was.

"That's what command said. Guess you were right. She must have heard you were here. No warning this time. They've done something to develop their Veil skills, something new."

"Estrella's probably had this up her sleeve for some time, just waiting for an opportunity to use it. She would take great pleasure in making this her welcome gift for the Khimeyr."

As they entered the hangar, Qiaolin tucked a datapad under her arm, Khimeyr flyers scattering in every direction around her, heading toward the Solarii ships. The last one fired up and took off as the two leaders arrived.

Qiaolin's slim figure turned at the sound of the commanders' boots on the hard plascrete floor. "I've assigned one of our personnel to each of your ships. We've got five Khimeyr ships functioning and off in addition to the Solarii. All flights green," she said, flushed with excitement, highlights of copper in her chestnut eyes.

"Good job," Catava said to Qiaolin with a nod. Then she turned to Trezanna. "Trezanna Len, this is Xiu Qiaolin, former Dragonfleet pilot and the closest thing I have to family. Qiao, the Solarii Administrator."

The women shook hands briefly, each obviously more concerned with the attack than proper manners.

"Let's get to the command center," Trezanna said.

Trezanna led them down the back hallway, which strobed with flashing red lights, and into the reinforced room that was now the heart of operations since their main post had been ruined by the pirate bombs. The engineers transferred as much of the sensor equipment as could be salvaged from the old command area and yanked monitors from any part of the base that could spare them. It looked rough, but appeared functional.

A felinoid Viorn, who looked to be a high-ranking officer, waited in the raised center seat, overseeing the defense initiative under the dimmed blue lights of Alert status. This must be Rumadan, about whom Darien had told Catava.

The large front screen exhibited a satellite feed that showed aerial combat maneuvers. Smaller screens shone from the console several steps down from the cat-woman's chair, manned by Solarii officers in a disarray of uniform. The Viorn glanced up to acknowledge Trezanna's presence, a ripple of violet running across her facial fur before attending to her headset.

"Circle round, all units," Rumadan ordered, as they watched the drama play out on the screen.

The Solarii and Dragonfleet ships engaged, trading laser fire and wheeling round each other trying to gain advantage. Catava knew the Khimeyr ships had a different game plan, so she wasn't worried that they remained incommunicado. Ten minutes passed, then twenty, as the battle continued. Rumadan's ebony eyes flicked to Catava with irritation.

"More shields!" Rumadan yelled. "Launch ground torpedoes!"

Catava and Qiaolin observed the monitor, tight-lipped, analyzing the battle unfolding. Catava could feel her second-in-command burning to intervene. Politics only went so far. Trezanna had given her the right to lead the offensive initiative. She couldn't do that from the back row.

"I need access," Qiaolin muttered.

"I'll handle it," Catava assured with a loaded look at Trezanna.

Trezanna turned to Rumadan. "Can we get another tie-in?"

The Viorn growled softly and indicated a chair in front of her.

Qiaolin second slipped into it with a curt nod, activating the headset as she assessed the picture before her. "Dare? This is Qiao. Are we on schedule?"

Trezanna stepped close to Rumadan. "Damage report?"

Catava looked over the half dozen officers in the room, noting the lack of chatter and the concise focus on the crisis with approval. *Whatever else I think of Len, she runs a tight ship.* Qiao's plan intended to hit Estrella where it would hurt. In her ego. And at the moment they didn't have time to share it with the Solarii. No one had anticipated Estrella would come for them so soon. Catava sensed Rumadan's vexation like a red-hot glow behind her as the Khimeyr drew a particularly heavy barrage of Dragonfleet fire.

Xiu repeated her call three times before she got a response.

"We're a little busy up here," Pomeroy snapped, voice cracking like a whip.

Rumadan pointed out the hotspots on her screen to Trezanna. "Ships are up and on attack status. Non-essential personnel have moved to underground facilities, but we've received no report since they've gone." She glanced up, expression unreadable in those eyes, though her posture was apprehensive, and her color reflected that.

Catava studied the Viorn with interest. The Khimeyr had only encountered a handful of her species on their travels in the sector. Tenacious, they were, and often dangerous as well. Trezanna was lucky to have one.

Her heart pounding, Catava knew it was time to launch their little plan. She turned her attention to the Khimeyr fighters, now receiving low, terse instructions from Qiaolin. They pulled away from the battle as one, swung wide in formation, gearing into hyperspace, jumping in the direction of the moon where they would find the Dragonfleet base of Miramar.

Monty Winston's voice came over the com, his aggravation clear. "Where they goin', eh? Thought they were on our side."

What sounded like McKinley's voice intruded on the speaker, engaged in a similar diatribe against the deserters.

Catava touched a finger to her lips and shook her head. "I know what I'm doing. Give us a chance."

Rumadan bristled, but gave Winston a stand-by. Those in the room continued to scan and report and give orders to the Solarii pilots, while Catava counted down the time it would take for Pomeroy and his people to reach Dragonfleet headquarters. If all went well, they would arrive in about fifteen minutes, a long time for the Solarii to continue holding up their end of the battle.

But when Estrella realizes what we're doing, the battle itself will change.

Catava held her breath. This was a test. Her own people objected to the alliance, as much as Len's did, but they must work together. Trust, so important, might have been better established if only there had been more time to prepare.

Damn Estrella. She ruins everything.

"Incoming call from the Dragonfleet forces," said one of the uniformed women at a console.

Had to love it when a plan came together. Catava allowed herself a smirk of pleasure, seeing the expression mirrored on Qiao's face. Trezanna's lips parted, as if she were about to indulge her curiosity, but she didn't speak.

"I thought we might hear from her," Catava said. "Now let's drop a few bombs."

"On speaker," Trezanna said.

"Visual, too?" Qiao asked. "It's time Estrella learned the truth."

Trezanna looked to Catava, who nodded. "All right. Show her who's here."

"This is Estrella of Dragonfleet," came a haughty, alto voice. As the visual caught up, the black-suited leader swung her oversized command chair to face the screen. Her wide dark eyes opened a little farther as she saw who greeted her.

Catava stared back, stony-faced, sizing up her enemy's reaction. From the surprise she read on Estrella's face, she guessed the woman expected to find Luca commanding the Khimeyr forces. Her second expression was one of dismay. She wasn't prepared to find Qiaolin with them either. Poor Estrella, she thought without pity. The blows just kept falling, one after the other.

"What do you want?" Trezanna asked, stepping forward.

The pixie-like commander of the Dragon forces quickly reined in her surprise and rose to her feet, looking taller in the frame of the viewscreen. She fixed Trezanna in her icy stare. "I demand an explanation of the invasion of Dragonfleet space by these ragtag Khimeyr junkers. It's a little late for them to return the equipment they *stole* years ago."

"You are in a position to demand nothing," Catava answered coolly, jumping in a beat ahead of Trezanna.

Trezanna bit her lip to contain her response and withdrew behind Rumadan's chair, refusing the Viorn's offer to give it to her. Catava noted with gratitude that the Solarii commander intended to honor her word to let Catava command, and glanced at the second screen monitoring the fight overhead. The Solarii ships kept up their barrage of fire. The Dragonfleet ships seemed to be distracted by Estrella's attention to her opponents on screen, and two perished in quick succession. Catava remained stoic, watching, waiting.

Qiao took a report over her headset, and then raised a hand. "They're primed to go, Cat."

Catava nodded to Qiao. "Execute."

The woman's fingers tapped commands into the keyboard. Qiao stared at the small monitor before her, reporting back when the confirmation returned from the Khimeyr ships.

"Primed?" Estrella said with scorn underlying her words. "Primed for what? More treachery?"

"You're one to complain about treachery!" Trezanna scoffed.

Estrella stalked away from the screen, arms crossed. A crewman behind her suddenly exclaimed. Catava couldn't hear what he said, but the way Estrella shrieked and slapped him out of his chair let her know she wasn't happy. The Dragonfleet bitch hadn't changed a bit.

Estrella came back to the screen, visibly shaken. "You dare attack my home? You're insane to think you could ever take the base!"

Catava managed to hide her delight over Estrella's distress. "Probably not. But you cannot conduct a battle on two fronts." She nodded to Trezanna. "I've heard enough. Kill the communications feed."

"Everything we've got," Trezanna whispered to Rumadan. "Now. And bring up the exterior feed from our ships."

Rumadan passed on the order to the Solarii fighters. The view on the screen switched from the interior of Estrella's ship to open space, where the monitor on Winston's ship showed the immediate exchange of fire, nearly blinding in its intensity. When it was done, the *Talon* vanished back under Veil, along with at least three of her companion ships.

Long minutes passed as the command post sensors scanned the debris that remained floating from three or more Dragonfleet ships, impossible to tell what belonged to which ship in its present state. Despite their few casualties, a clear victory for the Solarii. But they were not done.

"Report!" Catava and Trezanna demanded at the same time.

"Pomeroy says they've taken out the main rocket launcher on the ground," Qiaolin said. "They're still looking for obvious targets." She continued to listen. "No damage to our birds. They've aerially scouted the base and housing areas. Holos coming in now." She slipped a diskette into the computer. "So far so—wait! Estrella's just appeared, cannons blazing. Pomeroy's hit!" A worried flavor of panic entered her voice.

"We've proved our point. Bring them home."

An emergency alert sounded before McKinley's face popped up onto the main screen, magnified as he leaned in close. "Get sickbay ready stat! Injured coming in, plasma burns, and worse. Gods, it's horrible!" Over his shoulder, the viewer showed writhing bodies on the floor of the bridge of the *Whirlwind*, the anguished voices of the victims making Catava's skin crawl.

Trezanna pointed to one of the command personnel. "Pass that on to the doctor. Done, Julian. Get on the ground as soon as you can. I'll see you have priority."

"Aye, ma'am." As McKinley's transmission ended, the screen shifted from the flames inside his bridge to the blackness of space once more.

"Have all our pilots checked in?" Trezanna asked.

"They have, ma'am." The young woman at the console handed her a couple of datapads.

"Secure to general quarters." Trezanna seemed distracted as she read them over. The lights returned to their normal radiance, and the flashing alert lights extinguished.

Qiaolin's voice peaked as the rest of the command center returned to normal status. "Get hold of yourself!" she said to someone on the other end of the com-link.

Catava leaned close. Though she was pleased with the grandstand event, it would be worth nothing if their people didn't come home safely. "What's the matter?"

"Lily's navigator was knocked out by an electrical short. I wanted her to tag after Pomeroy, but she's let space fill her brain." Qiao sighed in frustration, and then returned to her com. "Lily! Listen to me, you've got to help Pomeroy get back here. He took one hell of a hit. He can fly in on your wing. Lily? Do you hear me?"

"Do you need me for this?" Trezanna asked. "If not, I'll head down to sickbay."

"We'll manage," Catava assured her, aware of Rumadan's dark gaze fixed on her.

"Very well. I want reports every fifteen minutes," Trezanna said to Rumadan, before leaving the room. The Ops Director nodded, her attention split between the viewscreens and Qiaolin.

Catava cast her mind into creative mode. How could they get Darien home? They couldn't afford to lose him. His heart pulled the others together. "Any of his crew injured?"

"Don't know. Pomeroy's not coherent enough to tell me, but look." Qiaolin pointed out his flight pattern. "He's relatively stable in terms of path. All we need is for someone to help steer him."

"Anyone have tractors?"

Qiaolin shook her head. "We only sent out the light fighters today. Nothing heavy enough to pull in the *Queen's Claw*."

Catava cursed aloud and turned to Rumadan, prepared to ask for help, just as the com crackled.

"Got it covered, mates," Winston announced. "Shelby and I, we just happen to be headin' out yon. Be back in half a time."

Rumadan leaned forward angrily. "Winston! Winston, you do not have orders to assist!"

A smothered, amused sound came over the speaker. "What was that, Rummy? Having trouble with the com, mate?" An artificial noise hissed, obviously meant mimic static. "Can't hear a word, now."

The Viorn growled and switched to the other channel. "Lieutenant Hussard, you have orders to return immediately." There was no response. "Hussard?"

They waited, listening to empty air, for several long minutes while Rumadan fumed.

"The best of intentions," Catava said with a conciliatory air. "You can't blame him. He knows we need to work together."

Rumadan glared. "And this is how you suggest we begin? By encouraging our officers to insubordination?"

"I suggest nothing." Catava walked over and placed her hand on the Viorn's chair. "I observe what is happening and think it's good. We must unite on this, if nothing else."

Rumadan stiffened at the touch. "We have suffered enough at the hands of Dragonfleet mercenaries."

"As have we all." Qiaolin eyed the Ops Director, her cheeks bright with hot emotion. "But *we* are not *they*." She gestured at the screen. "Estrella is no better than a she-wolf, killing her way through the sector, claiming whatever she can lay her hands on."

"And you?" Rumadan said. She stretched her tense muscles, catlike.

"How are you any better? Having destroyed your colony, you return here to take over ours?"

Catava blinked in surprise, and then exchanged a confused look with Qiaolin. She shook her head. "Is that what you think we're here for? We come for our rightful share of Dragonfleet space, not yours. You have nothing to fear, Solarii."

Rumadan snorted. "Words. Words!"

Catava turned away, rejection clear in her pointed focus on incoming reports. The Khimeyr officers waited, not wanting to rock the boat further.

"Winston has located your ships," the Solarii tech announced a few minutes later. "All other undamaged Solarii ships are in port. All but two Khimeyr ships accounted for and returned to base."

Qiaolin nodded. "Thank you." She approached the command chair and extended a friendly hand as Rumadan removed her headset. "Xiu Qiaolin. I'm sorry we didn't have the opportunity for formal words before this crisis."

"You must be Rumadan," Catava added softly. "I've never met a Viorn, though I've heard of your people. I'm Catava."

"I know who you are." Rumadan's black eyes sparkled with hidden knowledge as she looked at each of them. "I am quite thorough."

"No doubt." Smiling, Qiaolin watched the schematic representation. "We better meet the *Claw* down in the hangar, Cat. No telling what Pomeroy's up to."

Catava straightened her navy blue jacket and nodded. The Khimeyr comrades started for the door.

Rumadan cleared her throat, calling their attention again. "Even I am guilty of prejudice at times. But I must give credit where it is due. Today, we had fewer casualties and we shared the load. I cannot dispute the tide turned once you shook Estrella from her attack." Rumadan's posture softened, as did the defensive tone in her voice. "An odd alliance it is, but perhaps one that will bring a future for us all."

There it was, Catava realized. That beginning of trust. Like the first spark of a flame, it began so small but would grow and spread from one to another, the bonding of comrades as they worked together, covered each other's shortfalls, and saved each other's lives.

The thought warmed Catava, as she headed down to check on her wayward boys.

CHAPTER 9

TREZANNA Len slipped into the infirmary, finding it the chaotic mess she expected after Julian's agonized announcement. Half a dozen people, skin blackened and burned, lay on medical beds as the staff tended their injuries. McKinley himself was on the last bed, his worn hands a bloody mess. Over his protests, Dr. Boring treated him personally.

"Heal my people," Julian begged, pulling away. "They're in bad shape."

"Worry not, dear Julian," Boring reassured him, reaching again for the damaged fingers. "All are receiving treatment, as you should be. Your hands are important to our survival."

Trezanna examined the ranks as she came through the ward. She was no medical expert, but what she saw made her believe they would survive. "What happened, Julian?"

The technical director came upright as Trezanna approached, causing Boring and his nurse to struggle to keep him on the bed. "Dragonfleet weapons, ma'am. Took two ships at once, opened up the plasma cores." His eyes were empty hollows for a moment. "Nothing we tried stopped the plasma leak. Burns everywhere."

Trezanna laid a sympathetic hand on Julian's shoulder, one of the few places he didn't seem to be injured. "But you brought them all home, Jules." Julian was always protective when it came to his team. That characteristic had won their loyalty and devotion over the years, and hers. But he was the doctor's problem now. "Don't listen to him, Gene. Just heal him."

"Hoping you would say that, Len," said Dr. Boring

With a nod from the doctor, the nurse administered a prepared sedative.

McKinley protested all the way to the bed's surface, where his eyes closed and his words were reduced to a mumble. The doctor proceeded to his work with his usual good humor. "Chased the Harridan away again, I see, yes?"

"Again." Trezanna sighed. "Again. And again. One day it will end."

"Oh sure enough 'twill, one way or another. All things end, missy.

Even you will. And I." Boring nodded, smiling gleefully.

Trezanna looked at him and shook her head, but failed to come up with a crisp retort. "Send me a report, Doctor."

Frowning, she left the infirmary.

* * *

ESTRELLA returned to Dragonfleet base, flying blindly and jumping at every shadow.

Her engineer, Gus, had reported the withdrawal of the Khimeyr after the destruction of the Dragonfleet missile launcher. What tore at her gut was that she had not anticipated the attack. And it wasn't Luca, but Catava Rolon.

Catava.

Estrella was in a rare state of anxiety by the time she landed the *Talon*. Catava and Qiao, conspiring against her, her former comrades-in-arms now turned traitors.

She pulled up at the last minute, swerving into an alternate vector, flying past the boundaries of her base. Frowning, she punched up one land map after another onto her glowing monitor, scanning until she found it. *There.* She launched a barrage of laser fire at a building utterly destroying the remains of the house where Catava's father had raised his family. If she wanted it back now, she could have it.

In molecules.

The outburst provided sufficient release to let her return to the base. She pretended not to notice when everyone scattered from her path as she cleared the ship and the landing bay. Marching down the hall to her sanctuary, she cursed the assassin among the Khimeyr who failed to kill Catava.

Reports surfaced on her personal communications device as she walked. The damage to the launcher was extensive, weeks, perhaps, before they could hope to have its use for defense. Estrella felt suddenly vulnerable. She hated the feeling. Traditionally, the Solarii left Miramar alone. In the past, they fought over neutral territory, or at Induna. She thought her little piece of space was safe. Until now.

Estrella paced the length of the room, considering her options. Trapped. No, not trapped. She was free to leave. But it was her base. She would never leave. Never. Miramar was her home, her stronghold, her domain. Hers. *Hers.* She had lied, cheated, even killed to keep it. She refused to give it up.

The thought of losing her hard-won prize made her fingers tremble, and she stopped that by smashing her fist into the wooden table top. Her hand aching but not shaking, she poured herself a glass of green with the other. Its fast-acting fire warmed and reassured her. She was not losing control. A minor setback, nothing more. She would repay them for this betrayal. *Oh, yes.* She would take those asteroids the pirates thought were so valuable. Screw the negotiations.

At her worktable, she unrolled a sector map, preferring the physical comfort of paper to the coldness of the computer-generated model. This she could put her hands on, touch it and could feel what belonged to her.

"Let's see. Where shall I begin?" Estrella said to herself.

She examined their area of space, marking areas with a lightsnake that left glowing trails for several minutes. Strategically located asteroids here. Free passage through space corridors here and there.

Once the Solarii and Dragonfleet had been allies, fighting together against Arkosian pirates. They had once coordinated strengths and weaknesses and shared information about holdings. Estrella was well aware that Dragonfleet now lagged behind the Solarii in alliances and territory. Her plan had been to take the desired areas by force. But then the Khimeyr had defected, leaving her in a weak position.

Estrella didn't like being in a weak position.

It had taken time to build up her forces and equipment before she dared mount another fight for control over precious resources. The strongest survived. That was the law of nature. Dragonfleet was the strongest. She had made sure of that. Mistakenly, she had presumed her position was perfect for a strike, what with the pirates back in the sector.

She had been wrong.

Her former comrades were now her enemies. They had reinforced the Solarii forces and destroyed Estrella's primary defensive weapon. *Damn them all.*

"We have as much right to survive as they," Estrella grumbled. She stared at the map, plotting until the lights faded.

The door-com beeped.

Estrella's gaze flicked toward the interruption. "Come in."

The wooden door with its dragonhead carvings opened just enough to admit her weapons chief, Hawk Kenton, the closest thing she allowed to a confidant. A broad-shouldered man, husky, with thick black hair and narrow dark eyes, he owned a temper to match Estrella's own. She appreciated the fact he was honest, brutally so when necessary, unlike many of the other worms who served under her. She also appreciated his skills in her private chambers. He was pleasing enough on a mattress, when he was in her favor. When he wasn't, he might as well have been dead. Hawk was intelligent enough to stay out of her way then.

When Estrella needed someone to tell her the truth, someone she could let down her guard with, Hawk was the one she called.

Hawk stayed by the door. "Strey?"

She softened slightly at his pet name for her. "I'm deciding what revenge I shall take against the traitors."

Hawk leaned over her shoulder and looked at her map without touching her. "Rare prizes, those planetoids." After a short pause, he straightened and took a step back. "No chance we could find the same riches elsewhere?"

Estrella's heart skipped a beat. He wouldn't mislead her or play up to her just to curry favor, not at a time like this. She didn't look up. "You think they can beat us."

His foot scraped against the floor, as Hawk moved out of reach, a defensive instinct common to those familiar with her outbursts. "We'll be weeks repairing the launcher. And we lost two more ships today, Strey. Henry says the Khimeyr have joined the Solarii." His voice grew softer, more caressing. "I'm not saying you can't. But is it worth losing everything?"

Estrella stepped toward him, the maps rolling up with a snap as she let them go. "We will never lose everything! Never!"

Hawk moved warily to the other side of the desk, which pleased her. He dwarfed her, easily nine inches taller and a hundred pounds heavier, but he bore dagger scars that proved her fierce temperament could overcome the difference in their sizes.

"Your spirit's strong, Strey," Hawk said. "But I wonder if that determination will be the death of us all."

She watched his eyes, but his gaze never flinched. She looked away first, hiding hot tears of frustration. "Why did they come back? Why *now?*"

"Luca always did have a sense of timing."

"Not Luca. Catava and Qiaolin. They directed the attack against us, working with Len."

Hawk eyed her curiously. "That strike had Strada written all over it."

She thought the same thing, but she had not seen Luca and the bitch Catava didn't disclose any secrets, either. "He wasn't there. I don't know where or what." A deep breath as she felt her anxiety rising again. She must maintain control, even in the face of changing variables. Safe in Hawk's presence, she could admit small chinks in her personal armor.

"Whatever's going on over there, we've got to know."

"Send out someone?" he suggested.

She nodded. "Is there someone they won't recognize?"

"Neither group?" Hawk scratched his chin, thinking. "That's a tall order." His eyes lit up suddenly. "Wait a minute, there is someone, a young woman. Just arrived couple of weeks ago. No history with the Khimeyr or the Solarii. Just what we need."

Estrella nodded. "Send her. I want to know what's happening. And if she's a good candidate, we may have further orders." She smiled in a sinister way. "Very important orders."

"Understood." Hawk smiled and walked out. Estrella returned to her table, shoving the maps aside. Half muttering in a sing-song tone, half-humming as she wrote, her plans to attack the Solarii base formed under the point of her stylus. "The weak do not deserve resources," she reassured herself. She tapped the stylus on the tabletop as she debated the upgrading of ships.

Another knock enflamed Estrella's ire. "What is it?" she snapped.

The door opened and then closed. She stared in disbelief. Heart pounding, she slowly rose as the stylus slipped from her fingers.

Krainel, the leader of Dragonfleet she thought she had driven to his grave five years before, stood on her doorstep, smiling at her. He looked as if he could have stepped directly from the council room to hers. Longer legs were encased in the black leather leggings he favored. His graying hair was trimmed short, a jaunty beret sat on his head.

How could this man haunt her? Was she losing her mind under the pressure?

"You're dead. *Dead*, I say!" Hating her choked voice, she cleared her throat and slipped the dagger from her boot, feeling stronger with it in her hand. "Foul devil, why do you haunt me?"

Krainel gave a hearty laugh. "Haunt you? Why should I haunt you, temptress?"

Moving closer to study him, Estrella growled and held the dagger tight, not understanding how Krainel could stand before her, as real and substantial as her worktable. "Return to the dark realm where I sent you, devil, and leave me!"

Ready to cut through the space where the apparition waited, destroying the hallucination that persisted despite her disbelief, she stepped toward it. The laugh came again. Her brain finally kicked in. She realized the laugh was not in Krainel's deep basso. The sound was entirely familiar, impudent. Her eyes narrowed. "What trick is this?"

Krainel chuckled and then vanished, the form in the doorway shifting to that of Hawk Kenton. He took his hand and a small device from his pocket. "Amazing, isn't it? Gus came up with this last week. I wanted to surprise you. It's a personal holo veil."

Although tempted to kill Hawk for his insolence, she was intrigued enough to walk over and examine the mechanism.

"Why should I want to appear as old Krainel, anyway?" Estrella complained in pique of temper.

"That's the best part," he said with a grin. "You can be anyone. All you need is a sharp holo of them."

Hawk's finger made a few adjustments to the controls, and then he re-formed into Gus Henry's rotund jolliness. A spare moment after that his image changed into Estrella.

"Shut it off!" Estrella barked indignantly.

"Yes, my queen." The Estrella image faded and Hawk reappeared. "Just think how you could move among your people undetected. Hear what they say about you."

Her eyes lit up. The Dragonfleet leader had no interest in gadgets for the most part, not unless the instrument could personally serve her in some way. This one held many possibilities. "Yes. It would be a great weapon."

"Whatever makes you happy, Strey."

She grinned and held out her hand. "You shall be worthy to rule at my side."

His smirk held a trace of hesitation as he embraced her. Both knew she didn't mean it. He courted her as much for her power, as herself, or so it seemed. They danced along a knife's edge.

She allowed a single kiss, intending to return to her planning. But in the morass of emotion in which she drowned after the Khimeyr attack, the fire behind his lips took over, bringing her comfort and distraction.

She grabbed his collar and pulled him to her, kissing him again. Sensing assured victory, Hawk didn't need any further encouragement. He kissed her again and again as he carried her to the other room. "My queen," he whispered in her ear. "Command me."

"I will, my love, I will," Estrella assured him before they were both lost to the waves of passion.

CHAPTER 10

THE Khimeyr attack had its intended effect. The Dragonfleet offensive ceased.

Two weeks later, Trezanna brought her kafee to a breakfast table in the Solarii common room, which was filled with people who were actually relaxed and smiling.

"Morning, ma'am," Shelby said. At the far end of the table she whispered to Pomeroy, who eyed Trezanna without emotion.

"Ladies and gentlemen." Trezanna edged in beside Winston who grinned and made room for her at the table.

On Winston's other side, security chief Chase Austin cut a bowl of tartfruits. Dr. Talib was deep in conversation with a dark-haired man several tables over who Trezanna guessed was one of the Khimeyr doctors. Integration of the two groups seemed to be going better than anticipated. She didn't recognize a couple of the men across them, but smiled anyway as she drank her kafee.

As she ate, Trezanna listened to the small talk going on around her. Already the Khimeyr and Solarii were becoming friends.

Winston regaled the two men across from him with old war stories, and they returned the favor, at the same time shyly flirting with Chase. "You told us that one already, boyo," one of them scolded Winston as he produced a particularly poignant scene.

The tall one laughed, waving a finger at Winston. "Yeah, except last time it was you who got it in the arse."

Winton blushed, bringing a round of laughter from all of them.

Trezanna smiled and turned her attention to Pomeroy. His report on what the Khimeyr discovered when their ships flew over Miramar filled her with more questions. She wanted better results without appearing too demanding.

"Are the repairs completed to your ship?" Trezanna asked.

Pomeroy hunched his shoulders in the ragged Dragonfleet jacket and shook his head. "Took out tracking, nav, 'bout it. Snap new one in." He shrugged. "No worries."

"That's good." Trezanna noted Shelby's effort to make eye contact.

The Solarii pilot shook her head very slightly. Trezanna took the hint and a sip of kafee and smiled at Pomeroy. "We're glad to have you."

The saturnine Khimeyr only nodded an acknowledgement, though something tumultuous burned behind his eyes.

"Anything we can do for you?" Trezanna persisted.

He looked on the verge of a harsh retort for a moment and then his expression mellowed. He gave a smile and slid his empty cup across the table. "Yes, love, can you get us another cuppa?"

A gasp of disbelief came from someone at the table. That was not the way one usually treated the Solarii administrator.

Amused, Trezanna took the opportunity to gain points with the other team. She picked up the cup and glanced inside. "Black?"

Pomeroy's eyes warmed a few degrees to include a sparkle of approval. "Sweet, if you wouldn't mind."

Trezanna smiled. "No worries."

A buzz of conversation followed as she left the table to go to the galley port. She chuckled to herself. Pomeroy had certainly scored a point on her, but the gesture cost her nothing. She returned the kafee with sugar to him and gathered her things.

"Early meeting," Trezanna apologized, excusing herself.

The group murmured farewells, most of them still amused at the interchange. She left the room, feeling much better about the blending of Solarii and Khimeyr.

As Trezanna neared her office, Rumadan met her in the hall.

"Someone here asking for you," the felinoid Viorn said, twitching violet.

"What's your concern?" Trezanna knew the shade, if not the tone. Something had set off Rumadan's caution radar.

Rumadan shook her head. "I cannot identify my exact question. Just…you will see."

They rounded the corner nearest the administrator's office and found several chunky and worn pieces of luggage piled against the wall. Piled on them was a scruffy man in wrinkled clothes. Looking like he hadn't bathed or shaved in a week, he was asleep, or appeared so, with oily black hair drooping around his face.

Trezanna raised an eyebrow. "That?"

Rumadan nodded, her lip curling. She plucked some lint off her black jacket. "He says he must speak to you. A warning, he said."

"Then we shall see what he has to say." Trezanna walked down the corridor, heels clicking sharply. The noise caused a stirring of the pile and hasty muttering as the body wrapped in a tan sheepherder's coat slid off the luggage onto the floor.

"I'm Trezanna Len," she said, not offering her hand.

An odor arose from the man, as he fought his way to his feet.

Trezanna took a step back and held her breath.

Rumadan growled with disapproval.

"You'll have to forgive my appearance," the man said in a mellow pleasing voice. Wide-set hazel eyes flashed with good humor, as he gave a boyish grin. "I flew in with some cargo me Pop tossed in my ship. Cows or something. After fifteen minutes, you just don't notice the smell any more, ya know? But it makes you wonder what those cows ate."

Trezanna eyed him. "Is there a point to this?"

"Stefan Ciro. Ma'am." He gave a slight bow. "My father sent me. Yanoro Ciro of the Philean Waypass. He remembers you well from your days with Space Force. I have something of importance to tell you."

"Then get to it," Rumadan purred dangerously. The depth of her violet tinge indicated extreme irritation.

Stefan studied the Viorn a moment and then tossed a tentative smile at Trezanna. "Could we talk in private, ma'am?"

Trezanna thought about inviting him into her office and then caught another whiff. Not for all the lives of the Holy. "I remember your father. He was a good man. Had some problems with a neighboring colony, as I recall. A territorial dispute?"

"Yes, ma'am." An enthusiastic swell of color and animation illuminated Stefan's face. He extended his hand, releasing another cloud of disgusting odor.

Trezanna didn't take his hand. "I'd rather not have you in the office in that condition. Anything you have to say can be said here."

Stefan looked confused. The young man was obviously accustomed to getting what he wanted. Eyes flicking to the ceiling as he seemed to mentally regroup. Then he looked at her with more confidence. "Perhaps I could borrow a room here at your facility? Wash up? Prepare to meet with you properly?" As both women continued to cast him reproachful glances, he just grinned. "Come on now, I don't bite."

Rumadan muttered about wanting proof, but Trezanna took pity on him. "Very well. See Chase Austin in the main lounge." She pointed down the hallway. "She'll assign you quarters." Trezanna looked at the pile of suitcases, which reeked as much as their owner. "And you can take these."

"Yes, ma'am." Stefan bowed and grabbed up the bags, his coat nearly dragging on the floor. "Thank you, ma'am. Chase Austin. I'll remember. And I'll be back to see you, ma'am, I promise, to deliver my father's message. Don't you worry." He bowed more as he backed away down the hall toward the lounge.

"I shall notify pest control," Rumadan rumbled, as she disappeared around the corner.

Trezanna suppressed a smile. The newcomer reminded Trezanna of a traveling salesman. Nothing like his father, a businessman, who ran the Waypass station at a crossroads in space. The elder Ciro was a solid trader, unlike some of the other men at the Waypass, extended family that dealt in less acceptable merchandise. She would see this young man, find out what he was peddling, and move him on his way.

Entering her office, Trezanna checked her top desk drawer and her personal laser pistol to make sure it was charged. Just in case she chose not to buy.

After a knock on the door, Catava stuck her head in. "Got a minute?" Trezanna nodded and beckoned her in. The Khimeyr woman sniffed and made a face. "Waste removal problems?"

Trezanna laughed. "New guest."

"Ah." Catava crossed the room and casually sat in the brown leather chair before Trezanna's desk, relaxing back against the cushion.

"I've reviewed your report on the status of Dragonfleet," Trezanna said. "It's a fair guess Estrella's licking her wounds."

"I'm not sure what convinced her to stop, but I agree together we stand strong against her. While she's got a hangar full of ships, I doubt most of them are working."

Trezanna tapped a finger on her desk, thinking. *What would her old Space Force instructors have advised now? Did their rules even apply so far out in the black?* "Should we try to pin her down to peace? She's not likely to be more vulnerable."

Catava shook her head. "Estrella would spit in your eye. She'd take that as a sign of weakness. Let her stew about it. The scariest thing that woman owns is her own mind."

"If you say so. Plenty of work for us before the long cold. The outliers are bringing in the early harvest now. I'm sure they're glad for your people's help at their busiest time."

"Since they've lost the farms they tried to establish on Zeta, perhaps it's a little like home. Even if the land holds them by sufferance." Catava's voice lacked conviction. "From the holos Pomeroy brought back, it doesn't look like she's done much to maintain the crop-share areas at Miramar. Even if we get back there...." Her words trailed off into silence.

Trezanna knew that feeling of helplessness when it came to the care and welfare of the settlement that depended on her team for its safety. "Let's leave that issue for another day. Are ship repairs complete?"

"Coming along. Even bandaged to the hilt, your McKinley seems to be underfoot in our hangar every time I turn around, supervising refits and upgrades. Pomeroy said the two of them have cobbled together a reasonable supply of spare parts out of a few of the ships beyond repair. That should put us in a stronger position for the next round." A flare of defiance flashed in Catava's eyes.

"I have no intention of relaxing my guard just yet. I'm sure she has something else in mind, something less risky for Dragonfleet." Trezanna frowned, reviewing a mental checklist. "We should load up on supplies while our pilots can get out safely. Perhaps your people would like to make a raw material run to asteroid Delta-6."

"I'll put Pomeroy on it. He can choose a squad. You don't care if he takes Solarii?"

"Not at all. I'll send a team out to the fields to restock the galleys."

"I was thinking we could place some long-range perimeter buoys so we don't get caught unprepared like the last attack."

Trezanna heard a hint of accusation in Catava's tone. "The pirates destroyed our last ones. The Gandorians who sold them to us haven't been back again."

"We know how to do this," Catava informed. "Let me get some people on it."

"Fine." Trezanna tried not to sound defensive. "If Estrella's likely to take on a less protected target, we might offer the safety of the base to the outliers' families, if they want to send them. We've probably got enough personnel now to expand the classrooms." Even as she made the suggestion, Trezanna wondered whether she could realistically spare anyone from flying or mechanic work to oversee a bunch of frightened children.

"Hard to balance it all, Len. I'll check in with you later." Smiling in a way that showed she understood Trezanna's feelings, Catava got up and slipped out of the office.

Trezanna noted again how much more Catava resembled her old self, the worn lines on her face gone, the stress less obvious, now that she was discovering her place in the scheme of things. As were they all.

Satisfied, Trezanna started on the round of tasks she enumerated, continuing to bring her base back to fight-ready status before the next attack came. She did not know if it would be Estrella, or the Arkosians, but she knew in her gut the quiet would not last nearly long enough.

CHAPTER 11

STEFAN Ciro made short work of repairing his appearance.

A quick shower restored his raven hair to its normal unruly cap, framing a face his mother often described as *elfin*. Clean clothes from his suitcase completed his preparations to meet with the base commander. His goal was to impress her. His father would expect no less.

Stefan should have known better than to present himself right off the ship, but Yanoro emphasized haste. He appraised himself in the mirror inside the door of the tiny closet. A long, loose chestnut-colored tunic over black slickpants, tiny gold hoop in the left ear, polished black boots. A world of difference. He grinned, noting how it lit up his face. He needed that appeal.

He was ready.

His father obsessed about sending the ship half-full, until he had found a second commission, a load of livestock bound for Antla. He had not imagined the weight or the stink. As soon as the load had been dropped, Stefan headed to Induna with all haste, following his limited information. He had a sector location, a planetary description, and a name: *Trezanna Len.*

He had found her, but had forgotten about his shabby and somewhat smelly appearance. The wildcat bodyguard had tried to send him on his way, but he had wormed his way around her, obtaining an appointment with Len. His mission would soon be complete.

Stefan put some wares in his pack, along with the communiqué he prepared. Before he met with her, he wanted to get a feel for the base and the people who worked for her. The more he could learn, the better salesman he could be.

He ambled out, walking through the halls without being challenged and eventually arrived at the lounge. The late-morning common room held a lively bunch of folk in ebullient spirits. His impression of Len's crew improved. The smell of good, fresh food was more than he could pass up. Luckily, the galley port was self-explanatory. He acquired what constituted several meals' worth of his normal catch-as-catch-can diet with some simple requests.

Balancing three plates, extra bread and kafee on one arm, his pack over the other shoulder, Stefan made his way to a table at the far side of the room where he could observe the natives. He set down his food, then his pack, and began to eat as if he wouldn't get a chance for several days. Which under present circumstances, he never knew if he would.

Within a few minutes, he caught a pair of eyes on him from the next table. They belonged to a small boy dressed in red, no more than four or five, who sat on a chair too big for him, kicking one soft-shoed foot as he ate his soup. With each kick, the boy came just short of impacting a smaller girl next to him, who ignored him, licking the butter off her bread. Stefan winked at the boy and he froze for a few seconds, then grinned and waved his spoon.

"Chad." The boy turned back to look at the woman at the table as she spoke. Stefan followed the boy's glance and found the most stunning eyes he had ever seen, pale blue-green and clear, gazing into his. The blonde woman assessed him coolly and returned her attention to the children, urging the girl to eat her meal.

"Momma Cat, why that man have lots of plates?" the boy asked the woman, glancing back to look at Stefan.

"I don't know, sweet. Perhaps he's starving." Her tone, accompanied by another look at Stefan, implied that imminent starvation wasn't happening quickly enough. "You finish up, okay? We have things to do this afternoon."

Stefan noticed his fork hanging in mid-air. His jaw went slack, as he stared at the woman. A beautiful vision of motherhood, she was a Madonna to beat all the classical depictions, providing her children their daily bread, tending to their every need. He could almost picture a halo above her head. He fidgeted a moment and set down the fork, his appetite gone in an instant. If he could only speak to her.

"Can I help you?" someone said from beside him, nudging his elbow.

Turning in his seat, Stefan found a tall woman in a simple gray jumpsuit peering down at him. She wore a frown of disapproval and a weapon on a belt at her waist. She must be security.

He got to his feet out of respect. "Do I look like I need help?" Stefan asked, grinning at her. "Well, maybe I do. I'm sure you see all kinds around here."

"Exactly. When we don't know much about those kinds, we tend to keep a close eye on them."

"I'm harmless. Really. Even to little children." He spoke a little louder and glanced over in time to see the Madonna gathering her things and her children. Dismayed, he frantically tried to think of something to do to stop her from leaving.

"You look like trouble," the officer said.

The Madonna stopped a moment, assessed him with a suspicious eye and nodded to the security woman. "Trouble indeed."

The Solarii security officer nodded. "I'll take care of it, ma'am."

"Thank you, Ms. Austin." The unknown woman tossed a quelling look at Stefan and then departed with the girl in her arms.

The little boy trailed behind, watching Stefan over his shoulder. He giggled and waved as the family disappeared out the door.

Stefan dropped back into his chair, defeated. "Who *is* that?"

The security officer laughed. "Someone who's got more important things to do than deal with the likes of you."

"Now, Ms. Austin," he said, his voice mimicking the Madonna. "I'll have you know I carry important news for Trezanna Len. News brought at considerable expense to my health and dignity. Some respect, if you please." He pitched his voice to evoke clear self-mockery. That usually won women over. That or the bad-boy innocent look with which he followed it.

"Yeah, I heard about your manure-soaked dignity." The officer shook her head. "I'm Chase Austin, head of security for the Solarii. What was your name again?"

"Stefan Ciro." He reached for her hand, intending to kiss it with some grandiose notion of chivalry, but she pulled away.

"Well, Mr. Ciro, since you've had a chance to compose yourself, perhaps you could find time in your busy schedule of consuming our supplies to meet with the administrator. She sent me to find you when you didn't come straight from the quarters we assigned."

"Of course." Stefan glanced at his nearly empty plate. Gathering the detritus from his meal, he carried it to the port for recycling. "But, really. Her name?" he asked, pointing to the door behind them, adding a puppy dog quality to his eyes.

Chase glanced at the door, seeing they had gone. "Catava Rolon."

"Is that what they call angels on this side of the galaxy?" Stefan asked. "Thanks."

He shouldered his pack, the shining picture of the woman in his mind's eye. *Catava, an angel of light.* He thought back to what the child called her. *Momma Cat. Cat, yes.* He smiled at Austin. "Lead on, milady," he said with a charming smile.

"Save it for the Administrator," Chase said, shaking her head.

"Aye, ma'am."

Stefan followed Chase back to Len's office, studying the hall, the condition of the carpet, the freshness of the paint, the relaxed way Austin carried herself as she walked, comfortably, without pretense. What was this group called again? The Solarii? Lords of the Sun, a seat of power and myth. He grinned as the security officer opened the door. *Showtime.*

"Thank you, Chase." Len stood up behind the desk, her startled face marking her recognition of the transformation. "Mr. Ciro, I wouldn't have believed it." She offered him her hand this time. "A pleasure to have you here."

He took her hand, squeezing it warmly instead of kissing it. While that was the preferred greeting to women on his home world, he didn't get the impression the Solarii approved. He used the few seconds while their hands met to study the room, noting the absence of riches or the trappings of such. Nothing grandiose about them, even with Solarii reputation for a little arrogance. He liked that.

Trezanna waved Stefan to the leather chair across from her. The security officer stood near the door, her feet slightly apart, hands tucked behind her back but not far from her weapon.

Stefan eyed Austin a moment, certain she could kill him from where she stood. He turned the chair just enough to keep an eye on her and then sat, making himself comfortable.

"So what is this earthshaking news that brought you through hell and the digestive system of a hundred cattle to share it, Mr. Ciro?" Trezanna sat in the chair behind her desk, her back straight as a board, leaning forward to listen as she set her glassine cup aside.

He matched her posture. Best to get right to the worst. "My father says to tell you the Arkosian pirates have joined with several other thieving groups. They're determined to control the sector."

Her jaw set. He certainly had grabbed her attention.

"They've paid us a visit already," Trezanna informed. "Kind of hoping they were just passing through. Yano believes there's more to it than occasional harassment?"

"They're massing in the Rotaran Nebula," Stefan informed in a serious tone, watching her reaction. For the people of this sector, the news was of grave importance. "Our information is that they intend to re-establish their chokehold here."

"They've heard about the split with Dragonfleet." Trezanna rose slowly, slender fingers rubbing together. "They've regrouped and now expect to return here and crush whichever of us survives."

"Exactly." She looked across the room at Austin. "I'll bet they don't know about the Khimeyr."

"Khimeyr?" Stefan asked.

Trezanna nodded but didn't explain. "When are the Arkosians due?"

"Our informant wasn't certain," Stefan replied. "But there was no doubt the threat would be soon." He studied Trezanna's face, wondering how so many attractive women could live in one place. Or perhaps he had lived too long in a colony of mostly males. If he and his brother lived here, they would have quite the pick of choice woman-flesh. "You are prepared for them?"

Austin stepped forward, her face hard, rejecting the news. "Who was this informant, anyway? How reliable was he?"

"She," Stefan said. "A defector from the pirates. A young girl who'd been used for pleasure until she nearly died. She escaped in a sanitation barge and ended up at the Waypass. My father thought you should have this news, seeing how the small colonies like to stick together. And you all kicked their hind ends the last time." He chewed his lip, mindful of the destruction he had noticed upon landing at the base. Maybe these Solarii were not up to the task. "But the Arkosians are awfully strong. Even with these Cashmere? You've enough ships and fighters?"

"Khimeyr," Trezanna corrected.

Stefan observed the eye contact between the two women, so intent he wondered for a moment whether telepathy was involved. The thought left him unsure, so he waited, fidgeting.

"You're right," Trezanna said after a moment. "We've run them off before. When Dragonfleet was with us." She returned to her seat, sitting on the edge of it. "How is your father? Still peddling ice and bricks to the tourists at the Waypass?"

Stefan noticed the smooth change of topic. They didn't trust him. On such short acquaintance, he wasn't surprised. Best to remedy that. "Yes, ma'am, he is. You know it's his way. He's got the highest respect for you and the way you handled his people back when."

Trezanna nodded. "I remember. You were just a kid. Your brother, too. What was his name? Brian? Bren?"

"Brandon, ma'am."

"You're a long way from home," she said.

"Isn't my first time, ma'am." He leaned back in the chair, feeling less pressured. "Being at the way station, growing up the youngest of seven sons and cousins, my family didn't have much chance to keep track of me. I hopped lots of rides on transports going all sorts of places. As it's our way, I also apprenticed with my uncles, each of them, so I learned many trade routes and causes. Got more education from that than any real schooling."

"I wouldn't be surprised." She made notes on a pad of paper on her desk. "There's a lot to learn out there. Have you and your family had much experience with the Arkosians?"

"They're much more of a presence in our end of the sector, ma'am. We all do what we must to get along. The Waypass doesn't have much they need. They know they get more from us by leaving us alone."

"How's that?"

When both women focused on him, Stefan realized that he might have said too much. He didn't have to tell her about the relationship between the Arkosian pirates and the Philean Waypass. Everyone had the right to make a living, even trading with less than desirable partners. He cast about for an innocent explanation. "Sometimes they need skills we have, that's all. It can be a mutual benefit. Other than that, we try to avoid asking questions when the pirates come through. Does a lot to cut down on the glassware replacement, if you get my drift."

"Is there anything else you'd like to add?" she asked in a cool tone. "What did the informant tell you about new allies or weaponry?"

The Solarii leader's furrowed brow suggested she wasn't buying Stefan's explanation. So be it. Bottom line was his people would be just as happy to have the pirates destroyed once and for all.

"She said the pirates have hired on mercs out of the Nyaran system, strictly a business arrangement," he replied. "The Nyarans probably have the best weaponry of anyone around that part of space. Just about doubled their ship complement."

"Well. That's good information to have, if not to hear."

"You think you're going to take them on, ma'am?"

Trezanna stood. "Thank you for coming, Mr. Ciro. We appreciate the warning, and we'll let you be on your way."

Stefan scrambled up hastily and shook her offered hand of what was clear dismissal. "Thank you for seeing me, ma'am."

The security officer opened the door and Stefan was herded out, his head buzzing. Hopefully he had brought the news in time for the Solarii to do something about it, even if he didn't understand all the politics.

In the meantime, he had no orders to come straight home. Maybe he could prove useful to the Solarii if he would stick around a while. And while he was doing that, he would definitely see what he could do to get to know his angel.

CHAPTER 12

QIAOLIN squinted up into the guts of the Solarii craft *Tiboron*, frowning until she could adjust the light on the wires, tubes and hanging metal parts she endeavored to cobble together.

"Got any gum?" she muttered.

"What for?" Coveralls smeared in rank oil, Julian leaned over the top of the ladder that lifted him three meters above the floor. "What's the matter? Did you miss your mid-afternoon snack?"

"No, fool." Qiao scowled, adjusting her perch on a tall wooden stool. "Whatever hit you shook loose nearly every fitting in here. I need a dozen and a half bolts, a slew of washers and—Ow!" She pulled back as an exposed wire shocked her. "And some plaz-solder."

Julian slid down the outside of the metal ladder, his boots squeaking with the friction, and looked up at her with concern, dark eyes glittering. "You all right?"

"Yes," she said, irritated. "Just missed the hot lead here." She rubbed her wrist, then took the offending wire in a padded set of grips and tucked it out of the way.

Shaved bits of metal from where the cracked engine cover littered her black jumpsuit. She was not a trained engineer, by any means, but over the past years at Zeta she had managed to become a passable mechanic. "Hand me that wrench, would you?"

"You be careful. We don't have many who know their way around the inside of a turbo engine."

"Aye, sir." Qiao stopped short of a salute and allowed a smile.

It was a relief to be working without the tension that characterized the Khimeyr's first weeks with the Solarii. It had taken a while for the survivors to recognize their own kind. The two teams started to bond as they shared their histories and feelings. The Khimeyr, having been alone with each other for so long, were starved for fresh human contact, including Qiao herself.

Once Julian had worked through his prejudice against those of Dragonfleet, he turned out to be a pleasant companion and one very knowledgeable about ship maintenance. Qiao had learned much already from the young engineer, for whom she held a growing respect.

Qiao waved at Winston and Hussard, who passed on the way to their ships for an afternoon reconnaissance flight. Three patrols a day flew to keep them aware of what was happening in the skies over the settlement. Several squads were also set up as long range scanners between Solarii territory and the Rotaran sector, keeping them apprised of potential danger on many fronts.

A man name Stefan Ciro had brought news of pirates. He seemed a pleasant enough fellow. Qiao wasn't sure she believed his claims, especially when he seemed to be using them to leverage attention and time with her commander.

Catava appeared to have made an effort to discourage the eager pup, but Stefan's perpetual good humor seemed to deflect every slight or sour note. Good for him. In Qiao's estimation, Catava obsessed far too long on Luca's loss. Maybe it was time for Catava to look to the future, whether this particular young man was the answer or not.

Just as Julian climbed the ladder to hand Qiao some tools, a warning klaxon sounded, signaling an incoming craft without clearance.

Jumping down from the opening, Qiao dropped and rolled behind a crate. Julian scrambled for cover and his hand weapon. It took only a moment for everyone in the hangar to hunker down behind something solid, to wait with weapons drawn.

Surely if it was a Dragonfleet ship, that ID would have popped up. Could the pirates be here already?

Soon a long narrow craft the color of burnished brass came into view. It slid violently into the hangar, sparks flying across the runway, and nearly tipped as it skidded to a stop. The ship's hull was pitted with old battle scars. Qiao scanned the ship lengthwise and made out a name painted in faded black letters on the left flank. *Karma's Revenge.*

A door from the main base burst open, and a security team of four headed by Darien Pomeroy came running in. With weapons drawn, they slid to a halt as they approached the ship.

Pomeroy glanced around the hangar, and beckoned Julian, Winston, and Qiao to create a second line of defense about ten meters behind his team. Then he turned his attention to the ship, using his mobile communications set.

"Attention, unidentified pilot," Pomeroy barked. "Drop your hatch and toss your weapons out first! That's an order."

A burst of static from his unit was followed by an animated female voice. "Unidentified fascist wannabe, I'm not coming out of here with a dozen weapons pointed at me without more than a map in my hand."

Qiaolin smothered a laugh, recognizing a fellow rebel in that tone. But she knew Pomeroy would not be so amused.

"Want us to come drag you out?" Pomeroy growled.

"No." Another burst of static set in. "What—*hiss*—really like—*hiss*—repair my—*hiss*—equipment." The hatch opened and a young woman leaned down to peer out. She couldn't have been much more than twenty-two. Highlights in her long thick hair were nearly as brassy as her ship. Most of her body was still concealed behind various metal parts. "Now, what I would have said if I could have beaten my com into line is that my name is Piper Donovan, piloting *Karma's Revenge*, and I'd like to request permission to land." She eyed Pomeroy. "Sir."

"Fraggin' late for that," Pomeroy grumbled. "Who's aboard with you?"

"A friend," Piper replied. "Not a mass murderer last time I checked."

Qiaolin noticed gun barrels dropping a little all over the hangar, including her own. The girl might be a spitfire, but she didn't seem dangerous. Other than what they all were at that age, ripe with hormones and attitude.

The girl scrutinized them, apparently finding a welcome of sorts. She particularly reacted to the smile on Qiao's face. "I'll get him," Donovan said, and disappeared from sight.

They heard an exchange of excited voices inside the ship and something heavy clanged. Pomeroy looked at McKinley and frowned, then inched forward to the bottom of the ramp, his laser pistol drawn and ready.

"Hey! What's goin' on up there? You comin' out or not?"

"In our own good time." A tall man in a fancy gold overall stepped into the doorway. His jeweled turban reflected the lights from the hangar, and his skin was an unblemished rich chocolate brown. He stalked down the ramp past a nonplussed Pomeroy. "Difficult enough to survive an emergency landing without being treated as criminals. Is there a sane man present?"

Piper appeared in the hatch, adjusting tiny black boots, and then scooted down after her companion. She stopped in front of Pomeroy and held out her hand. "Piper Donovan."

After a moment Pomeroy holstered his weapon and took her hand.

Piper gave a rather impish smile and noticed Pomeroy eying the damage to her ship's hull. "Not a pretty picture, is it? Danged pirates shoot first and ask later." Her eyes swiveled back to Pomeroy. "Kinda like you guys."

Julian took the initiative in the awkward silence that followed to approach the green-eyed girl and introduce himself. The two started jabbering parts and metals before anyone else could join them and walked away to examine at the spoiled craft.

Meanwhile, Qiaolin moved forward to speak to Piper's companion. Adding the height of that turban, he was a good half-meter taller than she was, forcing her to look up at him with a craned neck.

The man smiled, teeth bright white against his dark face. "Not a sane man but a beautiful woman." He bowed. "My lady."

Qiaolin, unaccustomed to such compliments, cleared her throat with a cough. "I'm Xiu Qiaolin. Welcome to the Solarii base." Dwarfed by the nameless man, she looked at Pomeroy, a question in her eyes.

Pomeroy walked slowly over to them, dismissing the security team. "Darien Pomeroy, Khimeyr security, acting on behalf of Solarii Administrator Len. We have every right to defend our bit of space. We've had to take certain precautions."

"The first is to mistrust everyone," the man said in his deep voice.

Pomeroy nodded once, not flinching. "Damn straight."

The man looked at him and then smiled. "To each his own, Pom. You may call me Vanyakin of Myana." He bowed to Pomeroy. "We bring goods to trade. In particular, *weapons*."

Qiaolin's ears perked at his words, and she reached for her com-unit to notify Trezanna.

"Already done," purred a voice behind her. A quick glance revealed Austin and Rumadan, both staring at the *Revenge* with concern.

Pomeroy nodded to his Solarii counterpart. "No damage to the building and only these two aboard. You want I should take them for questioning?"

Austin shook her head. "I think they'll be fine. Trezanna will want to know about the supplies, at any rate. If you'd come with me, sir?" She gestured to Vanyakin to accompany her from the hangar.

"You are too kind," the tall, dark-skinned one replied, falling into step beside her as they walked out. "Tell me of these Solarii."

Rumadan exchanged glances with Pomeroy, whose face was unreadable as he watched Julian and Piper still chattering as they finished their circle of the damaged ship.

"It would seem important to corroborate the true status of the communication device," Rumadan said in deceptively idle tone of voice.

"Right it would." Pomeroy nodded. "I'll see to it."

Rumadan growled her approval and stepped back to study the newcomer. Winston and Hussard still waited by their craft to see if they were needed. Pomeroy, apparently satisfied, sent them on their way with orders to make sure no other lurkers waited overhead.

"Keep alert for more visitors. Powerful lot of strangers just happening by," Pomeroy said with a distinct lack of good humor.

"No worries, mate," Winston drawled. "I'll check first to see if they got bloody credits to lose at the chips game."

Pomeroy snorted. "You do that. Since I'm already planning to take yours later." He smacked his hand off Winston's ship and let them go.

Qiaolin watched the whole scene, feeling a little let down when everything turned out to be civilized. Disappointed, she climbed up into the engine cavity of the *Tiboron* to return to her work.

Perhaps I'm still holding a bit of Dragonfleet bloodlust after all.

CHAPTER 13

HIS ego still stinging from his encounter with the young pilot of the *Karma's Revenge,* Pomeroy returned to the Khimeyr wing.

In the Khimeyr common room he found the Philean Stefan Ciro on the floor playing a game with Chad, Catava's foster son. Both lay on their stomachs, feet in the air.

"Where's Momma Cat?" Pomeroy asked the boy and cast a disapproving glare at Stefan.

Chad pointed across the hall.

That was no kind of respect, now was it? Pomeroy thought. *Couldn't afford to be sloppy, not when you didn't know what was coming round the next curve.*

Pomeroy cleared his throat, rebuking without a word.

Chad dragged himself to his feet and straightened his back like a good soldier. "Momma Cat is in Miss Lily's room."

Much better.

Stefan returned Pomeroy's hostile gaze. "He's just a boy. No need to get red about it."

Already burning under the collar, Pomeroy was across the room in a couple of steps. He grabbed Stefan by the shirtfront and yanked him to his feet. "No need for *you* to interfere in Khimeyr discipline. You don't have business here."

Chad yelped and scrambled out of the way, the game pieces flying across the floor.

Stefan tried to get loose, keeping his hands clear and in the open. "Come on, friend, I wasn't hurting anything."

Pomeroy, seeing red, drew back a fist. "No, But I could show you how it's done."

"Let him go."

The icy voice behind him cut through Pomeroy's anger, causing his fingers to release Stefan. The men backed away from each other, confronted instead with the vision of a furious Catava Rolon. She beckoned to Chad, who scurried to cling to her leg, wide-eyed and silent.

"What's going on here, Dare?"

"Just handling discipline, ma'am." Pomeroy informed.

"I wasn't aware Stefan was under your supervision." Catava turned her aqua gaze on Stefan, a bare hint of amusement within. "Were you misbehaving?"

Stefan gave a roguish grin. "Just a misunderstanding, ma'am. I did make a mess on the floor there, playing dots with Chad." He gestured to the scattered game.

Catava gave a long sigh of impatience. "If you boys think you can play nicely, I have serious matters to attend." Her stare indicated they better figure out a way to do that.

"I'll send your report in writing then." With a snort of disgust, Pomeroy headed for the door.

"You do that," Catava muttered from behind him.

* * *

STEFAN watched Pomeroy stomp out of the room.

Catava stood like a statue for a moment and then ruffled Chad's hair. "Are you all right, sweet?"

Chad nodded wordlessly, still clutching her.

Stefan grinned and looked to the door where Pomeroy left. "He's loud, I'll give him that." He bent down and started picking up the red and white pieces. "Perhaps it isn't a good idea to play on the floor anyway. We could set up on the table, Chad. Would you like that?"

The boy looked at Catava for approval and then scampered across the room to the table.

Stefan smiled. "Your son's quite a boy," he said with some warmth as he set up the pieces for a new game. "Beat me three times already."

Catava didn't respond. Her eyes burned as she watched the boy gather his pieces. One was missing and the boy went to search for it on the far side of the room. She shrugged as she found Stefan's gaze on her. "He's not my son."

Stefan slid into a seat at the table. "Oh, I'm sorry. I thought—I mean, he called you mother."

"It's all right." Catava joined him, gesturing when Chad returned that the game should continue. "His parents are dead. I took Chad and his sister into my household."

The raw look in her eyes when she spoke of Chad's parents showed him her pain. Just as quickly, she looked away, revealing there was more to the story, something she hid from others.

"Not entirely a selfless act?" Stefan asked.

Catava looked at him, eyes hard for a moment as he pried, then softened. "No, actually, it wasn't." Her eyes flicked away, then back. "Perceptive of you."

"His parents were friends of yours, then?"

Catava nodded in response. She moved one of Chad's pieces into a strategic position with a wink. When the boy climbed back into his chair, he surveyed the board and then glanced quickly up at her. She smiled as he recognized what she had done.

"He seems happy enough." Stefan moved a polished white piece into direct jeopardy, putting on a face of mock outrage as the boy captured it. "Hey!"

Chad smiled and set up his next move. She whispered a suggestion, becoming a conspirator in Stefan's lopsided strategy. His eyes widened and then he took another piece and moved it.

Stefan was amused. "I didn't realize what an accomplished opponent I had."

"You're playing a four-year-old," the Catava said.

"Mm-hmm. I know exactly who I'm playing," Stefan said. Allowing a smile, he wondered whether entertaining the little boy was a way into Catava's heart, too.

She reacted to the smile with a slow flush before coming to her feet, feeling somewhat awkward. Lily called to her from the door. Catava leaned down to her boy. "I need to go. Chad. Mind Mr. Ciro. When your game's finished, come back to our quarters, all right?"

Stefan wanted her to trust him, but even as dense as he sometimes could be, he should have realized Catava carried with her a broken heart. He should have seen it. *Stupid, stupid.*

"Cat—"

"I need to go," Catava said, cutting him off. She shook her head and took her leave, walking briskly from the room, ignoring his deep sigh.

Somehow Stefan would get Catava's attention and win her heart. Of course, she was distracted with everything they were juggling at the moment. Pirates on the horizon and a heartless woman called Estrella Drake. Eventually there would be time to think about someday. They would get past this soon.

As the youngest of seven, patience had been drilled into him since the day of his birth. Stefan could outlast her any day.

CHAPTER 14

TREZANNA and Rumadan watched the main screen in the command center as one, eyes fixed on the blinking indicators as the ships appeared on the sensors from their outlying beacons.

The alert interrupted Trezanna's informal discussion with Piper, Lily, and several others in the lounge. She knew something was seriously wrong as soon as she entered the center. Rumadan's coloration alone warned that the crisis was real. Yet she had not ordered the fighters into the sky.

Not Estrella, then. Maybe worse.

Trezanna studied the screen, not wanting to believe what was before them. She asked Rumadan to alert the Khimeyr.

A few minutes later, Catava and Qiaolin burst through the door at a run, as astonished as the Solarii once they saw the screen.

"So Stefan was telling the truth about the Arkosians," Catava said, out of uniform, her hair hanging loose down her back.

Qiaolin bit her lip. "Apparently so."

Over the weeks since Stefan Ciro's arrival, his claims had been the subject of much discussion but not much hard fact. Not until Piper Donovan's independent confirmation of the pirates' attack of her *Karma's Revenge* lent credence to the tale.

"They are waiting outside our outer beacons," Rumadan growled. "It is a mystery to me why they have not come closer." She tapped the controls on the chair arm, sharpening the focus.

Ten ships of varying sizes hung in space at a dead stop, running lights blinking.

Catava looked at Trezanna. "Perhaps the Solarii are not their targets."

Trezanna pursed her lips and nodded, smoothing her pale green knit suit. "We're not currently the weaker of the groups. It would be a logical assumption."

"That would presuppose they know our forces have expanded." The Viorn studied Trezanna, ears twitching with speculation.

"Interesting point." Catava looked back at the screen. "We didn't tell them."

"You're going to let them kill her, just like that?" Qiaolin blurted.

"Perhaps you would rather we invite her for tea?" Rumadan's skin quivered lavender with purple splotches.

Trezanna crossed her arms. She agreed with Rumadan. Estrella surely showed no compunction about attacking the Solarii. "She'd let us hang in the wind."

Qiaolin spun back around and stared at the screen. "Will you even warn her?"

"That is not our responsibility." Rumadan eyed her coolly.

After an awkward silence Trezanna chose a course of action. "Double the patrols," she said, stepping forward and setting the logs. "Set the alarms down tight. I want to know when they make their move."

Rumadan rumbled agreement. A quizzical twitch of an ear and a look at Qiaolin posed the silent question of whether or not preventive action was necessary.

Trezanna shook her head no.

Catava stepped closer, speaking softly to Trezanna. "Scouts?"

The Solarii Ops director expressed her displeasure with a darkening of her fur. "I think we're better off that they don't know we know."

"Perhaps." Catava nodded absently, turning back to the screen.

The four continued to watch, but the ships didn't do anything worthy of note. Shortly afterward, Qiaolin left, her lack of composure evidence of some inner battle.

The Catava stretched and looked Rumadan in the eye. "Qiaolin's all right. She's passionate, but she'd lay down her life before putting any of us in danger."

"We must continue to believe that is so," Rumadan said in a tone that implied dire consequences otherwise.

"I've known Qiao a long time. She can be trusted." Catava turned back to the screen. "Do you think we can stand against the Arkosians without Dragonfleet?"

Rumadan cocked her head and examined Catava's face, lit by the reflected blinking colors of the screen. "It would seem we have no choice."

Trezanna had to agree.

* * *

TREZANNA left the command center with the intention of returning to her quarters, but instead turned into a corridor that led to an outside patio, too agitated now at the thought of more fighting to settle into sleep. Escaping into the crisp night, she filled her lungs with the cool air, trying to clear stagnation from her mind, preparing for a new crisis mode.

Trezanna had spent ten years of her life in Space Force, her leadership training providing the ability to conduct dangerous missions, captain ships, discipline personnel, and more. This side of her could be cold and a little calculating, could believe that some losses were acceptable and even necessary. A leader needed to be that way.

There was a time, years ago, when she believed that in order to be whole a conscience and moral sense must be satisfied, and that went for anyone, even a leader. Knowing that Dragonfleet could be doomed by her own inaction didn't sit well morally. She imagined that most Dragonfleet officers wanted nothing more than she or any of her own people did, to survive. Estrella was a special case, centered on her own desires and needs. But the others? Could she doom them as well?

She sighed as she glanced inside at the few remaining personnel gathered under the bright lights of the lounge for a last conversation or drink for the night. Since joining the Solarii, it seemed either they were fighting for their lives against outside enemies or battling to protect others in the name of survival. At some point, in some future, would it be so much to ask that life would be warm, cozy, rewarding, and even peaceful?

"Would it?" Trezanna asked aloud, leaning on the brickwork wall that surrounded the patio and its garden containers.

"Would it?" echoed the cheery voice of Dr. Boring. He walked up from the yard, his face illuminated in the reflection of lights from inside. "What troubles you, oh fearless leader?"

Trezanna shook her head at the subtle challenge in his tone. "Not now, Doctor. I'm not in the mood."

"Mood, you say?" Boring smirked as he joined her. "Trouble, it waits for no mood, it strikes when least expected." The doctor studied her face with a concern much deeper than a medical assessment. "Which is it, the Dragons or the pirates then?"

The Solarii administrator smiled reluctantly. The Eponans weren't telepaths, but the doctor certainly had some degree of right-on empathy. "Pirates," she said.

Boring gave a brisk nod. "Expected, from all reports, and Julian and crew have rebuilt the ships, some a little rough, for certain, but space-worthy. We should be ready."

Trezanna looked up at the night sky, the stars a comforting spread of white lights against the darkness. "Our equipment, our personnel.

Ready." She nodded. "We'll stand to the last man and woman, if we must. But best guess is they've got their sights set elsewhere."

"Elsewhere, you say?" Boring looked up at her. In the shadows his eyes were nearly dark as Rumadan's. He examined her face, and then a smile toyed with his lips. "Estrella, then? Irony, such irony. As ye sow, so shall ye reap."

Trezanna couldn't define how she felt, some mixture of fatigue, anxiety, and regret. She leaned on the edge of the wall, propping her chin up with her hand. "I guess."

"How fortunate we are that the Khimeyr came along when they did. A nourishment of both heart and mind, indeed." He patted her shoulder, passing on reassurance through that empathic connection. "Always think wisely, my dear. Remember, dwell not on the *what ifs* but the *what is*."

Trezanna smiled, feeling better. "I will, Eugene. Thank you."

He nodded and scuttled off to whatever evening plans lay ahead.

Trezanna spent a few more minutes breathing the calm of the night wind into her soul, getting in touch with her inner voices. It would benefit them all if she began the next day with a clear mind and focus. When she reached her limit of silence in the dark, she offered a host of prayers to any god who might know her, who might answer her, before she went inside to her bed.

CHAPTER 15

THE four-tone summons pierced Qiaolin's sleep.

The sound rattled her com-unit on the bedside table, a code she had not heard in years, the code assigned to her by Estrella. Fully awake in a snap, she reached for the unit, glad she didn't share her quarters with anyone.

Do I dare answer it? Would the pirates hone right in on the signal?

Torn, hoping she was right, she activated the com.

"Qiao?" came a breathless, panicked female voice. "Answer me, damn you! I know you can hear me!"

Could that be Estrella? Qiao thought it was. That biting attitude resonated with her memory. They had been friends, once.

"This is Qiaolin," she said softly. Knowing how the others felt about Dragonfleet, this communication might well be considered treason.

"Help. Qiao, we need help. Please. For all those battles we fought together." The voice rasped out wearily and then choked. After a long coughing fit, she gasped: "Arkosians...."

Sorry to have been proved correct, Qiaolin slid out of bed, spurred to action. But what could she do? Who among the others would provide Estrella any sympathy? Darien would laugh in her face. She couldn't think of even one person who would accompany her to Dragonfleet space to rescue Estrella and her people.

"You're hurt," Qiaolin said.

"Underground. Hiding." More coughing echoed.

Qiaolin kicked out at the shadowed air around her, frustrated. Could she beg Trezanna for her old friend's life? Not much percentage in that.

"Qiao, we were comrades once. All these years can't have changed that. We can help you, too, Qiao. I can spring at least a dozen ships, some good people, if the pirates get distracted. More important, I've seen what the pirates are up to. Qiaolin, please, you've got to help us." the voice said and then the channel went dead.

Qiao jumped back on the bed, keying the unit, trying to get her back. "'Strella?" She smacked the unit with the heel of her hand. No response. Staring up at the ceiling, watching patrol lights pass outside her window, she debated the best course of action.

Surely they would listen now, Catava and Trezanna.

Estrella had even offered help. She wouldn't humble herself unless she was in real trouble. Trouble eventually bound to follow a path straight to their doorstep.

Qiaolin wrapped herself in tumbled blankets, trying to decide what to do. Her first instinct was to honor that old friendship, to fly to the rescue of her former comrade. *Lousy idea.* But she couldn't come up with a better one. Maybe the leaders would do better.

She sighed and padded out to find Catava.

* * *

TREZANNA leaned against the counter cradling her cup in her fingers, taking the chill off her hands as she listened, too agitated to sit.

"She's finally flipped!" Julian sputtered. His expression vacillated between amazement and hysteria, as he pulled at the open collar of his navy blue over-shirt. "That leather-clad bitch really thinks we're going to come save her?"

The discussion of the joint council meeting wavered little after Catava's news of the mid-night contact with Qiaolin. Though it was early in the morning, news that the pirates had attacked Dragonfleet had given them all a burst of adrenaline and that, as much as the steaming carafes of kafee Trezanna set out in the lounge, stimulated both their thoughts and words. Many on both sides came to listen and to learn of their fate.

Qiaolin waited, silent in her black softsuit, her chestnut eyes blazed with divided feelings Trezanna understood very well. Darien and Julian traded cracks, debating what flavors of desperation would cause the Dragon firebrand to lose her nerve. Chase and Rumadan, both veterans of the fight, were thoughtful, aware of many implications, as was Trezanna.

Her check of the beacon readings at first light showed the dangerous proximity of the pirates, a number of them in orbit over the moon above them. Ciro was right. Their armaments had improved since the last encounter with the Solarii.

"So do we hang separately, or hang together?" Boring's ebullience seemed undimmed by the prospect of yet another armed conflict. He nibbled on some *torba* crackers that he brought to the meeting, amethyst eyes brilliant with good humor as he studied the others.

Trezanna wondered why she was surprised that he practically stole the query from her mind. He smiled at her, nodding merrily.

"It's not just a question, Trezanna, it's *the* question. Safety in numbers, this has always been a maxim." Boring turned to the others, waving his cup in anticipation of consensus. "Belated it may be that Estrella has decided she needs us, but that makes it no less true. To survive the pirates, it needed all of us once, and will again."

"You can't be serious," Pomeroy snarled. "The she-devil would flay us alive and leave us bleedin' in the street, you know. And laugh while she watched, eh?" His voice was rough. His scruffy beard was now gone, shaved clean, and his hair was trimmed. He must be feeling like less of a renegade.

Catava shot her muscle man a quelling look, and he dropped his eyes. But tight tendons in his jaw revealed his trepidation. "I vote no," he muttered.

"Are we voting?" Julian demanded. "If we are, I agree. Absolutely not. I repaired enough of our craft she used for target practice and I'm not about to suggest we should fly right into her arms!" His spoon tapped a nervous rhythm on the table top, which stopped as Rumadan growled her irritation.

"Have you installed those prototype weapons you developed, Julian?" Chase asked. "The ones that target shield generators?"

"I've got two of them, one on the *Amazon,* and one on the *Whirlwind.* The third one's not done yet. But there's no guarantee they will turn the tide." The engineer's chin seemed less firm, giving him an even younger appearance.

"It's the best we have for now," Trezanna said.

"What about that weapons trader? Ain't he sold us a batch yet?" Pomeroy demanded.

Catava deflected him. "That's a conversation for another day. Now we have to choose whether we should help Dragonfleet. Not all of those who remain are Estrella, you know. Plenty of people are trapped there who just couldn't escape as easily as we did."

All too true, Trezanna thought. She resented the thought of aiding the very people who had been trying to kill them for so many months, but not everyone at Miramar fell into that category.

Trezanna turned to Catava. "I know you hope to regain your hold on that territory. Easy enough to let the Arkosians do your work for you, especially if Estrella's in bad shape."

Catava didn't react, but Pomeroy's head bobbed sharply in assent, while Xiu clutched her cup until her fingers blanched.

"Qiaolin says she's offered help," Catava said without inflection. "We know she's a good fighter. Certainly it's in her best interest to help us."

Winston spoke up from a table near them in the lounge where he had been listening, though he was not a voting member of the council. "Just so we remember in two weeks or three weeks, she'll come round and cut our bloody legs off without so much of a thank you."

Pomeroy's dry, dark laugh punctuated the discussion. "Exactly. Mad dogs bite!" Catava reached a hand out in his direction, Trezanna guessed to calm him down, but he pulled back. "Is this a free and open discussion or ain't it? I got a right to express my opinion. Or does only Solarii word count for naught?"

Catava just shook her head. "Of course not, Dare. Speak your piece."

Pomeroy shifted in his seat now that he was the focus of attention. "Just thinkin' this is trouble we don't need. We know what she's all about. We're smarter than this." He looked to Trezanna as if he wanted to say more, but he visibly made the effort to control his tongue.

Trezanna waited several moments for further input after Pomeroy finished, and then glanced at Rumadan who simply nodded. The buzzing discussions of the onlookers would likely be unproductive.

Time to make a decision.

Trezanna cleared her throat. "Voice vote will do. Council members only, please. In support of aiding Dragonfleet?"

Chase, Qiaolin and the doctor gave their assents.

"Against?"

Pomeroy and Julian voted against. Trezanna eyed Catava, wondering what she would choose. Rumadan, withdrawn, her fur a pale lavender-gray, also had not chosen a side. A potential tie vote.

Qiao reached across the table to the Khimeyr leader. "Cat, you read the intel reports. The Arkosians are decked out and fit to fly. If we don't have the remains of Dragonfleet with us, we might not be able to survive, even with the Solarii."

As Julian bristled at the insinuation that his well-tended fleet might not be adequate for the job, the Khimeyr second-in-command held up a hand to cut off his comment. "Even if we were all at full strength capacity, both our groups, we'd be hard pressed to counter this challenge. And in all honesty, we're not. We need those extra ships and personnel. If we're not going to get them from your Space Force, or some other entity, or new recruits, all we have left is Estrella. We don't have to trust her. We just need her fleet."

"We have to consider the possibility that Estrella is setting us up," Julian replied. "She could have sent a false distress call to draw us into a showdown with allied Dragonfleet and Arkosians."

"Long range scans show heavy weapon fire in Dragonfleet space," Rumadan interjected. "Even though we cannot scan Miramar, it would be foolish of her to waste such amounts of munitions simply to correlate an illusion."

Pomeroy greeted Rumadan's comment with a cynical snort. "Ha! You know the devious little harridan. Wouldn't put it past her meself."

"We cannot trust her under any circumstances," Catava finally agreed, shoving her cup away with an impatient hand. "But I have to admit we are in no condition to take on a fully-equipped force. I'm leaning toward incorporating Dragonfleet into our units. Hell, we can send them out in the front row. Make sure they never get the chance to shoot us in the back." She glanced at Pomeroy. "Can you get on board?"

Her second rose to his feet, obviously angry. "To Hades with that old saw about the devil you know being better than the devil you don't. Estrella's still the devil! I've always been the good soldier," he said, emotion rending his deep voice. "But I don't...without a bloody leader with balls, I...." He glared at Catava and Qiaolin. Then he walked out of the room, slamming the door behind him.

"I'll handle him," Catava said. She gestured to Qiao, and the two of them followed after their irate comrade.

Trezanna was confident that Catava could handle him. Those who lived by the chain of command had a profound connection with each other, one that transcended differences of opinion.

As Julian will comply with my orders even, if he disagrees with me. Even if he's disappointed in me. Or hates me for it.

Trezanna straightened her shoulders and studied the faces of her people. "If I'm wrong about this, I'll take responsibility. But I'm not sure what chance we have unless we all hold together. We'll ride herd on Estrella and her people, and take every precaution. But I'll go with Catava on this."

"When do we leave?" Chase asked.

Trezanna glanced at Rumadan for the answer.

The Viorn shrugged, her muscles taut but her color returning. "No time like the present."

"Let's go then," Trezanna said. "She says she can make an escape happen, if the pirates are occupied elsewhere. We can do that." She watched Winston and Julian. "If there's any sign that Estrella betrayed us, give her what she deserves. No questions."

The two men nodded and shoved back from their tables, before leaving. Their boots marched heavily down the corridor outside on their way to the hangar bay.

Trezanna nodded. "I'll lead the mission. Rumadan, you stay and keep defenses up. We don't want the Arkosians sneaking past us while we're at Miramar."

"Of course. We shall be ready for them."

The two left for the hangars, Trezanna stopping to grab her flight suit and jacket from a locker outside the bay. She shoved her legs into the thick blue coverall and then wrestled her way into the sleeves, pulling it over her clothing. With a quick zip up the front, she swung her hair free of the collar and entered the hangar, her heart racing with the burst of adrenaline.

To all appearances, Rumadan must have given the orders to scramble the Solarii and Khimeyr ships as soon as she left the meeting. The bay was fully lit and personnel scrambled between the ships, stowing weapons and other supplies. The Solarii administrator stood in the doorway a moment, taking in the sight before her, admiring the earnestness with which her people went about the business of conflict.

Winston helped the engineer ready the ships, checking in the pilots, sharing words of encouragement and his crooked grin. Talib boarded the *Carapace*, her enthusiasm unhampered by her earlier injuries, as evidenced by her wave and a thumbs-up to Trezanna before she disappeared inside.

Trezanna returned the gesture and crossed the hangar to see Winston. "The *Galena*?" she asked.

"Second round, ma'am. Me and Qiao set it up earlier, whenever we was going to fly out, we got the troops lined up in order of gun power. Sending up twelve birds, best of both groups...."

Winston trailed off as Pomeroy entered the far end of the hangar, Qiaolin following after him, both yelling. Pomeroy's words were unclear from the distance, but his tone was angry and she finally broke off and went to her ship, with a defeated look. He glared after her and then climbed into the *Queen's Claw* after some irate words with a member of the Khimeyr ground crew.

"Can't blame him," Winston said, with just an underlying challenge in his tone.

Trezanna bit her tongue, buying time to be professional. "Get the first group in the air, now."

"Aye, aye, ma'am." Winston squeezed the button on the mike of his com. "First two roll!"

The hangar filled with the acrid scent of fuel igniting, as engines roared, near deafening in the enclosed space. Two ships, one Solarii and one Khimeyr, taxied out and then took off as soon as the runway was clear, circling to a pre-determined rendezvous point before departing for Dragonfleet space. The plan was to grab the pirates' attention, keeping the Arkosians busy while Estrella arranged whatever sleight-of-hand she had concocted to scramble her people in hiding. Only as a last resort would they go in to evacuate the trapped Dragonfleet people.

What would happen when they got back? Most would probably call for immediate retribution against Estrella for the crimes she had committed against both groups. That was still a possibility. She would deal with that later. Now, her eye was on survival.

Winston waved Trezanna on as the next two pair of ships rolled for the doors. "Your turn, boss lady! I'll have your back right enough in a few."

Trezanna surveyed the open hangar. The rush of people had cleared. The operation was underway. She nodded and continued to the *Galena*. As she crossed the open hangar floor, she waited for one of the larger Khimeyr ships to pass. Seeing it was the *Queen's Claw*, Trezanna eyed the bridge's port windows, pondering Pomeroy's state of mind.

To her surprise, she caught his eye on her. As she wondered how to encourage him, he suddenly grinned and tipped his worn hat. Surprised, she smiled in response and gave him a sharp salute before he pulled into the launch rotation.

As Trezanna reached the *Galena's* hatch, Shelby Hussard passed her, dashing for the *Whirlwind*, her hair flying loose behind her, still tugging on her jacket.

"Sorry, ma'am, I was in the shower!" Shelby was obviously distraught at being caught literally with her pants down.

"You're still on time, pilot. Good flying!"

With a grateful smile, the *Whirlwind's* pilot boarded her ship, and a few minutes later, her engine roared, as did Winston's *Tiboron*.

Trezanna crossed the hangar to her own ship and caught a glimpse of Piper watching all the activity. Trezanna found the slender girl to be bright and interesting, though closemouthed about herself. If only there was time to get to know her. Maybe she would stay on with the Solarii.

"Something I could do?" Piper asked.

"Sure," Trezanna said. "We need all the help we can get. See Rumadan up in the command center."

"You got it." Piper tossed a wrench into her open hatch and headed for the door.

Trezanna boarded her fighter and prepared for takeoff. Just before she lit the engines, Catava's voice came over her com.

"Len, I tried everything with Pomeroy, but I don't know what he'll do once he's up," the Khimeyr commander confessed.

Trezanna considered the impudent grin Pomeroy had given her. "I think he'll be all right. Save your worry for the pirates."

She flipped the switch, fired up and took off, the pressures of launch pushing her back into her seat. She piloted the *Galena* into a suborbital path, heading for the assembly point. Catava's *Liberator* was right behind her. When they arrived at the rendezvous, the force took off for Dragonfleet space.

CHAPTER 16

QIAOLIN transmitted the private four-tone code randomly to prevent detection by the Arkosian pirates. No answer. She commed Catava. "Still no response."

"It could be too late."

"I know." Qiao heard Catava pass on the news. She came back a few seconds later with a reply.

"Len says we'll send someone close enough to scan for survivors. Then decide."

"Copy." With a sigh, Qiao shut off the com and stared out at the stars. She had two interim conversations, brief and broken up, with her former flight-mate. Estrella knew they would be coming. Did the window of opportunity close? If so, at least they tried. Many of Estrella's people she considered her friends, or was before the break came. She would never forgive herself if they didn't try to rescue them. Fiddling with the dials, she waited for orders.

A ship ahead of her pulled out of formation and disappeared into Veil mode ahead of them, making the jump to light-speed. They all waited, ship-to-ship communication buzzing as the pilots discussed the situation pending his return.

Qiaolin let it all fade out of her active focus. The thought of combat with the Arkosians didn't excite her. A veteran of the last battle, she had lost many friends and comrades to the bloodshed. The pirates were every bit the murderous beasts their reputations described. She would have been just as happy not to deal with them at all.

Static rattled her com, followed by the four-tone signal Qiao had been waiting for. "'Strella?"

"Are you coming?" The voice was raspy, whispered, but held the faintest element of hope.

Qiaolin dared to take a relieved breath. "Status?"

A harsh laugh, followed by a burst of noise that sounded like an explosion. "Bad. Real bad. The Arkosians dropped troops, know that much. Several of us injured. Some dead. But we should be able to make a run for it." Static cut off her next words. "Careful, Qiao. They…."

The transmission faded away in unintelligible noise.

Qiaolin cursed under her breath and called Catava. "They're alive. Estrella says the Arkosians are on the ground."

"Understood. We're reading a power buildup now. Something's heading this way."

A few minutes later, the *Tiboron* burst into view in front of them, a couple of Arkosian cruisers on its tail. "Look out!" Qiao yelled, pulling her ship into a dive to get out of the way. The combined Solarii-Khimeyr forces scattered, spiraling outward like debris from an explosion to avoid the incoming ships, and then turned back, all guns blasting.

The battle was on.

* * *

HER protective shields on full, Trezanna took a position toward the rear, monitoring the fight on the small screen in front of her.

Two large cruisers belonging to the Arkosians took up the larger part of her screen as the Solarii-Khimeyr fleet arrived.

Space in front of her filled with tiny bursts of flame as exchanges of fire met their targets. She could differentiate between Solarii and Khimeyr ships by their signatures, but not by their fighting style. Pack mentality ruled. The shields of the Arkosian ships resounded with multiple attacks as the smaller ships spun in and out, their trajectories set to evade return fire.

Unfortunately, the pirate weapons were heavier, causing greater damage. Both Pomeroy's and Catava's ships took hits which sent them out of the rotation on long ellipses, taking time to recover before rejoining the battle. She made a run herself, feeling her heart pound as she passed between the lines of fire, trading shot for shot, the roar of the weapons under her rumbling through her feet, her ship bouncing around as her shields bore the brunt of the assault.

Passing behind them to circle around, she avoided most of the fire from the rear turrets and headed back toward the front in a smooth arc. McKinley's *Amazon* launched one of the prototype weapons at the pirate ship nearest, and Trezanna was thrilled to see it penetrate the shields and hit the hull with such force it seemed palpable even inside her cockpit. She was disappointed there was no following explosion, but the ship spit out no further fire and its shielding faltered.

That was half the battle.

Winston and Hussard tag-teamed the other Arkosian ship, taking turns on the offensive, blasting, then darting quickly aside. Xiu followed them in, but as Trezanna watched, suddenly swung wide, making a large detour around the pirates. A glance at rear sensors revealed eight ships coming at great speed along the route the pirates had come.

More pirates?

Who fooled whom here?

A second look grabbed Trezanna's heart and returned it to her chest as she realized these were Dragonfleet ships, chunking salvo after salvo at the Arkosians from behind the line. Xiu hooked up with them and the pack honed in on the disabled Arkosian ship, firing at a blinding rate.

Trezanna wrenched her attention back to the functional Arkosian ship, which was still firing. The remaining ships joined her, their pilots' cheers and war cries over the com a boost of adrenaline for her.

"Watch it now," she heard Winston admonish Hussard as she headed in a little too close.

"Spunky lass!" Darien Pomeroy called with a hoot.

Trezanna smiled and loaded another round of torps into the firing chambers. She had always liked that girl. The damaged ship began to list, and she considered giving an order to retreat. *Not yet. Not yet.*

She launched her torpedoes in the middle of a deep dive, and then yanked the rudder to the side to bring her under the ship. Passing beyond the reach of its return fire, she made a grand loop that gave her a view of the Dragonfleet ships, who launched their barrage, then pulled away from the ruined Arkosian vessel, surely aware that its time was limited.

The pirates seemed to be retreating toward the moon, and Miramar, only one still firing indiscriminately. The other triggered a warning klaxon denoting the detection of a radiation leak.

She sounded a retreat and hurried to catch up, flying on a higher trajectory to keep her sheep in line.

Suddenly a blinding flash of light signaled the pirate ship exploding. For a few seconds, Trezanna could see nothing out her front window. It was the sound she heard first, Winston's cry of anguish as the *Whirlwind* encountered flying debris from the demolished Arkosian. Jagged metal cut into the ship's machinery and opened its hull in a burst of silent flame. The ship and its feisty pilot Shelby Hussard were no more.

One moment of silence seemed to draw out into many, until the sky went black again. Stunned aviators realized one by one what had happened as the group pulled away to rendezvous. A burst of foul language came over the com as Winston turned his ship and headed straight back for the remaining Arkosian cruiser.

"Winston! Where ya going, man?" Pomeroy's voice was genuinely distressed. "Git your ass back here!"

Trezanna's direct order which followed was ignored, as was every other voice. The *Tiboron* made a beeline for the ship, which had stopped firing after its sister vessel exploded, taking Hussard. Trezanna even considered firing on Winston herself, long enough to disable the engine and tow him back.

How dare he waste his own life like that, and the ship they so desperately needed? This was a mission, not a chance to indulge personal feelings. Grief needed to be put off until they returned to the Solarii base. "Winston!"

She heard Catava order the others to continue the retreat, the Dragonfleet ships in their midst. Laying in a course for the *Tiboron*, hoping to somehow head it off, she pulled up when Winston's ship became enveloped in a green beam from the pirate ship, which pulled him closer.

"Tractor, Trezanna! Get out of there!" Catava's voice was sharp as a Hakian dagger.

"Damnation!" Trezanna, wise enough to know she couldn't break the beam, avoided a few wild shots from the ship and rejoined the others far enough out of range to escape the pirate weapons. Before she even reached them, she flipped on her rear sensors. The other ship swallowed the *Tiboron* whole. She had lost them both.

Forcing her emotions to a cold numbness, she counted up the remaining allied ships. She was not losing any more. Trezanna gave the signal to return to the Solarii base, and Catava led the pack in retreat, along with the Dragonfleet ships that had joined the fight.

The pirate ship, apparently satisfied with its cargo, turned for the base at Miramar. She watched after it, knowing her team achieved its goal to free the Dragonfleeters, but any joy she might have felt dissipated in the depth of their loss. Whatever benefit Estrella and her people may have brought to the alliance, she couldn't imagine that it was worth this.

And those who had dissented would not let her forget.

CHAPTER 17

NOW that they had rescued some Dragonfleet refugees, the real question Trezanna had to face was what to do with them.

The ships that escaped from Miramar flew back with them to the base, the radios empty of the excited chatter that accompanied their lifting off. The Solarii, devastated by the death of Hussard and Winston's capture, hardly let the Dragonfleet pilots out of their cockpits before the scrapping began.

Disturbed by what happened to her young pilots, Trezanna found herself caught up in the fracas a couple of times, pulling her people off unsuspecting Dragonfleeters.

"Knock it off!" she yelled at the third such unlucky officer. "None of us are happy about this, all right? Rumadan! Get security out here!"

Trezanna glanced around to see Catava and Pomeroy doing the same. Qiao stood with Estrella and the other Dragonfleet officers in the center of the tarmac, huddled in a circle. Estrella's gun was in her hand, but pointed at the ground.

Trezanna marched over to Estrella. "Put that away," she ordered through clenched teeth. "Now."

"Fine discipline you have among the troops," Estrella snapped, her dark eyes full of scorn. She shoved the weapon into a leg holster that fit tight over her black leather jumpsuit. "I'd have dropped half of these hooligans in the dust."

How could the woman be so arrogant after just being rescued? Had Estrella expected a hero's welcome? A parade?

"You're welcome," Trezanna said in a voice rife with sarcasm.

Pomeroy came to join them. "You want I should muzzle her like the rabid dog she is?"

Trezanna bit her tongue before she gave in to the compulsion to let him do just that. "Get her to the conference room. The others can go to D Wing. Make sure security keeps them there, no weapons, no com devices."

His sharp nod let her know that was handled

Trezanna went inside, stopping in the bathroom to wash her face.

The guilty eyes that stared back at her from the mirror condemned her choices. Her gut urged her to go after Winston and forcibly pull him from the jaws of the Arkosians. No way to do that without a frontal attack and further loss of life, a foolhardy and unproductive course of action.

But doing nothing just felt so defeated.

Finally she made her way to the conference room.

Rumadan, who had arrived first, laid a furry hand on Trezanna's shoulder. Her black eyes flickered like dark velvet curtains in moonlight. "You must move forward and quickly, if any chance exists to bring Winston home. Find out what the Dragonfleet people know. Use it."

"I know. I *know*. Pomeroy's bringing Estrella here so we can talk." Trezanna turned away, her arms crossed across her belly, protecting her from the pain. If she could be hard enough, if she could shove that guilt into a place she didn't have to feel it, then she could go on. She had done it before. She could do it now.

Within a few minutes, she heard footsteps and a babble of voices in the hallway outside. Pomeroy came first, his face rough and rigid, dragging the small, black-clad figure behind him. He threw her into the room.

Trezanna watched Estrella, who straightened from where Pomeroy tossed her, hot dark eyes burning with scorn. Catava followed them in, along with several other Khimeyr. Trezanna noticed that Qiaolin was not among them. Julian came to stand in the doorway, a silent sentinel. The line of his tight jaw, the tragic sorrow in his eyes, the hunch in his shoulders, all told Trezanna he thought of his own losses at the hands of Dragonfleet. *I told you so,* his look said to Trezanna. *I told you so.*

Catava and Estrella studied each other, stiff and unyielding, no love lost there. Trezanna could see that.

"Sit down," Trezanna said. "Everyone."

No one moved.

Rumadan growled softly from her place against the wall in the background, and crossed to lean on the table. "Time is wasting."

"Where's Luca Strada?" Estrella demanded. Her slight frame seemed too small to contain the amount of fury that vibrated through her tight voice.

"Where you can't touch him any more," Catava replied, her eyes hard as plasteel. She leaned close to Darien and whispered something. An interested look came over his face and he studied the dark-eyed virago more closely.

As the taut silence stretched out again, it was broken by a whistle heard from down the hall, coming closer and closer, and finally coming around the corner to the conference room. Dr. Boring walked in, cup in hand, and graced them all with a broad grin. "Hope I'm not too late." He took the closest seat at the table. "You can begin now."

The doctor's arrival broke the surface tension holding those in the room on their feet. Catava and the three others she brought with her moved around the table to sit on its far side. Pomeroy remained standing, waiting, until the Dragonfleet leader grabbed the chair closest to her and sat down. He sat within easy reach.

Time's wasting. The words echoed in her head. Trezanna sat at the head of the table, placing her notepad in front of her. After a deep breath, she turned her attention to Estrella. "What's the situation on the ground at Miramar?"

"Why are my people being locked up?" Estrella countered, hands out, palms up in supplication. "We ask for your help and you treat us as criminals?"

"Your people are in their wing for their own protection, Estrella. The Solarii are understandably a little worked up about their people being systematically blown up by you and yours."

With a set jaw, Estrella eyed Trezanna. "If you didn't intend to honor a truce, why rescue us at all?"

"Good question." Trezanna leaned back and crossed her arms. "Here's a consideration. Why don't you start answering my questions or I'll send you back? I'm sure the Arkosians would be glad to have you."

Pomeroy took out his firearm and laid it on the table, away from Estrella. "Does she have to be alive?"

Estrella looked from one to the other, and then bit her lip. An internal battle raged, evidenced by a twitching cheek muscle, clenched fingers and averted eyes. After a few moments, she spoke as though the words were dragged from her. "The Arkosians have two cruisers on the ground in addition to the ones we fought in the air. Some forty men occupy the place, heavily armed. They caught us off guard, overran the base three days ago."

"Rest of 'em must have stayed aboard ship," Pomeroy grunted.

Catava's attitude didn't warm one degree. "Do you know how many there are? Their ship's complements?"

Estrella shook her head. "They clearly didn't land everything and everyone. I'd have left the majority of my force in space, if it was me." She shrugged. "They're at least half as smart as I am."

Trezanna ignored Estrella's self-indulgent smirk. "What damage did the base sustain?"

"A couple of buildings took hits from some heavy weaponry," Estrella replied. "I lost twenty men in the supply building, which is mostly rubble now. But they didn't hit indiscriminate targets. I suppose they wanted as much of it whole as possible. So they could use it."

Rumadan leaned forward, arms on the conference table. "How exactly did you escape the attack?"

"We nearly didn't. There was a two-minute warning before the first bomb hit. No time to engage the anti-aircraft guns before they started landing." Her gaze flicked from Rumadan to the ceiling and back again. "Those of us in the hangar heard the invasion alarm and bailed for the tunnels under the base. We hid while the Arkosians swept through the base the first time taking prisoners. As time went on, we got the chance to rescue some of the others and they joined us below while the pirates were busy congratulating themselves on a job well done. Idiots."

Trezanna watched Estrella shift nervously in her chair. Was anything the Dragonfleet leader saying actually true?

"Once we heard from Qiaolin, we waited under the hanger," Estrella continued, with a frown. "Several ships were ready to fly, so we took them when the pirates were engaged with your forces. We sustained a couple bits of damage in the process. Where is Qiao, anyway? Did you lock her up too for helping me?"

"How many people did you leave behind? Where are the rest of them?" Catava persisted. "Did you leave them to die? A convenient way to punish those who didn't prove their loyalty?"

"Bitch!" Estrella's left hand slapped the table and drove her to her feet. Pomeroy matched the Dragonfleet leader, his weapon in hand faster than Trezanna could follow. Rumadan, seated between Trezanna and Estrella, rose, positioning her body between the two.

"Everyone, calm down!" Trezanna said. She noticed the little smile that tickled Catava's lip before it faded into a stern look. The others at the table were stiff with anticipation, all except Dr. Boring, who absently fiddled with the handle of his coffee cup. "Please, take your seats."

Pomeroy and Estrella stared each other down until they both returned to the chairs.

"I think that's a fair question," Trezanna stated. "What happened to those you couldn't liberate?"

Estrella remained stiff. "What we saw of Gus and the others, the pirates were using them for slave labor, making them stay at their posts to keep the place running."

Trezanna nodded. It made sense. With a minimal guard complement, the Arkosians would find it hard to maintain support services as well as keep a lid on the prisoners. If they had some hold over them, families perhaps, they could compel forced labor pretty easily.

Pomeroy fidgeted in his seat, lips twitching with words he must have wanted to say.

What was it he desired to know? Trezanna wondered. Probably the same things she did. All their speculations could now be laid to rest. This was the perfect opportunity to find out the true size of the Dragonfleet contingency, their number of ships and weapon capability. And it was an opportunity she was not about to pass up.

"How many of your people are left behind at Miramar?" Trezanna asked.

"Maybe one-ninety-five. Two hundred," Estrella answered, too quickly.

"Two hundred!" Pomeroy's rough face contorted with consternation. "When we left Miramar five years ago, there were almost four times that! Have you butchered them all?"

The other Khimeyr whispered among themselves, watching the petite dark woman with suspicion.

Estrella shrugged again and responded with an almost careless air. "Really, Darien, I can't be responsible for knowing the whereabouts of every little person who rag-tags around a powerful group like Dragonfleet. There may be more, somewhere. I prefer to devote my attention to those who are loyal."

Her words bled over into a long silence. Trezanna debated how much of this was a waste of everyone's time. Estrella was never one to be straightforward. They could only guess there were more survivors waiting for them, maybe as many as Pomeroy recalled. On the other hand, Estrella might gain some benefit by being honest. As potential allies, the Solarii could help her. It was possible that she would make a mental turnaround, play nice and be one big happy family.

When pigs fly.

"Any idea who's in charge of the pirate forces?" Trezanna asked.

"The same as last time. Yves Marcand. Big man, small brain. It's a shame I didn't get close enough to him to open his gut with my dagger. I could have—"

Trezanna cut her off. "Would have saved us all some time and grief, I'm sure. Better luck next time." She turned her mind to the thought of

Dragonfleet crew held by the pirates as workers. They probably needed every available body to keep the base running. So it was likely that they would find Winston at Miramar, too.

Pomeroy rose to his feet, hawk-like eyes flashing as he looked around the table. "Jibber jabber! Talk ain't savin' no one. Action's what we need here. If Winston is there, who better than us knows that base, hmm? All we got to do—"

"Is walk up to the door and knock?" Trezanna couldn't help the biting tone, but it was directed as much at herself as anyone. Guilt did that to a person.

"Better to sit here on your arse while they do god knows what to Winston?"

Rumadan's ears twitched with annoyance. "We cannot recklessly throw away more lives."

Trezanna looked around the table, seeing despair and frustration. If anything could tear the heart from her beloved Solarii, this could be it. "I don't at all concede the loss of Monty, Mr. Pomeroy." She regretted the emotional vibrato tingeing her voice. "At the same time, I will not countenance another hasty, half-cocked reaction. We have the gift of hindsight and the time to plan a response. I intend to take it."

"How *long*?" Pomeroy persisted. "He may only have a few hours, or a few days! How bloody *long*?"

Dr. Boring looked up from his fragrant marigold tea with a faint smile. "I must observe that Monty is a strong man with a broad back." The doctor peered at each of them in succession, ending up on the pacing Khimeyr security man. "One does not destroy valuable merchandise."

Pomeroy just stared.

"Best use of such a man would be as slave labor, yes?" the doctor added. "To get a good price in any market, they must preserve him."

Trezanna leaned forward, her lips pursed, her fingertips tapping together. There was time. Not much. But some. "We can only hope you're right, Doctor. That's all for now, people. Let's think this over for a few hours. When we meet again I want hard solutions." She stood up. "Anything else you want to tell us, Estrella?"

"Anything else you want to give me?" Estrella asked in a demanding voice, her sharp eyes fixed on Trezanna. "I came, understanding I would help you in return for my freedom. I've given you what you wanted. Now what are you going to do for me?"

"I'll consider that, once I verify some of the information you've provided." Trezanna cleared her throat. "Catava, take Estrella back to her wing."

"Of course." The slender blonde gestured to Pomeroy. The two leaders shared a knowing look, and then the Khimeyr and their 'guest' headed out.

Too much to do,

Trezanna returned to her office to bury herself in detail work. Tasks still awaited her, like the planning of a memorial ceremony for Shelby Hussard. The pert pilot deserved the recognition. People needed an opportunity to say their goodbyes. In her mind's eye, she envisioned the young woman, remembering her sharp tongue and willing heart.

What can I possibly say to do justice to all that she was?

Trezanna made some lame notes, but nothing she wrote really embodied Shelby's spirit.

Monty would know.

Maybe after he comes home.

CHAPTER 18

BACK in her office, Trezanna meant to bury herself in work, but she couldn't shake her guilt about Winston. She needed to walk off her ghosts.

She slipped on her brown leather jacket and headed for the lounge, hoping to hear some snippet of encouragement. Several people greeted her, both her own and some from the Khimeyr crew, before withdrawing to a respectful distance. Just as well. She didn't really want to discuss Winston or Hussard or anything about Estrella, either.

Getting some kafee from the galley port, she surveyed the room and was suddenly struck by the familiarity of Piper Donovan's expression as she talked to one of the Khimeyr pilots. The girl's subtle speech patterns jogged something in her memory. She noted the stubborn way her jaw jutted out, the deep green eyes. *Golden-green eyes, just like Greg's.*

Revelations flashed across Trezanna's consciousness like holo-stills, her heightened state of emotion putting the puzzle pieces together. The girl came looking for her. A woman disavowing her past. Those eyes, the lilt of an Irish heritage in her voice and speech. She looked, even sounded like McGregor Donovan. How could this woman so closely resemble the lover from Trezanna's past, the one who stole her child?

Unless this was *her.*

Could this be Trezanna's daughter Keridwen, lost for nearly twenty years? Ridiculous. It would have to be the most unlikely coincidence. But Piper turned to look at her, without surprise. She *knew.*

A shattering noise woke Trezanna to her surroundings. Shocked, she realized she had dropped her glassine mug. Kafee spread across the floor in a pool. When she turned to the counter for a towel to clean up, she caught a glimpse of herself in the mirror. The reflection was of a pale woman who felt the world shift beneath her feet.

Could it really be true? What could she say to her?

She bent down, soaking up the dark liquid with the pale blue towel, afraid to even look up, to encounter the eyes of the girl. Careful not to cut herself, she gathered the white pieces of mug. Moments ticked by in slow motion. What were the others thinking, watching her unravel? Did they know? Did her daughter?

"You missed one." The smooth-skinned hand with bitten-back nails held out the broken handle of the mug.

Trezanna took it, murmuring her thanks, and then tossed the remainder into the waste dispenser. When she turned around again Piper stood before her, arms crossed, and a curious look on her face.

"You finally figured it out, didn't you?"

Looking around to see the others studiously ignoring them, Trezanna glanced back, examining her daughter's face. The last time she had looked upon this face, it had been that of a toddler. A flash of memory, a laughing child with her blanket curled in a sling chair. It was hard to see that same child within the defiant young woman standing before her.

"You didn't say anything," Trezanna said.

The girl looked at her without mercy. "No. I didn't. Didn't figure it was my job to do your homework for you."

Stung by the unforgiving tone, Trezanna nodded and stepped behind the counter, giving herself some space, both physical and mental, to consider the situation. The girl moved closer, her elbows on the counter, stark black sweater complementing the ivory shades in her skin, the ones so like Trezanna's own. She cocked her head and stared at her mother. "Well?"

The Solarii administrator stared back. How could it be? All the years Trezanna longed for her, searched for her, considered all the things she would say if she ever found her daughter. Where the hell were all those words? She opened her mouth to speak several times, but each time nothing came out.

Piper's hard gaze faded as the moments passed. She put her head in her hands, mumbling so Trezanna could barely hear her. "He was right. I shouldn't have come."

"Who?" Trezanna forced the word out, as disturbed by the girl's distress as she had been by her hostility.

"My father." Piper swiped her sleeve across her cheeks, wiping away any evidence of tears as soon as possible. "He told me you left me and never wanted to see me again." She sniffled and bit her lip, as if she could seal her feelings inside. "I finally track you down, after all you've done to stay lost. I check you out, see what kind of person you are, what other people think about you, and I'm actually impressed by what they say. I almost think it's a good thing I've found you. But when you actually put two and two together, do you welcome me? Do you say you're glad to see me? No!" She banged a small fist on the counter. "You stare like you've seen a ghost! One you wish had stayed dead and buried!"

The outburst piqued the interest of the few left in the hall. A sharp look from Trezanna convinced them to collect their waste for disposal and bolt from the room. Reeling under her attack, Trezanna finally found some of her words. "When did you change your name?"

It was Piper's turn to be jarred from her train of thought. "What?"

"Why Piper? We named you Keridwen, in memory of your grandmother."

"Oh, that. Father called me Piper, after a little bird he remembered from Terra. He said I reminded him of one, the way I never stayed still."

Trezanna's hands clenched into fists. In her mind's eye she could still see the copper-haired baby, just learning to walk before she was taken. The true outrage of what the girl was saying finally hit her. Abandoned her? Trezanna never abandoned that baby. She was taken! How did Greg dare tell her such an outrageous lie?

"Greg told you I left you?" The anger she had kept caged for so many years began beating out a fierce rhythm within her. *Calm down,* she warned herself. This young woman wasn't at fault. She didn't dare release that pile of emotion on her, not when she might lose her again so easily.

The girl wiped her face and climbed onto one of the stools. She crossed her legs, not making eye contact, pretending she didn't care. "Didn't take a rocket scientist to figure it out, now did it? You weren't there."

"I wasn't where?"

"On Coronus III. With us."

Trezanna blinked. Not once had she ever come across that name in her search. "Coronus III? For how long?"

"From the time I was twelve 'til a year or so ago." The invisible chip on Piper's shoulder was clearly evident.

"And before that?"

The girl shrugged. "Some outposts, we never stayed long. Father worked two jobs all the time to make enough money to make sure there was food to eat, while you were out having your glamorous Space Force career."

Trezanna felt the anger explode. How could Greg tell her such bitter lies? "Glamour? Really? Have you looked around here? Any bit of precious you see?" When the girl didn't respond, Trezanna moved opposite her at the counter, leaning forward to look right into her eyes. "You're no fool. Think about it. Why did your father move so often?"

"Because he had a hard time finding work." Piper's defensive tone was steeped in proud loyalty.

Trezanna's pain pushed through the floodgates, now stinging her eyes with hot tears. The pressure of her command situation, the loss of Hussard and Winston, all the hurt of all the years poured through into her words. This battle she would win. If not, then she was lost.

"Your father was a brilliant politician. His education was scientific, but he could do a hundred things, carpentry, brickwork, chef, bartender, anything he wanted to. You name it, and Greg would tell you he could do it. There is no way under the open sky that he couldn't find work. He could have talked anyone into naming him king of their little community, if he wanted. He was just that good." She cocked her head, keeping their eyes locked. "He lied to me, Piper, and he lied to you. He kept moving for one purpose and one purpose only. To keep me from finding you."

"He said—"

"I don't *care* what he said!" Trezanna's hand slammed the wood of the counter, the impact enough to hurt her fingers. "I searched for *years* to find you after I came back to the outpost and you were gone. He didn't want a child! He wanted nothing to do with you the first six months of your life. He just wanted me to come back. When I didn't, he made sure I'd be well punished for daring to defy the great and wonderful McGregor Donovan!"

Trezanna trembled, the release of emotion built up for so long shaking her to her very soul. With the girl's rapt attention on her, she fought to make her chattering lips form words, to keep talking.

"Every scrap of information I could find about him, I chased down. I spent six months searching, and in the process lost my commission at Space Force." A hysterical laugh escaped her. "Yes, my *glamorous* career. I was drummed out of the service for dereliction of duty because I was running around chasing after my *baby*!"

Trezanna spun away from the girl, tears streaming. Trapped in the space behind the bar, she paced as best she could, trying to catch her breath between sobs. "Even once I found the Solarii, I kept my ears open, hoping that Greg's ego would trip him up, that he would step back into the limelight somewhere. Hoping to find him. To find you." Through the mirror she stared at her daughter, all pretenses gone. "I can't say what I would have done to him, if I had found him. But nothing could have been as terrible as what he did to me. To us."

Piper's tough attitude back to crumble, tears sliding down her cheeks. "No, he wouldn't." Her lips formed words of blind allegiance, but shadowed misgivings hung, like heavy curtains, in her eyes. "I asked him.

I asked him so many times."

Trezanna could hear the voice of a five-year-old, an eight-year-old, behind Piper's words, a young girl clinging to hope, hope slowly crushed as the memory of a mother she loved was destroyed. Greg surely caused the damage intended for Trezanna's heart, but in the process he hurt their child even more. Trezanna wanted to reach for her, but held back. "It's not your fault."

Piper picked at her cuticles, looking away, looking everywhere except at Trezanna. "He had letters, notes he said were from you. None of them said you were coming for me." Blood appeared on her fingertips, but she didn't seem to notice. "If you wanted to be with me, you should have…."

"I did. I did, Piper. I sent messages to people who knew him, asking them to forward them. I never told him I wouldn't return for you. Ever. He wanted a short visit with you, just a couple of weeks until I returned from an assignment. That was all. You were always with me before then. We only lived with Greg for a very short time before he left us. He could never deal with a woman who didn't find him the center of her universe. He wanted to show me how wrong I was. He ended up hurting us both."

Piper buried her head in her arms on the counter. Trezanna could only guess about her interior battle, the one between the father that filled her head with lies for so long, and the mother who stood before her, revealed for the first time. Trezanna's instinct was to grab hold of the girl before she disappeared again, but Piper was an adult now. She made her own decisions. *Best to concentrate on the positive.*

"But you came here looking for me."

The girl didn't move, her voice muffled against the counter top. "I heard you were with the Solarii. Took me awhile, a little roundabout, but I made my way here."

"I'm glad you did."

Trezanna wondered whether the truth was strong enough to overcome that loyal bond between father and daughter. Why now, after all this time? Why did the girl, hard to think of her as anything but Piper, come now to find her? Maybe she began to wonder, or found holes in her father's stories. Just enough to make her come see for herself. A suspicion settled into Trezanna's bones like a wet autumn chill.

"Where is Greg now?" she asked quietly.

After a long pause, the girl pulled herself upright, eyes red and puffy. Trezanna reached under the counter for a tall stack of paper napkins, placed them midway between them on the counter, before taking one to wipe her own face.

"My father's dead," Piper said. "He died of an infection last winter-turn."

Trezanna nodded slowly. So there would be no revenge-taking, no way to reclaim all those missing years. Her fist tightened again, then she forced it to release. Time to let go of the anger, the hurt. The full impact of the treasure she found, the one that found *her*, began to burrow beneath the surface of her exposed emotional armor. How she handled the gift would probably change the rest of her life.

She walked out from behind the counter, wanting nothing to stand between her and her child any longer. "I'm glad you found me, Piper. I'm truly glad. I want nothing more than a chance to show you the kind of life we can have together. If you're willing to stay."

Piper wiped her face and pushed bronzed curls off her forehead, running her hand back to clear her brow. "You really mean it?"

Trezanna reached for Piper's hand. "I swear it, on the strength of a mother's love."

With an expression of wonder, Piper took her hand. Her gaze moved from their hands up Trezanna's arm to her face, connecting with her eyes. What she saw there must have convinced her. All at once she became a ball of energy and long legs and pent-up loss, sliding off the stool and into Trezanna's arms.

"Mommy," Piper whispered close to her ear, holding tight as if Trezanna were a life preserver in a raging sea. The word caused the remainder of Trezanna's shaky defenses to crumble and she held Piper close, both of them weeping for the wasted years.

Long minutes later, the Khimeyr leader appeared at the door. Catava raised a curious eyebrow as she studied them. "I'm sorry to interrupt, but we've got a situation."

Piper disentangled herself, brushing her hair back and composing her face. "You go. Someone needs you. They always do."

Reluctant to let go, she squeezed her daughter's hand. "Come see me this evening. We've got some catching up to do."

"I will," the girl promised. She grabbed her jacket and slipped out of the room.

Rubbing her forehead in disbelief, the Solarii administrator looked up with a wistful smile. "Never give up hope. Never. Miracles happen."

Curiosity still burning in her eyes, Catava looked after the young woman. "Glad to hear it. Maybe we can get one for Estrella. She's demanding to see you."

"I don't have time for foolishness. Our rescue preparations are under way?"

"The team's meeting to iron out details. We'll be able to incorporate the Dragonfleet members once we've got everything the way we want it."

"Wonderful. Let's hope our luck's still running hot, shall we? Keep me informed."

"Will do." Catava headed out.

Trezanna took a deep breath, in, out, clearing her head. What changes the last twenty-four hours had brought! Would she be prepared for the next twenty-four?

Not if you don't get back to work.

The mental voice that scolded her reflection in the mirror behind the bar faded at the glimmer of a smile in her eyes. A miracle had indeed happened. Maybe things were starting to turn around for her, somehow, into the light. She felt better about this rescue mission already. It was a matter of time before Winston was back in the fold once again, too.

Just have to keep believing in miracles.

CHAPTER 19

IN the wing allotted to the refugees from Dragonfleet, Hawk Kenton managed to avoid his enraged commander most of the night, but the effort robbed him of any potential for sleep.

Grumbling, he wished for the hundredth time they would have just gone to ground at Dragonfleet instead of relying on the pseudo-generosity of the Solarii. At Miramar, he knew where to hide.

"I have never been treated with such disrespect! Locked in this tasteless gray wing like a prisoner? Like a caged animal?"

A crash of glass in the next room was followed by a string of curses that impressed him. *I wonder where she learned that particular biological function.* "You did try to kill them all," he called out dryly.

The sounds of destruction paused for only a moment before her heard her frustrated shriek and more crashing. "Whose side are you on?"

Hawk smirked, and then covered it quickly before she looked around the corner to catch him with his feet up on her table. "Yours, my Queen." As he heard her coming, he jerked his legs down and got up. Better to meet her standing.

Estrella, dressed in sleek black leather, stalked into the room, dark eyes blazing like a sun's corona. "This is not what I expected! Qiao used to be my friend! And besides, I never expected the accursed Arkosians to come after *us!*" Her boot tapped a frenzied beat on the floor as she paused for breath. "We're most like them! Why wouldn't they offer an alliance so we could wipe out these rabbits?"

She ran her fingertips through her short dark hair, absently spiking it, and then took up pacing again. "I would not have asked for help if I knew we would be treated like common criminals."

Hawk was not too keen on the fact that he and the other Dragonfleet officers had been confined upon arrival with the Solarii. Estrella would have done the same, if not worse, if some of the Solarii fell helpless into her hands. From his understanding, when they came to Induna Estrella offered her help to the coalition to fight the pirates.

But no one seemed to want their aid. After cursory medical treatment, they were left essentially alone. Stirred up, trapped, fully wired, all they could do now was irritate each other.

He shrugged and pulled down the back of his gold-toned shirt, setting his booted feet a foot apart for extra stability in case she came for him. "We talked about this, Strey. They're not going to lay out the best silver for you and crown you a hero. But you have to admit they did us a favor. If it were not for Qiao, you wouldn't even *have* a bed. Unless you wanted to share it with that pirate, the loud-mouthed one with the gold-dyed hair."

Estrella glowered. "Don't remind me how much I don't need you." She fingered the handle of her black dagger. Hawk didn't ask how she managed to keep it or where she hid it during the initial search of the Dragonfleet officers. She would never have relinquished the blade. The thing was like an extension of herself, a mythic symbol of her strength and cunning. She once confessed to him that if it left her hands, her power might waver. And she could never let that happen.

He shared a faint smile. "They'll warm up. They're weak. They forgive."

Something in her face softened. She would not admit it, was at least willing to allow for the possibility that he was right. But she didn't like it. "So. Patience."

He nodded, relaxing slightly. "There's my girl."

She continued to sulk as she prowled the open spaces in that room. "It's not like we had a choice, not really. Two evils, and the Solarii the ones less likely to destroy us at first glance. They *are* weak."

Hawk froze his smile, not wanting to show his satisfaction at her agreement. These things always worked better when she believed it was her own idea. "Exactly. We must look out for ourselves." The damned Khimeyr-Solarii inter-breeders had apparently let their *superior moral tendencies* overrule the better strategic decision to let the Arkosians wipe out the Dragonfleeters.

Good thing for us.

"Perhaps we should push for some concessions, as befitting our position."

Recognizing his spoiled darling's adrenaline rush as her scheming mind ticked on, he wanted nothing more than to take her in his arms, to divert some of that passion for himself. History, however, instructed that in this mood, she could turn murderous in a second. He would pass.

"Like what? They want your help. You can provide information they can't get any other way. Playing the brat won't get you the concessions you want."

"I want to be able to contact our base."

Hawk eyed her in disbelief. "Let me get this right. You want to alert the Arkosians to the fact that we have survived and we are in the bosom of the Solarii?"

"I want to find out from my people what the situation is!"

"Gus and the others are bound to be watched every minute, Strey. Those pirates aren't going to let them just sit about and chat." He stretched, the forced inaction getting on his nerves, just like the rest of the Dragonfleeters.

Safety just isn't in our genes, he thought. *None of us will live to a ripe old age to rock on the porch with the grandkids.*

"Am I not brave? Am I not resourceful? Did I not find a way to contact this base?" Estrella punctuated each question by sharply kicking a leather-seated chair away from the table, taking out three of the five, the remaining one between herself and Hawk. "Do you not think they will do the same?"

As she went to kick the last chair, he grabbed it out of her reach and came closer, towering over her. "Enough of this tantrum, Strey! Act like the commander you are. Summon Catava Rolon to do your bidding. Plan your revenge. But leave off with the fits of pique." He pulled her to him and kissed her hard. "You are a woman, not a child."

She allowed him to kiss her, swaying into him wantonly, then while his head was clouded with hormones, swiftly drew her dagger and sliced his cheek. "Leave my sight, cretin! I need no mere man telling me how to conduct myself!" She took two steps back, her jacket hanging open, eyes blazing.

His first thought, to strike her, was quickly withdrawn, even as his hand instinctively reached into the air. *That was never a good idea.* Instead, he stepped back out of reach not giving her another shot. He looked at her, other hand to his cheek to stop the blood. "I'm sure you'll find me when you remember just why you need me."

Before she could reply, Hawk turned his back on her and walked out.

* * *

THE Dragonfleet leader was consumed with emotion and even a little confusion.

Why did Hawk plague her so? What exactly happened with the renegade Dragonfleet people? Where was Luca? Why didn't Catava answer her? For that matter, why was she even here? And how was it that her personal assassin, the one she sent with Luca and his pitiful band to

Zeta, avoided killing her blonde rival?

"Just as well. I'll have the chance to finish her myself," Estrella muttered, wiping Hawk's blood off her dagger onto the window hangings before slipping it into her boot again.

She tried to subvert the nervous energy her passions engendered into a more practical direction. Outrageous, it was, for the leader of her faction to be imprisoned without any outside communication devices. She stalked through her temporary quarters to the front hall, rapping on the door which stood between her and the rest of the base.

Pomeroy's face appeared on the tiny monitor by the door. "Whatcha want?"

"I want a com installed in here," Estrella demanded. "Immediately."

"Mmhmm. Anything else? Some nice pat-ay, maybe? Classic vintage of green?" His eyes twinkled. The Khimeyr guard was tickled to have Estrella of Dragonfleet at his mercy.

"Solarii scum."

He laughed. "Sorry. I don't have to listen to your insults." The screen went black.

A hiss of displeasure escaped her lips, but she controlled her features, not sure if Pomeroy was still watching from his side of the wall. Her earlier thought of diplomacy crossed her mind, and she frowned. *Blast his eyes, Hawk was right. She must control her temper, especially among these weaklings.* It was no longer her own dominion where a reign of terror could keep her in control.

If I only had my com-unit.

She scowled, remembering the indignity she felt as all Dragonfleet officers surrendered their weapons and communication devices to the Solarii security team before being escorted to their new quarters. They complained bitterly, while Catava stood watching.

"We came here to help you!" Estrella said to Qiao as she stood by her commander. The louder she protested, the less likely the searchers were to suspect she still carried her dagger.

"Like as not you came to save yourself," Pomeroy muttered.

She ignored him. "Locking us in shabby, debris-filled rooms—"

Qiaolin didn't seem very sympathetic. "No different than ours. Most of the damage you caused yourself. Why not share the wealth, hmm?"

Catava interceded before tempers got out of control. "You can't expect to find a lot of love here, Estrella. I give Trezanna credit for being able to put aside the people she's lost because of you and look at the big picture." Arms crossed, she eyed the other woman. "If she has to decide what to do with you right now, you won't like the answer."

Twenty-four hours later, Estrella expected she still wouldn't. But she couldn't leave it alone. She buzzed for Pomeroy's attention again, carefully composing herself. When he appeared on the monitor, she forced her most appealing smile. "Come on, Darien, we're both warriors. It's not like we haven't fought side by side, you and I. You know it's tough to be locked up. I need to talk to Qiao or Catava. Please?"

Pomeroy shrugged. "I'll put a call in. Whatcha want? So's I can tell 'em."

"I need to tell them some things about the Dragonfleet base. Give them some ideas. If they'd put some equipment in here, let me help analyze the situation, I could contribute to the fight against the pirates. That's why they let me in. Isn't it?"

"Sure is what I heard. Ain't heard much from your pie-hole to justify it, though."

Estrella growled. Who left this idiot in charge? She would have skinned him in three minutes flat if she could have put her hands on him. She smiled at the monitor sweetly, knowing the time would come when she would retaliate for every indignity she received. "Please, Darien?" she asked, digging her fingernails into her palms to keep her smile pasted on.

"Right. I'll tell them." His face disappeared from the viewer.

With nothing left to do, she left her quarters to tour the locked wing and check on her people. Most were of the same ill-humor as she, while others complained to her as they dared.

"I've summoned Catava to meet with me," she explained. "I'll share our demands."

She encouraged their complaints, their heated words, knowing the people would be easier to command once the hard feelings were directed away from her decision to come here and more pointedly at their so-called hosts. She left her people with a consensus that soon the Dragonfleet chief would have things back under control. Satisfied, she returned to her disheveled room to await the Khimeyr's arrival, aching for a bottle of green to bolster her bravado. But it would not happen.

When she arrived back at Miramar in triumph, then she would have rights and privileges befitting a leader like herself.

She waited. And waited. And paced. And waited some more, until her temper was nearly frayed. Bitches. She would see that they lost that superior attitude. Yes, she would.

Hours later, Catava Rolon and Trezanna Len came to Estrella's quarters. Pomeroy accompanied them inside, drawn weapon in hand.

Estrella eyed the security man. "You think I'm dangerous?" she asked, slipping lazily onto a sofa. She had managed to straighten the place up a bit, setting up the chairs she knocked down, and making her little web look civilized, drawing in the prey.

"Why take chances, eh?" He shrugged, his gaze measuring the distance between them. Did he really think she couldn't jump him for that weapon? She was still in top form. He looked like he had wasted away on his doomed colony.

Catava took a seat on a softly padded green-toned chair across from Estrella, sitting stiff, tension evident in her posture.

Trezanna, standing behind Catava, seemed preoccupied, thoughts hidden in the depth of her eyes. Maybe their lack of focus could work in Estrella's favor.

"It's so kind of you both to come," Estrella said, hardly able to keep the irony from her tone.

"What do you want?" Catava asked, her voice sharp as an icicle in midwinter.

"I want to communicate with my base. I want to see about rescuing the rest of my people. I want some respect."

"Really." Catava leaned back in the chair, looking relaxed.

Estrella studied the Khimeyr leader, guessing the release of tension didn't in any way signal that she was about to give in. The chill in her eyes never flickered.

"Seriously, Cat. We need to know what's going on there. Helpful for you, too, right, to keep tabs on the Arkosians?" She looked at Trezanna slyly. "You know they're coming here when they're done with my base."

"I'm sure."

Trezanna wasn't any warmer. *Damn the bitches to Hades.* Maybe she really had pushed her luck too far this time. Did she need to resort to diplomacy? Kissing up and making nice. Not her style at all. Tyranny was so much cleaner.

Winning favor and play politics. At one time Catava was adept at this game, she curried favor with the best of them. But that was back when her father was in power.

Estrella sized up the other two women, felt them staring down on her, thinking they were so much better than she. At least Estrella retained the courage to lead. She could bring them all safely through the situation with the pirates. Then she could finish off both of them, when she no longer needed their numbers. "If given access to long range scanners and the ability to use heat sensors on the base, I could lay out for you an exact picture of the situation and who's there. Or you could let me watch for the rest of the fleet while you concentrate on securing Induna."

"We're running long range scans," Catava replied, not rising to a debate.

"Share the results. What harm can it do, Cat, while we're confined? We're wasting hours every day we could be putting into analysis." She studied both women. Catava still didn't bend, but she could see a change in Trezanna's eyes.

"What about your people?" Trezanna asked. "Do they have the ability, as you did, to contact us?"

Estrella shrugged. "I knew Qiao's personal frequency. Some at Dragonfleet have mine. It is possible they could reach me. If given adequate equipment." She diverted the hot glare that crawled into her eyes, directing it to the worn carpet, not allowing her anger to escape and confront them, to damage her chances of making this work.

"You'll have what you need in time," Catava replied, emphasizing the word *need*.

Estrella forced her face to keep smiling, as her hand slipped under the edge of her thigh, where the black leather of her pants indented the chair cushion. Her nails curved up, jabbing into the leather, dull pain against her skin. She pushed harder until she felt genuine hurt. "I *need* to contact my base."

"We could install some equipment in the next few days, just so you can monitor. I'm not sure we're ready for you to have equal access just yet, Estrella," Trezanna finally said. "I've got more important priorities. Anything else you've recollected about the pirates? Or the base?"

Estrella felt her glare flash and instinctively reached for her dagger. Darien's eyes narrowed and his arm stiffened. She pulled her hand back, idly scratching her leg, turning the glare on the Khimeyr strongman.

"Well?" Trezanna checked her chrono. When Estrella didn't answer, still burning, Trezanna shrugged. "I think we're done here."

Catava stood up. Estrella noted with a rush of pique that she never stepped between Pomeroy and the Dragonfleet leader. Pity. She might have tried an instant coup.

The two women started for the door. Estrella felt a rush of desperation. "Unless I can contact my people, you won't get good information!"

"Qiao heard your call. Maybe she'll get lucky again."

"They won't respond to you! Their loyalty is to me only."

Catava shrugged and cast a look at Trezanna. "We'll take that into consideration." She gestured Trezanna out ahead of her.

Pomeroy waited for them both to pass, keeping his eye tight on Estrella until the door resealed behind them, drawing the line once again between captivity and freedom.

The diminutive Dragonfleet leader waited until she was sure they were gone and then drew the dagger from her boot and stabbed the sofa cushion beside her repeatedly, viciously, imagining their bloody corpses under her, until she felt an almost sexual release. With a ragged breath, she felt cleansed, in control of her own destiny again, and then turned over the cushion to hide the damage from Pomeroy's cursed cameras.

They'll die, Estrella promised herself. *They'll all die*.

CHAPTER 20

SLEEP avoided Catava the night Estrella and her refugees arrived.

The next morning, she couldn't focus. Lily Renard took pity on her and finally volunteered to keep the children entertained for a few hours.

Not thirty seconds later the door-com beeped.

Still wearing her heavy red sleep-shirt which ended at mid-thigh, Catava opened the door. "Don't tell me. Chaddie left his fighter jet here."

It wasn't her quiet pilot, but Stefan Ciro.

Stefan blinked, his expression showing he was caught off guard by the Khimeyr woman's early morning dishevelment, though he couldn't take his eyes off her legs. "Oh. I'm sorry. I could come back when you're more...I mean...."

Embarrassed, she stepped behind the door slightly. "No, my fault. I was expecting someone else. Give me a minute."

He nodded, fidgeting with the datapad in his hand. "I'll, um, wait right here."

She eyed her raven-haired visitor a moment, then shut the door and walked to the sleep chamber. Her closet held her few belongings, including several one-piece jumpsuits that worked equally well for administrating, flying, planting crops and rocking children. Wiggling into a soft blue garment, she wondered what the Philean wanted.

Stefan managed to place himself in her path often. His mischievous eyes were always accompanied with a persistent grin. Qiao teased her about her not-so-secret admirer. As time went on, Catava found it hard to muster objections.

Her basic needs met and Luca's children safe, she actually began to relax a little. Stefan's teasing and occasional companionship was the first she allowed herself to enjoy since Luca's death. It was pleasant to be admired again. Winding her hair up into a loose knot, she pinned it in place and then checked her appearance in the mirror. *Much better.*

She returned to invite him in. "I should know better than to answer the door half-naked."

He grinned at her. "You'll notice I didn't complain."

She felt a flush in her cheeks, and cleared her throat, offering him kafee while she refilled her own cup. Maybe this second infusion would clear her head. "Your playmate is off with Lily."

His smile faded. "I saw them leave. I wanted to talk to you. Something serious." He set his datapad on the table, and slipped his hands into the pockets of his green jacket.

She studied his face, trying to read his intention. Surely he knew better than to make any sort of declaration of his feelings. Despite her slow thaw toward him, the Khimeyr were at war. No time for a real relationship, even if she might want one.

"Serious, is it? What do you want to talk about?"

"It's a peculiar proposal, actually. I've got no say in what goes on around here. But I've been listening to all of you talk since you came back with the Dragon officers, and I like Winston as well as the next person. I think I've got a plan."

"You do?" she asked, as she sat down and invited him to join her. She never thought of Stefan as strategist. Over his last few visits with Chad, he talked about his life at the Waypass and his family trade business. He also told how his father rode herd on the place, of the brother who idolized him, and of the mother who had died some time before. But she knew next to nothing about his education and training. What experience, if any, did he have in search and rescue ops?

His hazel eyes darkened just a shade. "The plan's risky. Especially for you. But I've thought it out."

"Me?"

"You're the best candidate," he replied.

Stalling, she sipped the kafee, letting the warmth from her cup heat fingers that had suddenly grown cold. "I don't let risks put me off, Stefan. But I've got responsibilities. Those children depend on me, not to mention the rest of the Khimeyr."

"I know they do." He joined her at the table, earnest as a little boy wanting sweets from his elders.

"What do you have in mind?" she asked.

He took a deep breath and activated the datapad. "Over the years the Arkosian pirates have had dealings with our Way station. The chief in charge of the commanding ship that raided Dragonfleet is named Marcand, right? He knows me. My family has done some, uh, business." His gaze faltered, and then returned. "He'd do business with me again, I'm sure of it."

Catava decided she didn't like the sound of this. She liked his hesitancy about his *business* even less. "Doing business with the pirates is the way to get Winston back? How? Will you trade them something?"

"Not exactly." He looked back at his notes, his tongue flicking out to wet his lips several times. He wouldn't look her in the eye, just kept staring at the notes as though they would save him. "The problem you all have is that you can't get in, right? If any of you fly over there, you'll be blasted out of the sky before you can do anything."

"Right. So there's no point in a frontal attack. Anything with our registries will—" Suddenly, she saw where he was going. "But your ship has Philean registry."

"Exactly. And a familiar one, as far as the pirates are concerned." He shifted in his seat, still not looking her in the eye. "So I can get inside their attack zone. What I don't know is the layout of the base—"

"Which we do," she said, finishing his thought. "I'm with you so far. I'm assuming your plan means once you've got a ship on the ground, we've got a shot at getting Winston out. So you'll deal with the pirates, drawing attention away from the ship, so the rescue team can access the underground tunnels at Miramar and find Winston. Hopefully they'll have time to break him out and get back to the ship while you're still wheeling and dealing."

He nodded, still watching her, still tense in his seat.

Getting to Winston wasn't the hard part, then. There was something else. Something worse. "What's the catch?"

Stefan coughed and squirmed. "For them to believe me, I have to have something to trade."

"All right. I'm sure Trezanna has all sorts of supplies, minerals and things, especially since that Vanyakin arrived. Piper's ship was filled with unique commodities. Have you asked her?"

He shook his head. "I haven't spoken to her."

"I'll take you to make arrangements."

Stefan was right. At their most basic pirates were businessmen. To deal with them, all the Solarii had to do was speak their language. Commerce. Clever.

Stefan shook his head again. "With the Arkosians, you need to deal in what *they* want."

Apprehensive, she examined his face. "And what do they want to deal in?"

"Beautiful women."

Catava opened her mouth and closed it again. "Please, tell me you don't intend for me to sell myself to the pirates for Winston's benefit."

"Of course not!" He jumped up, agitated. "But I'll have to tell

Marcand I have something worth his while before he'll even let me land. He'll want to see it." He looked at her, pleading in his eyes, and then smiled. "If you'll go along with it, pretend to be my captive, there's no question he'd find you bonny enough."

She bit back an urge to tell him to ask Trezanna, since it was her missing officer. She appreciated Stefan's delicate diplomatic style. He had just told her in so many words that she was the most attractive candidate for the job. But this job carried some definite negatives. "And how do we guarantee I don't end up in someone's harem on Alsatius Prime?"

"Ah. That." He scrolled ahead on his datapad. "I think I've got that worked out, if you'll trust me."

A nervous laugh escaped her. "Trust you? I hardly know you! And this is insane."

"That's true." He sighed and stepped back. "I haven't been much use around here." He shrugged. "I just thought maybe I could prove myself." He scuffed a foot and looked away. "Besides, you know I would never let anything happen to you. Not the way I feel."

She watched his boyish face take on a beaten-puppy look, and chewed her lip. The plan itself? Creative, determined, and best of all, apolitical. Stefan was not thumping his chest for the glory of his people. He just wanted to help. It wasn't a bad plan, in theory. The right people could use the hidden passages and take Winston with a minimum of trouble.

If the Arkosians were not expecting them.

If their guard was down.

If Estrella had told the truth about how many pirates there were on the ground.

The main Arkosian cadre would be distracted and involved in Stefan's primary motive, the sale of a worthy female. Any of the officers she had seen in action since her arrival would be adequate and ready for the hand-to-hand combat involved in taking out guards or corner units. She could already imagine Pomeroy's bulldog jaws clamping down on the plan, insisting they do it, insisting he lead the expedition into the bowels of the base at Miramar.

On a more philosophical note, a joint Solarii-Khimeyr venture would do much to cement the alliance between the two groups. Perhaps they could recruit some of the Dragonfleeters to their cause in the process.

But the danger could not be minimized. Although she was well versed in fighting skills, the way slaves were kept often created certain disadvantages, whether they were locked up or just not physically respected by their captors. Men like these pirates would think nothing of beating a recalcitrant slave woman, careful only not to permanently damage the merchandise. She would need some concealed weapon, something to even the odds if it came to life or death. Chad and Suzi couldn't be left alone.

She had made the promise, and she meant to keep it.

The thought made her realize she was seriously considering the plan, and she couldn't believe it. "I should just shoot myself in the head now," she said, her lips curving in a wry smile.

Edging toward the door, Stefan stopped and cocked his head, curious. "What?"

"You're right, Stefan, it's worth a shot. Maybe I'm crazy, but I think we should talk to Trezanna." As his expression lightened, she reached for his hand and squeezed it, whether for reassurance or courage she couldn't say. "I think we've got a plan."

CHAPTER 21

A shadowy rodent of some kind, heavy-clawed from the sound of it, scratched along the far wall.

Winston couldn't see it. He had not seen much since being dragged from the *Tiboron* and tossed into one of Estrella's murky basement hellholes. He thought it might have been a day. Maybe two. Maybe more.

The smell of hot metal and burning wood drifted through a six-inch grate near the ceiling. Earlier a dim glow had come from the grate, too. There was no way of telling how long ago that was. But he saw enough of his surroundings to realize this was no place he wanted to be.

He shuddered again and started over with the multiplication tables.

One times one is one. One times two is two. One times three is three.

Years before, in his days with the Western Alliance, soldiers learned ways to focus, to redirect thoughts, to offset brainwashing or other assaults on one's sanity. Like this. Structure. Logic. Progression. One fact followed another, which followed another, to a known point. Do not let the mind stray after that creature, the one that sounded small at first but might be larger, might have teeth, might have….

Stop.

He took a deep breath, felt it shudder out of him. The tricks only worked so long.

Winston had discovered that truth during the war. On a scouting mission, he encountered an enemy patrol. After being tied up, they dragged him to their headquarters and then locked him in a cell. An indoor cell, with bars on a tiny window that opened into the hall, no openings to the outside. Not like this one. Where that one was relatively decent place, this place had dirt floor and walls. And there was rotting smell coming from the corner.

A faint whimper escaped him.

Stop.

Concentrate.

Two times five is ten. Two times six is twelve.

His mind slipped away from the rote track, his gut twisting in panic. Trapped. He was trapped. Locked in, unable to get out, while other *things* could get in. His breath caught.

Two times eleven is twenty-two. Two times twelve is twenty-four.

He had been a good soldier, a strong soldier, until that locked cell of the Eastern Alliance. A full-out blitz hit the base, taking out his captors. After three days he lost his voice, his shouting unheeded by those with more important concerns than the survival of an enemy. He banged on the walls and the door and the small iron bars in the window, until his arms were mottled with black bruises. His stomach howled for sustenance. He managed to conserve a small bit of water for later. He was past prayer, past care and nearly past hope.

The liberating force didn't arrive for a week. He awakened from a ragged sleep one day to hear soldiers calling for survivors in the wreckage. They hauled Winston away under sedation to the army's mental ward. Two months of intense therapy finally brought him back to his senses, but his CO's granite face said it all. Winston was finished with military service. He lost his career, everything in his life, because of those days. He thought the claustrophobia and flashbacks were lost, too. But here, in Estrella's hell, they assailed his senses like the smoke overhead. He would fight to hold on to his sanity. If he lost it again, he didn't know if he could find his way back.

Three times four is twelve. Three times five is fifteen.

Winston thought about the explosion that took Shelby, but quickly sublimated that mental picture. He couldn't deal with that reality yet, not under this kind of pressure. He and Shelby were never lovers, but fellow freedom fighters, partners in the soldier's way, covering each others' backs, finishing each others' thoughts, halves of a fighting whole. Watching her die was like having his own arm ripped from his body.

Three times eight is twenty-four. Three times nine is twenty-seven.

He remembered his blinding rage, his blistering need for revenge. He set a course for the Arkosian ship that blasted the *Whirlwind*. The tractor beam had pulled him in. Once the pirates landed at Dragonfleet base, he held them off for an hour inside the *Tiboron*'s barricaded hatch, until they had finally blown it. Head reeling from the explosion, he had hardly seen the two dark men who hauled him through the hangar. *Focus.* He counted the steps they took, precisely one-hundred and seventy-five steps to the inner sanctum. Then down two flights of stairs. Then thirty-three steps to the door of his cell.

They had not beaten him. Had not asked one single question. They had just shoved him in a cell. He had neither seen nor heard anything from anyone since the cell door had been slammed shut.

Seven times seven is forty-nine.
Seven times eight is fifty-six.
Seven times nine is sixty-three.
He was alone, in the dark, and losing ground fast.

CHAPTER 22

"ARE you out of your mind?" Trezanna asked.

In her office, the Solarii Commander leaned back in her desk chair, not sure she had heard Catava and Stefan correctly.

Maybe it's too early in the morning. Another kafee, maybe. I swear he just said he was going to use her as bait to distract the pirates.

Trezanna eyed him. "You really think I can run this by the council with a straight face?"

He cleared his throat. "Pomeroy's already lined up a ground crew, including some of the less radical Dragonfleeters." At Catava's sharp look, he shifted his weight, looking uncomfortable. "Just asked around down there to see if anyone might be interested, that's all. Didn't want to waste your time if no one did. Estrella gave me a dozen names. We'll split into two groups. I'll deal with Marcand. Pomeroy will take the others in search of Winston."

She rubbed the back of her neck. "Catava, we can't afford to lose you."

"I know," Catava replied, slipping into a chair across from her. "I see this as more than the issue of Winston as a man. He's a symbol. One of the real blended members of this team, like Hussard. If we lose them both, we cut our heart out."

"I thought the same," Trezanna agreed. Stefan seemed harmless enough, but did they really know his motivations? What if his purpose was to turn the other woman over to her enemies, his deception winning her complete cooperation? "What safeguards do you have in place?"

"No guarantees, really." Stefan scuffed a soft brown boot on the gray carpet. "They won't allow many of us inside. Myself, Catava, and maybe one other. I'm open to suggestions who. We'll be responsible for getting ourselves out if anything goes wrong. If the timing is right, I'll get a signal when they've got Winston. At that point, I'll nix the deal with Marcand and we'll hightail it out of there."

"Doesn't take into consideration what happens if Marcand bites." She scowled at both of them. "If he makes a deal, the man will expect you to follow through."

"Surely," Catava proposed, "Stefan can make the price high enough it will be unreasonable."

He chewed his lip a moment before answering. "Marcand's a shrewd dealer. He'll know right off if we're trying to pull one over on him. I've got to make it at least sound legitimate. If I'm openly wasting his time, he'll keep us from landing, and he'll start wondering why I'm dealing this far from the Waypass." The trader's eyes darkened to a tawny gold. "Then we'll really have some trouble."

Impossible. Her concerns echoed were in Catava's eyes, but she also recognized an iron determination. How could she tell the other woman what risks to take and which to avoid? If she chose this despite the pitfalls, then so be it. "All right. If you're sure." Catava nodded. "Then we'll meet in one hour to go over final details."

Pleased, Stefan seemed to stand taller. "I'll make you proud, ma'am. We'll bring Winston back safe."

"And the rest of us, I hope." A slight scold in her voice, Catava uncurled from her chair gracefully, rising to her feet. "So who else shall we take, Trezanna?"

A wave of sadness flushed across her heart. "Normally, I'd tell you Winston was your man. I could send Chase or—"

"No, not her," he said. "Too pretty. Someone male. I don't want the pirates' attention distracted by other females."

Rumadan was chosen for Pomeroy's retrieval crew, along with Qiao. Who else would be unknown? The one who came to mind was Julian. Not a fighter or a trader, young besides. Could he pull it off, despite his feelings about Dragonfleet?

"Julian?" she suggested.

Stefan nodded. "He could do it, I think, with a little attitude adjustment. Most men dealing in that merchandise are a lot more cocky."

Trezanna scoffed. "Well, Mr. Ciro, you've got attitude to share."

His eyes widened just a bit, showing that comment hit the mark, before a sheepish grin responded for him. Catava's soft laugh filled the interim silence. "She's got you, Stefan."

She read the warmth between them and wondered if the Waypass man truly made inroads on Catava's closely guarded heart. More miracles? Perhaps.

"Best get underway then."

"We'll keep you updated." Catava left the office, Stefan planning before the door closed.

As she headed out to ask Julian if he would join the team, Trezanna wondered if their run of luck would hold out once more. She didn't like entrusting the mission to others, but this time, another choice was not available. All she could do was watch, wait, and pray.

* * *

AT mid-afternoon, the team gathered in the conference room, ready to risk their lives in the rescue of one of their own.

Catava could tell by the burning incandescence of Pomeroy's dark eyes and stiff carriage that he was adrenaline-pumped.

Since their return to Induna, Qiao carried a reserved air about her. Rumadan and Trezanna stood apart from the others, talking quietly. Rumadan came highly recommended, her Viorn feline heritage providing her with certain advantages for working in shadows. Julian stared out the window, his face giving little clue of his thoughts.

She waited with Stefan, a belated case of nerves making her edgy.

She would be weaponless. Nowhere to hide one in the skimpy costume pulled from a crate in his hold. She reviled its revealing nature, but Marcand would expect something like it. Stefan promised not to restrain her in any way so that she could defend herself, if necessary.

Shaking off her fears, Catava took the opportunity to speak with Dragonfleet second Hawk Kenton, who Pomeroy had approved as the only team member from that group, despite Estrella's proposal of several others, including herself. Catava and Trezanna agreed that if Hawk proved trustworthy, he would no longer be confined upon their return. He leaped at the chance. She didn't know whether he simply wanted out or if he wanted to escape from his commander.

Estrella didn't take the news well.

When Hawk alone was excused from the confinement area to come with them, Estrella threw a right proper tantrum, according to Pomeroy. They left her screaming obscenities, calling Hawk a traitor for helping them. He took the abuse in stride.

"She's not all bad," Hawk said. "She has days when she's sane. Besides, the woman's kept us alive over the years since she took over from Krainel, I'll give her that."

"Not all you give her from what I hear." Pomeroy made a suggestive gesture, sending the others into snickers and soft laughter, a much-needed tension release. Hawk's jaw worked into a scowl, but Pomeroy clapped him on the shoulder. "Small world, mate. Don't get your suspenders round your ears."

Catava stretched her shoulders, still trying to shrug away her anxiety.

Time to get started. "We'll take the *Mercantile*. He will have command until Miramar. Then Dare takes charge of the rescue squad, while Stefan and I move on to distract the Arkosians. If there's any chance to rescue more Dragonfleet personnel, we may take it, if we're not compromised by then. Let's go."

The others filed out. She turned to Trezanna, who seemed subdued. "I know you felt you should go along."

"It's my man that's lost. But I understand why Stefan wanted someone male. I think you've got the right people. We'll be ready to celebrate when you return safely."

"We'll do that." She added an impulsive hug, feeling a need for reassurance.

Trezanna held her close a moment, and then released her. "You better hurry."

The other woman nodded and slipped away.

* * *

STEFAN estimated the flight to Miramar would bring them into Dragonfleet territory at dusk.

The rest of the operation was hard to gauge. Stefan's hidden transceiver would alert him when the other team accomplished their task. At that point, he would be responsible for getting himself, Julian and Catava onto the *Mercantile* and away.

His ship carried high quality weaponry and a number of special adaptations useful to a man with cargo he needed to hide from time to time. If the element of surprise remained intact after the rescue, they could take flight before the Arkosians could trace them. Not that the Arkosians were stupid. They would likely know where the rescue team originated. Best case scenario, the team could find some way to sabotage the Arkosians' whole operation.

The *Mercantile* lifted off, a thick silver-toned freighter several decks deep. Stefan, dressed in gaudy teal jacket and slacks, piloted the vessel while Julian took the second seat, wearing a simple gray suit as befitted a male servant. Catava waited in the cabin behind them, dressed in the filmy peach-toned slave's garb Stefan had chosen. A short fitted piece trimmed in gold barely covered her breasts, trailing a gold chain to a short skirt she kept tugging under her. She also wore thin-corded gold sandals and gold ribbons in her hair, wrapped into a psyche knot.

Hardly abashed, he coached her on the comportment of female slaves, how they didn't speak until they were asked to and were no better than animals with natural urges. "You're expected to be hot," he said. "A slave covets the touch of men. So in situations where you don't know what to do, a seductive look is as good as anything."

She studied him a long moment. "Do you often sell women into slavery?"

He twitched as her words hit him like an open hand. "We're a small community, Cat. We deal in what pays, to keep food on the table and heat in our homes. We can't always choose our cargo."

"It's not right to sell human beings, Stefan."

Julian called him from the control deck, and Stefan turned away. "Can we talk about this when we get back?"

"Sure," she replied. "You have a jacket?"

His smile felt ghostly. "Of course."

He gave her an overcoat that she pulled close to her with a belt, and they went below, where the assault team changed into dark coveralls. They smeared black pasty oil on their faces and other exposed skin to shade them from Arkosian scrutiny.

Hawk spread a map on the table, revealing the path to the underground dungeon. "It's not a pleasant place. Strey doesn't pamper anyone."

Pomeroy frowned at the map. "How we gonna know where to find him once we get in there, eh?" He tapped the central control station. "Figure some bandy be sittin' in a chair here makin' sure everyone's sleepin' quiet."

Rumadan looked over his shoulder. "What are the chances of obtaining a uniform?"

Pomeroy shook his head and continued blackening his face. "Arkosians, not Dragonfleet. No tellin' what they'll be wearing."

Qiao paced at the shadowed end of the room, where old cargo blankets and rusty handling devices hung round the walls on the bay. Only the lights directly over the table worked, enough to illuminate the map, and reveal the expressions of those in the room.

"Sorry about the overheads," Stefan said. "Hadn't really planned to have the whole ship in use this trip. I'd have boosted a case from the Waypass."

Qiaolin scowled. "I hope the rest of the ship is in better working order."

"It'll work right enough when it's needed." His spine straightened, adding a snap to his voice. Stefan was not expecting them to grovel with gratitude, but a little respect would have been nice. After all, it was his plan. Right?

Julian ducked down from the upper level. "Contact. Arkosians within shouting distance, people."

"This is it," Pomeroy said.

The four warriors, Pomeroy, Rumadan, Qiaolin, and Hawk, gathered handheld weapons and sat on the single bench along the wall.

Stefan led Catava back to the room with a bunk. "They're likely to ask for a look-see. Just sit tight, all right?"

She shivered. "I'll do my best to look like a cheap slut."

"Better you look like an expensive one." The hint of amusement left his eyes. "If we don't get inside the perimeter, the rest can't complete their mission."

With a deep sigh, she slipped off the overcoat and handed it to him. She crawled up onto the bunk, arranging herself carelessly and concentrating on her fingernails with a lazy smile. "Better?"

"Best key for this sort of lock I've ever seen." He leaned close and stole a kiss. When he pulled back, his cheeks flushed with the knowledge of his impudence, his lips moved as though they expected an apology, though none issued from them.

"Stefan, now!" Julian growled from behind him.

"Coming." Stefan flipped a switch on the wall of the small cabin. "You'll be able to hear everything, Cat. Don't worry, all right?"

"Right," she said.

A squawk came from the com in the next room, and he ducked out. "Coming."

A few seconds later, he settled into the pilot's chair. "This is the Philean Wayfarer ship *Mercantile*, Stefan Ciro, pilot. I've got a little bauble I think Marcand would like. You know how he's always on the lookout for something particularly delicious."

"That so?" A mumbled exchange of male voices. "Let's have a look, shall we?"

* * *

SO Stefan had called that one right, Catava thought.

She did her best to appear demure and sexy at the same time, not looking directly at the holo-monitor.

"Here you go, friend," Stefan said. "Take a long drink of this."

Nothing changed in the cabin where she waited, but just knowing the men were able to see her in that barely-dressed state sent ripples of nausea through her midsection.

"Beautiful, isn't she?" Stefan asked.

A low whistle came across the speakers. "Like to get me hands on that."

"Yeah, so would Marcand, I'm sure. Get me clearance, and I'll add your two cents."

The man laughed. "That'll be worth something, I'm sure. Stand by." After a brief period of static, Stefan received directions to land the vessel. "Marcand's given you clearance to land in hangar A. See you on the ground, Philean."

"Looking forward to it." Stefan cut the ship-to-ship, and then turned to the ship's intercom. "All right, people. From here on in, I've got to concentrate on Marcand. Timing needs to be perfect so you can get to this dungeon and back. You best believe they're checking us out. If we don't pass muster, we'll be molecules before we land."

Catava got to her feet and paced, knowing the camera was off, knowing no one could see her. She resisted the urge to hold her breath all the way down. Chad and Suzi were in her mind's eye, their faces angelic, smiling without a bit of self-consciousness, bundles of pure joy. She would return to them. She had to.

Finally the long trip to the surface ended with a gentle touchdown. She peeked around the door to the command cabin, watching Stefan shove items into a pack, including an *object d'art*, a wooden statue that she knew contained two small dart projectiles because she had watched him put them there. Julian would have empty hands and pockets, but the rope belt he wore could easily choke someone. She would be the only defenseless one when they met the pirates.

Stefan looked up, his face pale, jaw tight. "Ready?"

"Let's get this over with," she muttered.

"My thought exactly." Stefan slipped out of the hatch.

She followed him out of the hatch. Julian followed closely behind her, his head hung down at a subservient angle. As they left the *Mercantile*, she noticed Julian's cautious surveillance of the area.

A patrol ship landed nearby, and a big man dragged himself out of the cockpit, followed by a second. "Ciro?" The voice was the one she heard over the intercom. She concentrated very hard on not letting her hands clench into fists.

He nodded, strutting across the deck to meet the pirate. "That's me."

"I sent a message ahead to Marcand. He be expecting ya." The man ogled her.

She did her best to convey an air of deference while suggesting the world with her eyes.

A quick flirtatious look showed her more than the pirates' lustful faces. Guards were not posted in the launch area, so Stefan must be trusted. A cold wave rippled across her skin. Did he in fact mean to trade her for safety, or worse, coin?

But her gut didn't tell her that.

Stefan grinned. "Good. I like efficiency. More time to make profit, hmm?"

The man laughed and preceded them into the main base. "Profit's good."

Recognition prickled as they entered the expansive stone-lined hallway leading to the main chamber, now only a place where memories lived. Her parents were honored here, her father a respected leader. Many changes had ensued, none of them good. Paint peeled in long strips from the walls and dirt piled in the corners, not at all like the glory days of Dragonfleet. Estrella was no steward. She cursed the woman a thousand times for allowing the noble institution to come to this.

As they neared the doors to the main hall, they encountered Arkosian personnel, all heavily armed, all with a lustful eye for her. One reached for her as they passed, and Stefan was quick to step between them.

"She's not for you, pal. Only Marcand gets this one."

The pirate lifted his hands and stepped away. "Right you are."

Stefan let Catava and Julian pass, and then followed. She allowed herself a quick glance up, finding his smile reassuring. In the antechamber to the throne room, they waited an inordinate amount of time, supervised by the two pirates from the patrol ship. Keeping silent, as befitted her character, she hid a smile, thinking Marcand wished to put a simple slave trader in his proper place. He probably wasn't even conducting business, as his minions said. Just making sure they knew how unimportant they were.

Finally, another of the pirate's men came around the corner and stepped before the door. He knocked, three resounding blows, on the large carved wooden door. At an answering knock from inside, the door swung open. The pirates waited until they entered, then walked away.

Inside, several burly men, dressed in a hodge-podge of dingy clothing, halted them, the tallest with a red bandanna on his head. Her gaze focused on the lethal-looking projectile weapons the two held in their hands, pointed at the newcomers.

"Drop your bags!" yelled bandanna man.

Catava's fear wasn't pretense at all, though she preferred to think her trembling was from the large unheated chamber where they waited, rather than dread. They anticipated a chance of betrayal when they landed. Was there a chance that the Dragonfleet's petite leader sent a warning to tip them off? She knew little of the Arkosians' ways. She knew all about Estrella.

Stefan nodded to Julian, and they both set their canvas knapsacks on the floor. The pirates grabbed the bags and pawed through them roughly. When they were done, they tossed the bags back on the floor at Stefan's feet. Bandanna man jerked his head toward the center of the huge room. "Don't keep the man waiting!"

"Of course not, my good sir!" Stefan picked up his sack with a nonchalant air, gesturing to a somewhat shaken Julian to do the same. He grabbed her by the arm, pulling her forward. He didn't turn to look at her. The game must be played to the end.

The tall wooden throne in the center of the council chamber turned slowly on its pedestal to face them, revealing a rail-thin man of medium height, a dark whip-like scar down the left cheek of his narrow face and hard ice-blue eyes. He wore a jacket of tanned leather and no hat on his sandy-haired head. He stared down at them from the height, some two meters above them. She remembered old Krainel in that chair, dispensing wisdom and punishments from on high. It looked worn and dusty. Perhaps Estrella had created something more regal for her own use.

"Master Marcand," Stefan said. "A pleasure to see you again."

"Is it?" the pirate asked in a voice that sounded like rusty chains rubbing together.

"Most assuredly. I heard you, ah, relocated." He emphasized the last word with a wink.

"And how did you hear that, boy?"

She felt Julian fidget behind her. Did he have the same eerie sense of imbalance as she? Five others in the room besides themselves, spaced evenly around the tapestry-hung chamber, and all armed to the teeth. The three of them could be dead in a matter of seconds.

Stefan forced a hearty laugh. "As if everyone doesn't know! You manage to overthrow Dragonfleet and take their base, and you think it's not the latest buzz on every com channel? So where is she?"

Marcand leaned forward, shifting his sharp gaze from Ciro to the half-dressed blonde, who quickly looked down. "She?"

"Estrella, of course." He winked. "I'll bet you had her stripped and chained to your bedroom wall, didn't you?"

The pirate slammed his hand on the heavy arm of the chair. "Blast her, she ran."

"What a shame." Stefan let his voice drop, thick with cunning. "I'll bet if you put out a bounty, you'll find her fast. She hasn't forged many friendships, you know."

"Could be, could be. How's your scoundrel of a father?"

"Drunk as usual." He shrugged, and then spread his hands wide. "Leaves me and my sibs on our own."

"I see you've come round to your uncle Antic's calling. Your old man never had the stomach for dealing in flesh. No matter what it pays."

"Aye, you're right. That's why the Phileans foster out their boys to all the relatives, my lord, so we get to learn the best ways of making our fortunes."

She wasn't sure if the exchange put her mind at ease about Stefan, but she didn't dwell on the point. The pirates' attention was suddenly focused on her bare skin.

Stefan squeezed her arm tight. "Juicy, isn't she?"

For the first time, Marcand smiled.

She felt the blood leave her face under his cold and hungry regard.

"She's just what I've been looking for," Marcand said. "I'll give you a hundred ecrons for her."

CHAPTER 23

THE assault team waited in the *Mercantile*, wanting to make sure Stefan and the others were clear before they slipped out to conduct their half of the mission.

Once the pirate guards had taken their comrades inside, Darien Pomeroy lowered the rear cargo hatch as quietly as possible.

He counted his blessings. They expected to be outside on the tarmac, which presented some challenges in terms of moving around unseen. But Marcand's man ordered them inside the main hangar. Likely wanted to make sure his prize didn't escape easily, if Pomeroy were to guess, but the reason didn't matter. They started out ahead of the game.

Stefan had managed to turn the *Mercantile* while landing, blocking the view of the rear hatch as much as possible, but there were no guarantees.

After the dust settled, Pomeroy waited for an alarm. Hearing none, he peered out around the edge of the ship, finding only one man on patrol at the far side of the hangar. If they were careful, they were clear.

"Right. Let's go then," he snapped.

Hawk slipped into the lead, as the four hurried along the shadowed wall to the underground vent they had determined would be most accessible to the dungeon. The vent cover unscrewed with a screech but a minimum of trouble. The dripping of water far below echoed in the stone hollows.

Pomeroy and Hawk stood guard, as Qiao and Rumadan descended first. He sent Hawk down next while he kept a sharp eye out for any patrols. The lack of obvious security nagged at him, but he had always been a fan of luck.

Just carry on, long as fate's smiling on you.

Reaching the bottom of the tunnel in near-darkness, he cracked his hand light torch open and used the compass to find their bearings. The air was stale, moldy-smelling. Clear that Estrella didn't care how her base was maintained. "Which way?" he asked Hawk.

"The tunnel's that way," Hawk replied, pointing behind them.

Rumadan eyes glittered. "Would it not be more prudent to divide our efforts and split up?"

"No." Qiaolin spoke softly but with great conviction. "If we have to leave in a hurry, we should all be together. No one gets left behind."

"Stick together, that's the way to play it," he agreed.

Rumadan's ears twitched with annoyance, but he was done discussing. Trezanna had designated him as commander of this little squad and, by the heavens, he would make the most of it.

Hawk came to the beginning of the tunnel and tried the door handle, finding it turned easily. "You don't think they've just ignored the tunnels, do you?" he asked. "We've got all kinds of stores down here."

The Khimeyr shrugged. "Hard to tell. They probably figure they got all the time in the world, since Estrella is gone."

"Yeah, maybe." Hawk led them into the tunnel, which sloped upward for a hundred feet or more to end behind an opaque windowed door. Lit from within, they could see illuminating piles of red-tinged rock along the tunnel where the cave wall was crumbling in. "Watch your step."

The team edged around the obstacles, moving quickly up the tunnel. He checked the door, top and bottom, unable to detect an alarm to give them away. *Might be someone inside*, he thought, watching for some of Estrella's boys to crawl away or for anyone coming in. He pushed the door open slowly, holding his breath, weapon in hand. No one.

So far, so good.

According to the maps and Hawk's recollections, they were far enough in. Next they would have to pass through the brig's control area. If that went well, they would go on to find Winston. He blew out some air, hoping his tension went with it. The stairs were just beyond the door. He herded the others to the top of the steps, watching behind them for danger.

During the descent, he brought up the rear of their little expedition, believing he could trust Hawk in the lead. They had known each other briefly in the time before Luca's ill-fated exodus. Hawk had been a team player, a good man. A little too interested in climbing the political ladder the easy way, to Pomeroy's mind, but dependable.

He took a moment to assess the other team members. That cat woman, Rumadan, gave him the creepy crawlies, but she focused on business. Qiaolin, on the other hand, her mind was elsewhere. Like as not upstairs with Catava, wondering what was happening.

When they came to the last step, Qiaolin stumbled, and gasped when Pomeroy caught her arm.

"Sorry," she whispered.

"Come on, girl, buck up. We'll be home for tea." He grinned and winked, as he slipped past her and joined Hawk at the bottom of the stairs. The two females came up behind the men as they peered out a small window in the door.

Inside they found a midsize room, brightly lit, the far wall lined with control panels, one with several screens lit with a greenish light, displaying shadowy images of the prisoners in their darkened cells. A round metal table sat close to the door, the floor around it littered with crumpled paper and other trash. Around the table, three men glared fiercely at cards in their hands. Behind them and to the right was the computer center, where he recalled the controls for the holding areas would be found. *And the men between them and it.*

Three versus four. Not bad odds, but Pomeroy's fingers tightened. No telling how many more there might be just out of sight, or in reach of the com-unit on the counter. "Damnation. Looks like we'll have a brush-up after all."

Hawk watched the three a few moments, eyes narrowed. "No, no, wait a sec. I know those guys. They're Dragonfleet."

"They know you?"

"Yeah. I think I got this covered." Hawk ran a hand through his rumpled hair, then shoved the door with a loud screech of hinge and stepped into the open before anyone could stop him.

Pomeroy cursed but waited, despite his urge to step out and start shooting. The less attention they attracted, the better.

Damn Kenton. If he blows this operation, I'll shoot him myself.

The men jumped to their feet, cards falling to the table and floor in a mad scramble for weapons. The oldest of the three squinted, his face twisted up as if he couldn't believe what he saw, blaster in hand.

His weapon tucked into his waistband behind his back, Hawk chuckled and spread his hands. "Fellas." He walked closer, standing between the men and the three outside. "Thought I'd never find my way out of that hellhole."

"Hawk? Where you been?" The man with the gun waved at the other two. "C'mon, lummox, it's Kenton, Estrella's...." His voice trailed off. A nervous look second-guessed if he caused offense.

Hawk laughed. "No problem. Been dragging around in there for days."

"What's he got all over him, then? He's smeared from one end to the other." The wiry, cocky one with the weasel face glanced over his shoulder at the open weapons locker.

"You ever been down the South 6-A tunnel, rummy?" Hawk made a face. He stepped over to the screens on the far wall. "It's full of stuff you'd never want to see again. Think someone must have emptied their ship's oil pan down there." He brushed at his clothing.

The upstart glowered, unconvinced, but the older one put his blaster back in his belt. "Enough, Ty." He looked back at Hawk speculatively. "Is Estrella with you?"

Hawk smiled. "No, man. I figured with the pirates in charge, she'd be in one of these." He tapped on the center screen.

Pomeroy watched the attention of all three swivel away from the door and toward Hawk.

Good lad.

In a whispered exchange, Pomeroy assigned Rumadan the third man and Qiaolin the task of determining in which room Winston was confined.

He would take the mouthy one himself.

"All right," Pomeroy whispered, "on three." He counted softly and thrust the door open.

CHAPTER 24

IN the great hall upstairs, Stefan's first sickening thought was that he might have underestimated Marcand.

He expected to have to bargain and cajole the pirate into considering the offer. But what they had gotten held no hint of equivocation. That was not supposed to happen.

Stefan froze, as he turned to find shocked expressions on the faces of his companions. He fumbled for a response.

Stall. Stefan, stall.

He slapped his knee with a loud guffaw.

"Marcand, you beast! You're slipping, you're slipping!" At the pirate's condescending look, he moved away from the other two slightly, accentuating the distance, drawing the pirates' attention. "What kind of merchant do you take me for? You think I come all this way just to see your pretty face?"

Chuckles came from the men behind him, but Stefan never forgot the half-meter sticks two inches thick in their hands. Catava held her ground, hands just behind her back at a softened parade-rest posture. Good girl. Stefan hoped Julian had the good sense to stay in character as well. The longer he appeared non-threatening, the longer he would be safe.

Marcand studied him, eyes never warming, but at last he smiled. "Perhaps you're right, young Philean." He stood and walked slowly down the sandy wooden steps from the throne, his gaze focused on Stefan's. "Perhaps this is a game." He stopped right in front of Stefan, a step above him, forcing Stefan to look up to him. "But whose game is it, hmm?"

He didn't flinch, though something in the pirate's tone was like icy water down his back. Did Marcand know? Stefan cemented that cocky smile onto his lips, willing it not to fade under the pirate's scrutiny, as though he were carefree and just waiting for a pocketful of coin.

Just as suddenly, Marcand turned away from him and approached Catava. After looking her up and down, he grabbed her around the waist, pulled her to him, and gave her a hard kiss, biting her lower lip.

Catava stiffened for only a moment, and then let him have his way. Stefan imagined what was running through her mind, a thousand deaths she could inflict on him, given the opportunity. They knew the risk upon taking this challenge. Stefan's concern now was for the odd tone in Marcand's voice. What did he think he knew?

He cringed, as Marcand continued to manhandle the woman. His heart dogged him, nagged that he shouldn't have allowed this, not under any circumstances. The fingers of his left hand clenched slowly as he counted off long seconds, trying to remain calm.

Julian had retreated into a stupid look, hands hung loosely at his sides as if he was not paying attention.

Marcand pulled the band loose from Catava's hair, then wrapped his hand in the soft blonde locks, holding her head at the level of his, searching her eyes. "You," he said at last. "You, I have seen somewhere."

From the first, he reminded her several times, *a slave has no voice*. Stefan prayed with his entire being that she would not respond. She didn't. She even fluttered her eyelids down so as not to meet his eyes.

"Where did you find this girl, Ciro?" Marcand demanded.

"A merchant brought her to the station along with several other girls. He wanted to retrieve the cargo he left in storage, but my father wouldn't let him have it without payment." Stefan came closer and pinched her cheek. "She was the best of the lot."

Marcand thought over his words, and then looked back at her. "Those eyes. I feel like I have seen them before. I will remember where and when." He released her so quickly, she stumbled. It was all Stefan could do not to catch her. "Come, we will dine together and work out a price for this lovely animal. I shall have my men secure your slaves." Marcand snapped his fingers and three men came forward to do the pirate's bidding.

"That won't be necessary," Stefan said, an edge coming into his voice. A twitch of Catava's fingers showed him she was wound as tightly as he, feeling the situation go from bad to worse. "They have been well-disciplined."

Marcand eyed the two. "I prefer security. It saves having to damage them if they disobey." He nodded and two of the men produced lock bracelets and chains.

His mind quickly considered the possibilities. The other team was probably still in route to their destination. Any trouble on this end would impede their mission. But if Catava and Julian were confined, they would be unable to help themselves if trouble ensued. How could he possibly dispute this with an already-suspicious Marcand? What would a slave do to avoid confinement?

As the man approached her wrist with the bracelet, Catava went down on her knees and clung to Marcand's leg. "Please, Master!" she cried in a desperate voice. "Let me serve you at your dinner! Let me show you I am worthy!"

Startled at her sudden movement, the guards jumped forward as Stefan and McKinley stepped back out of their immediate reach. Julian caught Stefan's eye, showing an equal concern for their welfare. Their success now hinged on the Khimeyr leader's performance. Stefan would have found her hard to resist.

Marcand reached down and pulled her to her feet by her hair. "You are an eager little wench." He grinned, kissing her again. "I have no doubt you are worthy." He assessed her once again and nodded. "Very well, little sweetness, I shall not stop you from fulfilling your function. You shall serve me."

Catava smiled and touched Marcand softly. "Thank you, my Master." She stepped closer to him and away from the guard.

To Stefan's dismay, Marcand reached for the metal bracelets, which were fastened together by about eighteen inches of silver chain. He locked them on her wrists with two sharp clicks.

"I like to see my women in chains," Marcand said. "It makes them more beautiful."

Not much Stefan could do for her now. With only a few seconds to contemplate his options, maybe he could at least save McKinley. Stefan forced a smile. "Chains do make a woman beautiful, particularly in this case." He turned to look sternly at Julian. "You there! Get my bag from the ship!"

As he hoped, Julian twitched, totally taken off guard. "Aye, sir!" he blurted out and stumbled in the direction of the exit.

"Stop!" Marcand eyed the drab-dressed Julian. "Is that not your master's bag there?" He pointed to the knapsack which Stefan brought in.

Julian bowed repeatedly, an accurate presentation of someone frightened beyond thought. "Just doing what I'm told, boss." He edged toward the door, not looking anyone in the eye.

"The blue one, inside the cargo bay," Stefan clarified. In the heat of the moment, he had chosen what he thought was a simple task fit for a servant. Damn the pirate for remembering.

Marcand eyed Julian. "Not very bright, is he?"

Stefan picked up the knapsack with his darts in it and slung it over his shoulder. "Female slaves bring a good price, so we keep our eye out for them. The males, though, we get stuck with what we can't trade." He nodded very slightly as Julian's eyes met his, and the Solarii engineer continued to inch away, still bowing and murmuring respectful words.

"All right. He don't look like he could cause much trouble." The angular pirate pointed at Julian. "Don't be long, or it'll come out of your hide!"

"Yes, boss, yes, boss." Julian scrambled for the door and disappeared through it.

If luck was on their side, Julian would not have to return. If both teams could complete their tasks on schedule, they would meet back at the ship before he was missed.

Marcand took the chain between Catava's wrists in his hand and twisted it between his fingers for a firm grip.

This was not going well. With the Khimeyr leader in chains, Stefan fumbled over every new lie. He hoped fervently that things were going better below. At least the risk would have been worth it.

Marcand beckoned Stefan to precede him into the next room, and pulled his new prize along after him. The heavy thud of the men's boot heels echoed off the stone floors and walls.

"Some wine, Ciro? Or better yet, have you tried green? I've found a stockpile of bottles in a cave below. You know it's illegal in several sectors because of its addictive qualities." Marcand laughed. "Perhaps this is what has rotted Estrella's brain."

Stefan returned the laugh, keeping careful tabs on the path. They were moving farther from the hangars, not closer. So much for a quick escape. He had hoped Julian could reach safety. Now he needed to save himself and Cat.

"I was surprised Estrella conceded this base so easily," Stefan said.

Marcand shook his head. "It doesn't sound like what I remember of her. She was quite fierce when we held this territory several years ago. The Solarii filth were feisty, but the women of Dragonfleet were outstanding. I'd have been proud to have any of them in my harem. Brilliant, hot-tempered, and beautiful. Most of them."

Stefan was prepared to respond in kind when Marcand stopped walking. He turned to find the pirate commander staring at Catava Rolon with recognition at last.

Seven damnations of Adam, he thought. *Now what?*

"You. *You* are Dragonfleet!" Marcand's eyes blazed as his fingers closed tight on the chain. "I saw you at the final battle. Here in this hall! A black uniform, and your hair was—" He pointed to the scar on his face. "Perhaps it was one of your sisters who did this, but today I will avenge myself for that humiliation! You will pay!" He yanked the chain, nearly knocking her from her feet.

Reeling, Catava stumbled upright as Stefan closed in from behind Marcand. The guards had not yet followed them through the doorway. No better chance.

"Now!" Stefan hissed.

Catava didn't hesitate. She kicked Marcand hard in the groin with her heel, shoving him away. The pirate staggered backward, pulling Catava to the floor with him. She rolled toward the pirate, her wrists twisted in the chain as her flimsy costume pulled at the seams and tore away.

Stefan glanced around frantically for a weapon. A broken pipe, half melted and damaged from some sort of weapons fire, hung from the wall ahead of them. He lunged for it, twisting it hard, struggling to tear it from its moorings.

The pirate groaned and his face contorted. He used the chain to drag the woman, kicking and fighting, toward him. Then with a final jerk, he got her close enough to grab her neck.

"How dare you, bitch?" he snarled, his fingers biting into her skin.

She pulled away from him. "I'd dare a lot more if—"

He let go of her neck and slapped her hard. "Shut up!"

Frantic now, Stefan yanked on the pipe, until it snapped loose. Weapon in hand, he spun to face Marcand, breathing hard, his stomach in knots. He couldn't figure out why the pirate hadn't summoned his guards, but he suspected it was a matter of pride. Marcand wouldn't let a woman and a skinny trader beat him.

"Let her go, Marcand."

"She's mine." Marcand caught her neck again and wrapped his sinewy arm across her throat, holding her between him and Stefan. "Back off, Philean, or she's meat." He paused, still trying to catch his breath from her assault. "I knew something didn't smell right about this. What's she, an assassin? Out to kill me for Dragonfleet revenge?"

"I'm not Dragonfleet, you bastard!" Catava raised her foot, kicking off her sandal, and then drove her heel down Marcand's shin, fury adding impetus as she raked his leg to the instep.

Marcand roared out in pain, his grip slipping. Catava twisted aside as Stefan swung the pipe right into the pirate's forehead. His skin split in a spray of blood and he went down. He didn't get up.

"Hey!" came a shout from the doorway. "What's going on in there?"

Two of the guards sprinted into the hallway, seeing their fallen commander on the floor.

Stefan, the pipe ready for another victim, remembered his other weapon. "Here."

He tossed the bloody pipe to Catava and ripped the statue from his knapsack, pausing just long enough to aim the first dart and pull the trigger. The barb hit the guard in the chest. His impetus carried him two steps forward before unconsciousness took him. Stefan aimed and shot the second before the first man had fallen with similar results.

"Three down," he said, breathing hard, jacked with adrenaline. "At least three more between us and the ship."

Catava eyed the pipe in her hands. "Let's hope we've given them enough time below."

Stefan realized she was naked. Really naked. In Marcand's chains.

Voices sounded in the hall beyond them.

"Right," he ground out. "Let's go."

He tossed the useless statue aside and took back the pipe, moving along the hall with it cocked at an attack angle. When the next guard came through the door, com-unit in hand, Stefan swung the pipe at his head, taking him out with one blow. His attention focused ahead, he frowned as he heard Catava's footsteps going in the opposite direction. "What are you doing?"

"Getting these damned chains off." Catava bent over Marcand's body to ransack his pockets, coming up with a whole ring of keys.

"We don't have time for that now! Come on."

Footsteps echoed in the hallway beyond them and she groaned. "Here, then." She tossed the ring at him. "I seem to be out of places to carry this."

Stefan couldn't help his physical response. "I noticed." Feeling guilty, he pulled his shirt off and wrapped it around her shoulders, since she couldn't put her hands in the sleeves.

With a growl, she shoved him toward the hangar. "Can we just get out of here?"

"Okay, okay!" Stefan mentally replayed the landmarks he had noted on the way in and followed them in reverse order out to the receiving chamber. Voices and other commotion echoed in the hallways, coming closer. He grabbed Catava's hand and ran for the hangar bay.

They nearly made it.

CHAPTER 25

UNAWARE of the chaos going on above, Pomeroy and his team continued into the underground detainment facility. From the moment they stepped inside, they were in control.

Pomeroy would have liked to think it was his forbidding profile and their aimed weapons that won the day, but in honesty, he would admit that Rumadan's appearance grabbed the attention of the Dragonfleet men immediately. While their jaws hung in various states of surprise, Pomeroy and Hawk took the leader's weapon.

"Over here, gentlemen," Rumadan purred. Pomeroy would swear she was smiling.

They stumbled to the place she indicated, still staring, and Hawk locked handcuffs he found in the desk onto their wrists, securing them around a pipe. When the leader looked as though he was going to yell for help, Pomeroy smiled.

"Go ahead, friend," Pomeroy said. "I'm trying to leave you alive out of respect between comrades. Don't really mean that much to me, though."

The man reconsidered and glowered at them all.

"Get on it, Qiao!" Pomeroy barked. "We don't have much time."

"Yes, sir." Qiaolin slipped behind the counter to activate one of the keyboards. She tried alternate codes until one finally unlocked computer access. With a triumphant cry, she pointed to the right. "He's in Hall A, third room!"

The two hurried down the hall toward the room she had located. Bare bulbs lit the hall intermittently, alternating blinding illumination and shadows. Filth, spider webs, even discarded trash was tossed haphazardly in this place no better than one of the Old Terran French *oubliettes*.

Qiaolin counted down the doors. "Lock code: Queen."

"She even named the jail doors after herself? What a bitch." Pomeroy key-coded the door. It clanged open, revealing a cold space in near-darkness. "Monty lad? You here?"

A moan followed by coughing sounded off to the right. The Khimeyr security man flipped on his hand light and shone it around the walls. The light fell on a man, lying in a heap on a makeshift cot. Pomeroy shook him by the shoulder. "Winston! Get up, man."

Another moan was the only response.

"Damn it," Qiaolin cursed. "He's going to be no help,"

"What did they do to him, the bastards? Guess they've got some arse-kicking coming," Pomeroy muttered. "All right, mate, let's take a little trip home, eh?"

Pomeroy bent down and maneuvered Winston onto his shoulder, carrying him like a sack of grain. "Out!" he said. Qiaolin scooted on ahead of him.

As they came down the hall, Rumadan met them.

"We have trouble," she growled. "Something is wrong upstairs. The guards have been alerted to hunt Stefan and Catava."

"Bloody hell." Pomeroy continued to the control room, surveying the lay of the land. "We better move then."

Hawk eyed his former comrades. "What about them?"

"What about them?" After he stopped moving, Pomeroy started to feel Winston's weight on his shoulder and hoped adrenaline would keep them both upright.

"Aren't we going to evac them back to the base?"

"They're working for the pirates!" Qiaolin said.

Ty bristled. "Only 'cause they have our families locked down. We got no sympathies for those rutting thieves."

Pomeroy hesitated for only a moment. "We got no way to rescue all the kith and kin along with them. If they escape, those babies are as good as dead."

Hawk's expression faded, less optimistic. "Oh, right. We'll make it a plan for another day." He looked at his buddies. "Guess you're better off looking like you put up a fight, hmm?"

The three men struggled to come to terms with being left behind, but in the end, agreed they were probably right.

Hawk swung around the console and plopped into the chair. "Let me run a quick download to see what the situation is."

"We don't have time to screw around," Pomeroy snapped.

He gestured with his head, sending Rumadan and Qiaolin toward the door from which they entered. They quickly obeyed his silent command.

"Won't take but a minute." Hawk grabbed a loose data chip and jammed it in the slot and punched up the download buttons. His knee bouncing nervously while he waited, he eyed Winston. "You think he's okay?"

"No clue. We're gone. If you don't catch up, you're on your own, my friend." Pomeroy lurched for the doorway.

"I'll be along in the shake of a hare's leg."

Qiaolin was halfway up the stairs when Pomeroy shoved his way through the door. Winston's weight shifted and Rumadan stepped close, slipping under one of his arms. The two half-carried, half-dragged the inert man up the stairs. Although Rumadan was stronger than Pomeroy anticipated, the pilot was a big man. Pomeroy's breathing was ragged as they reached the top. Hawk's footsteps came up behind them as they nearly reached the door, and Qiaolin held it for all of them to pass through.

They continued toward the hangar bay, retracing their steps, moving as fast as they could. About halfway through the downward tunnel, Winston came to enough to realize someone had hold of him and he began to thrash about.

"No! Get your hands off me, Eastern bastards!" He knocked Pomeroy loose, tossing him into the staring Hawk, and both crashed into the tunnel wall.

"Monty!" Qiao yelled. "Stop! We're here to help!"

Winston started to back away. His weakened state, however, brought him to his knees before he had gone three steps. "I don't feel so good," he mumbled.

"We have no time for this," Rumadan rumbled. She looked at the dazed men and made a noise which could only be amused. She lifted the struggling man onto her back and proceeded onward, oblivious of their pride. "We must hury!" she called back over her shoulder.

Hawk and Pomeroy looked at each other in amazement for a moment, and then followed, Pomeroy reaching for Qiao's hand as she tripped over a rough place on the floor. Seconds and minutes passed in the sounds of gasping breath as they ran for their lives.

At last they reached the hatch to the hangar bay. Hawk popped up to scout the situation. When he came back, his expression was grim. "There's guards milling around by the door to the antechamber. But Julian's in the ship, watching from the hatch. I say we make a run for it."

Rumadan agreed. "We are much safer there. If necessary, we can fly Ciro's ship ourselves."

Qiaolin stiffened. "We're not leaving Cat and Stefan here."

"Not if we don't have to." Pomeroy rubbed his face and took a deep breath. "Let's not jump the gun, hmm? Get above and cover us," he said to Qiaolin. She popped through the hatch, picking up a little energy.

After she was up, Pomeroy turned to Rumadan. "What are we to do about him?" He gestured to Winston.

"I can lift him," Rumadan said, "but I will be unsteady. I would not want to drop him."

Pomeroy nodded. "Right. Hawk, you help pull him up, and I'll keep an eye here."

The plan worked admirably and soon the team was skirting the wall behind the ships, Winston's dirty Solarii uniform the only thing visible in the shadows. Pomeroy checked a look past the ship, but the guards had vanished. McKinley waited inside the hatch, his head ducking in and out every few seconds.

It must be bad. If that raw pup allowed my commander to come to harm, I will have something to say and do about it.

They inched along the ship's hull, concealing themselves as long as possible. When they reached the hatch of the *Mercantile*, Qiaolin and Hawk went first, and then Rumadan carried in Winston. Once the others were safely in the ship, Pomeroy joined them.

Rumadan released Winston to Hawk and Qiao, who settled him in the cargo bay. She then joined Pomeroy and McKinley. "Report. What is the situation with Catava?"

Julian shook his head, dark eyes troubled. "Marcand suspected something, I think. He had Catava chained and she was trying to avoid his advances. Stefan sent me out on a pretext when he saw things were going bad. I heard some shots. Then all the guards ran inside. I kept expecting them to come for me, but they must have forgotten."

The Viorn growled softly, and then looked over at the instrument panel. "I thought it was a blessing to be sent inside the hangar but it may prove to be our downfall. Are there projectile weapons on the front of this craft?"

Julian nodded. "Yeah. I've been familiarizing myself with the set-up. In case," he added, a self-conscious twitch running along his jaw. "Laser guns and small missiles."

Looking out the front port with apprehension, Rumadan nodded and slid into the captain's chair as Qiaolin came into the control room. "How is Winston?"

"Out cold." Qiao's voice held no tone. "I can't see any real damage. Think it's in his head. I left Hawk with him."

"Probably the best place for him."

"What's happened?" Qiao asked.

"We are not sure. Julian claims shots were fired." Ears fluttering,

Rumadan glanced at Qiaolin. "Can you access the base com channel?"

"Maybe." Qiao took the second seat and fiddled with the controls. "They're not using the Dragonfleet code line."

Pomeroy paced outside the cockpit. Where was Ciro?

Qiaolin tuned the dial until they could catch snippets. The agitated voices called for more guards. They heard the words *Marcand*, *slave*, and *dead*.

Julian paced in frustration. "I shouldn't have left them."

"Nonsense. You followed orders," the Viorn growled. "If nothing else, Stefan knew when he was in over his head." She considered the instrument panel. "Julian, can you bring the ship's systems online undetected?"

"Probably not. In this enclosed space, the noise would reverberate."

"Whatcha got in mind?" Pomeroy leaned against the doorframe, rubbing his stiff neck.

"Assuming Stefan can clear the door. I want to be ready to fire."

Finally someone had a plan that sounded viable.

Pomeroy allowed a smile. "Now you're talking!"

CHAPTER 26

STEFAN knew their time was running out. They had to get back to the *Mercantile* before Pomeroy's team returned and before the pirates killed them all.

He had his hand on the door handle, as the shooting started. "Come on! We're nearly there!"

"Right behind you," Catava called.

Stefan's momentum carried him several steps into the bay before he heard the unmistakable sound of weapons charging behind him. Feeling like he moved in slow motion, his head came up to find half a dozen pirates drawing a bead from the hallway. Without thinking, his right arm shot out to shove Catava behind him, imposing himself between her and the pirates. The motion of his turn put him in profile for just a few seconds, but it was a few seconds too long.

The heat of a laser shot burned along his rib cage, a flare of pain, not a full-on hit, but a graze. It still hurt like hell.

Within the split second before the laser whine faded, he felt her jerk against his arm. A liquid red flower bloomed on her right side as the shot that only skimmed him tore through her abdomen. She stumbled backward and collapsed against the door.

"Cat!" He fell to his knees beside her, while laser blasts burned into the wall above their heads. His pack dropped. There was nothing left worth using for defense.

The only thing between the oncoming pirates and Catava was him. Stefan needed time to think. He held up his hands as if surrendering.

Damn it. So close. The *Mercantile* waited just across the hangar bay. If he could get to the ship, Julian should be waiting. *And the others, if we're lucky. Medical supplies, too.*

One of the oncoming guards yelled "Don't move!" The rest stopped about four meters away, targeting them.

"You should be going after the assassins instead of me," Stefan said softly. "Two of them, Dragonfleet men, they took off down the hall over there." He pointed toward the hall where they left Marcand. "We were lucky to get out alive ourselves!"

The one giving orders frowned briefly. "What did they look like?"

Stefan made up as ordinary a description as he could of two men who might be assassins, and then glanced down at Catava. The shirt he gave her now lay on the floor next to her fallen body. She was deathly pale and her breathing shallow and labored. "Let me tend to her," he pleaded. "If Marcand survives, I'll make her a gift to him."

The commander scowled but nodded, then sent half the team to scout the other hall for the alleged attackers. He then took two quick steps forward and smacked Stefan in the back of the head with the butt of his weapon. "If you're the one who offed Marcand, business will be the least of your worries."

Stefan fell sideways with a groan, his vision blurred and head throbbing. "I came here looking for profit, friend, not murder." he muttered, and was rewarded with a kick.

A sudden burst of laser fire from the other hall was followed by men's voices calling loudly for help. The commander eyed him for a final moment and assigned two men to watch them, before he took the rest of the squad to investigate.

Stefan put a hand to his head, seeing double, but more concerned about Catava. *I've got to get her out of here.* He rolled to his knees on the floor, allowing a whimper, managing to knock the door open several more inches before pulling himself to his feet, holding the outside edge of the door. His final act was to lean against it, swinging it all the way open as he leaned his head against the thick wood as if he was too dizzy to control his actions.

"Come back in here!" one of the dark-haired men ordered.

Stefan weaved, acting like he could barely stand up. "I think I need a doctor," he said.

The second man laughed. "You'll need an undertaker, is my guess." His blue eyes were cold, and his arm relaxed, allowing the point of his weapon to slip toward the floor, deciding, perhaps, that Stefan was no threat.

Bastard. Stefan cast a glance at his ship. The landing lights flickered, several times. Movement inside the cockpit, but no way to know whether it was only Julian or if the rescue team was safe as well. The hatch remained open, a dark hole which promised safe haven. He measured the distance with his eyes and decided to take the risk.

Stumbling back into the doorway, he lurched for his knapsack. "Bandages," he said, loud enough for them to hear. "She needs bandages. In my bag." He gestured to the knapsack, down the hall. "I've got her clothing, her jewelry in there. You can have the jewels, I don't care. I just need the fabric. Please."

The men exchanged a look, greed deepening their dark smiles. He thought for a moment it was not going to work, but then they lunged for the hallway. As soon as they turned away, he dragged Catava out the door and kicked it closed. He ripped his belt buckle loose and jammed it between the door and the frame just under the hinge.

Shouts and pounding from the other side of the door faded from his consciousness as he set his focus. Whispering an apology to Cat, he grabbed her under the arm and heaved her onto his shoulder, glad she was unconscious, hoping his rough treatment would not hurt her further. His shoulder now wet, warm with her blood, he stumbled in the direction of the open hatch, fixing his eyes on it as if it were the door to Paradise.

Come on, Stefan, move forward. One step. One foot and then the other. Faster!

The roar of the *Mercantile* powering up drew his attention. Laser fire, its whine muffled, sounded from behind him. Pieces of the floor around him tore loose in little twists of smoke and skittered like hep dancers.

When he stumbled up to the hatch, a shattering noise behind him made him turn for half a second. He shouldn't have. A searing burn tore up his arm and he nearly dropped the woman he carried. Hands reached for him and for Cat. They were pulled inside as the hatch closed, the ship reverberating repeatedly as it took hit after hit. He tried to orient himself toward the cockpit, but had to stop, black spots flashing in his vision.

"Sit down, friend," Pomeroy said, his tone indicating it was an order. "We'll take it from here." He leaned forward. "Go! Go!"

Stefan felt his ship lurch forward, the rumble of rocket fire and the sense of imbalance that went with liftoff. His arm hurt so much that he found it difficult to focus. He lost his pack. The pack was given to him by a passing trader when he was fourteen. The trader exchanged it for some worthless rocks, or at least that's what Stefan thought at the time. The rocks turned out to be star opals.

I'll miss that, he thought. *Where will I put all my secret treasures?*

Stefan fought the growing blackness as long as he could. Eventually, it won and he faded into the dark.

* * *

RUMADAN didn't need Pomeroy's urging to make a hasty exit.

The door to the interior spilled out pirates, nearly two dozen of them, all armed and firing. The Dragonfleet reports obviously underestimated their enemy.

Rumadan activated shields as soon as the power was up, so they weren't causing much damage to the *Mercantile*, but she didn't know how long they could hold out.

She retaliated, not with laser blasts, but small powerful missiles, which created huge burning breaches in the plascrete walls. She turned the craft for liftoff and continued to fire, crippling the nearby Arkosian and Dragonfleet ships parked in the hangar. Although their markings were distinguishable, at that moment she didn't really care which she took out.

The flares from those impacts cowed the Arkosian defenders, and they retreated inside the doorway. Rumadan guessed they would be looking for a way to fight back, and she wanted to be well away before they came up with one.

"Pomeroy!" Rumadan called. "I need you!"

Shrugging off his worn Dragonfleet jacket, the Khimeyr security man moved forward, sending Julian and Qiaolin to tend to Catava and Stefan. "Name it, Rummy."

"When we're clear, drop a bomb on the hangar opening. We don't want anyone following us. Estrella will have to forgive us later." Rumadan turned her concentration to avoiding debris and gaining enough speed to leave the ground.

"Yes, ma'am." Pomeroy pivoted, entering the command at the tactical console. "Standing by."

Rumadan maneuvered the ship through the hangar entrance, accelerating as soon as they were clear. A few moments later, they were airborne. She pulled the stick back and began to climb. "Now."

Pomeroy let loose, observing the rear monitor as the explosives hit the edge of the hangar. Upon detonation, they effectively caved in the roof over the majority of the structure. "Bingo!"

"Bingo?" Rumadan asked.

They may have made it off the ground, but they were by no means clear. Half a dozen or more Arkosian ships waiting up there. The Solarii team was certainly outgunned. The only advantage they had was surprise.

"Old Terran expression, Rummy. Not to worry."

He glanced back toward the cargo area, brow furrowed. Rumadan imagined he concerned himself with his commander's wounds, as well he should.

"Other tasks must take precedence now," Rumadan said. "I need another set of eyes to watch the monitors. You have delegated the injured to others. Trust them."

He blinked and nodded. "Course. Sorry. Just hate to see it." He turned back to face front. "What can I do, eh?"

"What communications have come from the base? Distress signal? Anything following us?"

"Nothing's bloody coming outta that hangar," Pomeroy declared. He studied the rear sensor readouts and tapped some keys on the control console. "Everything's silent. Hard to tell, though, how many of the buggers there are, up or down."

"Precisely." Rumadan set a course for Solarii space, feeling small pockets of uneasiness creep under her fur.

Though she could leave the tending of the wounded to those not flying the ship, she wanted to know about the confrontation with the pirates. Had Stefan and Catava manages to kill any before running for their lives? Were the odds now in their favor?

Rumadan was also mindful of the severity of their companions' injuries. Winston was clearly disoriented and damaged from his time in captivity. Stefan's torso was soaked in blood and one sleeve burned away to reveal an arm blistered red from shoulder to elbow. Catava. The Khimeyr commander's nakedness left nothing to the imagination as far as her injuries were concerned. The amount of blood loss probably meant they would arrive home with one mortal casualty.

Though it was not in a Viorn's nature to sigh, Rumadan sighed anyway and contemplated the damage with regret.

How would Trezanna accept the news?

* * *

IN the cabin below decks, the team had its collective hands full.

Hawk settled Stefan next to the unconscious Winston on a couple of hastily tossed brown wool blankets that had been ripped down off the wall. Cleanliness was not an issue at the moment.

Winston stirred and moaned, but did not wake up. He looked as if they had rolled him in sawdust and sulfured mud. Hawk wondered what hells Winston traveled in his day in Estrella's *oubliette*. And what kind of hell would he have to deal with when he returned to the real world, especially now with his comrade Shelby Hussard gone.

And Stefan? Hawk extrapolated how Stefan felt about the brave woman who risked her life to help the Solarii. He could recall, during his time with Dragonfleet, some of the gut shots. They seldom turned out well. Once Stefan realized that he had very likely taken Catava to her death, he would be a basket case.

Hawk couldn't object to the two men being out cold. It made things easier, as far as he was concerned.

Over the last several hours, he got a glimpse of all kind of bravery, the kind that exemplified what he wanted to be a part of. Not the kind of team he belonged to with Estrella. She sent them out with a laundry list of little errands to do, errands he accomplished while there was access to computers. It was the only reason she let him come, and then she covered it with a manufactured tantrum. No one suspected a thing.

Except his guilty conscience.

Julian knelt next to the men, rooting through a gray plastic box a meter square, dropping mild obscenities like rain. "Cotton balls, gauze, some old rags? What kind of med-kit is this?"

Hawk joined him, helping sort through the box. "This is first aid, my friend. For people working on the engine who cut a finger. Most cargo ships aren't geared for a knock down, drag out. I think Qiao took some with her to tend Cat."

Uncomforted by the explanation, Julian ranted on. "We should have thought about this. We should have brought a nurse, at least! I'm only an engineer. What am I supposed to do, wire them back together?"

"Calm down. We're all right." Hawk clapped him on the shoulder. "I have some field experience. Winston there appears to be in shock. All we can do is keep him warm and watch him. Ciro is a little banged up, fried in a couple places. Most of the blood isn't his." He glanced down the hall in the direction where Catava lay. "She's another story."

Hawk took off Stefan's shirt and vest, glad the young man was unconscious as he peeled some of the melted fabric from his skin. He laid a gentle layer of gauze over the burns on Stefan's stomach, attaching it with strips of tape, and then wrapped the arm.

"That's gonna hurt like hell later," Hawk said. "But he'll wait 'til we get back to the base. Let's see what we can do for the woman."

Catava was taken to the room which she had occupied on their trip to Miramar. The bed was now a place to perform what medical treatment they could offer, instead of nervous waiting. Qiaolin partially dressed Catava in worn loose blue trousers and covered the rest of her with a sheet. When they entered the room, Qiaolin stood next to the bed with its green wool blanket, smoothing the hair of her leader, her friend, as if she were a small child.

"How is she?" Hawk asked.

Julian stood in the doorway, looking uncomfortable.

"I don't know," Qiaolin replied in tight voice. "That's the third set of bandages I've put on."

Hawk drew back the sheet. Blood oozed through Catava's dressings, the bright red splash of color emphasized even more against her pale skin. He shook his head.

"Let me try something here," Hawk said.

He dug through the jumbled pile of medical supplies Qiao had tossed at the end of the bed, and made pressure bandages the best he could.

"She's bleeding to death, isn't she?" Qiaolin asked.

"Not if I can help it."

"Why the hell did she get hit? Why didn't Stefan take the lead?"

Hawk studied her for a moment, and then covered Catava with the sheet again. "It's not your fault."

That got her attention. She froze, stiff. "Of course it's not *my* fault!" Qiao snapped. "I wouldn't have let her get shot!"

Hawk shrugged. "Bet Stefan didn't have that intention, either. He's burned pretty badly, too. We won't know what happened 'til one of them's awake. Dragonfleet women tend to be a little headstrong."

"We aren't Dragonfleet women," Qiao replied in an icy tone.

Hawk realized his mistake as soon as the words were out. He meant them as a sort of compliment, but it was too late to drag them back into his throat. "Right. I'm sorry." He sorted through the supplies, looking for something else to stop the bleeding. "Julian, you have any ideas here?"

"I'm not a doctor, remember?" Julian shifted awkwardly. "If I only…." His voice trailed off and he shook his head. "Maybe. No." He straightened, a look of enlightenment crossing his face. "Wait. That I can do. Be right back."

Then Julian bolted from the room.

Hawk rotated his shoulders, stretching, feeling the tension in them. The ship vibrated beneath his feet, the noise of its engine steady. No sudden lurches or jolts. They must have made a clean getaway.

Had he earned his freedom? More important, had he demonstrated that Dragonfleeters were worthy allies? He had done what they asked.

Now what?

Catava's eyelids fluttered and her breaths seemed to fade away.

Qiaolin choked and bent over the bed. "No! Cat!" She shook the woman hard by the shoulders. "Come on, don't give up!"

The woman on the bed gave a long shuddering breath, and then fell back into a ragged but regular rhythm.

Qiaolin, trembling, looked up at Hawk, and he stepped closer and slipped an arm around her shoulders, half-surprised she let him.

"Good job," Hawk said. "Probably knowing you're here is helping her hold on."

"You think so?" The tension in Qiaolin's frame seemed to release just a little. "We can't lose her. She gave up so much, trying to make Zeta colony work. Everything she wanted."

Hawk shouldn't tell her the truth, but he thought it might help. "You know, she could have bested Strey if she'd stayed. With the support of her father and his friends, she could have pulled it off. Strey's made too many enemies. But after you left, there wasn't much of an alternative."

Qiaolin considered that as Hawk congratulated himself for finding a subject to divert her. "What happened to her father? Is he still alive?"

Hawk shook his head. "He died when he volunteered for a mission against the Galnites, about three years ago. He and the other elders proved the Old Guard were still worth their salt."

She nodded absently, watching Catava on the bed. "What do you think Julian went for?"

"Beats me." Hawk rolled his shoulders again, alert to a shift under his feet. Something was happening.

The sound of pounding footsteps came toward them. Then Julian burst through the doorway, energy practically flowing from his pores.

"I think I've got it! We've got to take her down below." Julian struggled to gather Catava in his arms.

"Let me," Hawk said, picking up Catava as gently as he could. "You just show me where."

"Come on, you'll see!" Julian was already out the door.

Hawk exchanged curious glances with Qiaolin. Adjusting the weight in his arms, he followed the Solarii engineer.

"Hawk, you be careful!" Qiao scrambled out the door after him too quickly, crashing into the opposite wall as the ship yawed. "Where are you taking her? Be careful, I said!"

"I'm trying, damn it." Hawk stumbled, the movement of the ship throwing him off balance. Something was now definitely going on above. Julian led them down a dim corridor into the back hold. A sheet of silvery metal lay in the middle of the floor. Piles of stuff tossed to all sides showed that the space had been hastily cleared. A few bare bulbs hung overhead, swinging with the motion of the ship.

"Put her there!" Julian ordered. "Then come help me with these connections."

Hawk crouched down and laid her on the cold metal. He had never seen anything like this set-up. Several power boxes sat at equidistant points from the metal sheet, hooked to it by clips and wires.

"What are you doing?" Qiaolin asked. Suspicion shadowed her eyes as she circled the metal sheet.

Hawk blindly followed Julian's direction, hooking red wires to left terminals and blue wires to right terminals of the power boxes, until there were half a dozen all around the metal sheet.

The only light in the room was directly over the floor where Julian knelt on the other side of the comatose woman. When he looked up to answer Qiaolin, his face in the halo of light looked like that of an angel.

"I'll tell you if this works," Julian said. "Everyone step back."

He flipped several switches. Connections popped and fizzled for a few seconds and settled into a deep hum. The space over Catava took on an opaque tone, as an oval shape reached a foot above the floor.

"Yes!" A smile lit Julian's his face. As Qiao continued to look puzzled, he ran over and grabbed her hands, spinning her around. "It's a stasis field. It'll keep her just as she is until Dr. Boring can get to her!"

"Julian, you're a genius," she said.

"Good man, McKinley," Hawk said, allowing a grin.

The engineer flushed at the praise. "I didn't know if the independent power packs could do this. But I thought if I hooked the power grid to the alternate supply, with the constant conductors in place…." Realizing he was not talking to fellow engineers, he trailed off and grinned at Hawk. "Guess I'm used to working without the right tools for the job." He patted Qiaolin on the shoulder. "She'll be okay now," he promised. "I'll stay here and make sure it keeps running." Julian's dark eyes sparkled, now that he was once again in his element. "Maybe I can find a De Vries generator in the hold someplace."

Hawk nodded with satisfaction. "You watch out for her and we'll make sure Winston and Stefan don't go bad, too." The ship lurched again, a hard port this time. "Damned pirates, most likely. Go on up, girl, and see if you can help. We've got this."

Qiaolin stared down at Catava and then hurried up the thin metal ladder. Hawk made sure Julian had the field in good working order, and then went to see what he could do for Stefan and Winston.

Hawk possessed a very narrow window for changing his future. He could deal himself into Estrella's good graces or perhaps accept the offer to join the Solarii. Either way, if he wanted to keep his freedom, he had best make sure all of the team came back as healthy as he could manage.

CHAPTER 27

"INCOMING! Four fighters!" Pomeroy cried, spinning around from the co-pilot's chair to the tactical board. "They're hot and fully loaded!"

He had not expected their flight to be unnoticed. Thanks to the destruction the Solarii-Khimeyr team caused while making their exit, the pirate ships on the ground didn't pursue them. But retaliation burst onto their screens as soon as Marcand's men established communication with the Arkosian ships overhead.

"Acknowledged." Rumadan swung the ship to starboard in a wide arc, then port again, in standard deviation evasive maneuvers. "I hope they are prepared below decks."

Qiaolin came onto the command deck, grabbing the nearest console to keep from falling down. "Julian has Catava in a makeshift stasis field, so she may live 'til we get back. What can I do?" She glanced at the array of monitors and winced. "Stars above. Isn't enough, enough?"

"Take co-pilot, Qiao!" Pomeroy barked. If they couldn't get home in one piece, all of the miracle working in the universe would be of no use. He took over the tactical panel, his quick fingers punching in the command to return fire at the oncoming pirate ships.

Qiaolin slipped into the second chair and glanced at Rumadan for instructions.

"Plot a course through the nebula in the Provost sector."

"Yes, ma'am," replied Qiaolin, setting to her task.

Pomeroy reviewed the data on the battle with interest. Stefan's ship might pass on the outside for a basic cargo transport ship, but the shields were substantial. The weapons were better than the ones on the old wrecks they had taken to Zeta years ago. He fired again, two blasts at a time, twice around, then sat back to watch.

The first round took out the closest cruiser at contact, the resulting fiery explosion so bright he blinked. Number two hit the second craft amidships. It veered sideways, causing the attacker behind it to crash in another silent blaze. The remaining ship avoided the explosion, but swung so wide it lost speed and the trail as Qiaolin's new course led the *Mercantile* away from the Solarii base and into the nebula.

"Wouldn't it be better to take a straight route to decent medical support?" Qiaolin asked.

"The pirates may not realize we came from the Solarii base, as this ship bears no such markings. If we escape thorough the nebula, we may buy some peace for those at home." Her expression warmed a few degrees. "I notified Medical of the team's casualties. They will be standing by."

The nebula was huge, covering several parsecs of open space between Induna and the Cryeron colony. Dragonfleet had launched little hit-and-run attacks from its concealing dust on several occasions. It could be treacherous, the regularly traveled corridors subject to the invasion of space debris and drifting asteroids. Sensors and instruments were easily clouded. But that worked in favor of those trying to hide.

Rumadan navigated the *Mercantile* into position behind a particularly large asteroid and cut the engines. "Shut down all drives and non-life support drains. We shall wait a few minutes to see whether the Arkosians have abandoned pursuit." Qiaolin nodded and complied, leaving the com channels open to monitor for chatter.

After the noisy rush of escape, the dwindling hum of the engines and other powered processes felt like silence. The three waited, still and quiet. Pomeroy chafed to engage the pirates, wanting to destroy them once and for all. But this was not the day or the ship.

"It seemed to me that Catava's injuries are quite grave," Rumadan offered. "If she does not survive, that will mean one of you must lead the Khimeyr."

Pomeroy straightened. His mind sharp as it turned to this new course of speculation. His experience at leading units on the field certainly qualified him. But he never expected to be in that position. He and Qiao shared the duties of second-in-command, neither seeking the power of leadership.

"She will survive," Qiaolin insisted.

"What about the others?" Rumadan asked.

Her face drawn with worry, Qiaolin counted off on her fingers. "Monty is in shock. He doesn't seem to have any obvious injuries. Stefan's left arm took a bad laser burn, and he's got another on his abdomen. Cat—well, you saw her. It's not good. Several laser wounds to her torso, and it took a while to stop the bleeding. Julian's done what he can with this stasis field."

"We shall bring them home." Rumadan's silky voice gathered a more philosophical tone as she looked out the front port. "Fate has taken a hand. You were the caregivers granted to them by the stars. We must trust if they are meant to survive, that this will be enough." She glanced at the instrument panels and then at Pomeroy. "No sign of them."

* * *

"WITH all due respect," Pomeroy reminded, "we can't read them any better than they can read us, ma'am. We best sit tight awhile longer." He found all that heebie-jeebie spiritual stuff downright creepifying.

A man could count on himself, and a few companions, if he was lucky. Trusting to gods or fate brought a lot of heartache. If there wasn't anything for him to do here, better that he went to see if the others needed help.

"I'll be back," Pomeroy said, getting to his feet. He pulled on his jacket and then stalked into the corridor that led to the cargo hold. "Too much to think about,"

As he marched into the back, he pondered the possibility of losing Catava. It was more than he could deal with for the moment. That was not supposed to happen. She could handle herself in a fair fight. Didn't look like there was anything fair about this, though. What was all that about chains and marks on her neck? Stefan hadn't protected her from harm. He had warned that pup, but decided to wait for a full debrief to see where fault lay. If Catava didn't pull through, there would be hell to pay.

In the small cabin, Pomeroy found Hawk speaking softly to Winston, who was propped up against the bland wall and holding a cup of dark steaming liquid. Now this was more like it.

"Hey, look who's peepin'!" Pomeroy called in a cheerful voice. "How's my boy Winston, eh?"

Winston jerked and spilled his drink. "Glad to see you, mate," he replied with a wan version of his usual grin. He looked into his cup. "Hawk's been telling me what's gone on. Guess what I did was a bloody fool thing to do?"

Pomeroy nodded and crossed his arms. "Guess it was. Didn't bring the girl back, no ways. If it wasn't for Ciro there, you might still be a guest of Estrella's Happy Hell. 'Twas his plan as got you out."

Winston glanced at the unconscious man. "I shall thank him, then."

"Any word on Catava?" Hawk asked.

"Julian's not reported any change," Pomeroy reported. "I'm headed there now. Check back with you later."

Below, Julian McKinley moved lightly from one power box to

another, checking each wire connection like a spider traversing its web.

The device was beyond Pomeroy's understanding, wires and clamps, buzzing and humming, but he would believe it was working, absent any evidence to the contrary. He studied Catava's pale face, recalling how she looked when he lifted her, naked and bleeding, from Stefan's arms at the ship's hatch. She actually looked a little better. The realization choked him up a little. He would hold onto that hope.

"Everything five by five here?" Pomeroy asked, trying to keep his voice from sounding ragged. Wouldn't do to get emotional now. Too much to do before they all got home safe and sound.

Julian's expression was troubled. "What's going on? Why aren't we home yet?"

"Hot pursuit. Rummy took a dive in the nebula 'til the pirates got lost." Pomeroy watched the makeshift monitors and tried to decipher what they meant. "Will that thing keep her in one piece 'til we get there?"

As a short caused sparks to fly, Julian frowned and bent to reattach the wire. "If we don't take too long."

Pomeroy shrugged. "Don't know when, friend. Can I do anything?"

"Tell them to hurry." With a sigh, Julian returned to tending the machinery.

"Right." Pomeroy glanced around the shadowed room one last time and headed back to the bridge.

When he arrived, Rumadan's piercing gaze caught him.

"We need to get a move out of here, soon's possible," Pomeroy said. "The equipment's failing, though Julian's holdin' it together with a lick and a stick." A quick glimpse at the monitors showed no intruders. "Seems to be working."

Rumadan nodded in agreement and plotted a course one-hundred-thirty degrees away from the trajectory which had brought them into the nebula. The roundabout path would further avoid any confrontation with anyone who might have followed them.

As the *Mercantile* approached the edge of the nebula, Pomeroy increased his sensor scans to see who might be waiting. "All clear," he said with surprise.

"They may have been hit in that barrage when the other ship was destroyed," Rumadan hypothesized, as she set the engines at full. "If that is the case, it would have been prudent to return to base."

They made good speed back to Solarii space. As soon as they were within communication range, Qiaolin transmitted the specific details of their injuries. Emergency personnel awaited them when they landed.

The three in the cockpit watched from the door. Catava and Stefan were hurried away and then Hawk came out with Winston.

A very pregnant nurse scanned Winston. "Don't you want a wheelchair?" she asked.

"I'll take him in," Hawk said with a grin. "Kinda become attached to the old boy."

The nurse sniffed pointedly. "Fine. Then you can shower in the infirmary. Come along."

Julian came forward, looking worn as old leather. His eyes met Qiaolin's as he paused at the open hatchway. "I hope she held on long enough."

"I couldn't have asked for more." Qiaolin took his arm, and they headed in the direction of a tight little group of Khimeyr waiting for information about Catava and the mission.

Rumadan left the ship last, surveying the busy hangar bay as she exited the hatch. She stopped for a moment and turned to Pomeroy. "Well done. We have accomplished those tasks which were purrs. Now it is to the others to take the torch and finish the race."

"Right," Pomeroy replied. *More idealistic claptrap.* He preferred the realistic. He needed a shower. Then he needed a drink.

Maybe two drinks.

"Hawk! Hold up! I'll go with you." Pomeroy nodded to Rumadan and slouched off after the medical team.

CHAPTER 28

TREZANNA had her hands full when the *Mercantile* finally returned.

She had to make sure her team kept on top of the sensors to watch for a counter-attack. While the team had taken a Philean ship, clearly the rescue attempt aimed for a Solarii officer. Even someone as dense as Marcand could put together that bit of math.

Piper nagged her to prepare, as well. "Vanyakin has crates full of new weaponry in the *Revenge*. You should install them here."

"And pay him with what, Piper? We're stretched to the limit, and your friend has the right to earn a living from what he's brought for trade."

"A sector cleared of pirates would seem to be a good outcome for the general economy, wouldn't it? I'll persuade him it's an investment." Piper's eyes sparkled with mischief.

Piper's jaw set with determination, a gesture Trezanna had seen in her own mirror too many times not to know what it meant. She enjoyed these moments of recognition, the proof that she and Piper were of the same stuff, that they belonged together.

"I'll ask him, Piper. I promise."

Preparing to go to the infirmary and check on her people, Trezanna silently lamented her lack of omniscience. Even her Space Force training didn't make decisions easier. In the Force, there was always a higher-up to make those hard choices. Pass the buck. That was why the officers wore those clusters pinned to their uniforms. But here at Induna, she was the one with that desk, the one where the responsibility rested.

It was a calculated risk to send Hawk with Stefan's group. What would happen if Hawk returned a hero? Estrella rejected him for helping them. Could he be persuaded to join the Solarii-Khimeyr coalition? Could he help persuade others to do the same? Could the Solarii's support of Estrella's second-in-command mean the others would reject Estrella's leadership? It was possible.

On the way to the infirmary, Trezanna connected with Rumadan. The Viorn was terse about the rescue of Winston, sharing spare facts and commendation for all involved.

"Even the Dragonfleet officer acted with the highest of honor," Rumadan said, ears twitching as she picked bits of dark oil from her fur.

Trezanna studied her Ops Director. "How long 'til the Arkosians come, do you think?"

"Unclear." Rumadan explained the destruction of the hangar at Miramar. Restless muscles rippled with tension, creating violet blotches on her fur. "Stefan was the one with direct contact with the leadership inside. We do not know how he left things."

"Understood. Thank you, old friend."

Anxious now to check in with the doctors, Trezanna hurried along the corridors. Pausing at the lounge door, she saw Hawk and Piper hot in conversation at a cluttered table. Piper's face was flushed.

Trezanna wondered what was upsetting her daughter, but a page from medical dragged her forward. Her question would have to wait.

The infirmary was decidedly in crisis mode. Personnel bustled in and out of the isolation room in the rear. A bloody Stefan Ciro lay on a monitored bed to the left, talking with the nurse. A burst of raucous laughter to the right drew her attention. Pomeroy and Winston, Winston obviously trying to escape and the other not allowing him.

Walking over to them, she caught Winston's eye. "Welcome home."

To Trezanna's surprise he hugged her, lifting her off the floor.

"I can't believe you did it, ma'am," he said. "But thank you."

She extricated herself from the man's arms with as much dignity as she could manage. "It was Stefan's idea."

"Oh, rightio. I know that. Wouldn't have happened less you gave permission." Winston hung his head. "It cost a lot. It was a damn fool thing to do. You would have been to rights leaving me there to rot. I'm sorry. Damn fool thing."

Trezanna laid her warm hand on the pilot's shoulder for a moment's comfort. "It *was* a damn fool thing. And it has cost us a lot."

Winston glanced back toward the isolation room. "Yes, ma'am."

Trezanna mentally ticked off the team members. "You and Qiao?" she asked Pomeroy.

The Khimeyr shrugged. "Fine. We're tough birds," Pomeroy said with a smirk. "Julian, too, walked out without a scratch."

"What about the others?" Trezanna asked.

She watched Ciro inch upright, wincing as the nurse, Bethany, removed his shirt and exposed white bandages.

Pomeroy shook his head. "Stefan was pretty fragged when he hit the hatch. Catava was—" His voice tangled in a choked whisper, and he stared at the floor. "Dunno, ma'am. 'Spect they'll have a story to tell."

"I expect they will." *If they lived to tell it*, she thought. "Glad you're back."

Trezanna moved over to the medical bed, noting the adjustments Bethany made to work around her pregnant belly as she scanned Stefan's blistered arm.

"That looks nasty," Trezanna observed. She watched Stefan's face, not wanting to jump into the questions she really wanted to ask. "Despite that, it seems like your plan worked."

Stefan's eyes flashed, as he grabbed Trezanna with his good arm. "Maybe you can get an answer! I want to know what's happening with Cat. No one will tell me."

Trezanna glanced at Bethany, wondering if no news meant they didn't want to tell him something bad. "Perhaps no one knows yet," she said, stalling for an answer.

The nurse nodded, her troubled gaze moving to the curtained area.

Stefan's eyes filled with tears. "It doesn't matter. I don't matter." He gestured to his body. "This is nothing compared to what she's going through! If I've killed her, then nothing else matters."

"Stefan, I have great confidence in my medical staff," Trezanna said. "Dr. Boring may drive me crazy, but he is very good at what he does." She turned to the nurse. "Can I get him something? Tea, perhaps?"

Bethany put away her instruments. "Of course. And I'll see what I can find out."

"Fine." Trezanna let her finish as she went to the galley port for two cups of strong, spiced tea. She returned and handed Stefan one. Then she sat on the doctor's stool next to the bed. "Tell me what happened."

Stefan stared off a moment. Then he drained his cup and set it down. He glanced over at the isolation room. "Everything went like we planned. At least, at first."

Trezanna's gut clenched as Stefan recounted the confrontation with Marcand, and then the nightmare unfolded, Marcand's death and the general bloodbath that followed.

His voice got quieter as he went on, until he came to those last desperate moments. "She didn't even say anything, it happened so fast. She just fell. She just fell," Stefan whispered. His tears fell, too.

Trezanna didn't respond. What could she say? It was too soon to know if he had lost the woman who held his heart, a loss that would be shared by the entire community. She sipped her tea in silence, letting him calm himself.

So Marcand was dead.

That would seem to be momentous news. He and some uncounted number of lackeys gone. That would surely put a kick in the side of pirate activity for some time. And likely prompt a vengeful attack against the Phileans. Time for that later.

Nurse Bethany popped her head in the iso-room and then returned to Stefan's bedside. "Doctor is still performing surgery," she said in soft, sympathetic voice. "But I got a look at the monitors. Her life signs were definitely better than when she came in."

Stefan sighed, his shoulders bowing even further.

Trezanna reached for his good hand, finding it cold and distant.

"Putting aside your personal stake in this, Stefan, your mission was a great success," she said. "You took a small crew who had never worked together before. You entered hostile space and talked your way inside a heavily defended garrison. Both teams completed their missions. Considering the perils, injuries were to be expected. You brought your ship and everyone aboard it home, including Winston." She squeezed his chilly fingers. "Most of our people will consider you a hero. Stop beating yourself up."

Stefan's tawny eyes widened. "A *hero*? No way."

"Absolutely. I know I am very grateful for the risk you took." Trezanna allowed a smile, as Winston limped toward the door. "That young man is a very important part of this organization." She turned back to Stefan. "As you could be, if you're interested."

"Me? Part of the Solarii? Oh, I don't know. My dad, my family—" The offer clearly had caught Stefan off guard. "I'd have to think about that, ma'am."

"You do that." She finished her tea, hoping he would say yes.

A sudden exodus of personnel from the isolation room ended with Eugene Boring. The doctor, his blue gown streaked with blood, removed his gloves and slowly walked over to Trezanna, stretching a little from side to side, his eyes weary.

"A strong heart she has." Boring turned his attention to Stefan. "And you? A hard head has saved many a fool." He picked up a diagnostic tool on the table next to the bed and waved it past Stefan's head. The scanner made mysterious noises. "No lasting damage."

"Cat? You've got to tell me!" Stefan demanded.

The doctor rubbed his forehead. "She lost much blood. We have attempted to replace it with artificial plasma and some of whatever stores we have. It is a rare blood type. The wounds themselves?" His tone sounded more pronouncement and less speculation. He shrugged. "The lacerations tore much flesh. Very bad. But recoverable."

"What are you saying? *Much blood?* You mean it's bad, right? She's not going to live." Stefan gripped the edge of the bed with his hands as if he would spring off without its weight to anchor him. "What blood does she need? I'll give her as much of mine as she can use. She can have all of it!"

Trezanna took it upon herself to interpret for the cryptic doctor. "I think the doctor's saying she'll be fine, without pinning himself to a firm diagnosis."

Boring scowled at her. "Conclusions are mine, not yours. I see no medical diploma on your office wall." Chewing his lip in a firm pout, the Eponan allowed an encouraging nod. He glanced at Stefan. "She's not ready to leave this plane, I suppose. Something holds her here."

"Can I see her?" Stefan asked, halfway off the bed before got out the question.

"For a few minutes only!" the doctor said.

Stefan sprinted toward the isolation room.

Trezanna watched the young man with a pinch of jealousy. It had been long since she had cared that much for someone or since someone cared that much about her. "She'll live?"

"She will," Boring replied. "Julian must be commended for his quick thinking. If it wasn't for his stasis device, the morgue is where we would be sending her."

"I'll be sure to let him know he was responsible. He'll be pleased." Trezanna glanced over at Pomeroy, who was watching them from under a thunderous brow. "I'll let you tell the others."

Boring nodded his thanks. "My opinion has not been asked, but this rescue was crucial. A blended team, a blended spirit it makes. Even the Dragonfleet contingent must admit this."

"Agreed. And you as a last resort, to deal with the results of our foolishness." She glanced toward the curtain. "I'll check back later."

"Very well." The doctor beckoned to the Khimeyr security man, who crossed the room with an impatient stride.

Trezanna began planning a staff meeting agenda for sometime in the upcoming days. They would need to consider their options now that the pirates had lost their leader. This could turn out to be an interesting development. Very interesting indeed.

CHAPTER 29

HAWK had noticed Trezanna Len's eye on him as she passed by the lounge where he sat with Piper. *Wonder what she thinks.* He turned his attention back to her daughter, now pleading with him.

"You've got to tell Estrella I can't do what she asked now," Piper said, a desperate edge in her voice. "I know I was angry and ready to do anything to hurt my mother and her Solarii then. But now it's different."

Hawk focused his dark gaze on the girl, her face so young and innocent. Just the sort Estrella would glory in sucking into some nefarious plan, working her until that innocence was lost forever. "Why don't you tell her yourself?"

"Because I would like to live." Piper frowned. "You know how she gets."

"Don't I, though?" Hawk gave a dry chuckle.

After his excursion with Pomeroy's team, he was not looking forward to having conversation with Estrella. He had not yet decided to whether to continue as Estrella's second-in-command. That was, if she would have him back. She had put on quite a show when he had been chosen to return to Miramar, but had her pique grown into something more serious? What percentage was there in returning to the glorious post of Estrella's whipping boy?

Probably stab me soon as look at me.

He was the one to discover Piper's true identity after she wandered into the Dragonfleet base, all full of vinegar and vengeance for the mother that had abandoned her. He cultivated her, hoping to turn her bitterness toward the Solarii leader into a real Dragonfleet weapon. Placing her here was a stroke of luck. If all went according to plan, she could easily have taken down Trezanna and caused a Solarii downfall. The self-styled empress would have given Hawk an appropriate reward, and a more secure position of power.

Now he wasn't so sure that was what he wanted.

He found, after the first awkward rubbings with the Khimeyr-Solarii corps, that they worked together well. No threats, no blackmail, no coercion, just a simple respect for the other's abilities.

At the same time, no one had real power. Here, he was just another face in the crowd with no control over others. He couldn't make them fear just by walking into the room. He didn't have the power of the dragon behind him.

He had a decision to make.

"So what do you want to do, then? Just walk away?" Hawk asked Piper and then took a drink of the cold ale before him.

"Why can't I? No harm's done, not yet."

"True enough."

Piper peeled strips of the label off her drink bottle. "I really like her, Hawk. I believe what she tells me about my father. I know what kind of man he was. He held grudges like that."

"She seems to be a straight shooter. Nothing like what Strey used to say about her."

"Exactly." Piper blew air out through pursed lips and shoved the ravaged bottle and its discarded label away from her, then slouched back in her chair. "So? Will you tell her?"

"What do you think the Khimeyr want?" he asked, his brain still grinding through the stuff of *what if*.

"Huh?" She blinked and sat up straight.

"Gus said if the Khimeyr came back, they'd try to take Miramar away from us."

"I know, but I haven't seen any indication of that since I've been here. They seem perfectly suited to co-exist with the Solarii."

"Yeah." Hawk pushed away from the table and went to the galley port, getting both himself and Piper another cold drink, his alcoholic, hers just another juice drink. His mind buzzed with possibilities. If the Khimeyr and Solarii could so easily unite to increase their strength, couldn't Dragonfleet benefit from an alliance?

Hawk thought they could.

Certainly after the Arkosian attack, they were in no position to stand alone. He remembered with regret the destruction Rumadan had caused to create their recent escape. It was necessary at the time, but a mess for Dragonfleet when they returned home. A partnership could be very welcome.

Estrella would never allow it.

Perhaps Estrella was the superfluous part of the equation. If she were removed, what might happen then? The thought pricked him with a hundred prospects.

His best alternative for self-advancement might well be to solidify his favorable position vis-à-vis each of the groups, buy time to see which way the current would ultimately run. Smiling at Piper, he realized how he could win points with her mother. Just in case.

"I'll talk to Estrella." Hawk leaned forward. "I'd like to tell your mother, too, if you don't mind. Not that she doesn't know how treacherous Estrella can be, but she needs to know how low she'd go."

Piper squirmed in her chair. "Do you have to?"

"Don't worry." He reached over to pat her hand. "I'll make sure Trezanna knows who to blame."

The young woman nodded, relieved, and got to her feet. "Thanks, Hawk. I owe you one."

"Not at all," he said with amusement, as she walked away.

You're the one who has done me a favor, little lady. When I explain this to Trezanna Len, Estrella's fate will be pretty much sealed. And when they look for someone new, someone reasonable, to lead the pack, I'll be right here to step into those shoes.

Grinning, Hawk grabbed his fresh ale and headed down the corridor to the outside, to get some fresh air before dealing with his soon-to-be former leader.

* * *

FINALLY free to pass through the sterile curtains, Stefan found Cat sleeping.

A wave of tenderness hit him at the sight of her blonde hair tangled on the pillowcase. Her left hand softly clutched the gray blanket. All evidence of her injuries was blissfully hidden under stitches and bandages and blanket. She was pale and beautiful.

He sighed out the pain in his heart and took a seat at the right side of the bed. The excitement in her eyes as they faced the pirates, the bond created by the quest connected them in a powerful way. That connection fed his attraction to her, the attraction felt from the first moment he had seen her.

She might not reciprocate his feelings. He knew that. She never said she did. But once they began planning Winston's rescue, she listened to him, talked to him, treated him as if he was worth something. And that meant everything to him.

He repaid her confidence in him by nearly getting her killed.

Despite Trezanna's glorious rendition of the events, he knew dealing with the pirates was a perilous proposition. Marcand was a dangerous son of a *jarquette*, always had been. Well, no one would fool Marcand again, that much was for sure.

With a sigh, he returned his attention to the sleeping woman, her skin nearly transparent in her vulnerable state. Dr. Boring confirmed what he already knew. She was a unique individual, right down to her blood type, and the universe was better with her in it. He should have never put her behind him. If he had stopped himself from turning, the shot would not have hit her.

"Stop it, Stefan," he muttered. He reached out a hand and caressed her cheek. Perhaps he could deflect some of his guilt by taking on her responsibilities. If he couldn't help her medically, if he couldn't help her lead the Khimeyr, at least he could care for the children until she recovered. This way of repaying his debt appealed to him. When the nurse came by to shoo him, he nodded and squeezed Cat's hand.

"I'll be back," he promised her, his voice catching with a flood of emotion. "Don't worry about anything but taking care of yourself."

She didn't move. With a shuddering sigh, he tore himself away.

He stopped in the lounge, needing a few moments to pull himself together before he spoke to Qiao about the children. He fetched another cup of the spiced tea Trezanna had brought him in the infirmary and leaned his elbows on the counter, inhaling its distinctive aroma as he formulated his speech for Qiao.

"But, Van, you have to. The Solarii need those weapons."

"You ask too much."

The intent female voice came from a table behind him. The negative reply came in a deep bass that Stefan recognized as belonging to the trader, Vanyakin. Stefan turned just enough to be able to watch Piper argue with the trader.

"It's only money!" Piper snapped. "We're talking about the lives of good people!"

The dark-skinned man laid a hand over Piper's. "There is no such thing as 'only money'. My life is as valuable as theirs. I need to eat, dear."

Stefan sipped the tea, tempted to interrupt. Vanyakin was known to him, having conducted business with his father for some time. His father and uncle talked about the substantial debt this trader carried at the Waypass. If the weapons were like those he had solicited for his father, then the Solarii could certainly use them. Even if Marcand was dead, someone would take his place. A superior offensive array would make the difference.

Piper persisted. "It's not like I asked you for a fee when you hitched a ride here with me from Miramar. I'm sure they'll pay you when they have the money. My mother said...."

Vanyakin shook his head in a negative response.

"How much?" Stefan jumped in.

"What?" Piper eyed him, irritated.

"How much?" Stefan reiterated, looking directly at Vanyakin. "For the weapons you brought?"

"More than the pocket change you carry, young Ciro." Vanyakin seemed mildly amused.

Stefan didn't expect the investment to be cheap. But with so many now allied to end Arkosian domination of this sector, maybe there was something more important than just coin.

"You *could* donate the weapons." Stefan suggested.

Vanyakin rolled his dark eyes. "You, too? You're a trader, like me. Your father hasn't raised a fool, now, has he?"

Stefan crossed to their table. "I've been raised to value a good trade since I could walk. But a real payoff isn't always made in money."

"What else is there?" Vanyakin scoffed.

"Look at it this way," Stefan said. "The Arkosians have decided to take the sector. They've recruited mercenaries. They've beefed up their attack force. Everything they're doing hurts trade in the sector. If they gain control, how long do you think they'll let you travel freely, making profit, hmm? Then how will you survive?"

Vanyakin frowned. Piper, however, flirted with a tentative smile, her eyes twinkling with admiration. Stefan continued before Vanyakin could dismiss him.

"What you've got now is an opportunity to contribute to the effort to wipe out the pirates permanently, without any real personal risk," Stefan added. "The Solarii and Khimeyr will do the fighting for you. Look at it as an investment in future profits."

"But—"

"Here, I'll tell you what." Stefan threw aside caution at the point. He had already risked so much that his father's potential wrath seemed minor by comparison. "You donate the weapons and I'll make sure your debt to the Waypass is waived."

"You can do that?"

Stefan didn't really believe he could, but nodded anyway. Immediate gain was more important to him now. If his father knocked him down later, he would deal with it then.

Vanyakin's eyes narrowed. "You know what I owe your father is more than what I'd sell the weapons for."

"It's worth it." Stefan set down his tea and held out a hand to seal the bargain. He was in up to his neck. Joining the Solarii, or Khimeyr for that matter, might be in his future. If his family disowned him for giving away their profits, he might be left with no other choice.

"All right, Ciro. I'll send you a contract. Just to make sure."

"I'll be here." Grinning, Stefan took his cup to the recycler.

Feeling a little better, he continued on his original heading to the Khimeyr wing. He found Qiao in the common area of the Khimeyr section, sitting on the floor amid a dozen small children of assorted ages. Dressed in bright shirts like a flight of butterflies, the children played with small toys and books.

Qiao looked up as Stefan entered the room. "You're up and around. So soon?" She adjusted her position, as Suzi crawled into her lap.

Stefan ignored the suspicious undertone to her voice. "They think I'll live." Chad came running, and Stefan picked him up, careful to hold the boy against his uninjured side. He sensed Qiao's unspoken question and answered it in a way to avoid alerting the children. "And your friend is doing better. Dr. Boring thinks she'll pull through fine."

Qiao's arms closed tight, hugging Suzi close. "I knew it. Julian promised."

Stefan hunkered down on the floor with the group. "These aren't all Khimeyr?"

"No. Actually, I volunteered to take the children from the day school for awhile. Thought it might clear my head of the negative undercurrent it's been in since we got back." Qiao smiled and handed a green-shirted tot a stuffed elephant to replace a toy he dropped. "I'm also reminded why we are here. These faces are those of the future."

"How true." Stefan settled Chad in his lap and opened the book the boy handed him to the first page. "Qiao, I wanted to ask if I could watch Chad and Suzi for a couple of days. I feel like I owe it to Cat, and to you all."

She frowned. "Do you know how to care for children? How do I know they'd be safe?"

Chad babbled about the pictures as he turned the pages.

Stefan half-listened, his attention on Qiaolin. "I've raised cousins and others at the Waypass. I think I can cope. I'm sure you have other things to do 'til Cat gets back."

She watched the children putter around them. "You really love her, don't you?"

Stefan smothered his first impulse to divert her with a light response.

His thoughts had become serious about Catava. Her friends deserved to know how he felt. "Yes. Very much."

"It's been a long time for her. She'll be afraid."

"I'm trying not to push her." Stefan sighed. "Or get her killed before I can tell her."

A warm chuckle escaped Qiaolin. "She couldn't talk about anything else once you'd shared your plan. She looked forward to it in a way I haven't seen her act about anything for some time. She almost sparkled." The Khimeyr second smoothed Suzi's hair. "She was well aware of the risks involved. If she wasn't willing, she would have said so."

His conscience assuaged somewhat, Stefan smiled. "Thank you."

"This mission succeeded. That's what counts."

Chad looked up at Stefan. "Momma Cat come back?"

His tongue fumbled for a minute before finding footing in a half-truth. "Momma's sleeping tonight at a friend's. She said I could have a sleepover with you. Is that okay?"

Suzi looked at him, a suspicious look in her wide-set dark eyes.

"We can make a tent. Read stories. Make cookies?"

"Cookies?" Chad echoed.

"Sure, why not?" Stefan replied.

"C'mon, Suz." Chad took his little sister's hand and pulled her toward the door. "Let's make cookies."

Qiaolin let him help her to her feet. "Do you know how to make cookies?"

"How hard can it be?" Stefan gave a shrug and then followed the children to the door.

Laughing, Qiao waved. "I'll be in my quarters if you need something."

"Terrific." Stefan took one hand of each child in his own and they made their way to Catava's quarters.

* * *

THE lanky blond guard outside the Dragonfleet quarters studied Hawk Kenton with a certain measure of curiosity.

"You want to go *in*?" the guard asked. "You just got out."

Hawk nodded. "Ought to make a report." He stood casually, most of his weight shifted to one leg, as he watched the monitor switch the view of the feeds of multiple holo-cams. The one holo that kept coming up was Estrella, berating a junior officer whose face he couldn't see, ending with a slap across the face. *Lucky fellow.*

"If you say so." The guard shrugged muscular shoulders. "But no weapons."

Hawk handed over the blaster given to him when he joined the rescue mission on Winston's behalf. The regret he felt as the weight left his hand was unexpected. He put on a grin to cover his disappointment. "I expect you'll come in and save me if Herself gets out of line."

"Not authorized to enter these quarters, sir." The guard smirked with no hint of apology. Clearly, he didn't feel sorry in the least.

"Guess I'm on my own then." Hawk rolled his shoulders to release some tension and stepped to the door, straightening the new black jacket he had picked up at the stores that morning. He selected a whole new outfit down to the shiny knee-length boots, one that clothed his well-toned body perfectly. He knew he looked good. His dark hair curled around the stand-up collar, hanging over it, the way Estrella always said she liked it. Hawk guessed he would be divested of his weapons. All that left him with was his personal charm. On many occasions in the past, that alone had preserved his life. He hoped it still would.

The guard opened the door and grinned. "*Bueno suerte, mi amigo.*"

Hawk recognized the Terran language. Smiling, he gave a jaunty salute and then stepped inside. The door slid shut behind him. From several doors down the pale gray hallway, he heard raised voices, and followed the angry sound to Estrella's anteroom. Inside, the Dragonfleet leader glared up at a red-faced Jack Skipper, an engineer who had escaped with them.

With a lazy grin, Hawk lounged against the doorframe. "Hi, honey, I'm home."

Estrella's head snapped around at Hawk's words. Dark eyes full of daggers, she dismissed Skipper in a poisonous tone. The engineer wasted no time shoving past Hawk to flee while he was still in one piece. Crossing the room, Estrella studied Hawk's posture, his demeanor and his cocky smile. Her expression was most displeased.

"You come crawling back here after abandoning me to help those weaklings? What did they promise you? Did you lay Trezanna? Bought you with some new boots and a belt buckle?"

Knowing her temper, he stayed out of arm's reach, to prevent her from outright attacking him as she openly seethed at his treachery. Maybe she could already see him slipping from her control. He couldn't afford to cut the ties just yet, though. "The question is, what do *you* want?"

Hawk watched her, seeing all the little signs which betrayed her volatility. When they first met, those signs made her exciting. Vital.

Unpredictable. Fascinating. But compared to the solid examples of female leadership he witnessed over the past few days, his heartfelt opinion was that she was unfit to command.

"I want nothing from you, traitor." Her eyes blazed with hatred.

"Traitor?" He laughed easily and dropped his voice, letting his broad shoulders block the ever-present camera. "I did what you asked, love. And won you points with your Solarii friends."

"You did?" She stepped close to him. "Where is it?"

Hawk slipped a small data disk into her hand. "That's all I could get."

Her eyes studied the disk, and then her gaze climbed slowly up his shirtfront, to his face, to meet his eyes. "Really. You get inside our base where you could set our people free, send me a message, even set the place to self-destruct, and all you do is bring me a measly data disk?"

"I didn't have access or time, my Queen."

"You didn't have the balls." She shoved him away from her. "You're no better than the damned Solarii." Estrella spit on the floor. "They'll all die a slow death. I have been treated worse than an Anthusian dog-wart by everyone. They fail to respect my position."

"My dear, I think you fail to respect your position as well. You are their prisoner and an enemy. As it stands, you don't deserve respect." He walked the long way around to her worktable, avoiding her, choosing a red fruit from the bowl, taking a bite.

Her cheeks red with fury, she leaped at him, her fingernails clawing for his face. He deflected her with a firm side-kick, knocking her hard into the couch. As she scrambled to her feet, breath knocked from her, he moved behind the table, keeping it between them. "I'm trying to help you, Strey."

"By selling me out?" Estrella pushed herself up with a gasp. She grabbed another fruit and threw it at him.

Hawk ducked, allowing the ripe globe to explode on the wall behind him. "I want to see Dragonfleet live. You must think of someone beyond yourself before we all go down with you!"

She watched him with sheer malevolence. "Which one was it? Trezanna or Catava? Or maybe my sweet little Qiaolin?"

"What?" He watched her shoulders, trying to guess from which direction she would attack next. Because she would attack. That much rage couldn't have been diffused in a single assault.

Her eyes blazed with incandescent jealousy. "Who got to you? Who did you sleep with?"

"You think that's what this is about? You believe me so petty?"

"Look at you! All dolled up in new clothes, smirking like a cat that got the cream. I've seen that look on you before." She prowled around the circular table toward him. "But it used to be me who caused it."

Hawk began a gradual retreat, staying a hundred and eighty degrees from her, shaking his head. "The only thing I've gotten from any of them is respect. They asked me to take them to our base, get them in and out safely. That I did." He was surprised to find his indifference to her had grown. "It actually felt good to work with people who believed in my abilities. Quite a change from your constant stream of trivial whining and blackmail."

Estrella's focus snap-shifted, as it often did when a conversation was not going her way. "So what else did you find at our base?" She tapped short, trimmed nails on the tabletop. "What's the situation?"

He breathed a little easier as she was diverted from her murderous thoughts. *That's why she was still in charge. She could at least grasp the important issues.* "The Arkosian leader is dead. His people were there, but several of their pursuit ships were blown as we escaped." He stepped even farther back. "Along with the main hangar."

"What!"

Hawk lied smoothly, leading her to think the Arkosians had done it to prevent the Philean ship from leaving. *Close enough.* She was unlikely to hear the truth, at least not until he could handle the consequences.

She growled. "Are the vermin removed from my base?"

"I don't know. Didn't stick around to find out. Too many casualties."

Her expression, always open like a child's, moved from outraged to thoughtful to vengeful to conniving, all in a few moments. "But that pig Marcand is dead. If that is so, and the below tunnels are still open, we could retake the base." She paced quickly between the table and the couch. "We still have ships. And pilots." She rubbed her forehead as she thought, as if it would stimulate her brain.

Hawk shook his head. "Strey, we only have seven ships here, and maybe fifty people. That's not going to—"

"How many did *you* take?" Estrella demanded, turning on him. "How many precious Solarii does it take to kill Marcand, hmm? One ship? And how many people? Four? Six?"

"That was different. There were other objectives."

She capitulated, almost too suddenly. "Of course you did. You accomplished them. You're right. I knew you would be valuable to the Solarii team." She smiled. "Now we have to decide how to turn that success to our advantage. If we get out of this damned jail, then we can get some ships armed and take our base back."

"Is that all you think about?" Hawk considered the hardships of the past days, the sacrifices so many made to reunite the groups. Estrella obviously considered only herself.

"What else is there? Catava and Trezanna can wail about their people and their fuzzy warm feelings all they want. Pirates won't respect that. The pirates will respect a strong leader who's got a firm grip on her base." Estrella came around the table. She laid her hand on his arm and looked up into his eyes. "You'll help me, won't you?"

She seemed so certain. He wasn't. His thoughts definitely ran more along the lines of replacing her, not helping her. He didn't answer right away. She seized on his silence, twisted it into mutiny.

"If you're not with me, then you're the enemy!" she cried, clutching at his throat.

Hawk felt his ties to her evaporate in the face of her senseless persistence, release washing over him and setting him free. This virago was no longer his only route to personal power. Grabbing her by the hair and the right arm, he spun her away from him, then captured her again, her back against his chest, his arm around her throat, tight, until she gasped for air.

"I'll let you go if you stop fighting me," Hawk said.

Instead, she continued to thrash and claw at him.

"Strey, I haven't betrayed you. But I won't see Dragonfleet destroyed. By the honor of my father, it *will* live. With or without you."

He shoved her away. She fell to the floor, choking.

"Get out!" she hissed.

Hawk stepped away, keeping his expression passive until he cleared the door. "After I get my things." He walked down to his room, others sharing a multitude of horror stories about Estrella's behavior during his absence. He just smiled, self-confidence building by the moment as he saw how they looked to him for guidance and leadership.

"Nothing I haven't heard or anticipated. But I expect things will be different around here. If you want them to be."

He studied them, seeing support in their eyes. Was that his answer?

The Queen is dead. Long Live the King.

* * *

MATTHEW Juri, a native Indunan guard, had watched the entire encounter on the monitor, his eyes glued to the fiery hellion who led Dragonfleet.

What a woman she was. Nothing like that chilly and aloof Trezanna Len. Estrella's personal charisma drew his attention, and he nearly violated his orders to enter when Hawk choked her. As Hawk left her on the floor, he focused the monitor on her, shocked to see there were actually tears on her face.

"Traitor, traitor!" Estrella pounded a small fist on the couch, then got to her feet and wiped her face angrily. "He's left me. They've all left me." She began to pace, her face set like stone, hugging herself tightly. "I don't need him. I don't need any of them!"

Juri's heart went out to her. He checked the time. Fifteen minutes before the end of shift, no one in sight, he opened the door, locking it behind him, and moved down the hall to the room where Estrella agonized.

"Ma'am? Are you all right?" This was the first time he had seen her in person. Facing her was a shock. She was so small. But power radiated from her bearing and her intense eyes.

She whirled around. "I thought you were not allowed to enter here."

Juri took a step back. "That's true, ma'am, and I don't mean to intrude, but I saw what happened, and I don't think it was right, ma'am."

He retreated toward the door, meaning to leave the room. She obviously didn't want him there.

A calculating smile crossed her lips so fast he was not sure he actually saw it. "That wasn't right, was it?" She came a little closer, glancing up at the monitors to the outside. "Hawk's left me now. He's been subverted by those damned Khimeyr. While my people have been attacked, now imprisoned, for nothing they've done." She looked up, vulnerable, hands open, palms toward him. "I'm so alone, Lieutenant."

This woman didn't deserve to be treated badly, no matter what she might have done before. She seemed no more dangerous than anyone else that had lost their home, or their normal lives.

"I'm not a lieutenant, ma'am," Juri said. "Just a corpsman."

She studied him. "Really? What a waste. Someone as talented at reading people as you? I think you deserve a promotion."

Juri's face grew hot, as he felt urges he knew he shouldn't. "I just wanted to see if you were all right."

"I'll be fine." Estrella walked around him, stopped between him and the monitor, and leaned closed to his ear. "I could use a man like you. One who wants to improve himself, one who will bend his orders to get a job done. Come see me when you're not on duty, Lieutenant."

The emphasis on the last word seemed very deliberate. Her warm breath on his earlobe gave him chills.

Nodding, Juri backed away. "You take care, ma'am."

He hurried back to his post before his replacement showed up, leaving the Dragonfleet leader with a mysterious smile.

CHAPTER 30

TREZANNA called the group to order, just as Dr. Eugene Boring scuttled into the conference room and handed her a folded piece of paper.

Thinking it was a patient update to share with the group, she opened it. *Keep in mind, my dear,* the note read, *all those ticking biological clocks among your staff and that of the Khimeyr. Plenty of new males in the mix now for all of you. A sprinkling of fresh DNA will strengthen both groups.*

Trezanna felt her brow furrow so deeply it pinched. *Seriously?* At this moment of crisis, when they gathered to decide a course of action against the pirates that would change all their lives, he was worried about baby-making?

Dr. Boring took a seat by the window. He smiled and gave her a small mocking salute, before turning his attention to a stack of papers in his hand.

With an exasperated sigh, she studied the faces of the others. Four days since the *Mercantile's* return, and most everyone recovered from the rescue effort.

Time to take action.

At the far end of the table, Julian tinkered with some machine part and a hotsod gun as Qiaolin watched, wrinkling her nose at the smell of burnt wire. Hawk paced along the far wall. A haggard-looking Stefan and a brooding Pomeroy leaned in almost identical positions against the wall, both holding cups of kafee. The others waited in various states of restlessness.

"The pirates are on our doorstep," Trezanna began. "They're well armed and dangerous. The destruction at Miramar reported by Hawk and Pomeroy was substantial. Even before our team got there."

"Let's cut to it," Pomeroy interrupted in a deep voice. "Do we go after 'em? Or wait 'til they come get us, eh?"

Trezanna saw Julian glance up and then back to his work, his fingers acquiring a slight tremble. Stefan had commended the young man on his conduct during the mission, but that twitch spoke volumes on how it had terrorized him. Qiao put a soft hand on Julian's arm and whispered in his ear.

"How long until Catava will be fit to fight?" Trezanna asked the doctor.

Dr. Boring shrugged. "Not easy to say. Her injuries, they are healing. Her spirit receives nursing from those close to her." He nodded to Stefan. "No sooner than a week."

"Could be dead by then, all of us." Pomeroy straightened, his feet spread a foot apart at parade rest. "I say we can't wait."

Trezanna checked her notes. "Data from Miramar showed that the Arkosians planned to transfer their forces to the surface at Dragonfleet before Stefan's mission interrupted them. We destroyed most of the ships they had landed there. And, at best estimate, removed their leader and a dozen men. Rumadan and Pomeroy then took out several more ships on the return trip." She consulted her pad. "Sensors showed more cruiser-size ships in outer orbit at Miramar."

"Not to mention what they left back on Prime," Stefan muttered, rubbing his eyes.

Trezanna thought he looked tired. He was keeping Catava's children while she recovered. Perhaps that was not going well.

"We sending scouts?" Winston asked, rubbing his unshaven face. "I'd volunteer."

Stefan raised a hand. "I could make a run home and see what's up. My da has regular commerce with the Arkosians, you know."

"I would not be surprised if he has more than that." Rumadan leaned forward in her chair, ears twitching. "A Philean ship fired on the pirates. I trust you figured that into your calculations."

All eyes turning to him, Stefan stiffened. "They wouldn't dare."

"On the contrary, Master Ciro, I believe they would dare quite a lot." With a muted growl, Rumadan settled back in her chair.

One of the advantages of using the *Mercantile* had been that it was familiar to the Arkosians. Perhaps they should have focused more on the corollary. Easily identifiable, the ship could be traced back to the Philean Waypass.

"We will warn your father immediately," Trezanna said.

"I've got to go!" Stefan bolted for the door.

A moment of shocked silence followed, and then Hawk and Pomeroy followed on Stefan's heels.

Trezanna hesitated long enough to turn the meeting over to Chase Austin, and she hurried after them. "How can we help?" she asked.

"Call 'em ahead, no doubt. Don't want to walk into some ambush."

Pomeroy tried to keep pace, but Stefan was far ahead of them.

"We'll do that," Trezanna managed, as she ran with him. "Can I send someone with you? How many ships do you want?"

"We'll move quicker with less. Do I have your permission to draft who I need?"

Trezanna felt her breath coming harder and faster, as she tried to keep up. "We owe this young man," she said as the hangar came into view. "We should assist him in any way possible."

"Hawk and I'll be right with him. You go make that call."

Pomeroy punched Hawk lightly in the shoulder. Then two of them took off in a run after Stefan.

Trezanna stopped to catch her breath, praying Stefan would find his family spared.

In a moment, she headed for the command center to place a call. She needed to assess Arkosian strength in the sector. Spread thin over two bases of operation with a leader dead and the loss of all they had begun at Miramar, it might be possible to beat them.

* * *

POMEROY burst through the swinging doors into the hangar bay, Hawk right behind him.

"Ciro!" he called. Then he spied Stefan climbing into the hatch of the *Mercantile*. "There!"

With Hawk at his heels, Pomeroy came up the ramp into the cargo hold, where Stefan chunked large tubs from one side of the hold to the other, obviously looking for something.

Pomeroy and Hawk exchanged looks, as Stefan hurled empty tubs.

"I can't believe what an idiot I am," Stefan mumbled. "Didn't even think what might happen, brain all in my pants. Mayhap I can trade myself for all of them back home."

"Hold on now, friend," Hawk said. "What are you doing?"

"Had some heavy weaponry in here." The young man's face was drawn with worry. "I don't want to land at the Waypass with nothing but my personal equipment in my hand."

"Actually, me boy," Pomeroy said, shaking his head, "I don't think you can land there at all."

"What do you mean? You can't tell me I'm not going, because I am!"

"Oh, we're going, all right. But not in this boat. They'll be watching for it a parsec away and we'll be space dust afore you know it." He glanced out the open hatch and nodded. "Be right back."

Pomeroy exited the ship and crossed the open bay to the *Karma's Revenge*. He banged on its metal hull, waiting for its pilot. "Piper?"

The girl stuck her head out from under the engine cover, her long hair tucked up in a knitted cap. When she saw him, her eyes took on a twinkle. "Yeah?"

"I see Julian has you all fixed up here." He looked over the hull, remembering the near-wreck it had been on her arrival. Now the brassy bird seemed shiny and serviceable.

"What do you want?"

Pomeroy grinned at her directness. "Your ship."

"Oh, really?" Piper swung down gracefully out of the engine hold. "What makes you think I'd give you that?"

Pomeroy shrugged and glanced over at the *Mercantile*. "Fact that you said the pirates shot you up. We're going scouting, and there might be some chance to shoot back. Thought you might be interested."

Her face lit up. "I can go? I mean, you want me to? Seriously?" She began shrugging out of her work coveralls.

"Wouldn't have asked otherwise. Get her hot, and I'll get the others." Pomeroy waved to the engineering crew to fuel up the *Revenge*. Then he loped back to *Mercantile* while Piper fired up her pre-launch. "All right, mates, it's time to go."

"Go where in what?" Stefan asked. Suspicion flavored his voice like a hint of smoke.

"Piper's agreed to take us. Same theory you had. Different ship, less likely to get blown out of the sky at first glance."

Stefan stalled, thinking, but then shrugged. "Could work, I guess." He tossed Hawk several laser rifles with straps. The Dragonfleet officer hung them over his shoulder, and tucked a hand weapon from an open box at his feet into his belt, too.

Pomeroy eyed the box of weapons. "What's all this?"

Stefan eyed him like he was a fool "Something to shoot with. You want some or not?"

Pomeroy doubted they would have the chance to use any of this. A ship-to-ship battle with the Arkosians was much more likely. All the same, he took three, and put them into a worn green knapsack he took off the wall. "Let's fly."

Hawk, halfway up the plank into Piper's ship, turned to see if the others were coming. Pomeroy waved him on. Stefan dragging alongside him, his brow clouded with brooding preoccupation.

Pomeroy leaned close. "If you chase two rabbits, both will escape."

Stefan blinked. "Rabbits?"

"Focus, mate," Pomeroy said. "Focus."

He guided Stefan into the *Karma's Revenge*. Then appropriated the tactical console, while Hawk took over engineering.

"Coupla changes I want to make. You mind, Piper?" Pomeroy already had the cover off the panel of his console, knowing the girl was too far gone in her launch sequence to come stop him.

Piper growled and turned back to her instruments. "You best not break or degrade anything."

"Nah, you'll be better than ever, sweetkins." Taking a seat on the floor in front of the console, Pomeroy removed a handful of wires and chips. Then he pulled some mem-units from his pocket and tucked them in before reassembling the whole panel. Slapping the cover back on, he grinned and crawled into his seat as Piper lifted off. "Now we'll be able to see 'em coming a long way."

"What's the co-ords for the station, Stefan?" Piper asked.

Stefan watched out the front port, a sigh leaving him as he told her. Guilt accumulated like the clouds of a sandstorm on the young man's countenance. He needed something to do.

"Ciro, make us a map, eh?" Pomeroy gestured to Hawk to hand Stefan a datapad and stylus. "Layout of the station, floor plan, whatever, so we've got some familiarity before we arrive."

Stefan took the instruments, his movements almost dreamlike, and he began to sketch. Pomeroy studied him, hoping he would pull himself together by the time they arrived. The success of this mission might depend on it.

Working off Stefan's coordinates, the *Karma's Revenge* made the hour-long hyper-jump and flight with no troubles. Even when they arrived in Philean space, they found no sign of the pirates, even at the farthest reaches of their scanning capability.

"Something's wrong." Stefan frowned, coming forward to stare at the blinking indicators on the instrument panel. "No one's hailed us."

Piper lifted her slim shoulders in a shrug. "We didn't hail them, either. If they've been under attack, they may not want to be waving flags, you know." She flicked on the com and requested permission from the Waypass station to land.

Static flared into the speakers, a voice behind it fading with every fourth or fifth word. "Roger, *Karma's Rev*…landing…thorized in sector 2-3." A map flashed on the com monitor, a blinking indicator showing the designated spot.

"Understood, Waypass station. Thanks." Piper cut her transmission. "Sound all right?"

Stefan's eyes narrowed. "I don't recognize the voice. But it was hard to tell."

Pomeroy felt an itch on his lower back, the one he got when things were about to go south. But there was nothing solid to go. *Balls to the wall, then.* "Looks good to me. Take her down."

Hawk started to gather the weapons he brought, but stopped, concerned, as he watched Piper bring the *Revenge* in to the coordinates they were given. His frown deepened. "Not here."

Pomeroy leaned forward to get a look out the window. The open space in which they had been directed to park was near the buildings. One other ship in sight, showing no activity. But Hawk was right. They would be in a clear line of fire from anyone inside, and if anyone else landed they stood a chance of getting boxed in. "Right. Over there." He directed Piper to an open space on the edge of the tarmac. They might be exposed a little longer crossing the field on the in-and-out, but if it was a trap, at least there was an escape route now.

As the ship powered down, all eyes gravitated to Stefan. Pale but determined, Stefan grabbed the barrel of his own gun and led them out. They made it across the tarmac without incident, but Pomeroy couldn't shake the feeling that everything was too quiet. Even the birds perched in the trees surrounding the broad buildings were silent.

Inside, indications were even stronger.

Their footsteps echoed in the empty halls. Lights flickered, as if the connections were loose, giving the hall an eerie appearance. "There's usually dozens of people walking through here," Stefan whispered, clearly spooked.

Guns at the ready, Pomeroy split them into two teams, Hawk with Piper and Stefan with him. "You take left, we'll take right, and we'll meet up in the lobby, right? See who finds the welcome mat first."

"You got it," Hawk said.

"Remember, these are my kin," Stefan warned. "Don't be shooting anything that moves!"

"Don't worry, my friend. I'll keep Piper under control." Hawk grinned and avoided Piper's irritated elbow aimed at his ribs. "Come on, gal. Let's go sting us some pirates."

Pomeroy watched a moment as the others took the opposite hall, then let Stefan lead the way. "Maybe my da's hunkered down in his office," Stefan said. "Least the whiskey's there."

Pomeroy clapped the young man on the shoulder. "Now there's the spirit. We'll have one with him, right enough."

The lights were on in the room Stefan indicated as the senior Ciro's office. Pomeroy drew close to the wall, and then moved along it until he reached the door. He counted to three, and then whirled around the corner, laser pointing from side to side in the office.

It was empty.

"Pop?" Stefan followed Pomeroy in and gave a little gasp.

The desk was partially cleared, but paperwork that must have been stacked on it now cluttered the chair and the floor.

"Someone's been through all that, looks like." Pomeroy checked the closets and the back entrance to the office. "He keep anything valuable here? Certificates, papers, securities?"

"I suppose." Stefan's eyes were focused on a small 3-D holo on the desk, a picture of a couple of boys and a pretty dark-haired woman. It was undamaged, but sitting in a clabbered brown pool that appeared to be dried blood.

Pomeroy saw what he was looking at and frowned. "Come on, kid. Let's see who we can find." He pulled him, stumbling, away from the desk and back out into the hall. "Now how many people are supposed to be about?" When a dazed Stefan just mumbled a response, he took his arm and shook him. "Stefan! You have four lives depending on you now, maybe more. Don't you dare fade on me!"

Stefan blinked, visibly holding off some sort of breakdown. "I'm sorry. It just—wait a minute." He pulled away from Pomeroy and dashed back into the office. He grabbed the holo, deactivating it, and then tucked it into his pocket. When he came back out, he took a deep shuddering breath and shouldered his weapon. "If there's a gathering, it'd be in the dining hall. Biggest room we have."

Pomeroy nodded. "Show me the way."

As they approached what Stefan said was the center of the complex, they found the halls strewn with debris, boxes, chairs, emptied drawers. The lights were out in scattered sections of the corridors, making progress treacherous.

"Bloody hell." Pomeroy turned the corner and walked up to a hole in the plascrete wall at least eight meters across with chunks of building material all around it. "What could have done this?"

Stefan inspected the jagged edges of the hole. "Talwyran cannon." He nodded. "My father did this."

Pomeroy raised an eyebrow. "Your father? Blew up his own bloody hallway?"

Crouching down, Stefan pointed at some blue liquid under one of the lumps of rock. "To kill this? Yes."

"What's that?"

"What's left of a flatfid." Stefan's face was hard. "It's a tracking animal the Arkosians import from the Galtaran sector. Vicious thing with teeth that'll rip through cowhide jackets." He stood up, looking at the hole. "It's worth the repairs to take one out."

"Think there's more?" Pomeroy reached for his com-unit.

Stefan shrugged. "Could be." He brightened a little. "But a flatfid wouldn't track something that wasn't alive." He pointed down the lighted hall to the right. "The dining area's that way."

Pomeroy stole another look at the damage and then called Hawk and Piper to warn them to watch out for such a creature.

It was bad enough dealing with bloody pirates. No one warned him about rampant wildlife.

But maybe Stefan had a point. Time to find survivors.

CHAPTER 31

WITH soft booted steps, Piper followed Hawk down the hall, keeping an eye behind them for stragglers.

She'd had enough of the pirates, who had used the *Karma's Revenge* for a dartboard. *Let them show themselves.*

Charred evidence of laser fire scarred the walls. They picked their way through debris that showed the aftermath of battle. Remembering Ciro claimed a thousand people or more populated the station at any one time, it was eerie to see no sign of life. This odd echoing silence just pricked her nerves.

She also felt a little awkward partnered with Hawk. This man held the future of her relationship with her mother in his hands. Did he have the promised conversation with Trezanna yet? She watched Hawk's back, pondering how to ask him.

Several late nights Piper spent castigating herself for her years of blind hatred of Trezanna. *I should have known.* No matter what his motives, re-defining her father as a liar was a struggle, but that at least was a personal matter. Estrella's plan to send Piper to destroy her mother and the Solarii, feeding into that hatred Piper's father started, that was something else. She loathed even the thought of Hawk revealing her secret. What would Trezanna say when she knew?

A large crash sounded ahead, clanging like a stack of metal boxes falling over. Hawk waved her back against the wall. Piper checked her weapon for the third time, making sure it was fully charged. The Dragonfleet officer stepped forward, laser rifle pointed in the same direction.

"Who's there?" Hawk shouted, and then ducked back.

The answer was a patter of footsteps headed in the opposite direction and a baby's cry.

"That must be some of Stefan's people!" Piper hissed.

Hawk nodded and motioned her forward. Whoever ran ahead continued to make noise in their quest to find safety, and the pair moved ahead, tracking them.

"When we catch up, you talk to them," Hawk said. "We'll explain we're with Stefan."

His words were cut short as a rope sprung taut, catching them across the knees. Both were knocked from their feet and surrounded by four men in rugged, earth-toned wool jackets and pants and muslin shirts. Piper struggled up, only to have a young man with Stefan's hazel eyes and black hair grab her and point his weapon at her head. She felt like an idiot. Had they really been stupid enough to fall for a trick like that?

"Be wary, trespasser," the oldest of the men cautioned, as Hawk reached for his weapon. "One more death here shall hurt us in no way."

Hawk handed over his rifle without protest. "We have no quarrel with you. If you're people of the Waypass station, sir, we're here with Stefan Ciro. We came to help."

The man holding Piper gasped. "Stefan? He's here?"

"Silence!" the first man barked. He looked over the two of them, his gun never wavering. "Who are you, then?"

Piper choked back the sharp response that first came to her, trying to be more diplomatic. "We're from the Solarii base. Stefan brought us to help with the pirates."

The man holding Piper trembled.

"Stefan was very concerned for his family," she offered.

A third man spat on the floor. "So concerned he led the cursed Arkosians right to us!"

"Hush!" the leader ordered. "Where is he now?"

Hawk shrugged. "We split up just outside the hangar wing. We're supposed to rendezvous with him at the central core."

The leader nodded. "Would make sense." He looked both ways down the hall. "Bring them," he ordered to his men and then stalked away.

The young man holding Piper pulled her along after him.

"Hey, be careful," she grumbled. "You're hurting me."

He held her tight, as they maneuvered around some of the rubble. "Lot of people hurt today."

"Stefan's father?" she asked softly.

"My father is dead."

The flat tone of his voice ended her questions. She went along, trying to make it easy for him. She couldn't remember if Stefan had ever shared his brother's name, or she would have tried to be friendlier.

"There more of you alive, then?" Hawk asked.

One of the other men nodded.

"Children apparently." Hawk smiled. "Glad to hear it."

The leader stopped at an open doorway and flipped on the lights. The room appeared to be some sort of communal dining area, but most of the tables were shoved askew. He ordered Piper and Hawk seated on a table in the middle of the room. Then he and the others moved into concealed positions near the door, weapons still trained on the two who sat exposed, weaponless and in bright light.

"Are the pirates still here?" Hawk asked.

Piper couldn't see beyond the room where they sat, the hallways outside dark. Just Hawk and Piper, clearly set out as targets. Who were they bait for, that was what she wanted to know. Hawk moved restlessly on the table beside her.

The leader shrugged. "We haven't heard them for the last two hours or so. I figure they're hiding here someplace." The gray-haired man pulled back behind the doorframe and eyed the door on the other side of the dining hall.

"Two hours?" Piper frowned. "That's about when we would have come into range."

Hawk looked at her, eyes glittering with realization. "They knew it. They pulled back, waiting. This is a trap."

Piper slipped off the table. "We've got to tell Stefan." A laser blast that practically singed her hair made her scoot back up quickly. She glared at the Phileans. "Look, the Arkosians aren't done here. They were just waiting for Stefan! We have to get out of here, all of us!"

The younger Ciro eyed the leader. "You think that's true, Enoch?"

The man's brow furrowed and he chewed his lower lip. "Could be a trick here, too. We don't know who these people are or how they got here. Maybe the pirates sent 'em."

A large clatter sounded behind Piper, immediately followed by the door on the far side of the room swinging open. As the Waypass crew aimed at the movement, Piper allowed instinct to take over. She rolled backward off the table and ducked underneath when she hit the floor.

Hawk did the same. "Pom, it's a trap!"

The door swung closed again amid muffled shouts. Someone in the Waypass group aimed for the table over their heads, and it split in two, hit with a laser blast. As the wood splintered, Piper cursed and scrambled under the next table.

Hawk scrambled toward the door instead. "Piper! C'mon!"

Enoch and Stefan's brother ran for the door, cutting them off.

The third man, limping, grabbed Piper by the hair, making her scream with the sudden pain. "Someone will pay for what's happened here, witch!"

Hawk raised his hands and backed up to the window.

Piper hoped the team would see him before the shooting started again. She, meanwhile, had enough. Tears in her eyes from the force with which the man pulled at her scalp, she grabbed the wrist that held her hair and bent at the waist, tucking herself small and yanking that arm forward. The man flipped over her, but he didn't let go. She fell with him. The wrist twisted in her grasp as he hit the ground and she felt it snap. He released her with a yell.

Before he could move, she grabbed his gun and knelt across him. She held the weapon to his head.

"I think someone needs to teach you manners," Piper said, no hint of humor in her voice.

From the corner of her eye, Piper saw Hawk lunge for one of the others. He took a weapon and swung the barrel in their direction.

"Drop your weapons," he ordered.

As Enoch hesitated, the door opened again and Stefan and Pomeroy rushed in, adding their potential firepower to Hawk's.

Stefan's eyes opened wide as he saw his brother. "Brandon!"

Getting up, Piper moved away from the fallen man and closer to her companions. Brandon dropped the barrel of his gun and started for Stefan, but the elder man grabbed his arm and pulled him back.

"Enoch?" Stefan looked from one to the other. "Where's my father?"

"You killed him." Face cold and eyes hard, Enoch stood firm.

Stefan faltered and took a step back, his eyes widening in shock. "Pop? No."

Pomeroy put a hand on Stefan's shoulder. "Buck up, son. Mayhap none knows the whole story here."

"He didn't do it intentionally. He couldn't have." Brandon shrugged off the elder's hand and went to embrace his brother. "It's not his fault."

"Bran, I'm sorry," Stefan said. Tears spilled from his eyes. His brother clung to him, shoulders shaking.

The Phileans, still angry, murmured among themselves as they tended to their fellow's broken wrist.

Hawk sidled over to Pomeroy. "More bad news. The Arkosians were here. Pulled out about the time we got into range. Odds on they're just waiting 'til we get comfortable before they make a return engagement."

Pomeroy frowned and looked at the other men. "How many refugees are here?"

Enoch set his weapon aside. "We've saved most of the people. Many of the women and children are down in the tunnels. But we easily lost thirty men today, including Yanoro, two of his brothers, other friends."

"We can take some. We can provide cover for another ship to escape if it will carry you all."

"We shouldn't have to *escape* our homes!" The injured man was outraged. "If the idiot boy hadn't provoked the accursed pirates, his father would be alive and so would my brother!"

Stefan, stricken, closed his eyes and turned away.

"Stefan led an impossible rescue mission that saved a man and gained us information on the pirates which can help defend us all," Piper said, her temper sizzling. "How do you know they wouldn't have turned on you anyway? They're *pirates*, for Lara's sake! Murderers and thieves! Maybe it did come sooner because of what Stefan did, but don't condemn him for it!"

Enoch's face didn't change. "He will live with the consequences on his soul."

When Piper would have started again, Pomeroy waved her into silence. "Do you want our help or not? We're willing to defend you against the pirates, or evacuate you into safety. Your choice." He stared down the old man until Enoch looked away.

Brandon looked around at the destruction and sighed. "We can't leave here, Stefan. Father would have wanted the station to remain."

"I know he would." Stefan looked at the other Phileans. "I guess we make a stand."

"No." Enoch raised his weapon again. "You leave. All of you. Or we'll kill you where you stand."

Hawk raised an eyebrow. "Excuse me?"

"You have five minutes to make your ship." Enoch looked at the chrono on the wall. He stalked over to grab a pack on the floor near Pomeroy's feet and shoved it into his arms, yanking on the front of his jacket. "Take your crap and go."

Stefan blinked, confused.

Enoch shot into the ceiling, plascrete chips littering them like snow. "Go."

Pomeroy shouldered the pack without comment, and then pulled Piper behind him and out the door. "You heard the man."

Hawk protested, but Pomeroy ordered him out as well. "The man's right. Nothing we can do here. The Waypass is an independent place. Can't harbor a criminal like young Stefan here if they want to survive. Ain't that right, friend?" He turned to Enoch.

"Don't want the pirates knowing we gave him aid and comfort." The man's cold gaze flickered for an instant as he looked at Stefan's stricken face. His head gestured in the direction of a mounted camera near the door.

Piper realized Pomeroy called this one correctly. The pirates could be monitoring them right now and the Waypass folks needed this to look good. She felt sad for Stefan and his brother. The two of them locked in a pained stare as they, too, realized that to save Brandon, Stefan must leave him.

A long moment of silence and the loaded glances they exchanged said much more than words. Finally, Stefan stepped away from them, raising his weapon.

"So that's the thanks I get for what we did? Then the hell with all of you! I should never have come back here."

Enoch nodded slowly, his gun swinging slowly to aim at them, too. "You shouldn't have come here. You've betrayed us all. The next shot is for you. Get out, now."

Hawk, prodded into action by the threat, started away, down the hall. Pomeroy kept himself between Enoch and Piper. "Go on, now, girl," he said.

Even as she followed Hawk, she couldn't take her eyes off the scene, watching Stefan as he backed away from the others, his brother frozen with his hand held out to Stefan, but unable to follow him. When Stefan would have tripped, Pomeroy grabbed his arm and pulled him down the hall.

"We've got to run," Pomeroy warned. And they did.

Piper scanned the air above them as they hit the door, but saw nothing. The four of them sprinted across the tarmac toward the *Revenge*, footfalls echoing against the sides of the concrete buildings. All of a sudden, the birds flew up from the trees around the compound in a huge flapping of wings, the air filled with the sound of panicked squawks. Piper turned to look over her shoulder and spotted the first Arkosian ship, coming in low over the horizon.

"Go! Go!" Pomeroy hurried them across the last fifty feet, dragging the hatch open.

Piper headed for the flight deck, Hawk right after her. Pomeroy pulled Stefan up the last few feet, and then secured the hatch.

"Get us out of here now!" Pomeroy yelled.

Piper forced a cold start, as fiery blasts hit the ground around them. The *Revenge* started to roll, picking up speed. The motion dropped Stefan, still in shock, into a seat. Pomeroy marched up behind the pilot's chair and grabbed an overhead strut for balance. Piper winced as the barrage continued.

"Hawk, get the damned shields up!" she called.

"Shields up, full," Hawk called from his seat a few seconds later.

Pomeroy muttered. "We're gonna get it from both sides anytime now, gal. The Phileans are going to make this look good." He tapped Hawk on the shoulder. "Protect the ass end, boyo. Otherwise, we're gonna have a torpedo enema!"

"Like hell they're shooting up my bird again," Piper muttered. She careened into a wide-angle ascent, slicing a curve through the air toward the approaching vessels.

"What are you doing, miss? Trying to get us fragged?"

"Just watch and learn, old man." Piper pulled across the path of the incoming pirates. The missiles from the base passed by, taking out the frontrunner of the pirate wing.

"Piper, don't be too clever here," Pomeroy warned. "They've got a point to make."

She squelched a surge of inner rebellion and glanced at Stefan. "Aye, sir. Leaving Waypass sector."

Heading for Solarii space, Piper kicked the ship into hyperdrive. The sleek bird easily outdistanced the cruisers, and they were gone.

* * *

STEFAN sat in the chair where Pomeroy placed him, numb. He didn't speak. There was nothing to say. His impulse-driven stunt to save Monty Winston cost him in ways he never thought through, the same way he always did, the same way his father often scolded him for. This time his carelessness came home. His home.

Piper tried to jolly him up when they arrived back at the station, but he could only think of his father's empty office, his brother's wounded eyes. Pomeroy, his worn face knotted with nerves, ordered Piper to cart Stefan along to the infirmary. She spoke with the doctor a few moments, and then left Stefan with him.

The doctor took Stefan's arm and smiled. "Come sit down. Tell me." He led the young man to a chair in his office. Setting out some kafee for them both, he took a seat behind the desk.

Stefan stared for a few minutes, and then reached for the kafee, though he just let his fingers touch the warm china. He didn't want a drink. At least not this kind. "My father is dead."

The doctor nodded. "This I am told."

"They chased me away with guns. From my own home." Stefan's eyes were dark gold, haunted. His fingers twitched. He nearly spilled the hot drink in his cup. He put his hands in his lap, but they seemed to take on a life of their own. They would not rest, his fingers moving helplessly.

"Many losses, all a part of the one. But such we expect in troubled times." The doctor drank his own kafee, waiting, watching. "The ones who are gone, you cannot bring back." He nodded his head toward the other room. "The ones who are still here, those you can help."

Stefan stared for a moment. How could he have forgotten the other casualties on his conscience? "How is she?"

"She improves. She asked for you not so long ago."

"She did?" Catava was awake? Speaking? Not dying? The rush of hope overflowed his heart. He got to his feet, shoving the cup aside, spilling its contents. "Oh! I'm sorry." He looked for something with which to wipe up the mess.

The doctor chuckled. "I can get this. Go to her. She needs you now."

Stefan, guilt sucking at his mid-section, bowed and barely managed a "Thank you, Doctor!" before he headed for the row of sickbeds. They had moved her from the iso-room to the last of the row. Cat was asleep, the light shining down on her face like that of an angel, Stefan thought as he approached the bed. He just stood there, staring at her, studying the depths of her breaths. Over the past few days she regained the faint pink glow to her cheeks. She would survive. Even with all else going up in flames around him, he held that fact close.

As if in response to his gaze, her aquamarine eyes fluttered open and she looked up at him, first without recognition and then a sharp awareness. "Stefan!"

He reached for her hand. "You look beautiful."

Catava took his hand, her fingers cool in his. "I'm told I'm improving. Qiao said you were taking good care of the children." She gingerly propped a white-jacketed pillow behind her.

"That's good." He just realized that he had left base without making arrangements for the children. Surely, Qiao had looked after them. He couldn't stand it if his half-cocked actions contributed to harm coming to anyone else. Had his actions not caused enough destruction?

"What's happened? You're upset." Catava pinned him with a look that warned him she would recognize any deception.

"I've managed to get just about everyone I care for killed, or nearly so, in the last week," he said, feeling his throat choke up again, threatening not to let his words escape. Struggling to contain his emotion, he shook his head. "My father, he's…."

Catava touched him on the shoulder. "Tell, me, Stefan. It's all right."

The contact with her fingertips tingled like an electric current. Some nerve deep inside reverberated in echoing sorrow. "Gone. He's *gone.*" Pain, guilt, and emptiness erupted in deep ebbing sobs, as he told her the whole story. "They made me leave. I'll never see him again. Or my brother. Or my home."

He felt guilty even talking about his own problems with her lying there in a bed. He whispered an apology and pushed himself away from her. "I'm sorry. I shouldn't burden you with my mistakes. You have so many important things."

Catava took him by the shoulders, looking into his eyes. "Don't be sorry. Be yourself with me."

"Myself? Who am I? No one. I'm alone. I have no home, no family. I very nearly didn't have you."

"Hush now." She gathered him to her like she would Chad, as if he had a skinned knee rather than a broken heart. "You're not alone."

He felt so safe in her arms. He prayed she would never let him go. But he still felt ashamed that he was the one who had placed her in danger and then failed to protect her. He wasn't ready yet.

"Thank you for understanding." Disentangling himself, he took a towel off the end of the bed, wiped his face, and then ran a hand through his hair. He cleared his throat. "I thought we were talking about you."

The way she watched him, he knew she could read him, knew that he created distance between them on purpose. Her tone when she replied was much lighter, almost teasing.

"Yes, it is all about me." The soft touch of her hand reassured him. "Trezanna was in earlier. I can see we'll need all the warm bodies we can when it comes time to deal with the Arkosians. So I'm busting out of this place no later than tomorrow."

"That would be wonderful," he said. In his mind's eye, he saw a picture of her quarters as he had left them. For the last several days the children ran wild through the rooms, making it look every bit as ravaged as the Waypass station. Maybe he could hire a cleaning crew.

He sighed. "Just take your time."

CHAPTER 32

HAWK trailed after Pomeroy on the way down to debrief with Trezanna, something nagging at him.

"Hey, Dare?"

Pomeroy grunted in response and held the door for Hawk to enter the corridor to the conference room.

"What did that Enoch fellow give you when we left the Waypass?" Hawk asked.

"Hmm?" Pomeroy shrugged. "Naught in that sack but some dusty old data disks. No clue what they might be."

Hawk held out his hand. "Can I see them?"

Pomeroy gave them to Hawk, but no label or marking on their outward appearance hinted at what they might hold. He would have to play them to figure it out.

Slipping past Rumadan into the conference room, Hawk told Len where they got the disks and asked permission to check them in the computer. She agreed, and came to stand next to him as he inserted the first one.

"Marus, scan disk," Trezanna said. The blue screen blinked a couple of times and then started scrolling memorandums, communiqués and specifications almost faster than they could be seen.

She frowned. "Marus, review data and restart at beginning. Run at half speed." She beckoned to the Solarii engineer. "Julian, can you make sense of this?"

With some device in hand, Julian wandered over and studied the screen as the replay began. After a minute, his jaw snapped shut. "Great gods of the heavens, do you know what this is?"

Pomeroy gave a deadpan look. "No, that's why we asked you to look at it."

Julian's face broke into a grin. "These are the parameters of the Arkosian pirate ranks." He pointed out each category as it appeared. "Ship count, troop strength, weapons allotments." He shook his head. "Incredible. This gives us the battle. Where did we get it?"

Hawk studied the information, wondering how many lives had paid for this information. But he agreed with Julian. This could put the pirates out once and for all. The Phileans had come through for them. He would have to let Stefan know.

This also signified that a sector without pirate raiders, a sector of peace was now possible. What did that mean for Hawk himself and the potential for him to lead Dragonfleet?

The buzz that broke out in the room at Julian's excited utterance covered Pomeroy's explanation, which led only to more, louder questions. Rumadan finally asked Julian to project the data onto one of the big screens so they could all see it.

When it finished, Pomeroy nodded with satisfaction. "Glad it was something special. It cost that lad plenty."

Trezanna asked Pomeroy to share an account of their visit to the Waypass. As the others listened, sympathy for Stefan bubbled up in the room. Trezanna assured them that the Solarii would stand with Stefan, since he couldn't stand with his own people.

"Stefan has suffered a great loss and we will support him, as he supported us in our time of need. We must remember this is war. Each of us may be asked to sacrifice for the good of the whole. None of you have failed to make us proud to date."

Qiao cleared her throat. "Just because we have this information doesn't mean we should head out to attack them. We still have plenty of organizational problems to clear up before we are strong enough."

"I agree with Qiao," Julian said. "We're slowly getting the ships up to par, and we're fitting them with the new weapons Vanyakin has provided as quickly as we can." He looked at Trezanna. "But you're going to have to do something about Dragonfleet."

"That's why we brought them here," Trezanna said, glancing at Hawk. "But it's a touchy issue."

If Hawk could show her there was an alternative to Estrella, perhaps Dragonfleet would survive. "Trezanna, I have some suggestions in that area to discuss with you. In a more private setting."

Trezanna agreed to speak with him after the meeting. She assigned Julian the task of sorting through the new data with Piper, Qiaolin and Winston to assist him. Dr. Boring announced that Catava would make a full recovery, news brought a round of cheers. Then she dismissed everyone but Hawk.

As the others went about their business, Hawk poured a glass of ice water from a clear pitcher. He had to approach this just right. He would likely have only this one chance to solidify his position, to launch himself into command of those with whom he previously served. His foot tapped nervously, as he chose his words.

Trezanna Len took a seat at the table and looked up at him. "Mr. Kenton, you have something to say?"

"Yes, Miss Len, I do. I know you don't have much reason to trust me. But you have." He looked her in the eye. "I appreciate that."

"Pomeroy trusted you." Trezanna gave him a slight smile. "I trusted *him*."

She had him there. A sheepish grin crept onto his lips, almost embarrassed to be seen. "I want to live up to your trust, ma'am." He took a seat, so they were on the same level. *Here goes nothing.* "Piper Donovan didn't return here by accident."

Trezanna stiffened. "What do you mean?"

"Estrella sent her here to finish the Solarii." Hawk shifted in his chair, hoping for a more comfortable position. "Once Estrella found out she was your daughter, she did everything she could to turn her against you and use her as a weapon."

Trezanna's fingertips tapped the table with staccato rhythm. "But Piper hasn't done anything of the kind. That I know of."

"No, ma'am. Piper came to me the other day, that day in the lounge when you saw us together, remember? She told me she no longer wanted to be part of Estrella's plan. Now that she is here and has gotten the chance to know you, she condemned Estrella and wanted nothing more than to be allowed to continue here, to re-establish your relationship."

Well, at least that part of it was true.

"I took it upon myself to tell you about this, since Piper felt so badly about it." Hawk studied Piper's mother. "Please, ma'am, I wish you wouldn't say anything to her. She's hardly slept nights, worrying you'd find out. It's caused her enough pain. I just thought you should know Estrella's been plotting against you from the get-go."

Trezanna nodded slowly. "Thank you." Her expression far from pleasant, he imagined she was contemplating what revenge she could take. "What shall we do with Estrella then?"

Hawk gave his best smile. Now came the hard sell. "Listen, ma'am, I know many Dragonfleet officers are of a mind to try an alliance with the Solarii and Khimeyr, but Estrella has refused. Even though she's made it look like she's collaborating, I know that woman doesn't have a cooperative bone in her body. I have the pledge of the others that they would follow me, were I the recognized leader of Dragonfleet." He paused a moment to let that sink in. "If Estrella is the impediment to true progress and unity, then she needs to be removed."

"Removed?" The Solarii administrator pursed her lips, her tone surprised as much as anything. "Shall we just take her out back and shoot her?"

Hawk knew that would have been an acceptable solution at Miramar. But here, they liked to believe they were more civilized and genteel. He managed a laugh. "Of course not. Better that she could be confined where she won't hurt anyone for awhile, until she sees the futility of continued rebellion."

A long silence followed, during which he could almost see the thoughts racing through Trezanna's mind.

Suddenly, she got to her feet. "I'll have to discuss the matter with Catava once she's recovered. After we've talked, I'll let you know, Mr. Kenton."

He stood and walked with her to the door. "Thank you for hearing me out."

"Thank you for being honest with me." Trezanna opened the door to see Piper waiting outside.

"Trezanna, I was just wondering if—" Piper stopped mid-sentence, her now wide-eyed gaze fixed on Hawk. "It's nothing really. Just wanted to make sure you were all right." She darted forward to give her mother a hug and then disappeared down the hall.

"You see," Hawk said softly. "Poor girl. I wouldn't want to be in her shoes."

"We'll deal with Estrella," Trezanna said, her jaw set tight. "Leave that in my hands."

* * *

ESTRELLA lazily traced a light design on the cheek of Matthew Juri, as they lay side by side on the bed in her quarters.

Juri was the one she needed. She was impressed with both his ability to short-circuit the security holograms to hide his presence here as well as with his enthusiasm and stamina in her bed.

Like Hawk, in the beginning.

"When do you think we can go, love?" Estrella said softly to the drowsing Juri.

"Tonight." He smiled, eyes still closed. "I've found a ship you can use to escape, just off the end of the regular field. It's not the best, but it's space-worthy."

Estrella smiled, the expression first icy, then warming as his eyes opened. It would not do to let him suspect she was using him. "Yes, that will do just fine. You have been very clever."

He looked at her. "It is only what you deserve. A woman like you should be free, not caged like a pet harstral." He touched her face. "It is my honor to serve you."

"It is," she said. She left the bed, pulling her uniform on roughly. "There is much to do before the evening. I shall have my people at the rear entrance. You are sure you can disable the alarm on the door?"

"Yes, ma'am. The security grid has been altered and a timer set."

Laughing wildly, she leaped on the bed and kissed him hard. "You shall be rewarded for your vision, Matthew. Rewards beyond your wildest dreams." She sprang back off the bed and went to the other room to make her preparations, leaving Juri to recover his clothes.

* * *

CATAVA returned to the Khimeyr wing the next day.

She moved slowly, leaning on Stefan's arm. Her wounds needed more healing time, but she refused to remain in the infirmary any longer. She invited Stefan to stay on to make sure she didn't strain herself lifting or otherwise dealing with the active youngsters.

As Catava came through the door, it was all Qiao could do to keep the children from launching themselves at her.

"Momma!" Chad narrowly escaped collision with Stefan as he deftly slipped between them. Stefan picked the boy up and let him hug her. Then did the same with Suzi, who covered Catava's face with kisses.

"How are my favorite little ones?" Catava made her way to the sofa, where she slowly lowered herself onto the cushion. The children cuddled up to her, chattering. She sat back and listened, realizing how much she missed them. She hugged them to her with sudden longing, ignoring the pain the movement caused. She couldn't help a hissing intake of breath as Chad jumped against her, jolting the shoulder that still pained her.

"Sit, now, love," Catava scolded him softly.

Chad complied, taking the space on her left, and Suzi on her right. Their small warmth and familiar smell reassured Catava in ways the Solarii doctor could not.

Qiao said that in Catava's absence Stefan had dedicated himself to the children. They had been wild, loud, and rambunctious. But with Stefan, they had been children once again. He was good for them.

From what Qiao said, she believed he was good for Catava as well.

Stefan and Qiaolin put together a tray of tea and snacks at the room's galley port, conferring in low voices she couldn't hear. From the frequent looks over their shoulders, she guessed they were talking about her, and her premature departure from medical.

"I'm fine," Catava said. "You can stop worrying about me."

Qiao looked up from her preparations. "Like hell I can. You've got all of us on your mind, and those two children, and the pirates, and Estrella. I know you. You're raring to get going again. But you've got to remember that you're the one who pulls us all through these hard times. We need you in one piece!"

"Qiao, stop it. I'll be a little slow for a day or two, but I'm ready. I need to be ready for all those reasons you just laid out." She smiled as the two brought steaming glassine cups to the small table in front of the sofa. "Besides, Stefan will take care of me. Won't you, Stefan?"

"Anything you need, Cat. I'll be here."

"See? It's handled, Qiao. Quit worrying and tell me about McKinley's upgrades to the ships. I want to be able to tear those pirates up the next time they show their ugly faces."

* * *

JURI slipped along the hall that ran behind the north end of the hangar, which was buzzing with activity as Vanyakin and Julian supervised the installation of the new weaponry in the Solarii and Khimeyr ships.

Wearing all black, he blended into the shadows as best he could. His future awaited him, along with the love of an exciting vital woman who would lead him to glory. Her eyes promised him the moon and more. Trezanna Len hardly noticed he was alive. Now he would have the opportunity to be someone.

The security schedule revealed the time when his compatriots would be at dinner break. Estrella and her people had been on their best behavior for the last several days, just as she warned them to be. They lulled the Solarii guards into complacence. Juri expected as much. The security holo now played a pre-programmed loop, which showed a card game in Estrella's quarters. He made sure his tracks were well covered. All the possessions he felt they needed were in the dark pack on his back. Once he released Estrella and her crew, they would steal the ship he had picked out and return to her base.

What was to happen then, Juri was not sure. Estrella desired to return to Miramar to rebuild her base after the Arkosian occupation. Juri would be a valuable part of that process, she assured him. She needed him to help enforce her rule, and would compensate him accordingly.

Feeling a glow of pride, Juri slipped outside and continued around the building to the door at the rear of the Dragonfleet wing. Ambient light barely let him read his chrono, but it was enough that he counted down until the programmed shorted out in the security grid. At exactly 2100 hours he put his hand on the door handle and pulled.

The bright light from inside blinded him for a moment. He froze until his eyes adjusted to the light. By then, footsteps approached him, many of them. He stepped outside and Estrella came through the door, followed by four men. He closed the door before the grid reactivated, eyeing the tiny group with concern. "This is your entire force?"

"The others betrayed me to follow Hawk," Estrella growled. "I shall avenge myself on him soon enough." She glanced over her shoulder. "These are my finest men! We shall ride to victory regardless of the traitors. Lead me to the ship!"

"Yes, ma'am." Juri led them along the outside of the building, avoiding the security lights and the trip sensors. "The ship, the *Deliverance*, Estrella, it's an old one. The Dragonfleet ships have all been disabled, and they're inside the security perimeter anyway. The Solarii ships are all being primed for the attack on the Arkosians. This was one of the Khimeyr ships that McKinley pushed aside as not ready for battle."

"We should be able to fly it if it was Khimeyr," Estrella muttered. "I'm not taking it into battle. Yet." She glanced behind them.

"No one should know we're gone until we're off the ground," Juri said. "Don't worry on that account."

The dark beauty turned to him, eyes flashing in light reflecting from the building ahead. "I trust no one. I don't intend to let those *tzang-huo* lock me up again. You promised they wouldn't." Estrella reached for his cheek, caressed it lightly with a leather-gloved hand.

"They won't. I swear it. Quickly, now." Juri started to run as they crossed the one open space where they risked detection.

Swiftly and silently, the others traveled behind him. The hatch was on the far side of the ship, so their actual entry was disguised by the bulk of the ship itself. The four men entered first, not speaking to Juri as Estrella watched the main building with hesitation.

Juri stepped up on the ramp and held out his hand. "We shouldn't delay. We must go now."

She eyed him a moment. Her lips opened a moment and then pursed again. She walked past without touching him.

Was she pleased? Displeased? Confused, Juri followed her in and secured the hatch.

Estrella went straight for the bridge, where her crew was already checking systems. "We take off as fast as we can. No time for the usual niceties." She sat in the center seat, and then pointed Juri to the communications console. "We're running silent," she said. "I want to know anything they broadcast, but we do not reply." Her grave expression made it clear without words what would happen if their escape was discovered because of an error by one of them.

"Yes, ma'am." Juri sat in the torn seat and activated it, monitoring the usual Solarii frequencies for chatter. As far as he could tell, then, he ceased to exist on the woman's personal radar. She was focused on only one thing: escape.

At a nod from Estrella, the makeshift crew powered up and started to roll. She took a deep breath of anticipation and turned to her tactical officer. "Be ready for anything these scum will throw at us."

"Ma'am." The officer saluted and fixed his strict attention on his assigned task.

One of her men maneuvered the *Deliverance* away from the group of second-rate ships, heading on a course oblique to the activity near the hangar. As soon as they reached take off speed, she ordered them skyward, tearing up the bare dirt with the wheels until they were off the ground. Then they were bound for Miramar.

Juri looked back at the base, dwindling into the distance behind them. He was not sure what would happen now that he was in charge of his own destiny, but he knew it would be something exciting and unanticipated. He had never felt more alive in his life.

CHAPTER 33

IN the Solarii hangar, Pomeroy's ears picked up the sound of an engine running hot for takeoff. He frowned and glanced toward the hangar door. "Whose ship is that?"

"What?" Piper crawled out from under the *Tiboron,* where she and Pomeroy had been trying for over an hour to connect the unfamiliar weaponry. She squinted into the distance. "I thought all of ours were in here."

Winston came in at a run from the control room upstairs. "Who the bloody hell was that? Refused any communication and disappeared. Some Khimeyr ship by the markings!"

"One of those over there? Nothing in that lot worth much more than a weekend drive, is what Julian said." Pomeroy frowned as he stood, a groan of pain accompanying the movement. The last five months certainly reminded him he was getting older with each passing day. His gaze flicked around the hangar. "No one requested a launch?"

"No, sir," Winston said.

"Blasted odd." Pomeroy crossed to the nearest computer interface and ran a first-level security check. "Nothing logged in. Get Julian up here. Let's find out what's going on."

Winston paged the Solarii engineer, who scowled his way into the room a few minutes later.

"A ship called the *Deliverance,*" Julian said, after being briefed. "We decided not to upgrade it because it wasn't as structurally sound as some of these others. No one's authorized to fly it. Who took it out?"

"That's what we're trying to find out," Pomeroy grumbled. Surely wasn't a ghost at the helm, so who could it be? Anyone with a legitimate purpose would have signed out a ship that stood ready. Something was definitely not right here. He hit the intercom and called the command center. "Get me Len."

As he was waiting for Trezanna, Pomeroy called Qiaolin on his personal com. "Qiao, do we have any scheduled flights this evening?"

"No. Last I heard, no one was going up again until they were all wired with the new gear."

"That's what I thought."

"Trouble?" Qiao asked.

"Oh, I think so." When the Solarii administrator's voice came on the intercom, he clicked Qiao off. "Stand by."

"This is Len," came through the intercom.

"Pomeroy, down in the hangar. You have any information on a ship called the *Deliverance*? The bastard just took off without so much as a request for clearance."

"One of ours?"

"A Khimeyr bird. One of those not scheduled for the upgrade."

"Not ours, not yours...." Her voice trailed off. She was probably coming to the same conclusion he reached and one he hoped they would avoid.

"Estrella," he growled. "Bloody hell! Somebody find Hawk Kenton and have him meet us at D wing!"

Pomeroy sprinted for the door, Winston right after him. How could this have happened? They posted a guard on that wing every hour of the day, knowing the wily leader of Dragonfleet would do whatever she could to set herself free. Heads were going to roll.

When the men arrived from different directions, panting and guns drawn, the security officer jumped to his feet and grabbed for his own weapon. "Halt!" he called, but stood down when he saw Pomeroy. "Is there a problem here?"

Pomeroy pushed him aside and the three men studied the monitors.

Hawk loosed a string of curses. "There. Look." He pointed to the holo screen. "It's staged. Right there, the tick? The loop starts over."

The security man's eyes widened as he looked at the screen. "By the Holy, I should have noticed that." He glanced at Pomeroy. "I'm sorry, sir."

The man appeared surprised, but Pomeroy was not sure of anything at the moment. For all they knew, this could be the man who let Estrella escape. If she had indeed escaped. Or maybe this was just one of her stupid head games. Best they find out. "Sorry may not be enough to cover this one. Open the door."

Hawk looked troubled, raising a thread of suspicion in that corner too.

Pomeroy eyed the man. "What do you know about this?"

"Me? Nothing. You called me down here, remember? I've been in the lounge the better part of two hours with Lily and some of the others!"

Pomeroy, faced with two potential suspects, growled with frustration. "All right, then. You two watch each other. Winston, you're with me."

He took Winston inside. Both slid their weapons from their holsters and held them pointed business end toward the ceiling, ready for use. The halls were empty. Had they all escaped? How could more than fifty people vanish? He marched to Estrella's designated rooms and stopped before the door, wondering if he should knock. If she was playing a game and he violated her privacy for no reason, she would turn that on him at the drop of a hat. He listened, hoping for music, voices, even snoring. Nothing.

Bloody hell.

Pomeroy silently counted to three on his fingers, then nodded to Winston, who swung around and kicked in the door. The room was empty.

His obscenities growing more colorful, Pomeroy moved on down the hall, kicking in more doors. Still no one. Where the hell were they?

Winston moved ahead of him, checking the other side of the hall. The last door was locked. "Showers," Winston said.

The only room without monitors. Great. "I don't have a key. And I don't want that clown from the desk down here covering his tracks."

Winston shrugged. "No worries." He pointed his weapon at the door handle and blew a hole through the door, lock and all, before Darien could even duck. "Problem solved."

"I guess," Pomeroy mumbled.

Annoyed, he shoved the door open with his foot. A sickly odor lingered in the room, along with unconscious men and women, more than he could count at a glance. He felt a little woozy, the longer he stood there, and finally connected the smell and the unconsciousness. These people had been poisoned. He yanked the curious Winston back from the door and glared up at the monitor in the hallway.

"Get this room vented," Pomeroy bellowed. "Now! And call the Doc down here!" He took deep breaths, trying to clear whatever that was from his system.

"They dead?" Winston asked.

"I don't think so." Pomeroy shook his head. "I don't understand. If she wanted to escape, why wouldn't she take her people with her? Where in Hades would she go?"

Winston shrugged. "Back to Miramar would be my guess."

"So she'd want as many of her people as possible to help her end the pirates, wouldn't you think?" He felt a little better when the fans kicked on inside the open door. If he had a real security squad, he would have requested samples of the poison to make sure who was responsible. As it was, he would be better off interviewing some of the victims inside.

"You'd think. What if these 'uns wouldn't go? Hawk was sayin' how he thought a bunch would rather follow him instead."

"Could be, could be. Then she wanted to make sure no one would blow her cover. My guys aren't allowed back here, so, no way for them to know these poor sods were in trouble."

"Think Hawk was in on it?"

"Gut tells me not. That little lady has her very own agenda." And it was clear her agenda no longer included Hawk Kenton.

The door at the base end of the hall opened, admitting the doctor and two staff people who hurried down the hall toward the two men.

"What happened here?" Boring peered into the shower room, clicking his tongue with disgust.

"Estrella happened, mate." Winston held the door as the medical personnel stepped inside.

Boring's violet eyes narrowed. He didn't miss much. "So she's gone?"

"Looks like it." Pomeroy gave an abbreviated version of what they found in D-wing. The doctor fussed and scanned them.

"You two catch any of the gas?"

"We're clear, doc. You take care of those and get me a full roster of who's left, all right?"

"Of course." Boring joined the rest of his team inside the room, and Winston and Pomeroy made their way back to the D-wing door.

Hawk's sharp eyes studied them as they came out. "Gone," he said, his tone showing it was a foregone conclusion.

"Gone," Pomeroy confirmed. "Where do you think she's headed, eh?"

Hawk Kenton crossed his arms. "Home."

CHAPTER 34

THE *Deliverance* screamed into Dragonfleet air space, barely holding together but for the sheer will of her commander.

Estrella walked to the front portal as they approached Miramar at first light. She wanted a good look at her situation. The wreck of her hangar made her cry out, her pain almost physical, like a punch in the solar plexus. "Cursed bastards! Look what they've done!"

"Incoming, ma'am!" The tactical officer was the first to notice the pirate blips on the screen.

So the pirates wasted no time. "Very well," she said. Time for the biggest gambit of this little war, she thought. Estrella looked coolly at Juri. "Hail them. Tell them I have a proposition."

Juri snapped to attention. "Yes, sir. Ma'am." His fingers tapped the com. "Khimeyr ship–"

"Dragonfleet ship!" she interrupted sharply, hand raised in reflex.

"Aye!" He cringed as she came close enough to hit him. "Dragonfleet ship *Deliverance* hailing the Arkosian ships, come in."

"Stand down or be blown from the sky!" came the terse response.

"Tell them we surrender. For now." She watched the port with a mysterious smile. All heads turned to look at her, dumbfounded. She growled at Juri, who hesitated, unsure. "Tell them!" He nodded and passed on her message. "*Now* tell them that I will meet them on the surface to discuss giving them the Solarii base."

Juri looked at her, his eyes wide, showing he was caught off guard. His gaze quickly dropped to his console. No reply yet from the Arkosians. He relayed the new message.

Estrella turned to the others, who were grinning, their respect for her clear, respect for the power she took into her own hands. Victory was nearly within their grasp.

"Response being received, ma'am."

Estrella smirked with satisfaction as the pirates agreed to her terms. "Meet them at the coordinates they provide. There, our plan for revenge will begin."

The navigator retook his seat, nodding. "Plotting coordinates, aye."

Now Estrella waited as the ships came together, the soon-to-be allies who would wreak destruction upon the Solarii and Khimeyr, the wolves among the sheep. Hours she spent alone, locked in her cage at the Induna base, where she plotted and planned. News of Marcand's demise filtered to her through gossip. The pirates were in need of a new leader. As it happened, she knew someone who would fill that void.

As the Dragonfleet leader paced, the navigator took the ship in as requested, setting it down in the open field beside the main building of Dragonfleet. The ship which flew parallel with them veered off and up, not landing. She studied the welcoming committee through the front portal. None were her people. The next thing she noticed were the big guns they carried.

"No one provoke hostility," Estrella warned as they waited inside the still-closed hatch. "We have much to win, and little to lose with this alliance. Do not fail me."

She stopped in front of Juri, looking him hotly in the eye and then grabbing his collar and pulling him to her for a brief kiss. He stumbled back when she released him, a confused look in his eye. Good. She liked keeping men off balance. It suited her.

Estrella walked out of the ship and stood on the grass, her boots firmly planted on her own soil at last.

"Where is your leader?" she asked one of the pirates.

"Inside. He's not dragging himself out here to see the likes of you." The man looked up into the ship. "Tell your men to come on out here."

"Boys? The gentleman would like to see you." Estrella eyes moved past the annoying middle man, checking her land as far as she could see for other damage or wreckage. Her companions filed out, taking their place behind her, almost as if it were rehearsed.

"Take me to him," she commanded.

One of the other pirates laughed. "Sassy bit, ain't she?"

They would take her seriously, damn them! "Only the fact that I know I can benefit your master keeps you from being a dead man right now."

"Oh, right, I'm worried." The man rolled his eyes. Two of her men glowered and tensed, ready to go after the man who showed such disrespect, but Estrella turned to them.

"We need them now for strength," she whispered. "But when we are finished?" She clapped her hands. "They can be disposed of that fast."

The pirate was unfazed. "C'mon." He motioned them forward.

Estrella walked forward, head held high, watching, always watching, to make sure she was in no real danger. She studied those who held them at gunpoint, seeking any sign of weakness.

They were led into the main chamber, the throne room where leaders of Dragonfleet had forever held audience with those lesser than themselves. A scattering of men in the room turned their eyes to the newcomers as they walked in. Catcalls echoed in the chamber as Estrella was recognized, and she gifted those present with her most regal smile. She would have addressed them, but all conversation in the room was quickly silenced as a tall black man entered through the doors behind the large, regal seat.

He crossed slowly, studying Estrella and her companions, making eye contact with his own people in a way she recognized from her own days on that throne. He climbed the steps, taking his time, and then sat down. The Dragonfleet officers were stopped at the foot of the stairs, and other pirates moved in behind them, waiting for them to try anything unacceptable.

"So interested in forfeiting your life, witch?" the man asked in a smooth bass. His sharp eyes dissected her.

"So interested in helping you take the Solarii base, milord," Estrella countered. She crossed her arms, her stance solid, feet shoulders' width apart. In her black leather, she knew how tough she looked. Now all she needed was to impress him.

He laughed. "To your advantage, not mine. I have no worries about the puny Solarii."

"If that is so, why haven't you destroyed them yet?"

The amusement faded from his eyes. "Perhaps I have better targets before me."

"Like the Phileans?"

A flash of recognition on his face told her she scored a point. How fortunate for her that Juri kept her informed on every little detail that passed through the Solarii security deck.

"They have been punished for their transgressions." The pirate sat on the edge of the throne, stiff, angry.

"And yet the Solarii harbor the man who killed your leader. They celebrate his accomplishment, while they plot to come here and finish what the Philean started."

Estrella bit her tongue, keeping a tight control on her voice. *So hard not to urge the pirate on with a flood of angry rhetoric.* She was known for stirring her people to any purpose with words. It was her gift of a gilded tongue. But this one, she could sense he was predisposed against her. He would not be pushed. He would need to be persuaded, like a new lover.

He pushed himself upright with a growl and came halfway down the steps. "And what would this alliance gain you?" Staring at her a moment, he came down level with her, gathering the hair on the back of her head in one huge hand and slowly bending her backward, forcing her to look up at him. "We all know Estrella of Dragonfleet does nothing that does not serve her!"

Estrella's men reacted, trying to protect her, but the guards made them kneel, a laser rifle pointed at each of their heads.

"Tell me!" he demanded.

"When I offered to help Len and Rolon, they locked me up as a prisoner." Estrella fought to keep a disinterested smile on her face. Her back muscles aching, she took a deep breath. "You and I, milord, we could band together and take them."

"Why do I need you?" He released her suddenly. She fell to her back on the filthy floor. When one of the others would have kept her there, the pirate leader waved him away. She scrambled to her feet and looked at him boldly.

"Because I've been there. Because I've won one of their security men onto my team." Estrella gestured at the men behind her, careful not to indicate which one she meant. "We escaped with our lives despite all their security precautions. We could get you in with a minimum loss of ships and personnel."

He studied her, his dark gaze a calculating one. "And once we have accomplished this great feat?"

"Who knows?" Estrella shrugged. Was it too soon? Could she appeal to him with her usual currency? She allowed a small, flirtatious smile. "Perhaps we shall part ways. Perhaps we shall share the territory." She looked at him with interest. "We could be very close neighbors."

Watching her, speculating, the man finally nodded. "You may call me Andaeus Meda. Come. We shall talk."

Estrella nodded and turned to the others. "And my men?"

"I have no need to speak to them," he said. He glanced at two of the guards. "Hold them in the dayroom." The man who navigated their ship protested and was promptly struck down by the pirate guarding him. He and the others were dragged to their feet and out of the room.

Meda led Estrella out of the room to the small private dining area behind the grand chamber. "This idea of teamwork fascinates me, my little poison pot," he said. "Tell me more."

* * *

THE news of Estrella's escape rattled Trezanna.

First, her security system had been compromised by a traitor. Second, an alliance between the Arkosian and Dragonfleet forces would create a formidable foe.

Matthew Juri. The name was vaguely familiar. The computer records generated a face to go with the name, a young man, blond-haired, brown-eyed, medium build, nothing to catch attention. He was relatively new to the Solarii, mostly kept to himself. No way to know. Estrella was known for making good men turn bad. Trezanna knew it was as much her fault, if not more.

The remaining Dragonfleet members survived Estrella's treacherous attack, nursed back to health by the Solarii doctors and reunited with their former friends in the Khimeyr ranks. They expressed their wish to ally with the joint venture under the leadership of Hawk Kenton.

Another item of unfinished business remained was Shelby Hussard's memorial service. It might be the perfect vehicle to counter this latest event, something more positive, more directed to unification. A service could take a few minutes to affirm the good nature of their people, this cause, before the next battle.

Trezanna set the service at two p.m. that afternoon in the common lounge. Not the traditional place for such an event, but she knew Shelby would have appreciated the informality. Winston appeared in her doorway shortly after she made the announcement. "I'd like to speak for Shelby, ma'am."

"Of course. It is important to celebrate the lives of our heroes. She gave her life in defense of this group—"

"She gave her life to save that bloody Dragonfleet bitch!" Winston interrupted.

Trezanna sighed. "I don't minimize what happened. It was a tragedy in every sense of the word. The mission could have been the door to a new alliance, Monty. It might have." She saw the condemnation in his eyes. "Now we know better. Every day is a risk. She knew that. And she would do it again."

His face struggled with emotions, his mouth moving with unspoken words.

She felt the depth of his pain in what he didn't say. "I'll see you this afternoon."

After he left her office, she stared after him, knowing the purpose of such a service was to allow people to let go of the departed, to find closure. But it never got easier.

The same thought threatened to drag her down at the appointed time, when she found the room packed to capacity. A holo of Shelby was on the bar next to a glass of her preferred ale. Candles burned nearby. Trezanna looked around the room and took a deep breath, then smiled.

"Thank you all for coming. I hope Shelby knew how many of you cared about her." Her gaze traveled around the group, lighting with recognition and sympathy for many of them. She read from her notes the standard information about their fallen comrade, the facts, names, dates, training, and service record. But what kept returning to her mind was her mental picture of Hussard the night of the tragic incident.

"I remember Shelby as an effervescent young woman, who lived each day with one-hundred percent of her energy and spirit. The night of this mission, she was in the shower when the alarm went out. Didn't stop her, though. She joined the effort to make our lives safer without a thought for herself. I admired her for the way she inspired others by her example."

Trezanna paused, giving a moment for contemplation. "I invite anyone who would like to speak, please do so." She moved aside, leaving the floor open.

Several people rose to their feet.

Pomeroy cleared his throat and looked around. "Shelby was one of the first Solarii I met. She showed me what was good and true here. I found it in her, but she warn't the only one." He coughed, as if the sharing something personal had choked him, and sat down again.

Bethany came forward. "Shelby was like a sister to me from the first day I came here. Her love and friendship inspired me every day, and I miss her." Her last words were caught in tears.

Trezanna found the young woman's poignant remembrance pulled at her own heart as well. Others followed, nearly half of those in the room taking the chance to share some warm thought or moment they shared with the departed. Last was Monty Winston, the man who had almost thrown his own life away for hers.

Winston chewed his lip a moment, traces of wetness obvious on his cheeks. The room hushed as the gathered waited for him to speak.

"Shelby was my friend." He looked around at the faces before him, his big hands shoved in his pockets. His jaw twitched and his mouth opened, but nothing else came out.

Trezanna debated stepping up to rescue him from his pain, but something stopped her. He needed to do this.

"She was my friend," Monty said again, his voice liquid with emotion. Then he returned to his seat.

Trezanna allowed a few minutes more, and then she moved back to the front of the room, amid the sounds of muffled sorrow. "We celebrate the life of our friend. May her way be lit by the knowledge and protection of the Holy. Amen."

She lit the last candle on the bar and added a silent prayer. Then she stepped back and closed the ceremony. She mingled with the others, her people, making a point of real eye contact, a personal word.

Somehow Juri had become disillusioned and uninspired enough to follow Estrella. Trezanna would not let such a thing happen again.

* * *

"THEY'VE changed the Veil detection codes," Juri announced.

He worked the computer console aboard Andaeus Meda's personal shuttle, as it cut through Solarii space, headed for the base.

Estrella snorted. "Finally, Len begins acting like a leader." She paced like a caged animal behind Juri's chair, and then glanced at Meda. "A slight obstacle."

"So I see. How do you intend to correct it?" The pirate sat in the command chair, every bit as tense as Estrella.

"Without your input," Estrella snapped. Juri winced. Clearly she forgot who she was addressing.

Meda was out of the chair in the blink of an eye. "Silence, woman!" He grabbed the Dragonfleet leader by the upper arm and shoved her aside, then stepped over to Juri. Studying the dataflow, he counted off options out loud as he pointed out the best landing site. "Take us to near-ground coordinates. Here. Increase your Veil cover to one hundred-ten percent and cut engines by one-half to delay detection." He looked to the tactical officer. "Prepare to release the barrage."

Juri nodded quickly and did as he was told. He had learned in the last week that Andaeus Meda liked immediate compliance. That was why he was one of two men, out of the five that arrived with Estrella, who remained alive. From the corner of his eye, he saw her seething as she shared command with the Arkosian.

Meda turned back to Estrella. "You have your little toy?"

She nodded, eyes hot with resentment. "Get me in and I'll make sure the job is done."

Juri watched as she reached in her pocket and took out the small device again, stroking it with her fingers. He was not sure exactly what the thing did but Estrella destroyed her quarters searching for it. When she found it, she actually danced with joy. "Gus Henry made this little beauty for me," she confessed. "This and the store of holos inside, this little bit will win the war, you'll see. Then Dragonfleet will be back in business once again."

Meda eyed her for a moment, and then turned his attention back to the readout. "Once we let all the debris and missiles fly, no one will notice one little shuttle in the incoming shower. They'll be too busy hiding their heads." He nodded to tactical. "Now."

The pirate kept his focus on the monitors, and then grabbed the back of Juri's chair. "We're through. Get below, the two of you. Our attack will begin when the defense net is blown."

Juri and Estrella hurried to the hatch area, hastily pulling on dark coveralls with Solarii insignia. Estrella transferred the device to her pocket. They crouched, waiting for touchdown. The ship would land just long enough to deposit them close to the command center, and then retreat to a safe distance, leaving the two to bring down the security and weapons systems.

Estrella promised him she could.

Juri was not so sure, especially since the pirate was perfectly satisfied to send Estrella out to get shot first. *What do I have to lose? If this little venture doesn't work, Estrella and I will be dead anyway.*

The countdown came and the hatch opened on schedule. The codes Juri hoped to use were changed, but the adjustments Meda ordered would cover their arrival long enough to get to a place of safety. They hit the ground, rolling to break the impact, then ducked and ran to the nearest building entrance, a hail of metal bits and explosives falling all over the base amid warning sirens. The shuttle veered away, its passing a shimmer in the sky.

Juri dragged a weapon from his pocket, watching for someone to challenge them, but the timing and the Veil had been flawless. He turned to comment on the absence of opposition and found Piper Donovan staring at him.

"Jupiter and sons!" Juri raised the weapon in response.

"Put that away, you fool!" came an irritated Estrella's voice from a face which was definitely Piper's.

Juri blinked. "By the Gods." It was a perfect illusion.

"Come." The likeness of Piper headed down the hallway, a relaxed gait taking over her stride, Piper's easy smile on her face. Juri, wishing he had a similar disguise, followed her, half-concealing the weapon. When they entered the auxiliary command center, Juri stunned the two officers who rose before they could speak. "Matthew, the net."

He headed to the appropriate terminal, first entering commands to transfer control to the auxiliary center, bypassing the new codes by a deeply implanted command he had installed before they left. Once they were in control, he nodded to Estrella.

"We've got about three minutes tops before someone gets here to stop us. Piper," Juri added as an afterthought.

"All right." The Dragonfleet leader smiled at him, a bright reward, then surveyed the panel before her and began entering commands, grinning with delight as the lights flickered off, one behind the other. "That's it! Nighty-night."

"Meda will be monitoring, won't he?" Anxiously, Juri watched the time and the door. When the shield net fell, Meda planned to bomb the Solarii facility, crippling the hangar as that of Dragonfleet had been, taking out supplies and communications. This would set up the Solarii-Khimeyr coalition for a permanent takeover within twenty-four hours when the rest of the Arkosian fleet could arrive.

Estrella nodded. "So he said." The last control light flickered. When the overhead lights didn't go out fast enough to suit her, she fired several blasts in their direction, and added a couple of shots into the computer decks as well. As the lights slowly dimmed, she nodded with satisfaction. "Done."

"Piper?" A shocked voice came from the door, drawing both the saboteurs' eyes. Hawk Kenton was framed in the still-lit doorway, weapon in hand. "What are you doing?"

Juri went to fire, but Estrella knocked his weapon aside and modulated her voice to be lighter and younger than it was. "I'm doing what I should have done when I first arrived and you talked me out of it," she said with a smirk. "I'm bringing this base to its rightful owners."

Hawk looked Estrella, then at Juri, and then back at Estrella. "Piper, you never said that."

She glanced at the security holo-cam and laughed. "You'd like to think people don't know what you're really about here. You're a traitor of the worst kind."

Hawk cocked his head as if he were listening to something, replaying it in his head. Then a look of comprehension came onto his face. He pointed his weapon with one hand and grabbed his com-unit from his belt with the other.

"Juri, you've made some mistakes here, pal. But joining up with her is your biggest one yet." He thumbed the unit. "This is Kenton in auxiliary control! I've got them!" A furious babble of voices issued from the unit before he put it back on his belt. "I don't want to hurt you. I cared for you! They'll be here any moment. Surrender and live."

"Never." Estrella thumbed the setting on her laser to kill and pointed it. "I'm a survivor. Ask my mother." She pulled the trigger.

"Strey! No!" He jerked and fell, a burnt hole smoking on his left shoulder.

Juri's fingers hesitated, their owner shocked at the coldness of his new leader. The lights flickered back into life and power hummed into the controls behind them. "It can't be!" Juri pushed Estrella aside and checked the console, punching it in his frustration as the systems rebooted one by one. "I had the override in place!"

"Another failure?" Estrella chided. "I'm very disappointed. I really expected more of you, darling."

He watched in horror as she pointed her weapon at him and pulled the trigger. The burning pain lasted longer than anticipated. He felt his heart jerk several times before it stopped and his world went black.

* * *

HAVING dispatched the two men, it was time to activate phase two of her plan.

Estrella pocketed her own weapon, snagging Hawk's as she passed, and ran out into the hall.

"Help!" she cried. "They've killed Hawk!"

She moved aside as the second wave arrived and then blended into the confusion, returning the way she had come, Gus's device in her hand. When she left the building, the appearance of Piper fizzled and faded, and that of Monty Winston stepped out.

'Winston' headed across the grounds to the secondary hangar bay and barked some quick warnings to the people manning the control booth. "Keep everyone else on the ground so we get a clear shot!" he cried in a voice which seemed deeper than his usual one, and ran into the hatch of the *Talon*, Estrella's ship, its security system still intact, voice-activated. Lighting up the engines with a delighted laugh, she launched before the ground crew could react.

Once off the end of the tarmac, Estrella cut power to Gus's device and the prickly air of the holo projection disappeared from around her. She hailed the Arkosian ship, alerting them to her return so they would not shoot her as an attacker. Meda was furious that her plan had not succeeded. But she reminded him that he ordered her to get the defenses down. He was to take out the power himself after she broke in. She had gotten inside and done her job. It was he who failed.

"Now we have another sleek ship to play with," she said. "One less for their defense."

Estrella smiled at the device in her hand. She would keep this secret to herself. There was no need for Meda to know. Pushing a button, her appearance faded into a perfect copy of the Arkosian commander.

Soon, milord, it will be me giving the orders.

CHAPTER 35

SPEECHLESS, Trezanna watched the holo play a third time as Pomeroy scowled over her shoulder. "I can't believe it."

"What is there not to believe? The evidence is clear before you." Rumadan prowled along the windows, her deepening purple fur showing she was uncomfortable. "Your daughter was in league with Estrella and shot two men to further an invasion by the Arkosians."

"Bull!" Pomeroy was furious. "Piper would never help Estrella."

Rumadan gestured at the holo screen. "Then how do you explain that?"

He glared at the screen. "I can't. Yet. Hawk's still unconscious in the infirmary. Guess we can ask him when he wakes up."

Trezanna fiddled with the controls. At the time of Estrella's arrival and the concurrent attack, the base experienced such power fluctuations that the audio feed was sketchy. They could see what happened, but not hear what was said. "Has anyone spoken to Piper?"

"Chase Austin has confined her to quarters." Rumadan rumbled her displeasure at being put in such a position. "You will have to mete out justice, your child or not."

"I know that!" the Solarii administrator snapped. How could she be surrounded by traitors upon traitors? Had Piper been angry with Hawk for sharing the information about her early plans to help Estrella? She rubbed her forehead with both hands, wishing she could erase the headache creeping in, or the image of her daughter shooting Hawk and Juri in cold blood.

Pomeroy shook his head, rubbing an unshaven chin. "Piper said she was in the garden. Tools are scattered round the plot. She could have been using them. The security holo-cams were down all over the base because of that." He pointed to the screen. "Just because we don't have a holo proving she was somewhere else doesn't mean she wasn't."

"Really. Pomeroy, would you admit you had been the murderer of your commander's troops, given an option? She has every reason to lie."

"She's not lying!" Pomeroy's fist splintered the cabinet nearest his head. As Trezanna and Rumadan looked at him, he stepped back, a little surprised at his own vehemence. "I'll, ah, take care of that."

"I understand, Dare. Believe me." Trezanna tapped the play button again. She watched as Piper walked in with Juri and reprogrammed the computer, listened to her conversation with Hawk blurred by static on the audio, and then saw the shooting of the two men. "It is unfortunate. We shouldn't let this distract us from our focus on the Arkosians. They will not delay much longer, now that this plan has been foiled."

"Then let me handle this," Pomeroy said, intensity burning in his eyes. "Up my alley anyway."

Trezanna nodded despite Rumadan's disapproving look. "All right. You have twenty-four hours. Maybe in that time, Hawk will be able to shed some light on the situation."

"Right." Pomeroy stalked out, muttering to himself.

As Rumadan started to speak, Trezanna cut her off. She didn't need to hear any more recriminations. "Has the power been fully restored? Are the ships ready for launch?"

"All systems are working," Rumadan purred. "There is an additional oddity. Austin reports that the *Talon* was taken from the field by Monty Winston immediately after this incident. Winston hasn't left the base, and claims he has not logged flight time for two days."

"If Winston is still here, then there are two impersonators."

"If one believes in an impersonator, then it is possible to believe in two." Rumadan's ears twitched. "Or one able to take on multiple appearances."

Trezanna decided at that moment she believed in Piper's innocence. "Notify Pomeroy at once. He'll need to speak to anyone who was in that corridor."

Rumadan assented with an unhappy growl and left the office. Trezanna played the holo again and sighed. This insanity must be associated with Estrella somehow. *It must be.*

* * *

DARIEN Pomeroy walked to Piper's quarters, his step and his soul heavy. The spirit of the pert young pilot had attached itself to his heartstrings. He physically ached to see her in such a predicament.

He nodded to Chase Austin, who stood outside the closed door. "Trezanna's given me permission to investigate, ma'am."

"I hope you can do something for her."

"I plan on it, eh?" He gave her a grin powered by a confidence even he found it hard to sustain, and then entered.

The room was dim, lights off with curtains partly closed. He found Piper sitting at a desk in the corner, watching her computer monitor, her expression blank. He could see it was a loop of the incriminating holo.

"Little bird told me I could find you here, girlie."

Piper didn't look up. Fingers tangled in the hair near her forehead. "I haven't worn that shirt for three months. I didn't even bring it with me from Dragonfleet."

"Really?" Pomeroy crouched down by the desk and watched the holo replay again. Then he tapped the monitor. "Where were you exactly when that happened?"

She shrugged. "I was outside getting some produce for the galley. There was a loud explosion and things started falling from the sky, so I ran inside."

"What door did you use to exit and enter?"

Piper frowned, green eyes clouding over. "The southwest door, I think. The one by the alcove."

"Both times?"

"Yes. Yes, I remember it stuck while I was trying to get back in." She looked at Pomeroy and then back at the monitor. "*That* is not me."

"I know, love. Let me work on it." His com-unit buzzed with a message from Rumadan about Winston and the missing ship. "Well now, that adds a layer to things." He pondered the mystery of Winston leaving with his ship and remaining at the base as well, realizing it lent credence to the imposter theory and told Piper so. "It's got to be Estrella. Juri was with her, but he was no more use, so she'd waste him. I'll wager Hawk could have exposed her. That's why she shot him."

"He's going to be all right, isn't he? Chase said they pulled him through." She sighed and reached for a brush, running it through her hair, and then braiding it tight, almost as though she needed something to keep her hands busy. "What can I do to help?"

"Nothing, I'm afraid. They want you to stay here 'til they're sure." The fading of the sparkle in her eyes stabbed him like an ice pick. "I'll do everything I can to break it open, right? Don't worry. We'll take Estrella down. She'll pay for this. For all this."

"Please let me know as you find out things, okay?" Piper looked at him, wistful, biting her lip. "Did my mother say if she'd come to see me? Is she upset? Does she believe I did this?"

"I don't think she does. She gave me twenty-four hours to clear you while the rest prepare for the pirates. Maybe there's something you can do from here on that effort." He grinned at her. "Keep you from becoming a stark raving Looney, eh?"

"Yeah. Yeah that would be nice." She pulled her knees close and hugged them tight.

She looked so pathetic, his heart nearly broke. "Now that's not the attitude I'm used to from you, young 'un." He looked at her sternly. "I'll prove it. Somehow I will. Even with bits and pieces of security holos I'll be able to track down a general history. There must be something she did in Aux Control to reveal her identity." He patted her cheek. "Now be a good girl and smile."

Under his intent scrutiny she finally did. "All right," she said. "Get me something to do."

"I will." On the way out, he asked Chase to find Piper some useful task. Then he went to Auxiliary Control.

The room was fully staffed today, making sure the repairs were completed expeditiously. Two armed guards stood by. Julian lay under one console, wires and chips dangling every which way, and muttered a mile a minute as the lights blinked randomly. Darien walked over and bent down, ignoring what he heard. "You mind if I look around, mate?"

Julian peeked his head out. "No. Just stay out of my way."

"You got it." Pomeroy stepped back and ran the holo on his handheld again, moving around the room to look at it from different angles as the holo did. Nothing looked out of the ordinary. The visual image of Piper never flicked or faded as she shot Hawk and then Juri. Several referents in what conversation he could recover pointed toward the administrator's daughter, the point about her mother and survival, even Juri calling her Piper.

But the stance wasn't right. The way the woman stood was not Piper's relaxed carriage, but someone pulled tighter than a geisha's hair bun. The voice was not right, either. The voice. That was it.

Pomeroy found an unoccupied console and connected the handheld holo player to it, then demanded a computer analysis of the voices.

While he waited, he watched the activity in the room, proud of the crew, mixed bunch that it was. Over the years he had heard about the Solarii, growing into a bit of a legend, a scary one at that. In the next few days, the two groups would be in a battle for their lives against the pirates and what Dragonfleet personnel remained at Miramar. He was confident that his life would be safe in Solarii hands as in Qiaolin's or Catava's.

The computer beeped, analysis complete. The readout confirmed his theory. The face was Piper's, the voice belonged to Estrella.

He sent a report to Trezanna and Rumadan.

Then he went to give Piper the good news. He wanted to see the smile in her eyes for himself.

* * *

DESPITE the repeated drills and exercises and no matter how ready the people were for combat, Trezanna knew the arrival of it was frightening and exhilarating all at once.

Nearly thirty-six hours after Estrella's escape from the Solarii base, the proximity alarms went off in the command center. Julian rang the emergency alert bell, sending the base to battle stations.

Trezanna and Catava hit the command center at the same time, and he briefed them in a hurried jargon. If the Philean information was correct, they would receive the entire Arkosian complement, two dozen heavy cruisers and twenty or more smaller flyers, most coming in on a trajectory from their main base, joined by those left at Dragonfleet. "*She*'s with them," Julian said, bitterness lacing his tone.

"Her loss," Catava said flatly, zipping her gray flight jacket. Watching the monitors, she tracked the blip designated as the *Talon* arcing toward the Solarii base. She leaned forward and punched the com to the hangar. "Status?"

"No contact by the Arkosians," came Rumadan's calm purr. "Ready to launch."

Catava looked at Trezanna, who nodded.

"Go," Catava said into the com.

"Launch, aye," Rumadan replied and cut the com.

The two women looked at each other, eyes liquid with emotion.

"We've prepared as well as we can," Catava said, breaking the silence. "Either it's enough or—" She took a deep breath, her aqua gaze finishing the sentence more eloquently than words would have expressed.

"It's enough," Trezanna reassured. "We have to believe that."

"See you on the other side."

Trezanna placed a hand on Catava's shoulder. "One way or the other."

Then they turned together and ran for the hangar. There the panorama seemed at first glance one of mass confusion. Over the last week, the fighting force had drilled for this kind of scenario. The crews divided into four teams, each with a chain of command in case anyone was lost. Alpha team was led by Darien, who commanded Piper, Winston and two other Khimeyr fighters. Catava commanded Beta squad, with Lily Renard, Stefan and the majority of the remaining Khimeyr. Qiao drew Julian and several of the other Solarii in Gamma section.

Hawk was to have steered Delta, but Trezanna stepped into his shoes, pulling Dr. Talib with her dual training and Chase Austin. Hawk was healed enough to fly along, although even he admitted he was not up to command. He seemed grateful to hear that Estrella's attempt to kill him had actually led to the active defection of the Dragonfleet officers who remained there with him. They filled out the Delta team. All in all, the combined groups controlled nearly fifty ships and three times that many personnel, each aware of the life and death nature of this endeavor.

Anticipating casualties, Trezanna exempted Dr. Boring and his staff from the defense force. Rumadan remained behind with a skeleton ops crew of non-pilots. Each control room chair was assigned a list of duties to provide support service to a team in the air. They had flown the missions a dozen times in preparation and everyone knew his job.

Trezanna saw that Gamma squad was loaded and ready to roll. Rumadan gave them the go-ahead as Beta was scrambling for their birds. The *Queen's Claw* and *Karma's Revenge* were notably absent, so the first team was obviously already up. She checked with the Viorn for any last-minute concerns, and then headed for the *Galena*. The rest of her team were suited up and ready to roll. Her hands shook as she went through pre-launch, but she tried to release her inner control, letting her body take over on automatic.

What seemed like a few short minutes passed, and then Delta got the nod for takeoff. Feeling the roar of the ship beneath her, she flew skyward as fast as she could. The other squads flew ahead of her, and further, but not nearly far enough. The Arkosian ships were already launching missiles at the base below. Shields deflected most of the fire, so far. Vanyakin was clear in his advice and counsel regarding the best use of the lasers, missiles, mines and other weapons they got from him. If they couldn't stop the Arkosians in the air, the ground attack would be long over before they could return to protect the base.

* * *

THE first wave of the Solarii-Khimeyr coalition joined the battle with Pomeroy's war cry, broadcast over the common frequency.

The sound seemed to galvanize the others, as Alpha squadron spread to choose their targets and engage, Gamma close behind. Trezanna's ten-ship contingent powered their weapons, flashes of light appeared all around as the exchange of fire began. Beta, just a jump ahead of her own group, had the *Mercantile* and Catava's heavier ship, and they focused on the cruisers, strafing them with laser fire as they came within range.

Rumadan reported updates from the large screen, coordinating data from all four squadrons. Everything seemed to be rolling along. Trezanna acknowledged the report before launching her own first attack.

Pomeroy cheered quietly as his fire on the lead cruiser flashed, then caused the lights on the cruiser to go out. "Get 'em, Winston!"

"Right, mate." Winston was close behind, flying one of the Khimeyr ships Julian had repaired. He lit a pair of missiles and sent them into the side of the cruiser. A burst of flame billowed out from the Arkosian ship and it listed heavily to port, into the path of a couple of the lighter pirate flyers. They avoided the collision and came around, sending a volley of blasts at Gamma's Julian and Qiao.

Qiaolin's power went out for a split second and she gasped in disbelief. "Julian!" she cried into her dead com. When her board came back to life, she read from the sensors that Julian had placed his ship between the Arkosian attackers and hers, taking flak for both of them. "I'm all right, I'm all right." She signaled, and he pulled ahead, out of her line of fire. She dropped several mines into the path of the pirates, who were too close on her tail to veer away and they were vaporized instantly.

Trezanna's squad was having a harder time. The more persistent Arkosians singled them out for pursuit. The pirates also seemed to have upgraded weapons that could read and modulate frequencies of the Solarii shields. She could recall seeing something to this nature on the Philean disks, but they had not had the time to adjust their shields. No chance to prepare for every eventuality. Trezanna set her jaw and urged her people to shoot faster.

Dr. Talib sent out a warning as her ship maneuvered wildly, trapped in the sights of an incoming attacker. Before Trezanna could get a clear shot, Talib lost the battle for escape in a flash and trail of debris.

"Damn them!" Chase cried out. She followed behind the successful Arkosian attacker, launching round after round until it too exploded.

Beta squad was now past the last of the marauders and had turned, herding some of the smaller flyers back toward the other teams, lasers hot on their tails. Delta and Gamma ships swung wide and returned in curving trajectories, coming in from the sides to aim for the cruisers' weapons launch areas, the Dragonfleet pilots some of the fiercest fighters seen yet. Lily followed her orders to take the *Odyssey* in front of the other ships, as close as possible, releasing more of the mines. Her efforts had resulted so far, in the loss of a cruiser and three of the small ships.

"Good show, Lily!" Pomeroy called out over the com, after seeing what she managed to accomplish.

He was able to pull out of the conflicted area for a few moments, watching for several things. First, the brassy color of the *Revenge*. Second, a sign that the Arkosians were concentrating on the surface. Third, the *Talon*, which vanished after the initial sighting by Julian.

"I know you're here somewhere, witch," Pomeroy muttered. "You're here, and you're laughing. Enjoy it while you can." His eyes narrowed with hate and he re-engaged as Lily picked up an invader following much too close for his comfort.

* * *

POMEROY was not the only one watching for the Dragonfleet leader. Trezanna was also very aware that the *Talon* had not been spotted in the rush of oncoming ships.

Could she have been destroyed by the pirates?

The Arkosians seemed as cold and unforgiving as Estrella. Perhaps her failure to bring down the defenses of the Solarii provoked the pirates to give her the ultimate punishment.

We could only hope.

"Status!" she barked in a direct channel to Rumadan.

The Viorn's tone was calm and unshaken. "Khimeyr at full strength and running within expected parameters on weapons and power. Solarii down one ship, running low on missiles. Advise conservation of missiles. Arkosians have lost three cruisers and seven light ships."

One for ten. Not bad, as things went.

Trezanna pushed her regret for the loss of Talib aside until they returned, then shared the report with the other teams. She gasped as Piper narrowly escaped a flare of laser as she left a mine in the path of an attacker.

Step back, step back, Trezanna nagged herself and put the *Galena* on a path returning to the action.

In his briefing, Vanyakin provided them with information on the physical location of the weapons launchers in the structure of the Arkosian ships. As a result, Catava's unit, her squad's ships loaded with enhanced shield-piercing missiles, enjoyed particular success in blocking the cruisers' ability to fire. But they agreed to do more than keep the pirates from shooting. All plans passed on by the Phileans showed the Arkosians intended an all out annihilation of the Solarii-Khimeyr coalition. They must assume, having encountered the strong wills of this group before, that the pirates would throw every weapon possible into this clash. None could be permitted to leave alive.

"Stefan, look out!" Catava shouted, as the *Mercantile* nearly collided with one of the cruisers. Ciro pulled up at the last moment making sure his torpedo was firmly launched at close range. A flower of hot flaming gases bloomed upward from the cruiser as the *Mercantile* sped away to starboard.

Another one down.

Pomeroy avoided debris, trying to stay close to the pirate chasing the *Odyssey*. Lily was fighting like hell to pull out of his sights, even heading back into the hot area, trying to scrape him off on one of his comrades' ships, but without effect.

"Hold on, Lily, girl, I'm coming!" Pomeroy called.

"Dare, come on, he's—" Her words cut off in mid-sentence as the Arkosian released a deadly blast that splintered the *Odyssey*.

Pomeroy blinked, blinded for a moment, and then bore down on the attacker with a laser approximation of an inferno and sent the attacker's into oblivion.

Trezanna kept an eye on the monitor inside her ship with a wide angle. Several ships exploded within seconds of each other, and she prayed they were pirate ships. She did a quick vertical loop to avoid incoming fire from a cruiser, and then watched with relief as the cruiser was derailed by one of Piper's mines. Rumadan gave her an update showing ten of the cruisers were gone, three carried disabled weapons and twelve of the smaller pirate ships were lost completely.

"It is not enough," the Viorn cautioned.

Trezanna bit back a sharp response that Rumadan was welcome to come take her place. "What about our people?" With a mumbled curse, she shot at a pirate ship that wheeled in front of her, sending it spinning.

"One Solarii and three Khimeyr ships lost." Rumadan's voice was somber. "Our crews are fighting well."

Trezanna nodded as she shut off her com and beseeched the Holy silently to see the right of their cause. Distracted a moment, she blinked with alarm when she next looked up and saw the Arkosian forces splitting into two detachments, two cruisers and six smaller ships headed straight for the planet surface. "Darien!"

"I'm on it!" Pomeroy alerted Piper, Winston and the remainder of Gamma squad to follow him, and they plunged toward the base after the pirates.

As Catava's team took out another cruiser, worrying the bigger ship like a pack of hyenas on a lion until it died, Trezanna ordered Chase and the remaining two Dragonfleet pilots to concentrate on the smaller fighters, pairing up to distract and destroy. She prepared to follow them when the *Talon* shimmered into view on the outskirts of the battle environs.

Trezanna's com crackled with static and then Estrella's laugh, silky and dangerous, filled the cockpit of the *Galena*. "Haven't you given up yet, Len?"

"Surrender isn't a likely option, unless you would like to take advantage of it," Trezanna said quietly. Glancing at the monitor, she saw the others were handling the responsibilities they were given. She set her course for the *Talon,* priming her weapons.

"Did you like my little surprise?" Estrella's ship didn't move, and Trezanna guessed that her shields and weapons were being readied as well. "I hope you didn't treat poor Piper too badly."

Not deigning to give her a reply, Trezanna launched a burst of laser fire at Estrella's ship, most of which faded in the repellent of her shield.

Estrella returned the favor, and then pulled away faster than the *Galena* could turn.

Trezanna wheeled her ship to follow and set a heat-seeking torpedo to launch as soon as she could be sure nothing else was close enough to attract it. "Let's see who surprises whom, shall we?"

* * *

WINSTON put on a burst of speed to catch up with the birds assigned to him by Darien Pomeroy and let loose nearly everything he had.

Pomeroy warned him if the pirates got to the ground it would be all over, and he meant to see that didn't happen. A blur of brass slid by to the side of him, it was Piper. He could only guess she was of like mind.

Right smart skirt, that one was.

Over the last couple of days Winston noticed the bond between her and Pomeroy, their sharp tongues poking insults at each other. But they never took offense.

"Pull up! Pull up!" Pomeroy yelled. "Incoming from the surface!"

"Bloody hell!" Winston swerved to starboard, the hull screaming as the G forces pulled at it.

These Khimeyr ships were never held together too well from the get-go. 'S all I need...blow apart and never get touched.

Pomeroy cursed at the late release. Rumadan must have held back until the last possible moment to discharge all the base defenses at once, creating a hail of missiles, torpedoes, and laser fire. The Arkosians had managed to get off a few token shots but were easily decimated, having been lulled into a false sense of security by the lack of resistance. He saw Winston pull away, and then looked around desperately for Piper.

"Damn it, Dare, I'm hit," Winston heard her say over the com.

"Piper?" Winston swung back around, looking for her and found her drifting down toward the surface, a huge score down one side of her engine, coolant leaking as a blue gas into space.

"I'm all right," she assured him, irritation lacing her tone. "Just didn't expect to be dodging bullets from my own people."

"Can you land?" Pomeroy demanded.

Her laugh came across loud and clear, as did her disdain for his question. "Can I land? On a dime, Pomeroy, on a dime. See you when you get back."

Winston hastily covered his sigh of relief, as Piper glided toward the base. She then rejoined him, heading back to aid Beta wing, arriving just in time to see the exchange of fire between Trezanna and Estrella.

"Well, look who showed up to send us off," Winston said bitterly.

"Dragonfleet's finest." Pomeroy's words were thick with sarcasm. "Should we help Len?"

As Winston was about to answer, Stefan Ciro interrupted with a request for assistance. A quick scan of the area saw four of the cruisers hanging at canted angles in space, but shields preventing them from final destruction. Pomeroy decided the greater good was in wiping out the other attackers and turned his ship to assist as requested, with Winston following.

"Qiaolin, drop some of the Christmas gifties," Julian urged over the com, as they caught up with the others.

"They're gone. Must have spent them all."

"Lily…." Julian's voice trailed off.

"No, not Lily. Piper's hit too, but she's bound for home," Pomeroy cut in. "We're on our own, ladies and gents. Let's give 'em hell."

* * *

TREZANNA counted down the timer on the missile, keeping up token laser fire to divert the attention of her opponent from her true purpose. Estrella seemed to be leading her away from the others on purpose, and as that suited Trezanna's intent, she followed without much thought.

Just a few more seconds and I can let this fly.

"So trusting you are," came Estrella's voice again. "Like a lamb to slaughter." She laughed, a harsh sound that grated along Trezanna's nerves. "I'd stop firing if I were you."

Frowning, Trezanna noticed too late the warning light blinking to let her know she had wandered into a field of rhonacton gas. Cutting her lasers immediately before the interaction between them and the gas incinerated her own ship, she watched helplessly as the field began to drain her power, halting her progress on the spot. She tried to reprogram her board for propulsion, without success, glancing up to see the *Talon* turning on a course straight for her.

"A sitting duck. How appropriate," Estrella said, her amusement clear. "Any last words?"

One shot. That's all I'll have.

Trezanna watched and waited, her finger itching to send the torpedo flying. She cut all other power, leaving whatever remained of the quickly draining resources for the weapons battery. As the *Talon* reached the edge of her targeting range, she pushed the button for missile launch. "How about goodbye?"

She could hear Estrella's cry of disbelief as she detected the late launch and pulled away in an effort to escape, but the torp did what it was programmed to do. The *Talon* was reduced to molecules.

CHAPTER 36

POMEROY stepped in to lead the last of the coalition ships in the battle with the remaining Arkosian ships.

As the last pirate vessel detonated, a cheer went up from the throats of the pilots.

"Well done," he called over the common frequency. "Gamma and Beta squads head back to the surface. Alpha and Delta." He paused a few seconds. "Trezanna?"

All of them listened, but there was no response.

"She went after Estrella," McKinley offered, swinging around to the last vector where he had seen them.

The two ships were out of sight.

As Pomeroy, too, scanned for them, a dull flicker appeared at the edge of his vision. "There. One o'clock. Something just went up! Winston, McKinley, you're with me!"

When the three ships arrived on the scene, they discovered the cloud of rhonacton gas and Trezanna's ship inside it, dead in space.

"She can't be—" McKinley burst out.

Pomeroy scanned the ship. "Faint life signs. Get a tractor beam on that ship now!"

McKinley locked on and pulled the *Galena* from the cloud, then maneuvered the airlocks of his ship together with Trezanna's, sliding through the hatch to drag her out. Her air was nearly gone, but she was only unconscious. "She'll be all right," he announced to the others.

"Smashing," Pomeroy crowed. "Let's go home!"

* * *

THE colony on Induna took several weeks to recover from the pirate attacks. Memorials had been held for those lost. Trezanna hoped this would be the last need for such services for many years to come.

She finished clearing her desk of the detritus that had accumulated while they had lived in chaos. At first their new circumstances seemed like so much to manage, but she'd had to surrender to the inevitable. She was no longer in control of everything. Once she realized she no longer had to be responsible for each moment, each event, it became a relief.

Joint work crews repaired the physical damage to their ships, buildings and grounds. She'd also accompanied Pomeroy and Hawk to the Dragonfleet base, where a small Khimeyr force rid Miramar of its final pirate inhabitants. In the process, they set free the families of the Dragonfleet captive workers, who adjusted quickly to the loss of Estrella. Hawk agreed to take the lead role, pledging to work with the Solarii and Khimeyr to form a tri-partite association rather than continue the sniping and war of the previous administration.

All that was left was the big decision. Would the Khimeyr and Solarii remain united at the Solarii base or split the sector with the Khimeyr dream of returning home coming true?

Trezanna and Catava puzzled over the solution in the spirit of close cooperation engendered by their time together. It was obvious the two groups would depend on each other for survival. Other enemies existed who would be as dangerous as the Arkosians, if not more so. Input from the line officers was mixed. But as the weeks passed, the decision hadn't become clearer. They had called a meeting to force the issue.

It was time. Trezanna slipped on her uniform jacket and left her office, bound for the hangar bay to meet the others.

The hangar bay bustled with activity as the troops gathered for the event. Fresh from an inspection tour of the revamped Dragonfleet base, Catava and Stefan greeted Trezanna when she arrived. Catava seemed particularly enthused. "The team's done good work. I think the base is ready. Hawk's agreed we can return home."

"I'll miss you," Trezanna said, finding the realization ironic. The thought of Catava leaving seemed to create a huge, dark void in her life. Who would have believed the two groups, and the two women, would have gone from former enemies to fast friends in just a few months?

"Don't make too much of it, Trezanna," Stefan said with a grin. "The two bases aren't more than a hyperspace jump apart. Each group can specialize, create trade. Induna's got superior soil and can grow enough food to feed everyone. Miramar's got Henry's machine shop in the basement."

"You sound like a merchant," Catava teased.

Stefan shrugged, looking embarrassed. "What can I say? Besides, my brother's promised to help."

"I'm glad the power of forgiveness has found your people, as it has found ours."

Stefan nodded. "Victory over the Arkosians won't bring back my father, but at least my family has rescinded its edict. I'm not disowned any more."

"So, what are you going to do?" Trezanna asked.

"Cat wants me to join her and the Khimeyr at Dragonfleet." Stefan reached for Catava's hand. "I've gladly accepted her invitation. I promise I'll take care of her and make her happy."

Catava slipped an arm around Stefan, and look as relaxed as Trezanna had ever seen her. Chad and Susie came galloping up, ushered by a crewman. Chad threw his arms around Stefan, who tended to him just like a father.

That decision felt right, and warmed Trezanna's heart. She knew that Qiaolin had chosen to remain on Induna to study engineering under the tutelage of Julian McKinley, and others had made up their minds as well.

One by one, the members of the Khimeyr and Solarii came before them to declare their intentions. But when Darien Pomeroy announced he was leaving with Catava, Trezanna was hit with the loss she least expected. Piper was going with him.

"It's not so far, Tre—Mother." Piper smiled warmly. As the wounds of the conflict healed, the two had made up for lost time, becoming close. The mother had finally bonded with the daughter she'd lost. But Piper was not a child any more. "Now that we're all allies, anytime we want, you'll come see me. I'll come see you."

"I thought you could learn the ropes of command here. I mean, in case...." Trezanna trailed off, seeing the warm emotions in Piper's green eyes, the eyes of her father, the man who Trezanna once loved and lost for sake of duty.

Can I insist that Piper's duty should come before her happiness, knowing how our lives have changed because of it?

Piper hesitated, her hand in Darien's, but Trezanna forced a smile through her tears and hugged her daughter. "No, you're right. I'm just glad you've come home. Follow your heart, love. Be happy."

As Trezanna assimilated that loss and the groups separated to do their final packing, Boring paged her to the infirmary. Guessing another of the injured pilots was about to pass on, she sighed and headed down to be present.

But on arrival, she was greeted by a joyous celebration.

"What's going on?" she asked.

"The Solarii have contributed to the next generation," Dr. Boring said, bursting with pride. "Come, come!"

He took Trezanna's arm and nearly dragged her into the isolation room. As they came close, the cry of a newborn baby echoed.

"Bethany?" Trezanna asked.

"Yes, ma'am." The new mother looked up, tired but happy, cradling a tiny bundle in her arms. "Guess she wanted to feel like part of the excitement."

Trezanna pulled the pink blanket aside with her finger to see the wrinkled little girl, dark eyes like raisins, with feathery brown wisps of hair. "Oh, Bethany, she's beautiful. Have you named her?"

The nurse smiled. "I asked Monty if it was all right. I named her Shelby."

"I pray she may have the spirit of that young woman, and all the others who've built this place." Trezanna smiled at the mother and child. "You get your rest now. Congratulations."

"Thank you, ma'am," Bethany said.

The doctor fussed like a mother hen, as others came to view this evidence of their new hope. Trezanna Len greeted her people and headed back to work, feeling lighter at heart than she had in a long time. Walking the main corridor, she looked out the tall windows to spy a group of children playing in an open green area in the warm sun. It was hard to remember anymore which were Solarii and which were Khimeyr.

For our future, it doesn't matter, Trezanna thought. *And that's the way it should be.*

THE END

About the Author

Lyndi Alexander dreamed for many years of being a spaceship captain, but settled instead for inspired excursions into fictional places with fascinating companions from her imagination that she likes to share with others. She has been a published writer for over thirty years, including seven years as a reporter and editor at a newspaper in Homestead, Florida. Her list of publications is eclectic, from science fiction to romance to horror, from technical reporting to television reviews. Lyndi is married to an absent-minded computer geek. Together, they have a dozen computers, seven children, and a full house in northwestern Pennsylvania. Other publications include the "Clan Elves of the Bitterroot" fantasy series titles: *The Elf Queen* (Book I), *The Elf Child* (Book II), *The Elf Mage* (Book III).

www.ingramcontent.com/pod-product-compliance
Lightning Source LLC
Chambersburg PA
CBHW050736180626
46814CB00002B/773